ANGELS
from
ASHES

HOUR OF THE WOLF

ISBN: 978-1-68313-001-7
First Edition
Printed and bound in the USA

Shrine of Our Lady of Good Help photo by author Karen Hulene Bartell
Cover photos courtesy of:
Ashley Webb: www.flickr.com/photos/xlordashx/10591921436
ID 51281511 © Alarich | Dreamstime.com

Cover and interior design by Kelsey Rice

ANGELS
from
ASHES

HOUR OF THE WOLF

Karen Hulene Bartell (signature)

BY KAREN HULENE BARTELL

P
Pen-L Publishing
Fayetteville, AR
Pen-L.com

SHRINE OF OUR
LADY OF GOOD HELP

PHOTO BY AUTHOR

In October 1859, young Belgian immigrant Adele Brise saw three visions of Our Lady of Good Help in a forest near Champion, Wisconsin. When the site of these Marian apparitions became a place of pilgrimage, Adele's father built a small wooden chapel on it. Soon after, a larger wooden church was erected over the exact location.

Twelve years after the vision, the Peshtigo Fire destroyed well over a million acres of the land surrounding the church, but the chapel and the people who took refuge inside survived the fire unharmed.

On a par with Lourdes and Guadalupe, in 2010 the Shrine of Our Lady of Good Help was the first Marian apparition site approved as a holy place "of solace and answered prayer" in the United States.

Visit www.ShrineOfOurLadyOfGoodHelp.com
for more information.

OTHER BOOKS BY
KAREN HULENE BARTELL

Christmas in Catalonia

Sacred Journey Series

Sacred Choices - Book I

Sacred Gift - Book II

Belize Navidad

Sovereignty of the Dragons

Fine Filipino Food

The Best of Korean Cuisine

The Best of Taiwanese Cuisine

The Best of Polish Cooking

American Business English

DEDICATION

With all my love to my husband, Peter William Bartell

In remembrance of the unnamed souls incinerated in the Peshtigo Fire, whose charred remains were placed in mass graves or never found

Special thanks to the Hadd family, descendants of Peshtigo Fire survivors, for sharing a family story

CHAPTER 1

"The early Celtic Christians called the Holy Spirit 'the wild goose.'
And the reason why is they knew that you cannot tame him."

– JOHN ELDREDGE

Arms clasped around her knees, Chloe Clark sat on the dock overlooking Green Bay, watching the sky lighten just as she had so many other summer mornings. *But how different this year.* From a deep-purple flush stretching across the horizon, the sky transformed into luminous shades of crimson, turning to rose and ginger as the sun dawned a shimmering gold.

She glanced at the water below, so still it seemed a mirror, reflecting the sky, doubling its splendor. Then she caught her own reflection. A serious face with a shy smile stared back through dark eyes. Shoulder-length, tawny-brown hair the sun had lightened to sandy framed her face.

When the honking cry of a Canada goose broke the stillness, she turned to watch its swooping touchdown on the water, creating a V of waves. She stretched, arching her back, and then checked her watch. Time to get back.

Kicking up sand with her sandals, she walked along the path to her Great-Aunt Edwina's weathered house. Waves of nostalgia washed over her. So many carefree summers here. Not like this one. Sighing, she pushed open the screen door leading into the kitchen and inhaled the fresh coffee's fragrance. She poured two cups, placed them on a tray, and headed to her great-aunt's room.

Tapping lightly at her door, Chloe called, "Are you up yet, Aunt Ed?"

"Come on in," she answered.

Chloe smiled at her favorite relative—the white-haired, eighty-year-old woman in bed, whose blue eyes were as clear and sharp as her wit. Her great-aunt wore a black bed jacket and a white cast up to her elbow on her right arm.

"Good morning." Chloe set her great-aunt's cup on the night stand. "How's your wrist today?"

"Ornery, like me." Edwina's snort serving as a laugh, she reached into the top drawer, pulled out a flask, and liberally poured into the hot coffee.

Chloe turned a blind eye. Her great-aunt had been adding brandy to her coffee for as long as she could recall, whether eight in the morning or eight at night.

"Would you like pancakes for breakfast?"

"You needn't go to any fuss." Her forehead puckering, Edwina glared at her cast.

Chloe recognized her bitterness at the enforced convalescence. Edwina had been her role model growing up. Self-determined, counter-cultural, her great-aunt had never married. Instead, she had earned a doctorate in the 1950s, something few women had attempted, let alone achieved, in that era. Chloe understood Edwina's pride in self-reliance.

"No fuss," said Chloe as she sipped her coffee. "Have to make breakfast for myself, don't I?" She shrugged. "No more trouble to make it for two than one."

Chloe thought of all the summers she had spent in Door County with her great-aunt instead of cooped-up in her parents' cramped Milwaukee apartment. Without those welcome escapes, her childhood would have been bleak. *You've made me hundreds of breakfasts. Glad to pay it back.*

"In that case, how about pancakes with fresh raspberries?" Edwina's eyes lit up like a child's.

Chloe grinned. *Self-reliant, but not above small indulgences.* "Sure, it's raspberry season. They're everywhere for the next week or two. Then they're gone. Might as well enjoy them while we can."

The light faded from Edwina's eyes. "Gather ye rosebuds while ye may . . ."

⁂

Chloe grabbed a quart container and took the sand path to the nearest raspberry patch, a dilapidated fence overgrown with brambles. Lush with raspberries, the briars sagged under their weight. Aunt Ed had taught her to reach among the thorns and pick fragile berries without getting scratched. Musing about summers past as she picked, she heard a young girl's voice.

"Do you live here?"

She turned toward her. "Just for the summer."

"Did you move in with Miss Ed?"

Chloe nodded. "Just 'til the cast comes off my great-aunt's arm. Do you live around here?"

"Yup, over there." She pointed farther down the path. "I'm Rose Beaulieu."

"Pleased to meet you, Rose. I'm Chloe Clark." Tilting her head, she asked, "Beaulieu, isn't that French?"

"My great-great-grandfather was French-Canadian." The corners of the girl's dark eyes smiled. "Beaulieu means beautiful place."

Chloe glanced up at the clear sky and then scanned the surrounding greenery and wildflowers. Within eyeshot, she recognized wild strawberry blossoms and wild roses.

"Door County is a beautiful place, isn't it?" At the girl's nod, she added, "Must be a great place to grow up." *Compared to Milwaukee.*

Rose stooped to pick something. "Do you know what this is?" She phrased the question as a challenge. Then Rose lifted her eyebrow as she held up a ten-petalled, pale-yellow flower.

Chloe shrugged. "A buttercup of some sort?"

Rose shook her head and grinned proudly. "It's a small-flowered crowfoot, and it's poisonous. Although the Menominees, the Native Americans who lived around here, used to grind up its roots to make an antiseptic."

Chloe opened her eyes wide, impressed with the girl's knowledge. "How would you know something like that?"

"Pop-pop taught me, and his grandma taught him." Rose straightened her shoulders. "She was a Menominee."

"Pop-pop?" Chloe scratched her neck.

"My grandpa."

"Your grandpa must be a smart man, a good resource for you."

"He is." The girl grinned. "If you want, I can teach you what he's taught me."

Chloe chuckled at the idea. "Sounds like fun, but I have to make breakfast and then go to work."

"When are you through?"

"About five."

"Okay, I'll meet you at five." With a wave, the girl was off.

Chuckling to herself, Chloe waved and finished picking her raspberries. Back home, she added half the berries to the pancake batter and smashed the other half with sugar to make a simple sauce, the way her great-aunt had taught her when she was Rose's age.

As they ate breakfast, Chloe told Edwina about her little friend.

"What did you say her name was?"

"Rose, Rose Beaulieu."

Edwina's eyes clouded over. "You said her grandfather taught her. Did she mention his name?"

Chloe shook her head as she studied the older woman's reaction. "Why? Is anything wrong?"

"No." Edwina poured herself another cup of coffee, lacing it with brandy from her flask.

———— ◇ ————

At five o'clock sharp, Chloe heard a knock.

Opening the screen door, she saw it was Rose. "C'mon in. I'll just be a minute while I shut down my computer."

"What kind of work do you do, Chloe?"

As she logged off, she turned toward the girl. "I'm a technical writer for a Milwaukee software company."

"You work from here?" Rose looked around the dining room that Chloe had hijacked for her temporary office—her laptop on the table, stacks of papers and user manuals surrounded it.

"While Aunt Ed heals, I'm telecommuting. I can work from anywhere."

"Even outside?"

"Only if there's Wi-Fi, which there isn't here."

"I'm supposed to give my brother these." She held up a bag. "And along the way, I can show you the wildflowers. I know a shortcut." Her face brightened. "Ready?"

"Lead on."

They started on the packed-sand path. Then they turned off onto a narrow rabbit trail through a stand of white birch trees. Dried leaves covered the young forest's floor. Chloe saw a tri-petal white flower, and then another and another among bright-green, tri-leafed plants. Soon the area was a green-and-white carpet of delicate blossoms.

"What are these?" Chloe stooped for a closer peek.

"Trillium. Aren't they pretty?"

"Beautiful. I've heard of being given the red-carpet treatment, but I'd prefer this white carpet any day." Standing up for a better look, she gazed at the flower fairyland.

"It's also called birthroot."

"Birthroot? Let me guess, can it ease childbirth?"

Rose nodded. "It was a sacred female herb." Her voice was serious, hushed. "Only medicine women could speak of it."

Chloe smiled. "Then how did your grandfather learn about it?"

The girl grinned and then turned away, trying to hide it. "Come on. If you like this, I'll show you something even prettier."

Chloe followed Rose along the path until they came to a patch of white flowers with dainty, yellow stamens.

"These are gorgeous. What are they?"

"Goldthread." Rose made such a sour face, Chloe giggled. "It's also called mouth root because it's good for canker sores. Just chew its bright-gold roots, and the sores go away." Puckering her lips, she closed her eyes, scrunched her nose, and shuddered. "But it's bitter."

"I'll remember that." Chloe chuckled. "Your teaching style makes things . . . unforgettable."

Just before she saw the bay through the trees, the rocky path gave way to a sandy mix and then to a packed-sand beach. As they walked out of the woods onto the shoreline, Chloe gazed up at the expansive sky. After the leafy canopy, it felt good to see the sun again.

Ahead, stacked canoes and kayaks lined the banks. Rose led her onto a wooden pier with a sign at its end reading "Sunset Cruises."

"This is where my brother works." She turned to give Chloe a knowledgeable nod. Then, spotting a bare-chested man wearing a captain's cap over a dark mane of hair, she waved.

The broad smile from his finely-chiseled face caught Chloe's eye as he started toward them. His lean body moved sinuously, like a tawny cat's. From his taut pectorals, Chloe could see he worked out. Not what she would describe as brawny, his upper body was toned, well-defined. She caught her breath. *Just about right.*

As he approached, she noticed where his tan line ended, just above his jeans. He took off his captain's cap and ran his fingers through his shock of silky, dark hair.

"Hey, Rose, what brings you here?"

She held up the bag. "Mom wanted you to have these."

He peeked inside. "Strawberries. Thanks." Then he gave her a hug.

"The first of the season," said Rose. "She knows you like them."

"Appreciate it." Then he turned to Chloe. "Who's your friend?"

"Chloe. She's staying with Miss Ed 'til her cast comes off."

His warm smile faltered for a moment. Then it returned, and he held out his hand. "Pleased to meet you, Chloe. I'm Hud Beaulieu."

"Chloe Clark," she said. An electrical jolt ran up her arm as their hands connected. Again, she caught her breath. "What an interesting name," she said, finding her tongue. "I've never known anyone named Hud. Is it Native American?"

He shook his head. "Okemos is my Native American name."

"What's that mean?"

"Little Chief."

"And Hud?"

He smiled. "I was named after my father. My grandfather gave him his Native American name, and my grandmother nicknamed him Hud for Hudson."

She watched his flashing, dark eyes. "Hudson, what's it mean?"

This time he blushed as he glanced at his sister.

"Go ahead." Rose shrugged. "It's nothing I haven't heard before."

"Technically, it's Old English for Son of Hugh." Rubbing his nose, he chuckled ruefully. "As the story goes, my father was conceived in the back seat of a Hudson at the drive-in." As he hooked his thumbs under his arms, he grinned sheepishly. "The nickname stuck."

Hunching her shoulders, Chloe chuckled. "So . . ."

"Back then it was called a shotgun wedding." Sighing, he shook his head. "Apparently, it was a stormy marriage, but it was strong." He gave a fervent nod. "It lasted until she passed away two years ago at the age of eighty."

"I'm sorry." She blinked, sobering. *The same age as Aunt Ed.*

"She had a good life."

"Then your grandfather's still living?"

"Oh, yes. Very much so."

"I wonder if my great-aunt knows him. What's his name?"

"Jake."

She opened her eyes wide. "Jake Beaulieu?" *I wonder . . .* The name jarred her memory, but she couldn't place it.

His eyes lingered on hers for a moment. Then he turned to Rose. "How would you two lovely ladies like to go on a sunset cruise?"

Chloe felt at her pockets. "I didn't bring any–"

"As my guests. I'm taking a group out right now."

Rose's eyes lit up. "Oh, yeah. Chloe, you'll love this."

Chloe mentally reviewed her to-do list as she studied his finely-chiseled features. *Got to make dinner. Don't want to worry Aunt Ed. Besides, this isn't going anywhere. He's out of my league.* "I shouldn't leave Aunt Ed alone too long."

"We'll be back in less than two hours." Hud's dark eyes bored into hers. "If you haven't seen the Door Peninsula from the bay, you haven't seen it."

She tried to stifle the timid smile she felt creeping at the corners of her mouth. "Though I spent summers here as a child, my great-aunt never would let me near the bay." She looked at Rose. Then, as she looked at Hud, she made her decision. "I'd love to."

He escorted them to the end of the pier. Then, giving her his hand, he helped Chloe up the plank. At his touch, a tingling sensation raced up her arm again as his energy flowed into her. She gazed into his eyes and saw they were locked on hers. *He feels it, too.*

Her eyelids fluttering, she felt a combination of triumph and terror. Since her breakup with Aaron, she had lost confidence in her ability to attract anyone's attention. *Admit it. You've lost all self-confidence. Period.*

Letting go his hand, breaking the link, she wondered if the real reason she had come to her great-aunt's aid was to get away from Milwaukee—sneak off, tail tucked between her legs, and hide. Maybe that scenario was closer to the truth than the one of the caring, dutiful niece.

But I love Aunt Ed. I want to be here for her. She shook her head, trying to shake off the memories and aftereffects of Aaron. *See? I don't even know how I feel anymore.*

Then she glanced at Hud. He was still staring at her. She blinked, not believing her eyes. The attraction was unmistakable . . . and mutual. Despite the warm afternoon sun, a shiver ran down her spine.

The assistant unhooked the ropes tethering the boat to the pier, tossed them to Hud, and jumped aboard. As the boat powered off from shore, Chloe felt her qualms slipping away. A breeze caught her hair, clearing her mind, carrying away her regrets. She took a deep, cleansing breath.

Hud pointed out the wildlife and told legends about Green Bay while the boat plowed through the water.

"On your right, look high into that group of oak trees, ladies and gentlemen. If you have binoculars, get them out for a rare treat. A bald eagle's perched on the tallest tree at three o'clock."

Murmurs came from the passengers as they opened backpacks and carrying cases, uncapping their binoculars and camera lenses.

As the bird took flight, Hud added, "And just below the eagle, do you see what looks like white flags waving? That's a herd of white-tailed deer."

Farther up the coast, he spoke into the microphone. "Those craggy rocks along the shoreline and the bluff above it are part of the limestone outcroppings of the Niagara Escarpment."

"Does it have anything to do with Niagara Falls?" asked a passenger.

"What you're looking at is the same cliff you'd see at Niagara Falls." He grinned, his white teeth flashing against his tanned face. "Just a tad smaller, of course. The Escarpment runs from New York State, arching through Ontario, Canada, Michigan, and down the Door Peninsula of Wisconsin."

He pointed out cherry and apple orchards. "If you're here in July, you can pick your own cherries. Then you can stay and, depending on the variety, pick your own apples from August into October."

As the sun began to set and the sky glowed a fiery, salmon color, he turned the boat around, heading back to port. All the while, he told them Door County legends and stories of haunted lighthouses, ending with a tale of the aurora borealis.

"How many of you have seen the northern lights?" Half the passengers raised their hands. "The Menominee people believed the lights showed the location of the manabai'wok, the giants, who were the spirits of great hunters and fishermen. Think of that the next time you see those color-ful displays."

Then he handed the wheel to his assistant and joined Rose and Chloe. "Enjoying the tour?"

"You're an excellent guide," said Chloe. "Listening to you, I've learned a lot. How long have you been doing this?"

"Every summer since high school," he said.

"Summers?" She studied him. "What do you do the rest of the year?"

"He teaches history at the university," said Rose.

"Really?" Opening her eyes in surprise, Chloe did a double-take.

Smiling proudly, Rose nodded. "He just became an associate professor."

He tousled her hair. "She's my biggest fan."

Chloe was unsure how to word it. "It's none of my business, but I'm curious. Why are you giving rides to tourists when . . . ?" *You could be doing more.*

He filled in for her. "When I could be doing something more academic, like research?"

She shrugged. "Research, teaching summer school . . . I don't know."

"I'm helping our grandfather. He's always helped us." He reached for his sister's shoulders, hugging her to him. "Now it's my turn." He looked into her eyes. "Something like what you're doing for Miss Ed."

Again, she examined her motives. *But am I helping or hiding?* She shook her head. "I don't think I'm as selfless as you."

"What do you mean?" His eyes probed hers.

She grimaced, her lips pressing into a tight line. *How do I put it?* "This is as much a vacation for me as a vocation. In many ways, coming here's an escape."

"Where are you from?"

"Milwaukee."

His eyes twinkled, teasing her. "City slicker, eh?"

"Hardly." She scanned the wide horizon over the bay, watching the changing colors of the sunset. "You can take the girl out of the country, but . . ." She turned back to Hud and took a deep breath. "I spent summers here as a kid but grew up in Milwaukee. After I graduated," she shrugged, "I simply stayed where the jobs were." *Did the "smart" thing.*

Hud turned to Rose. "Let's see if we can't persuade Chloe to stay here a little longer."

She nodded. "I'm teaching her about herbs."

"You two have a lot in common." Chloe smiled, looking from one to the other, noting the family resemblance. "You're both good at sharing knowledge."

"You hear that, Rose?" He gave her shoulders an affectionate shake as he let go. "Maybe you can teach Chloe about the northern lights?"

The girl's eyes lit up. "Sure."

He turned toward Chloe. "Have you ever seen the aurora borealis?"

She shook her head.

"Then you're in for a treat." Rose grinned.

"Midnight's the best time. Are you game?" His dark eyes teased, seeming to imply more.

Chloe's heart beat faster as she recognized the challenge. "Sure."

⁘

After dinner, Chloe stepped outside to test the temperature, then quickly stepped back in. "Once the sun goes down, it sure gets chilly fast." She turned to Edwina. "Do you have a jacket I could borrow?"

Edwina set down her cigar. "Look in the back of your closet. There's a second rack with jackets and coats."

Chloe pushed aside the front rack of clothes and walked to the far end of her closet, where the light did not penetrate. The floorboards creaked as she stepped cautiously in the dark. Suddenly, icy chills swept down her spine. She chafed her arms, trying to rub away the goosebumps. Her fingertips felt like she had dipped them in ice water. Then they began to numb. Her teeth started chattering. Cobwebs brushed against her face. Yelping, she swept them away with both hands, grabbed the first jacket she touched, and scrambled out.

As she stepped into her bedroom, the temperature felt comfortable. The numbness began leaving her fingertips, but a sense of dread persisted. *What was that?*

She looked at the jacket and saw it was a winter coat, way too heavy for a June evening. Shaking off the sense of panic, she psyched herself to go back. *Only this time I'll bring a flashlight.*

She found a pocket flashlight on her keychain. Gathering her courage, she took a deep breath and strode toward the back of the closet. Again the floorboards creaked, and the same icy fingers crawled up her spine. More spider webs brushed against her. She shuddered, but forced herself to put back the coat. Then her toe stumbled against something. She heard it slide aside, and she stepped away. Her fingertips shaking as they touched the clothes, she felt for a lighter-weight jacket.

Just as she pulled one from its hanger, her flashlight flickered and went out. *Good time for the battery to die.* She swallowed as she retraced her footsteps in the dark, the boards creaking when she stepped on them. As she groped her way along, something brushed against her arm. She screamed and ran out, knocking clothes off their hangers as she passed.

Once back in her room, she took a deep breath, letting the warm air revive her, but nothing could touch the chill at her core. She noticed the flashlight's beam of light. *Sure, now it's working.* She set it on the bedroom floor, its beam pointed at the fallen clothes inside the closet. Then she began hanging them up.

What am I, a child? She breathed deeply, trying to regain her composure. Then, in the flashlight's reflected beam along the floor, she saw a small box pushed to the very back of the closet. *That must be what I kicked.*

Groaning, wishing she had not noticed it, she felt more compelled to search it with every article of clothing she rehung. *What's in it? What if it has black widows or brown recluses?* She shuddered, hating spiders, knowing there was a distinct possibility she would find one.

Finally, the urge overcame the fear. She swallowed, pushed her clothes to one side of the rack, made a beeline to the box, and dragged it out into the light. Even moving swiftly, the floorboards creaked.

Rather than risk spider bites, she dumped the box in the middle of the floor. Picture albums and scrapbooks tumbled out, but no spiders. *Thank God!* Breathing a sigh of relief, she nestled the books back into the box and carried it to the living room.

"Aunt Ed, look what I found."

"Goodness." Edwina's eyes lit up as she lifted out an album. "I'd forgotten about these."

"I don't think I've ever seen them." Chloe helped her hold it open, as the older woman used her good hand to turn the pages. "Who are these people?"

"That's your great-grandmother, Maria O'Dell." Edwina swiveled in her seat to look at Chloe. "She was just a baby at the time, but she survived the Peshtigo Fire."

"Really?"

She nodded. "Her parents, your great-great-great-grandparents, are the ones who homesteaded in Door County." She turned a page. "This is the only picture we have of their daughter, your great-great-grandmother, Teresa Malone."

"I'm sure I've never seen these," she looked at her aunt, "or even heard of these people. Why?"

A cloud came over her aunt's eyes, and her shoulders sagged. "Their stories give me the blues."

"Why? Were they horse thieves or outlaws?" Chuckling, she tried to lighten her aunt's mood.

She shook her head. "No, nothing like that, but . . ." Wearing a faint smile, she met Chloe's eyes. "If you're interested, I'll tell you about them."

"I'd definitely like to hear their stories. Why don't you start at the beginning, with my great-great-great-grandparents?"

"I don't know much about them. Martin Malone and his wife came to Door County by boat in 1857. They'd come from New York State, originally. Then they relocated in Ohio for a short time. After that, they moved to Milwaukee, then Manitowoc, and finally they settled in Door County. They had three small children. One of them was your great-great-grandmother, Teresa Malone."

Repeating the name, Chloe thought for a moment. "The name rings a bell."

"After living in Champion a short time, they blazed a trail with a team of oxen and moved to Egg Harbor. As the story goes, Native Americans were frequent visitors at their cabin, and wildlife was so plentiful, they could see it nearly any time of day, right from their doorway."

Chloe shook her head. "It's hard to imagine now, isn't it?"

"That's about all I know of them, but their daughter, your great-great-grand-mother, Teresa Malone, was quite a woman. She was—"

A knock at the door startled them. Chloe checked her watch. *Midnight already?*

"Who's that at this time of night?" Edwina scowled.

"It's Rose and Hud." She crossed to the door. "Remember, I told you we were going to see the northern lights. That's why I needed the jacket."

"Oh, that's right." Edwina grunted.

Chloe opened the door. "Come on in."

Hud stuck his head in the door and nodded to each. "Hello, Miss Ed, Chloe."

"Hi, Miss Ed," said Rose, stepping inside. She looked at Chloe. "Are you ready?"

Chloe grabbed her jacket and keys. "All set." Then she turned to her aunt. "We should be back in about an hour or two. Will you be all right? Do you need anything before we go?"

Scowling, Edwina snapped at her. "I'm not an invalid. I can put myself to bed. Go on, and don't forget to lock the door behind you." She picked up her cigar and, puffing on it, relit it with her lighter.

Chloe was not sure what to make of her great-aunt's attitude. *She's getting cranky in her old age.* "Aunt Ed can take care of herself. She's a tough cookie," she told Rose and Hud with a wry grin. "I come from hardy stock." Then she thought of her closet's spider webs and creaking boards. *Hardy stock. Didn't say I was tough.*

They climbed into a pickup truck. Hud at the wheel, Rose between them, she turned toward Chloe. "You've really never seen the aurora borealis?"

"Nope. I've only seen pictures, not the real thing."

Keeping his eyes on the road, Hud tilted his head toward them. "There's no guarantee we'll see it tonight."

"It all depends on the sunspot activity," said Rose.

"I hope whatever causes it happens so we see it." Chloe gave Rose a warm smile.

"Hud's taking us to a cleared field away from town," said Rose. "The less light scatter, the better the view."

Ten minutes later, they turned off the highway onto a grated, dirt road. From there, Hud unlocked a gate and turned onto a tractor path in a field. He parked, grabbed a few quilts from the back seat, lowered the tailgate, and smoothed out the quilts on the truck bed.

"Climb up," he said.

Rose grabbed a thermos and some cups before scrambling up, taking the center.

Chloe hesitated, then laughed to herself and climbed beside her. Hud climbed on the other side of his sister.

"Now what?"

"Just look at the stars." Putting her hands behind her head, Rose lay back and watched the sky.

Chloe followed suit. As her eyes became accustomed to the dark, she saw a star shoot across the sky and gasped. "Did you see that?"

"A bonus," said Hud, looking at her over Rose's head.

Chloe chuckled.

"Just wait," said Rose. "I have a feeling we'll see the northern lights tonight." Within seconds, her arm shot up, pointing. "What's that over there? Isn't that swirling light I see?"

"Yup," said Hud. "Here it comes."

Chloe could not believe her eyes. Rosy-purple and lime-green lights shimmered and swirled across the sky, ebbing and flowing like thick liquid. The lights danced, creating a fluid pattern that flickered, twinkled, shot out, and curved in on itself, creating new swaths of colors, ever new displays. A kaleidoscope, always flowing, always tumbling and whirling, the lights leapt and frolicked like a living creature.

From the horizon to the zenith, churning colors filled the sky. Wave after wave flowed over itself, wiggling, cavorting. At other times, the lights seemed like colorful spotlights, waving back and forth at a Hollywood premier. Sometimes, the lights began at the horizon and climbed the sky. Other times, they appeared from above and danced down to earth.

A ray of white light shot across the bands of color. *Another falling star.*

Chloe sighed. Barely a whisper, she said, "I've never seen anything like this. It's . . ." She scanned her memory for any comparison. "It's like food coloring swirled in a giant glass of water."

Smiling, Hud sat up, using the truck's body as a backrest. Then he found the thermos and cups. "Who could go for some hot apple cider?"

Chloe realized her fingertips were numb. "I could, thanks." Sitting up, she took the cup from him, warming her hands on its heat before drinking. Then she looked up at the sky. "It's so beautiful, I hadn't realized it was getting cold." She tucked the quilt around her.

"Yeah, there's nothing quite like it." He nudged his sister. "Rose, you want some cider?"

When she didn't answer, he chuckled as he pulled a quilt over her. "It's past her bedtime."

Chloe turned toward him, keeping her eyes on the swirling lights overhead. "Have you always lived in Door County?"

He nodded. "On my great-great-grandmother's side, always. I live about a hundred miles from where my family's always lived, where the Menominee tribe originated."

"Really?" She sipped her cider, savoring its warmth. It was cozy under the quilt, talking quietly beneath the shimmering sky. She saw his profile outlined in the faint moonlight.

"According to our creation story, our five clans were created at the mouth of the Menominee River. This is where our people's story began."

"You said five clans. What are they?"

"There's ancestral Bear, Eagle, Wolf, Moose, and Crane."

"Which is yours?"

"The Wolf clan."

"So are you born into a clan, or does something have to make itself apparent to you?"

Though it was dark, she could see him turn his head toward her, observing her. "Why do you ask?"

"I've read about totems."

"You mean power animals?" It was too dark to see his expression, but his tone was sharp.

"From what I've heard, it involves dreams or meditation."

"I consider that slant spirit-wolf symbolism. Though it may have its origins in Native American cultures, New Age concepts usually distort it. The Menominee believe the wolf's a creature of great wisdom and should be revered as a spiritual guide." His tone softened. "You're either born or marry into a clan."

"So you don't receive a sign in a dream . . . or a blog."

She heard his soft chuckle.

"It isn't like a horoscope." He was quiet for a moment. "It's more like a coat of arms or a plaid tartan that symbolizes your family."

"Then what about people who're descended from a particular clan but haven't been taught about it?"

"You bring up an interesting situation." He sat quietly. Then he spoke in a confidential whisper. "I've had a similar upbringing. Although my father was one-eighth Menominee, he taught me very little about our heritage. However, I've had a special connection with wolves since I was small."

"How so?" She found herself leaning toward him—partly to hear better, partly because his tone drew her into an intimate circle.

"When I was four, I went on a hike with my grandparents and got lost in the woods. Not long after, a pack of gray timber wolves discovered me." He rephrased it. "It's closer to say they seemed attracted to me."

"What do you mean?"

"What I suppose was the alpha female approached me, stopping just inches in front of me. She began licking my face, cleaning off the sweat and grime. It was a caring gesture, not aggressive at all. I felt safe. Then, when my grandparents called out to me several minutes later and I answered, the wolves left silently. My grandparents never saw them, but over the next ten years, I occasionally caught a glimpse of a white wolf puppy. It seemed to grow up with me, from then until I entered high school."

"What happened to it?"

He shrugged his shoulders. "In the wild, wolves rarely live more than eight to ten years."

"Did you sense anything when you saw it?"

"I just felt a deep bond, a connection. I finally asked my grandfather about it, and he said I had the wild but disciplined spirit of the wolf. That was when he told me I was a member of the Wolf clan." His white teeth flashed in the moonlight. "It was the first I'd heard of it." He studied her face. "Someday, I'll ask him to tell you about his experience with a wolf."

She nodded. "I saw a juvenile wolf once. It was in one of the Milwaukee County parks. It sauntered onto North Avenue and then loped out of sight. I only saw it for a minute, but I'll never forget it."

"Did you sense anything?"

"Besides awe? And fear?" She chuckled. Then she paused, thinking. "I felt privileged to see such a noble creature, but nothing beyond that."

"Native Americans believe the wolf's a teacher. Even its presence is a message of guidance. At the time, were you faced with a difficult choice, or did you lack the information you needed to make some important decision?"

Unwilling to reveal any personal information, she felt her smile disappear as her muscles tensed and her mind skipped back to Aaron.

"If the wolf appears to you," he said, "ask advice from someone you trust. Think it over. Take the knowledge you need, and then take action with confidence. You'll do the right thing."

She was about to answer when she heard a wolf howl in the distance. She gasped. Then she began chuckling in nervous relief. "Talk about timing."

"Did you know wolves howl in the key of E, just like whales and dolphins, yet every wolf has its own unique sound?"

"Interesting. I didn't know that." She shook her head and then looked at her watch. "It's after two. Maybe we should start back."

"Morning comes early, especially in late June. The sun will be up in three hours."

Hud carried his sister to the back seat. Chloe nestled a quilt about her and folded the other quilts. Then, as they rode in silence, her thoughts turned to Aaron.

"Have you ever been to a fish boil?" His voice jarred her.

"What?" Flinching, her mind replayed his words. "No, what is it?"

"It's more than a dining experience. It's an event, something everyone ought to experience at least once." She watched his cheek dimple as he spoke. "Basically, it's whitefish, red potatoes, and onions boiled in a huge kettle over an open wood fire. The finale's a tourist favorite. They pour kerosene on the flames to make it flash up. Then they serve it with plenty of melted butter, lemon slices, and parsley."

"Sounds delicious."

"It is." He took his eyes off the road long enough to look at her. "They're having a fish boil at Fish Creek tonight. Would you like to go?"

She gave him a sidelong glance, debating. *Watching the northern lights with his sister is one thing, but a date?* She thought of Aaron but surprised herself at how quickly she said, "Sure."

CHAPTER 2

"Now had Aurora displayed her mantle over the blushing skies,

and dark night withdrawn her sable veil."

– MIGUEL DE CERVANTES

The next morning over breakfast Edwina asked, "Were you able to see the aurora borealis last night? It wasn't too cloudy, was it?"

"It was beautiful. In all the summers I spent here as a kid, I don't ever recall seeing anything like that."

Her aunt nodded knowingly. "Then you must have driven away from the town lights."

"Yes. Hud knew where there was an open field. The colors were absolutely astounding."

"There's nothing quite like it. I remember as a girl . . ." Wearing a thoughtful smile, her aunt was silent a minute. Then she blinked and focused on Chloe. "Did you have fun?"

"Yes. Hud and I had an interesting conversation about wolves."

Edwina scrutinized her. "Hud this and Hud that."

Chloe chuckled self-consciously. "It's nothing like that. We're just friends."

"Uh-huh." They locked eyes for a moment. Then Chloe looked away. After a moment of strained silence, Edwina poured another cup of coffee, lacing it with her flask's brandy. "I started going through the albums last night."

"You did?" Chloe looked up expectantly.

"If you have a minute before you log in to work."

"Yes. Let me clear away these dishes."

A few minutes later, as the two pored over the albums, Edwina pointed to a picture of a thin woman wearing an old-fashioned apron.

"This is your great-great-grandmother, Teresa Malone. She was five years old when her family moved to Door County. Originally, they moved near the town of Champion. In fact, they were neighbors of the Brises. According to the family story, on October ninth, 1859, when Teresa was seven years old, she was walking to Mass with Adele Brise and her sister, Isabel, when Adele suddenly stopped and stared at something."

"What are you looking at?" asked Teresa.

Adele didn't answer at first. She just gazed silently for several minutes, as if in a trance. She finally turned to them, her face white and her lips pale. "Did you see that?"

"See what?" Teresa looked around but saw nothing unusual.

"She's gone now, but didn't you see her standing between the hemlock and maple trees?"

"See who?"

Adele's tone was hushed. "The lady."

"I didn't see anyone." Creasing her brow, Teresa looked at Adele's sister. "Did you?"

"No." Isabel shook her head.

Adele's eyes were wide as she pointed to two trees. "She was standing right there, between those trees, for several minutes. You must have seen her."

Both girls solemnly shook their heads.

"You had to see her! The light around her glowed so brightly, it seemed to come from her, and the snow-white gown with the brilliant-yellow sash she wore sparkled, glittered. She had long, golden-blond hair, and she wore a crown of stars."

The girls glanced at each other and then turned back to Adele, shaking their heads.

Sighing, Adele sagged against the maple tree, seeming to collect her thoughts. "That's the second time I've seen her there." After a moment, she took their hands in hers. "Come on. We'd better hurry, or we'll be late."

After Mass at the Bay Settlement church, Adele asked to see the parish priest. She told him about the apparition, and he advised her what to say if she saw it again.

As they walked home later that day, Adele saw the lady a third time. Following the priest's advice, she asked, "In God's name, who are you? What do you want?"

Although Teresa and Isabel heard no response, they watched Adele kneel, listen, and nod in the direction of the two trees.

"Who is it?" asked Isabel.

"Why can't we see what you see?" asked Teresa.

"Kneel down," said Adele. "She says she's the Queen of Heaven."

The two girls looked at each other and knelt on the mossy ground.

Later, Adele told them what the lady had said. "'Blessed are they that believe without seeing and pray for the conversion of sinners.'"

Adele said the lady also gave her a mission. "'Gather the children in this wild country. Teach them the Good News.' Then the lady slowly vanished, leaving only a white cloud behind."

"According to Teresa's recollection," said Edwina, "Adele was twenty-eight at the time. She devoted the rest of her life to teaching children about God."

"What did she do? Join a convent?"

"Remember, these were the back woods. Not many people had access to education then, least of all women. As the family story goes, Adele started her vocation by walking from house to house, offering to help the overworked mothers in exchange for room and board. During her free time, she'd teach the children from the *Bible*."

"She certainly was resourceful." Chloe sipped her coffee.

"And apparently convincing. People began believing her and visiting the site. It became such a frequent pilgrimage, Adele's father built a small log chapel by the hemlock and maple trees, where she had seen the apparitions."

"How can they be so sure of the exact location? Even if they'd known the location at the time, wouldn't the chapel or trees have burnt down in the Peshtigo Fire?"

Edwina gave her a wide grin. "Peshtigo's another tale for another time, but it's interesting you mention the Peshtigo Fire."

"Why?"

"The fire occurred twelve years to the day after Adele's first sighting of the apparition."

"What a coincidence."

"There's no such thing as coincidence." Edwina waved her hand, dismissing the idea. "But to answer your question about the location, they found proof the chapel was built on the exact spot of the apparition."

Chloe narrowed her eyes. "What kind of proof?"

"You're right to be skeptical. People had forgotten the exact location, as well as the fact that the main altar had been built directly over it. When they built the fourth chapel of Our Lady of Good Help in 1942, the one that's there today, the excavators found the actual stumps of the hemlock and maple trees where the apparition had appeared."

"No." Chloe's raised an eyebrow.

"Yes." Edwina chuckled. "They preserved those stumps and built a crypt in place of them, just below the present main altar of the shrine. Two small relics of the actual trees are still on display in the gift shop."

"The stumps were better than GPS coordinates for finding the exact location." Chloe smiled. "You'd mentioned Adele worked from house to house, teaching the children. Did she do anything else?"

"According to your great-great-grandmother, my grandmother, Adele's mission was a demanding one. She would walk as far as fifty miles up and down the Green Bay Peninsula, despite the ridicule, weather, or wild creatures of the forest. Nothing stopped her."

"What a determined woman." Chloe shivered just thinking of Door County's frigid winters. "I can't imagine walking fifty miles alone through the forests. At least, I assume she worked alone. Did she?"

"Initially," said Edwina. "Later, Adele began a small boarding academy, and over time, several other women joined her mission. Although she never took formal vows as a nun, she started a community of sisters according to the rule of the Third Order Franciscans. Our Lady of Good Help has grown over the years, especially since it became the only approved apparition site of Mary in the country."

"Really?" Chloe blinked, processing her thoughts. "We should go to Mass there one Sunday. I'd like to see it."

<hr />

Hud stopped by at five o'clock sharp wearing jeans and a starched, button-down shirt.

As she opened the door, Chloe could not help noticing the tantalizing chest hairs peeking out behind his shirt's lowest open button. Catching her breath, she looked up into his face. She smoothed her hair and pulled at her collar, feeling outclassed. *What's he see in me?* Then she remembered her manners.

"C'mon in."

He leaned over and lightly kissed her cheek. "Hi."

As his hair tickled her neck, a shudder raced down her spine.

Then he held up a small bunch of irises. "These are for Miss Ed."

Edwina was just finishing dinner—drinking her brandy-laced coffee and smoking her cigar. "Hello," she said coldly, scowling.

Crossing to the table, he handed her the delicate amethyst and lemon-yellow blossoms. "Rose picked these for you."

"Thanks," she mumbled, barely moving her lips.

Still recovering from the kiss, Chloe took a moment to react. "They're gorgeous. Let me find a vase for them."

"Nonsense. I can put my own flowers in water, can't I?" Edwina gave her a stern look. "Go on. Run along."

Chloe stared at her, watching as Edwina turned her back on them and dropped the flowers on the table. *What's gotten into her?* She started to ask, but then thought better of it. "We should be back around nine thirty. Do you need anything before we leave?"

Her back to them, the old woman shook her head as she puffed on her cigar.

"Okay, then we'll see you in a few hours. Bye." She waited, but Edwina did not respond. Finally, Chloe called from the door. "See you." Walking outside, she turned to Hud. "Those irises were thoughtful. Please be sure to thank Rose for us."

"Definitely."

As Chloe swung into Hud's pickup, she asked, "Is a fish boil a Native American dish?"

He chuckled. "Could be, but it's advertised as a lumberjack special. It's a combination of a traditional Northwood meal, pyromania, and a French-Canadian booyah."

"What?" She looked into his twinkling dark eyes as he got behind the wheel.

"As the story goes, the lumber camps needed a quick way to feed a crowd of hungry lumberjacks. They tossed the red potatoes and sweet onions into a huge kettle of boiling water. Then, just as the vegetables got tender, they lowered a basket of whitefish steaks into the mix."

"Then it's not a stew or soup. They remove the fish?"

"Exactly. They'd cook the fish just long enough to let the oils boil out, leaving the tender steaks with a mild flavor. They could have ended the cooking process there, but they wanted to remove that fishy oil from the water's surface before pulling the basket back through it."

"Is this where the pyromania comes in?"

Glancing at her, he grinned. "They learned if they threw a bucket of kerosene on the fire, the flames would flash up, letting the kettle's oily water boil over, leaving behind a mouthwatering seafood dinner without a fishy flavor." He grinned as he kept his eyes on the road. "It's something you've got to see."

She watched his dimple deepen. "Sounds like the show's as good as the food."

"It is." Hud parked in front of a crowded restaurant. Then they walked around to the rear of the building, where a large crowd was gathered. "Good, we're just in time to see the flare-up."

She stood on her tiptoes, trying to peer over several people's heads. "Let's stand closer. I don't want to miss anything."

"Not too close." Wearing a comical smile, he pointed to his forehead. "I've had my eyebrows singed watching this."

She had to chuckle. *He's so much fun.* He met her gaze, and they became quiet as each studied the other's eyes.

Suddenly, the crowd gasped. Chloe spun around in time to see the kerosene thrown on the fire. A blaze engulfed the entire kettle. Flames shot ten feet in the air, leaping out several feet in every direction. Hissing steam bubbled over all as the oily water frothed and splashed out over the inferno.

Opening her eyes wide, she gasped. "Ohmigosh. You described it, but you didn't prepare me for anything like *this!*"

Laughing at the scene, they again caught each other's eyes. Chloe found herself entangled in his gaze as she tried to read him. The pause lengthened until she cleared her throat. "If the fish boil tastes even half as good as it looks, dinner will be delicious."

"Judge for yourself."

As he gently took her hand in his, Chloe felt sparks dart up her arm. She gave him a sidelong glance, assessing the move. *It feels right.*

The maître d' seated them near the fireplace. Despite it being June, Chloe was glad for the warmth, as well as the ambiance. Their cozy table for two boasted a starched linen tablecloth, while a tapered candle lent a soft glow.

When the waiter handed them a wine list, Hud said, "No, thanks." Then he turned to her. "Nothing goes better with a fish boil dinner than cold beer." He glanced at the waiter. "Am I right?"

Hiding a chuckle, the waiter nodded. "Yes, sir."

Hud looked at her. "Are you game?"

"When in Rome or Fish Creek . . . sure." She smiled. "Why not? Is there any dark local beer?"

Repeating her words with a smile, Hud laughed. "A woman after my own heart." He ordered two stouts and turned back to her. "How do you like Door County so far?"

"What's not to like? Fresh raspberries straight from the briar, sunsets that fill the horizon, northern lights that dance in the heavens, fish boil pyrotechnics that serve dinner with a 'flare.' It's got it all."

"How about the natives?" Arms crossed, dark eyes twinkling, he sat back and watched her reaction. "How do you like them?"

She swallowed a smile. "Rose is a sweetie, and Edwina's my favorite aunt."

Lips pressed together as he suppressed a smile, he silently nodded. "Anyone else?"

She tried to keep a straight face. "Everyone here's been very friendly. Can't say a bad word about anyone."

The waiter set down their chilled beer. Lifting hers, she looked Hud in the eyes and proposed a toast. "To new friends."

He stifled a grin as he clinked his bottle against hers.

The waiter brought a basket of fresh rye bread and a bowl of coleslaw. Then he set sizzling platters of whitefish, red potatoes, and onions in front of them with side orders of sliced lemons and melted butter.

Chloe inhaled the fragrance. "Oh, this smells wonderful. Suddenly I'm starving." She picked up her fork and was about to taste her dinner when Hud gave her a gentle smile.

"Shall we say grace?"

Noting his hands were folded, she swallowed and quickly set down her fork. Folding her hands, she bowed her head and mumbled, "Sure."

When he finished the prayer, he crossed himself. Peeking at him, Chloe followed his lead.

"This does look good." He squeezed lemon over his fish, dipped a forkful in the melted butter, and popped it in his mouth. "Cooked perfectly. They always time it right here—potatoes tender, fish flaky."

Chloe tasted it and groaned. "This is delicious." She looked up at him through her lashes. "Have to admit, you've shown me more of Door County than I'd ever seen as a child."

"Glad to hear it." He grinned at her. "If you're not fond of me as a Door County native, maybe you'll like me as a guide."

She grinned back. "You're the best."

"I'll drink to that." He held up his bottle, and she clinked hers against it in a toast.

She paused, becoming thoughtful. "Last night, when we heard that howl—"

"You mean this morning."

Snickering, she nodded. "This *morning* . . . was that howl really a wolf's?"

"Yup."

"It was." She blinked. "Door County's so isolated. I wouldn't think wolves could get here."

"Though it's cut off from the rest of Wisconsin, wolves can walk or swim here. They were hunted, trapped, and poisoned nearly to extinction by the late fifties, but they're starting to make a comeback. In fact, wolves are literally at the 'Door.'" He grinned.

"Door County." She rolled her eyes. "I get it."

"They've had a bumpy ride, though. In the fifties, they were painted as the big, bad wolves. In the sixties, they were an endangered species. Then they were reclassified from endangered to a threatened species. Then there weren't enough of them, so they were endangered again. Then there were too many. Then not enough. And all this in rapid succession. Their fate has depended on their federal classification."

"Let me rephrase that, see if I understand you." She gathered her thoughts. "They depend on the way the political winds blow—not only the way they're classified, but the way they're characterized. 'Big, bad wolf' conjures an entirely different image from 'endangered species.'"

"You're so right." His lips pressed together, he nodded. "Public perception plays a big role. Until 1957, while they were considered 'big, bad wolves,' bounty hunters earned five dollars for every pelt. By official counts, no wolves remained in Wisconsin."

"What a shame." She shook her head at the decimation. Then she looked up at him and smiled. "Obviously, there's at least one wolf here now. What changed?"

"After they passed the Endangered Species Act in the sixties, wolves were protected, and they gradually began returning to their native habitat. By 1980, there were about twenty-five wolves in Wisconsin. That's when the Department of Natural Resources began tagging and tracking them with radio collars."

She grimaced, following that line of thought. "It's good for keeping track of their numbers, but it's like fishing in a barrel if they decide to hunt them."

Nodding, he agreed. "On the upside, it's helped ecologists learn a lot about wolves and their habitat."

"I'll bet." She paused as she buttered a slice of rye bread. "Wouldn't they need wilderness to survive?"

"Scientists used to think so, but wolves really only need two things: food and isolation."

"I understand food. You're talking prey, in this case, white-tails, but what do you mean by isolation?"

"Basically, it's any area that isn't crisscrossed with roads."

"Few roads." She snickered. "You're describing Door County. In other words, you're saying they need to be left alone."

"Exactly," he said. "Low road density is the key to their survival." He helped himself to coleslaw.

She nodded as she squeezed lemon on her fish and then dipped it in melted butter. "Fewer roads, so fewer people and less interference."

"The question is carrying capacity. How many wolves can Wisconsin support?"

She sat back in her chair, watching his reaction. "I'll bet everyone has a different theory."

"Oh, yeah. From the environmentalists, who say there aren't enough wolves, to the hunters, who say there are too many, everyone's got their own opinion." His crooked half-smile told her which side he favored.

She leaned across the table toward him. "There's got to be a balance, a happy medium."

"There is: nature. Some years, there are more deer, so the wolves thrive. Then, as their numbers increase, the deer decrease in direct proportion. When the wolves can't feed themselves, they don't breed, so the deer population recovers—"

"And the cycle repeats itself." Understanding his point, she finished his sentence. "It's the way a predator-prey relationship should work—give-and-take, first one, and then the other. It's nature."

"Take Isle Royale, for example."

"Where's that again?"

"It's near the Minnesota-Canadian border, in Lake Superior. The wolf population had nearly died out there. Just a few females remained, and the moose population had gotten so large, it was stripping the land of vegetation. Then, one winter, the lake froze solid from the mainland to the island."

"Let me guess." She held up her index finger, interrupting. "A male wolf crossed the ice?"

He nodded with an approving smile. "'Old Gray Guy' they called him, and he repopulated the island's wolves. Now that the island has a good balance of wolves and moose, the vegetation's returning."

"Sounds like you have to look at the whole picture," she said, "the entire ecosystem, vegetation as well as wildlife, not just pieces of it."

"The ecosystem's only the sum of its parts. Remove a piece of it, and you break it."

"Nature's got a plan." She shrugged.

He shook his head. "Nature has instinct. God's got the plan."

She nodded to herself. "Guess it's man that spoils it." She sat back in her chair, thinking of Aaron as she studied Hud's strong face. *How different they are.*

Their waiter began clearing away the dishes. "Have you saved room for cherry pie?"

"You've got to try it." Lifting his eyebrow, wearing a winsome smile, Hud turned on the charm. "It's part of the experience."

She chuckled, knowing she'd already lost the battle, but she still pretended to debate, making him work for it. "I'm awfully full."

"They use fresh, Door County Montmorency cherries to make the pies here." He grinned until his dimple showed. "Gives it just the right amount of sweet-tartness."

"Sweet-tartness. Is that a word?"

"It makes your mouth water, doesn't it?"

"Oh, yes," she laughed. "But after your hard sell, I hope it's worth the calories."

Head resting on his hand, he stared at her, grinning. "You be the judge."

A moment later, the waiter returned with two slices of deep-dish cherry pie. A sprinkling of large crystal sugar on the top glittered in the candlelight. Once Chloe bit into its sugar-crunchy crust, she knew it was worth the calories. She rolled it over her tongue, savoring the textures and tart cherries.

"Well?" His dark eyes watched her expectantly.

She groaned as she swallowed. "It's worth every last sit-up I have to do to wear it off." Pointing to it with her fork, she added, "This is delicious." Then she looked him over. "How do you stay so trim eating this food?"

His eyes shone softly as he appraised her. "For one thing, I swim." Then he sat up, as if getting an idea. "How would you like to go swimming with me tomorrow?"

⁂

Taking the long way home, they drove along the lake in the moonlight. Then Hud dropped her off at her door, kissing her lightly on the cheek. When his lips slowly moved toward hers, brushing against hers, his breath tickling, she met him in a kiss that felt like they had been separated and had just now found each other.

They lingered in each other's arms until Edwina flipped on the porch light.

Giggling, Chloe extricated herself from his arms. "Could be wrong, but I think that's a subtle hint."

He laughed and gave her a chaste peck on the cheek. "See you tomorrow at four."

Smiling to herself, Chloe waved and then let herself into the house. She mentally reran the evening's events, remembering the kiss with a pleasant shudder.

Edwina sat in her rocking chair, a grim expression on her face. "You're late."

Chloe glanced at the clock. "It's nine thirty-one." She studied her great-aunt, noting the flaring nostrils, the high chin. "What's really bothering you?"

"I don't want you seeing that boy."

"What?" Chloe said, not believing her ears.

"I said, I don't want you seeing that boy."

"Aunt Ed, first of all . . ." She paused, controlling herself, choosing her words carefully. "Hud's not a boy, and I'm not a child to be told who I can or can't see." She pulled a chair closer and sat down. "Obviously, something's upset you, and it's not because I'm one minute late." She looked at Edwina's red face and cold, flinty eyes. "I've never seen you behave this way." Her voice softened. "What's wrong?"

Edwina pressed her lips together in a tight grimace. "I've tried to tell myself the children don't inherit the sins of the father, make myself believe it, but . . ."

"But what?"

"Have I ever told you the circumstances of my sister, Celestine Chloe's . . ." Edwina's bloodshot eyes looked into hers. "You're her namesake, you know."

Chloe nodded. "Tell me what about her?"

"You've never gone by the name Celestine, always Chloe, but my sister was called Celestine. Has anyone ever told you how she died?"

28

Chloe shook her head. "I don't recall anyone ever *mentioning* her. I'd always wondered why I was named for her."

Nodding, Edwina bit her bottom lip. "Then it's high time you found out." Edwina began rocking in her chair. The movement seemed to relax the tightness around her mouth, and she almost smiled. "Did you know I was once engaged to Hud's grandfather, Jake Beaulieu?"

Chloe's jaw went slack. Open-mouthed, she shook her head. "But I knew I'd heard that name somewhere."

"Jake and I were childhood sweethearts." Edwina's lined face took on a youthful softness. "He proposed at Christmas during our senior year at high school. We'd planned to marry the following June, but Jake had to drop out of school to help his family. We postponed our wedding for a year, while I started normal school."

"Normal school. I've heard of that. What is it?"

"It's a two-year college to train elementary teachers." Edwina sighed as she shook her head. "I'm not even sure they have those anymore. Anyway, Jake and I were inseparable. Where you'd find one, you'd find the other. Though sometimes Celestine would tag along with us to the root beer stand or drugstore to get a milkshake."

Chloe grinned. "An image from *Happy Days* just popped into my head. Did you and Jake ever share a milkshake with two straws?"

Edwina chuckled a hoarse, throaty laugh. "Oh, yes, many times." Looking without seeing, she smiled into space, seeming to remember happier days. Then she sighed. "I was a bobbysoxer, wearing poodle skirts and penny loafers. We'd go to the drive-in every Saturday night and then go to church every Sunday together. We were so in love." Again, she gazed off into space.

After several quiet moments, Chloe softly asked, "What happened?"

Edwina flinched as if jolted from her daydream. "Celestine was so fond of Jake." She chuckled to herself. "I think she had a crush on him in the beginning." Her smile drooped. "Then, she started gossiping about him."

"What do you mean, gossiping?"

Edwina took a deep breath. "Celestine began calling Jake uneducated because he hadn't finished high school. Then she started asking questions like what would my future be with him and what kind of life could we have together. She began calling him names like half-breed, saying he wasn't good enough to marry into the family." Edwina shook her head. "I don't know what got into her."

"Wow." Chloe raised her eyebrow.

"After I told her he wasn't a 'half-breed,' that he was a quarter Menominee, a quarter French-Canadian, and half German-Swedish, not that it mattered one whit to me, Celestine's behavior toward him became malicious."

"Did they have a fight or something?"

Edwina shook her head. "Not to my knowledge. Jake never mentioned anything to me, but she began planting seeds of distrust. After he left one time, she asked, 'Did you see that lipstick on his collar?' I tried to ignore her and walk away, but she kept on. 'Don't know how you could've missed it,' she called after me."

Chloe opened her eyes wide. "Was there lipstick on his collar?"

"I don't think so, at least, I didn't at first. Then one Saturday, when he stopped by to take me to the drive-in, Celestine said, 'You should be more careful about kissing him. Look. You got lipstick on his collar.'"

"So?"

"I wasn't wearing lipstick." Edwina stared Chloe down.

"Ah."

"That started the first of our fights. He tried to deny it, but I wouldn't listen. I could see the evidence. Finally, I asked him to leave, and he slammed the door behind him. Celestine then asked me if I'd heard the rumors around town. She said, 'He's two-timing you. He's going out with Beverly Kohler.'"

"Was he?"

"At the time, I don't think so. She'd just moved to town, but Celestine wouldn't let up. She kept asking, 'What was that lipstick doing on his collar?' When I wouldn't respond, she said, 'Ever since Beverly took that job at the hardware shore, he's been spending a lot of time there.' I told her he was outfitting the boats and canoes. Of course he'd be at the hardware store. Where else would he get the oar locks and paddles? But she planted seeds of doubt."

Chloe blinked, thinking it over. *Sour grapes.* "From what you're saying, it seems like she had a grudge against Jake. Did she?"

Edwina sighed and then pressed her lips together. "I don't know. So many years have passed."

"Is that why you two broke off your engagement?"

"No. There was more. My grandmother Teresa, your great-great-grandmother, had left me a hundred-dollar savings bond." Edwina seemed to struggle with herself. She opened and then closed her mouth, as if she could not find the words or bring herself to say them.

"What happened to it?"

"When it came time for my normal school tuition, I cashed the bond into a hundred-dollar bill." She looked pointedly at Chloe. "That was a great deal of money at the time, the difference between going to school that semester or not."

Chloe nodded.

"I'd left it on the dining room table," she turned and pointed, "right over there and weighed it down with the cut-glass fruit bowl my mother always kept on the table. Jake stopped by on his way to work to pick up a book he'd loaned me. Then I walked him out the door and kissed him goodbye." She took a deep breath. "When I got back, the hundred-dollar bill was gone."

Chloe raised her eyebrows. "Was he ever alone with the money?"

"Only for a moment, when I stepped into the kitchen to get his book, but it was long enough to cast doubt. Celestine accused him of stealing it. She was relentless. She kept bringing it up, hounding our parents and me about it. I knew there had to be a simple explanation, so I asked Jake on the phone."

"He denied it?"

"Absolutely. He rushed over from work to help me look for it. Nothing in his attitude or actions implied anything suspicious, but Celestine wouldn't let it go. She accused Jake to his face, finally saying she had seen him stealing it."

"What did he do?"

"Trying to prove his innocence, he pulled everything out of his pockets and laid it on the table, but that wasn't enough. Celestine accused him of stashing it somewhere. The more he denied it, the more vehement she became. Things became heated. Finally, I told him to leave."

"Did you ever find the hundred-dollar bill?"

Shaking her head, Edwina drew a long breath. "We searched everywhere, but it never turned up."

"So Jake did steal it?"

Pursing her lips, she said, "I don't think so, yet there's no other explanation." She lifted her shoulders in a feeble shrug.

Chloe rolled her eyes as her shoulders slumped. "That's why you're so adamant about my not seeing Hud?"

"No, there's more." Edwina's eyes reddened and then filled with tears. She swallowed. "Three days later, Celestine drowned."

"What's that got to do with Hud or his family?"

"It was Jake's fault. His negligence killed her. He let her take one of his canoes out on rough water."

"How do you know that?"

"No one knows for sure, but the investigators' report said the waves were too strong for a fourteen-year-old's arms. Her canoe capsized, and she drowned."

"That doesn't prove negligence on Jake's part." Chloe raised her hand, palm up, gesturing futilely. "Why do you blame him?"

"There were witnesses. People saw him rent her a canoe." Edwina's hands began shaking as she raised her voice. "He shouldn't have let her go out on the Bay in such stormy water."

Chloe shook her head. "I can understand how horrible her death must have been, how shocking that your fourteen-year-old sister drowned, but the proof is all circumstantial. How can you blame him for her death?" She stared at her great-aunt. "It's been sixty years. It's time to let it go." *She has to, or any future with Hud will be tainted.*

"You don't understand." Edwina's head sagged onto her chest.

Chloe ran her hand through her hair, shaken by the story. "Don't turn Celestine's tragedy into a feud that continues into the third generation. Whatever happened, it wasn't Hud's fault. For your own sake, let it go."

"You don't understand." Her shoulders slumped.

Sighing, Chloe stood up and kissed her great-aunt's cheek. "I'm sorry telling me the story has made you relive Celestine's death. Is there anything I can do to help?"

The woman silently shook her head.

"Then I'm going to bed. I've got to be up early tomorrow for a conference call." Her heart went out to her great-aunt as she gazed at her slumped posture. *Her pain's obvious.* "Can I get you anything before I turn in?"

She silently shook her head again.

Chloe patted her shoulder and crossed into her bedroom. Suddenly, she felt chilled. Shivering, she looked at the thermometer. Better get a quilt. Then she remembered where Edwina kept them . . . in the back of her closet. Chloe grabbed the flashlight, confident the new batteries would work, but as soon as she entered the closet, the light again flickered and went out.

She gasped and rushed back into the room. The flashlight flickered back on. Cold though it was, she felt perspiration running down her neck. Again, she lay the flashlight on the floor, moved aside her clothes on the front rack, and peered into the back of the closet, where Edwina kept the quilts in a cedar chest.

She shuddered. *It looks like a coffin.* Her mind began playing what-if games. *Stop it. It's a chest, not a coffin. This is ridiculous. What am I, fourteen?*

She took a deep breath and began humming Tchaikovsky's "1812 Overture" to blot out the sounds of the blood rushing in her ears and the creaking floorboards underfoot. Then she dashed under the front rack of clothes and raced to the chest. When she lifted its lid, she couldn't see anything inside. Her humming got louder as she groped blindly with her hand. Finally, she grabbed what felt like a quilt. Then, slamming the top down, she raced back to her bedroom, gasping and shivering from more than the cold.

"Euwww." *Feels like spiders crawling down my back.* She shivered like a dog shaking off water. Then she unfolded the quilt and spread it on top of the bed.

Changing into pajamas, she slipped between the covers, but sleep escaped her. She lay in the dark, wondering whose bedroom this had been. *Celestine's?* Finally, promising to investigate the closet in the daylight, she drifted into a troubled sleep.

CHAPTER 3

"Do you girls have hope chests?" Lloyd asked.
"We certainly do."
"I don't," said Betsy. "My husband and I are going to use paper plates and napkins."
"Poor Joe!"
"Lucky Larry!"

– MAUD HART LOVELACE, *THE BETSY-TACY TREASURY*

The next morning, after her conference call, Chloe opened the blinds in her room, pulled all her clothes off the front rack, and set them on her bed. Then she got an extension cord and a lamp that she placed inside her deep closet. It was still gloomy, even with the combined daylight and lamplight. Despite her jagged breathing, she forced herself to stay and investigate.

Starting at the back, she looked at the large letter E carved into the cedar chest's lid. *This must have been Aunt Ed's hope chest.* She lightly ran her fingers over it, wondering what memories it contained for her. Inside, although shadowy, she saw neatly folded blankets and quilts. *Wonder if she bought these for her marriage that never was?* She closed its lid gently, no longer afraid of its imagined contents.

Although the dimly lit closet was chilly, it was not spooky in the daytime. Shaking her head, Chloe laughed at her earlier fears. She saw jackets and coats hanging on the back rack but nothing unusual. She took a deep breath, glad she had forced herself to confront her fears. *Even if it took daylight and extension cords.* She pressed her lips into a thin, white line. *If only it was that simple to shake all my fears.* She wrapped her arms around herself, thinking of Aaron.

Just as she was about to leave the cold closet, she stepped on a floorboard, and it creaked. *This again?* She stepped from board to board, rocking back and forth, isolating which was the offender. When she pinpointed it, she marked it with her shoe and went into the garage for a hammer and nails.

When she returned, she held a nail on the corner of the board and raised the hammer. *Your creaking, my friend, is soon to be a thing of the past.* When the hammer hit the nail, the entire board jumped. She flinched. "What the . . . ?" Then, experimenting, she tried pressing down one end of it. The other end rose slightly. *Could this board be intentionally loose?*

On a hunch, Chloe took the other side of the hammer and gingerly pried the board loose. As she lifted it out, she saw a small compartment beneath. Inside lay a petite jewelry box. She gasped. *How long has this been here?* She brushed away the accumulated dust and cobwebs and picked it up.

Anticipation growing, she breathed faster, then she hesitated momentarily before opening it. *Whose is it? Was it?* The cold surrounding her became icy. Her numb fingers shook as she lifted the lid. Then she heard something. *Was that a scream? My imagination's running rampant again.*

Inside lay vintage costume jewelry and several photos of a young woman. As she handled them, chills started at the back of her neck and ran down her spine. She closed the box and took it into her warmer and brighter room. She shuddered. *What is it about that closet?*

"Chloe?" called Edwina.

"In here," she called.

The older woman looked around the room at the clothes piled high on the bed, the extension cord stretching across the room, and the hammer and scattered nails.

"What happened? Did a tornado come through here?"

Chloe chuckled. "Spring cleaning." Then she held up the jewelry box. "Look what I found."

Edwina's mouth formed an O. "Is that . . . ?" Chloe handed the box to her. Tears started sliding down her cheeks. "Yes, this was Celestine's." As Edwina opened it, she slumped against the bed.

Chloe jumped to her feet, catching her great-aunt's arm. "Are you all right?" Chloe moved aside some clothes, clearing a place for her to sit.

Nodding, Edwina settled onto the bed and then began sifting through the photos. Looking at one picture in particular, she smiled through her tears and handed it to Chloe.

"This must have been taken just before she drowned. This is what my little sister looked like."

Chloe studied the adolescent girl, who smiled back through time. A pretty girl, Celestine wore her sandy-brown hair in a pageboy with bangs. A blue headband held her hair in place. Chloe stared, analyzing the expression. *Haughty. She seems to sneer, as if she knows something no one else does.*

Chloe returned the picture to Edwina. "Your sister looks like the cat that caught the canary."

"Why do you say that?"

"I don't know." Chloe shrugged. "She just looks like she's got a secret she's dying to tell."

As Edwina's expression drooped, Chloe realized what she had said.

"I'm sorry. It was a slip of the tongue."

"If it was a secret she was dying to tell, she took it to the grave with her."

Chloe grimaced. "Why don't we close this box for now? I'll make breakfast, and then we can sort through the photos when we finish eating."

⁕

After she had cleared away the breakfast dishes and brought out a fresh pot of coffee, Chloe carried the jewelry box to the table. Edwina laced her coffee with brandy and then began taking out the pictures, one by one.

"Here she is at her eighth-grade graduation." She took a deep breath and shook her head. "Smart kid. What a shame Celestine didn't live long enough to reach her potential."

Chloe frowned as she glanced at it.

"I remember this one." Ed shook her head. "That's the day Jake found a silvery-black rock she liked. Hematite . . . no, galena."

"She looks happy here." Chloe set it down with the other pictures.

Edwina nodded. "She was. She liked Jake . . . at least, at first."

As Edwina's smile drooped, Chloe quickly changed the subject. She picked up another photo. "Who's this in the picture with her?" She studied it. "He looks so familiar."

Edwina's eyes widened. Her lips began trembling. Then, swallowing, she cleared her throat. "That's Jake."

"That's Jake?" As Chloe took a longer look, it dawned on her. "Ohmigosh, the resemblance is amazing. He looks like Hud."

"Just like him," said Edwina. The two women stared at each other.

"That's why you objected to—"

"Yes. Hud's the spitting image of his grandfather at that age." Edwina looked away as she placed the photo back in the box, face down.

Chloe took a deep breath. "Wow."

When they finished with the photographs, they began going through the costume jewelry and other personal effects. One square, metallic looking stone caught Chloe's eye.

"Didn't you just mentioned something about galena?" She held up the stone for her great-aunt to see.

"Yes." The word came out like a long sigh. She hungrily held out her hand for it.

Something caught the corner of Chloe's eye on the floor, but as she handed the stone to Edwina, the image seemed to disappear. *Now I'm seeing things. Great.* She shook her head, trying to clear it.

"This is the very stone Jake gave her that day we had the picnic. She loved this stone. It fascinated her." Then Edwina paused, staring into space. "Maybe it was the fact Jake gave it to her."

"What makes you say that?"

"She had a schoolgirl crush on him." Edwina sighed. "She used to follow him around." She handed the stone back to Chloe.

The moment the cold stone touched her skin, Chloe heard a voice. "Did not."

Chloe looked left, looked right. She looked under the table. Opening her eyes wide, she gasped. There sat a girl with a pageboy. *Celestine!*

The girl looked up and met her eyes. "You can see me?"

Chloe blinked. Speechless, she tried to move her lips.

"You can see me!"

"What are you doing down there?" asked Edwina.

"N . . . nothing." Chloe swallowed. "Just dropped something." She sat up straight.

The girl scrambled out from under the table and stood between them.

"You're as white as a sheet," said Edwina. "You feel all right?"

"Fine." The girl was in her direct line of vision when she looked at her great-aunt. Then the girl flicked her fingers in front of Chloe's eyes.

"Made you blink. Made you blink." Putting her hands to her mouth, she giggled. Then she became serious. "You really can see me, can't you?"

"Let me see that stone again," said Edwina, holding out her hand. Her arm reached through Celestine's spine and torso.

Chloe gasped and began choking.

"You sure you're all right?" asked Edwina.

Nodding silently, Chloe placed the stone in her aunt's hand. The moment she lost contact with the galena, Celestine vanished. *Ohmigosh. This is too weird.*

"I'd really better get to work. Maybe we can look through the rest of this tomorrow?"

"Of course." Edwina set down the stone and began gathering the photos and memorabilia.

"Just leave everything, Aunt Ed. I'll put it away." When her hand touched the galena, Celestine appeared again. Chloe caught her breath and threw the stone in the jewelry box. The minute the stone left her hand, Celestine vanished again. *I have to think this through.*

But the day got busier as it wore on. Back-to-back conference calls kept her mind on business, not the jewelry box. When she heard a knock at the door, she flinched and then checked her watch. "Four already?" She looked at the clutter on the dining room table and remembered the mess she had left in her room. Silently groaning, she finger-combed her hair and pinched her cheeks before answering the door.

"Hey, Hud, come on in."

"Hey." His eyes warmed into a smile the moment he saw her, and she felt the day's tension melt away. "Hello, Miss Ed," he called toward the living room, where she sat, rocking, slowly browsing through photo albums.

She said a brusque hello and then dipped her head. A beat later, she added in a friendlier tone, "Please thank Rose for the irises last night." She smiled shyly first at Chloe and then at Hud. "They're beautiful."

"Will do, Miss Ed." Then he turned toward Chloe with his intense, dark eyes. "All set?"

"Almost. Just have to change into my swimsuit. Should I wear it my under my clothes?"

He grinned. "It'd be easier that way." She dashed off. "And bring a towel," he called after her.

⚬

Fifteen minutes later, they turned into the Peninsula State Park. The ranger saw Hud's annual sticker on his windshield and waved him through. As they drove toward the beach, Chloe noticed a tower.

"What's that? A fire lookout?"

"Originally it was, when they built it a hundred years ago. Now, Eagle Tower's an observation platform." He looked at her. "It's got phenomenal views of the Green Bay islands and even Michigan's Upper Peninsula. Want to climb it?"

"Sure." She was game for any adventure when his smoldering eyes challenged hers. *With him, I feel I can do anything.*

"Though you have to work for the view, it's worth the climb. It's seventy-five feet of stairs, but at two hundred and twenty-five feet above the water, nothing tops it."

"If you say so, I believe you." She smiled bashfully. "You haven't steered me wrong yet."

After he parked, he took her hand. "C'mon."

Her calves ached, and she was breathless by the time they reached the top, but she forgot all that once she saw the vistas.

"Oh, this is gorgeous." She peered out over the bay. An eagle soared above the treetops but below them.

Standing slightly behind her, he used his body to shield her from the winds. When he reached his arm over her shoulders, she could follow its line, seeing where he pointed.

"That's looking north toward Washington Island."

"Washington Island. I've heard of it, but never been there."

"It's a great day trip. Maybe Saturday, if you're not busy, we could make a day of it."

"Sounds like fun." She turned around to see his eyes and found herself inches from his lips. Pressed against him, she shuddered.

"Cold?"

"A little," she fibbed, not ready to tell him the reason.

He put both arms around her, warming her with the heat of his body. Because his chin was even with her forehead, he leaned down to kiss her, and his hair tickled her neck, sending shivers down her spine. She lifted her arms around his neck, returning his kiss.

Finally, her arms still around him, she drew away and looked into his dancing, dark eyes.

"Maybe we should go swimming before the sun sets."

"Good idea."

A few minutes later found them at Nicolet Beach. Several people were sunbathing or beachcombing. Two were kayaking, and most were splashing in the clear water. Though it wasn't private, they had no trouble finding a secluded part of the sandy beach to claim as their own. Towels marked their territory.

After they stripped down to their swimsuits, Chloe started running toward the water.

"Last one in's a rotten egg!"

"No fair," he called, taking off one sock and hopping on the other foot. He still nearly beat her into the water.

They waded out until the waves lapped at her thighs.

"It's cold," she said, hunching her shoulders.

"Refreshing." He grinned. "It's like ripping off a Band-Aid. The faster you do it, the less painful."

Screaming, she dove into the waves and paddled around. When she surfaced, she grinned.

"It is refreshing. After the initial plunge, it feels good."

They swam and splashed until the sun began to sink, but Chloe did not want the day to end. Being with Hud seemed so right. *Not like anything I've ever felt.* Again, she had the sensation she had known him before and then lost him.

Now reunited, she began to resent anything that separated them, even the day's end. As they walked back to his pickup, she turned toward him.

"How would you like to have dinner with Aunt Ed and me tonight?"

"I'd like that." He gave her shoulders a friendly squeeze. "But only if I bring dessert."

"Okay." She gave him a sidelong smile.

They stopped to pick up an ice cream cake and were back at Edwina's before sunset.

Chloe removed the salmon steaks from the marinade as Hud got the gas grill working. She tossed a green salad with strawberries and avocadoes, then drizzled a honey/poppy seed dressing over all.

Setting up a card table on the back porch, the three of them sat down to dinner just as the sun dipped below the horizon. Edwina cut into her salmon with her fork, but before she could taste it, Chloe spoke up.

"Hud, did you want to say grace?"

Wearing a quizzical half-smile, Edwina set down her fork and folded her hands. After the short prayer, she said, "Amen." Then she looked at Hud, studying him.

"You know, you're the image of your grandfather when he was your age."

He met her stare with an easy-going smile. "I've heard that before, but I've seen very few pictures of him at any age. He isn't one to look back at his past."

Edwina cocked her head to the side and gave a shallow sigh. "Then you're in for a surprise. Chloe found some old photos this morning that you might find interesting."

Hud looked back and forth between the two of them, but neither said more, so he let the subject drop.

After dinner, they had dessert and coffee at the dining room table. Chloe set the jewelry box before Edwina.

"You hadn't finished going through these pictures this morning. Why don't you tell Hud and me about them?"

As if choosing memories, Edwina carefully selected which photo to narrate first. Finally, she picked up a picture of several people sitting at a table.

"This was taken at Celestine's fourteenth birthday party." She passed the photo to Chloe, who shared it with Hud.

"Ohmigosh," said Chloe, studying the round, oak table. "This is the same table." Pointing to the people in the picture, she glanced at Edwina. "This is you. This must be Celestine, right?" Edwina nodded.

"And this must be my grandfather," said Hud, studying the details of the man's face. "You're right. I do look like him."

"The spitting image," said Edwina, lacing her coffee from her flask. She selected another photo. "This was your grandfather and me in 1955." Again, she passed the photo to Chloe, who shared it with Hud.

Staring at it, he turned toward Edwina. "Have you noticed a similarity between you and Chloe?"

"Really?" asked Chloe, studying the young Edwina in the photo. *She's beautiful. I can't possibly look like this.* She shook her head as she looked from Hud to her great-aunt. "I don't look like this, do I?"

Edwina scrutinized her face and then looked at the picture. Slowly nodding, she said, "Now that Hud's mentioned it, you do. I just hadn't realized it before." She gazed at Chloe and Hud. "Looking at you two is like looking at Jake and me sixty years ago." She nodded her head and then sipped her coffee. "It's not as if time stood still. It's more like it . . . moved sideways."

"Like an alternate universe." Chloe nodded, grasping her great-aunt's meaning. "The same, yet different." She glanced from the picture to Hud to Edwina. *Looking at the photos is almost like picking up where they left off.* She stared at the picture, examining the faces for clues. *Since I met Hud, I've felt I'd known him before.*

Edwina took out the costume jewelry and the piece of galena, laying them on the table in front of her.

"What's this?" Hud picked up the galena, rolling it in his hand, studying it.

I forgot about that. The morning's memories rushed at Chloe like an Arctic blast. Catching her breath, chills ran down her spine.

"That's galena," said Edwina. "Your grandfather gave it to my sister Celestine."

Hud set down the stone and looked into space, seeming to recall some lost memory. He started to speak, hesitated, and then said, "I vaguely remember hearing a story about your sister." He shook his head. "But I can't recollect."

Chloe glanced nervously at her great-aunt, wondering how she might react.

Edwina calmly set down her cup, looked Hud in the eye, and said, "She's the girl who drowned in your grandfather's canoe."

Hud inhaled through his mouth and nodded. "Now I remember."

"Jake never told you about it?" asked Edwina.

"He's never mentioned it. I just recall my aunts' whispers in the kitchen."

Nodding slowly, Edwina sipped her coffee. "Hand me that stone, would you, Chloe?"

She hesitated, afraid of what she might see. *How silly.* She picked up the stone and instantly saw Celestine hovering over Hud.

"Jake," said the vision, trying to pull at his collar. "Jake." Then, as if she felt Chloe's eyes on her, Celestine turned and looked her directly in the eye. "Tell Jake I'm sorry."

Gasping for air, Chloe handed the stone to Edwina as if it were a hot potato. Just as quickly as it had appeared, the vision vanished.

"Are you all right?" Edwina studied her.

"I'm fine, just . . . yawning." At her own suggestion, she yawned, proving her point. Then she grinned self-consciously. "Sorry." She turned to Edwina. "Can you tell us anything about this stone?"

Edwina lifted an eyebrow. "There isn't much to tell. Jake, Celestine, and I had gone on a picnic. We went for a walk after we ate, and then Jake found this rock. From the moment she saw it, Celestine was attracted to it." She turned to Chloe. "The fact that she kept it in her jewelry box shows how she treasured it."

"Could I see it again?" Hud held out his hand.

"Sure." Once more Chloe was the conduit as Edwina passed the stone to Hud. For the fraction of a moment it touched her hand, Chloe saw Celestine. "Tell Jake."

Beneath the table, Chloe rubbed her hand on her thigh, wanting to wipe off all traces of the brief connection. Though the rock intrigued her, it also frightened her.

Hud rolled the stone in his hand, examining it. "I can tell you a little about its gemstone properties. This is the stone they used in crystal wire sets a hundred years ago. It's found in lead ore and contains traces of silver. It's also used in herbal, holistic, and homeopathic remedies, as well as crystal healing."

"Really?" Chloe wanted to hear more. *There has to be a reason it affects me this way.* "Does it have any metaphysical properties?"

As if weighing the stone, he bounced it in his hand as he spoke. "Galena's known for communication, receptiveness, and insight. Mystic tradition views it as an aid for shamanic journeys. Supposedly, it helps people face and overcome their deepest fears, as well as recover their personal power." He glanced at her laptop and then grinned at her. "It's also believed to counteract any electromagnetic pollution or computer radiation from sitting in front of laptops for long hours."

Chloe laughed. "That I could definitely use."

"Try it. Keep it by your computer." Starting to hand it back to her, he withdrew it. "Wait, I have a better idea. Can I keep this until tomorrow?"

"Of course." She spoke quickly, glad to have it out of her reach until she could think it through, accept it for the marvel it was. At the moment, it scared her.

He glanced at his watch and then turned to Edwina and Chloe. "I really should be going. To thank you ladies for this delectable dinner, how would you like to be my guests tomorrow night at the Theatre Under the Stars?"

Edwina hesitated. Holding up her casted arm, she shook her head. "One broken bone a summer is enough, thank you." She gave him a wry smile. "Besides, I'm getting a little too old to be traipsing over park trails in the dark."

"They have golf cart transportation from the parking lot to the amphitheater." His cheek dimpled as he smiled.

Again, she shook her head. Then she turned to Chloe. "Why don't you go? Enjoy it for us both."

"I'd love to." Catching Hud's eye, she smiled, hoping he sensed the anticipation mounting in the pit of her stomach. *Can't wait to see you.*

"Great. I'll pick you up tomorrow at sunset."

At noon, Chloe's phone buzzed with a text. See you at one. Aaron.

What? She texted back. Where are you?

Green Bay. Just landed.

She felt her heart racing. Not a good idea, she texted.

Don't you want to see me?

She groaned inwardly. No. She rolled her eyes as she texted. I'm busy.

I spend all this money, take all this time to see you, and you can't spare a few minutes.

She sighed. *He hasn't changed.* She texted No, not now, but her heart screamed *Not ever.*

I get it. You're seeing someone else.

DO NOT COME. STOP TEXTING ME.

Her cell phone rang. Rather than answer, she turned off the ringer, but she knew that was not the end of it.

An hour later, he rang the front doorbell. When she did not answer immediately, he rang twice more.

Edwina called sleepily from the back porch. "Someone's at the door."

Yeah, whether I like it or not. She sighed. "I'll get it."

She looked through the peephole, watching him pace back and forth. As he reached for the doorbell again, she cracked the door.

"You're disturbing my aunt's nap, Aaron. What do you want?"

He gave an expression of utter exasperation, scrunching up his face and then releasing, as if struggling to regain his calm. After a theatrical sigh, he brought out a bunch of daisies from behind his back and held them out to her. When she did not open the door wider, he shoved them through the small opening, breaking one of the stems.

She let them fall to the floor. "What do you want?"

"What do I want?" He heaved another great sigh. "I want you to know the trouble you've caused me."

"That I caused you?" She shook her head. "And what imagined trouble is that, Aaron?"

"I had to track you down, take time off from work, fly here, rent a car, and now that I'm here, look how you treat me."

"Track me down." She grimaced. "What'd you do? Go to HR for my forwarding address?" She knew from his scowl that was exactly what he had done. "And it took you what? All of five minutes. I'm sure the time, plane fare, and car rental are all business expenses you'll write off, so I repeat. What do you want?"

He stepped closer to the door. "What I want is what I've always wanted: to see you happy." Stepping closer, he pushed against the door. Surprised when it did not open, he scuffed his shoe.

"I like things the way things are. You've seen I'm happy. Now leave." She tried to shut the door, but he had wedged his shoe in the crack.

"You can't be, not in this Godforsaken outpost. I know you." He homed in on her eyes, staring her down. "You're incapable of taking care of yourself. You need someone to look out for you. You know it as well as I do. You can't manage on your own."

When she tried to shut the door again, squeezing his toes in the process, his tone changed. "I'm only telling you these things for your own good. I don't want to see you living in some unrealistic la-la land."

She gave him a sickly smile. "I can take care of myself and my great-aunt just fine, thank you."

"You can't even be honest with yourself," he scoffed. "You're not here to take care of your great-aunt any more than I am. You're here because you're running away from me."

She caught her breath, cringing at the truth, but she struggled to keep up a brave front. "There were good reasons why I left you."

"You couldn't even do that right. You snuck off without so much as a goodbye."

"I'd said goodbye a week earlier when I broke up with you."

"You can run, but you can't hide." Then, smiling his most charming smile, he used his favorite term of endearment. "You Big Dummy, you know you need me." He chuckled. "You need a user's manual just to turn on the light switch."

She rolled her eyes. "That's it. I put up with your emotional abuse for three years, and I'm done. It's over. We're over. And if you don't leave the property this minute, I'm calling the police."

His eyes challenged her. "You wouldn't."

"Watch." She began dialing 911.

He backed off toward his parked car. "This isn't over."

"Yes, it is."

She slammed the door and locked it, catching some of his daisies in the doorjamb. Then, drained emotionally, she leaned back against the door, taking a deep breath.

That felt good. Where did I finally find the strength to stand up to him? Now, if I could just undo the three years' worth of damage he's done to my self-image.

Just before the sun set, Hud knocked on the door. Seeing his warm smile brightened her mood.

"Hey," he said.

Closing the door behind her, Chloe stepped outside to kiss him privately. "Oh, I'm glad to see you."

Holding her in his arms, he kissed her back. Then, squinting, he peered into her face. "What's wrong?"

She shrugged. "Nothing. Why?"

He shook his head. "You just seem different. You sure you don't want to tell me about it?"

Her chest heaving, she took a deep breath as she stared up at him through her eyelashes.

"Maybe we're reaching the point where you should know." Then she smiled. "But how about after the show? This story might take some time."

"Fair enough."

"I'm almost ready. Want to come in a minute?"

As they stepped inside, Hud noticed Edwina drinking her after-dinner coffee, paging through a scrapbook. "Hello, Miss Ed."

"Hello." She puffed on her cigar.

"Are you sure we can't talk you into joining us at the theater?"

She smiled but shook her head. "Thanks, but you young people will enjoy it more without worrying about me."

He pulled a small box from his pocket. "Then maybe you'd be interested in seeing this." Holding Chloe's hand, he walked toward the table and presented the box to her under Edwina's watchful eye.

"What is it?" Chloe looked from the box in her hand to his dancing eyes.

"Open it." He grinned, his irresistible dimple deepening.

Chloe felt like reaching up and kissing it. Instead, she took the lid off the box. There was the galena, wire wrapped in an intricate design and hung on a silver chain. She lifted it out and looked at it in the light.

"It's gorgeous." She kissed his cheek. "Thank you." She looked at him in disbelief. "Did you make this yourself?"

He glanced uncertainly at Edwina and then turned to her. "No, my grandfather made it."

Edwina's coffee cup crashed to the floor. Though nearly empty, it splattered across the oak floorboards, scattering ceramic shards and coffee. Simultaneously, Chloe and Hud knelt down to pick up the larger pieces.

"Let me get some paper towels from the kitchen," Chloe said.

"Sorry, Miss Ed. I didn't mean to startle you."

"Nothing to apologize for. You just surprised me. That's all." She looked at Chloe, mopping up the coffee and ceramic splinters. "I'm the one that's sorry to have made such a mess."

"No harm done." Chloe stood up. "Let me dump this in the trash and get you another cup of coffee." She smiled at Hud. "Then let's get a proper look at Jake's handiwork."

She returned with the coffee, setting it by Edwina. Then she lifted the chain, letting the wire wrapped galena rotate so she could see all sides of the square stone. She grabbed Hud's hand.

"It's beautiful. Please thank Jake for me."

"I can, or maybe you'd like to thank him in person."

"I'd . . ." Chloe glanced at Edwina and swallowed. "I'd like that." Handing him the chain, she lifted up her long hair and presented her back to him. "Put it on me?"

As he clasped it around her neck, the loosely-wrapped stone touched her skin, connecting with her, and she saw Celestine.

Pointing to Hud, Celestine asked, "Isn't this Jake?"

Chloe shook her head in silent answer and then turned to Hud and Edwina. "How does it look?"

"It hangs at just the right length. My grandfather was worried about that. He thought it might be too short or too long."

"Grandfather?" Her eyes narrowing, Celestine scrutinized Hud. Then she turned to Chloe. "Jake couldn't be his grandfather, could he?"

Chloe nodded. She put her hand to the stone, feeling where it hung in relation to her neckline. "It fits perfectly." *But how am I going to wear this necklace without constantly seeing and hearing Celestine? I'll just have to learn how to tune her out.* Then she had an idea. "Be right back."

A moment later she returned, smiling, wearing a blouse with a high, jewel neck collar. The necklace rested on her blouse, not her skin. *No visions or dialogue from Celestine.*

"All set?" asked Hud.

"Am now."

⸺ ❦ ⸺

In the pickup, Chloe turned to Hud. "This really was so sweet of you to think of turning a memory into a work of art. And of Jake to make it. It's one of a kind." Unintentionally fondling the stone as she spoke, she suddenly saw Celestine sitting in the front seat between them. With a gasp, Chloe quickly took her hand off her necklace.

"My grandfather was glad to do it." Hud took his eyes from the road momentarily to glance at her. "He said he's wanted to make peace between the families for a long time, and you gave him the opportunity. He said to thank you."

"Me? I didn't do anything. I'm just the lucky one who gets to wear this fine piece of jewelry."

"You're the link between the families, the mediator."

She gave him a sidelong glance, thinking of Celestine. *What will her role be in all this?* "I really would like to meet Jake, thank him."

"Then let's set a date. How would you like to come to dinner at Pop-pop's tomorrow?"

She smiled at Hud's use of Rose's name for Jake. "I'd love it."

After Hud parked, they walked the short distance to the amphitheater, rented cushions, and found their seats. As they sat beneath the twinkling stars, Hud put his arm around her shoulders. She leaned against him with a sigh. *I've come home.*

An hour and a half later, they applauded the one-act musical comedy, turned in their cushions, and walked back to his pickup, arm in arm.

She looked up into Hud's eyes. "Could we go somewhere to talk?"

Even in the dark, his eyes glimmered like the stars overhead. "I know just the place."

She chuckled. "Somehow, I knew you would."

"Sven's Bluff has terrific views of northern lights and starry skies."

As he pulled her toward him in a kiss, her heart started beating faster. She caught her breath and lightly placed her fingertips on his chest as a gentle restraint.

"Seriously, I mean talk."

They drove to the lookout and gazed at the moonlit bay far beneath them. The stars shone brightly, but tonight Chloe saw no dancing northern lights.

Turning toward Hud, she figured the best approach to her subject was direct. "Do you believe in ghosts?"

Momentarily stunned, he broke into laughter. Then he shook his head. "Got to admit. You have an interesting lead-in to conversations." He thought for a moment. "I don't discount ghosts. I've just never seen one."

"What would you say if I told you I have?" She studied him as he stared at her.

"Have you?"

She nodded.

"How long have you been seeing them?" Eyes narrowing, he watched her.

"Since yesterday."

"Yesterday? What happened yesterday?"

She held the chain out from her chest. "Yesterday, I found the stone. It had been hidden since before Celestine drowned."

"Is she . . . ?"

"I have a ghost following me that looks fourteen and is convinced you're Jake." She raised her eyebrows at his questioning expression. "Yes."

His eyes darted around the truck's cabin. "Is she here now?"

Chloe took a deep breath. "I think so. Let me see." She touched her hand to the galena, and she saw Celestine sitting between them.

"How can you refer to me as 'she'?" She jabbed her finger into Hud's arm. "And if he isn't Jake, who is he?"

Chloe pulled her hand away from the stone to still the sights and sounds. "Celestine's here."

"Well . . . what does she want?"

Again Chloe touched her wire wrapped galena. "What do—?"

"You don't have to repeat what others say," she snapped. "Just because you can't hear, doesn't mean I can't."

"Okay, so what do you want?"

"I messed up Edwina's and Jake's lives. I want to set the record straight."

Chloe whispered to Hud, "Sounds like she wants to make some sort of confession."

"It wasn't Jake's fault I drowned. It was an accident." The vision and her voice died away.

After a pause, Chloe glanced at Hud and asked Celestine again. "What do you want?" She encircled her pendant with her hand to make sure she was making connection. Then she felt a tap on her shoulder.

"Look," Hud whispered.

Chloe gasped as her hand lost its grip on her necklace. The northern lights were starting their evening dance. Losing her focus on the galena pendant and Celestine, she stared up in wonder as the fuchsia and lime lights swirled over their heads.

Several moments later, when she remembered her mission, she held her pendant and asked again. "What do you want, Celestine?" But there was nothing: no sound, no picture.

"What's going on?" Hud whispered.

She shook her head. "Nothing. There's nothing. It's like a television that's lost power." Chloe hunched her shoulders, unable to explain.

She tried contacting Celestine several times more, but it was useless. As her eyes followed the twirling lights of the aurora borealis overhead, she began wondering.

"Rose said the northern lights were caused by sunspot activity, which is what causes geomagnetic storms. Could that somehow interfere with contacting Celestine?"

"You're asking me? I've never seen her." He chuckled. "But heck, yeah. Why not? Though few can see another plane, we can all see the northern lights. During sunspot activity, I know the solar wind's magnetic field interacts with the earth's, causing an increase in plasma movement." He shrugged. "Who's to say whether one affects the other or not?"

"So maybe the geomagnetic storms 'short-circuit' Celestine's ability to appear." She chuckled. "At least, that's the 'technical' answer you're getting from this technical writer."

He looked through the windshield at the swirling lights. Then he turned to her. "In the meantime, let's just enjoy the show."

When she got home, Edwina was still paging through the scrapbooks.

"How was the show?"

"Which one?" Chloe chuckled. "After the performance at the Theatre Under the Stars, the aurora borealis put on its own show. Tonight was a double feature."

Edwina's eyes fell on the galena pendant. She gave Chloe a wistful smile and called her over. "I found something that might interest you about our family."

"Really?" Chloe pulled up a chair. "What is it?"

"You'd mentioned the Peshtigo Fire the other day." Chloe nodded. "You recall my telling you about your great-great-grandmother, Teresa Malone. When she was seven, she accompanied Adele Brise at two of the Marian sightings at Our Lady of Good Help. Then, ten years later, on February twenty-fifth, 1869, Teresa Malone married Dan O'Hare and moved to Williamson's Mill, where Dan worked."

Chloe quickly calculated. "The apparitions occurred in 1859, so Teresa Malone must have been seventeen when she married."

"Yes." Edwina opened to a bookmarked page of the scrapbook. "Two years later, just after Teresa gave birth to her first child—your great-grandmother, Maria O'Hare—the Peshtigo Fire swept through Door County, Northeastern Wisconsin, and Upper Michigan, destroying millions of dollars' worth of property and timberland. Depending on the account, it claimed between twelve hundred and twenty-four hundred lives."

Chloe squinted, trying to recall elementary school history.

"Didn't that happen on the same day as the Chicago Fire?"

"Yes, October eighth, 1871. To this day, the Peshtigo Fire remains the worst recorded fire in North American history."

"You mean, the legend of a cow kicking over a lantern wasn't what caused the fire?" Snorting, Chloe gave her a wry half-smile.

As she pressed her lips together in a grim line, Edwina shook her head. "That legend helped the Chicago Fire become part of American history, but the Peshtigo Fire didn't get the same media coverage. Except for a handful of history buffs, like myself, and a couple academics—"

"Don't forget Wisconsin's elementary school children. As I recall, state history's part of the fourth-grade curriculum."

"With those exceptions, the Peshtigo Fire slipped into obscurity. Although, recently there's been interest among astronomers, conservationists, and meteorologists. It's even been a subject of novels and plays."

"Astronomers? I seem to recall reading about someone's theory of a comet or meteor hitting the Great Lakes area and starting the fires. Is that what caused it?"

"Spurious astronomy. That impact theory was debunked years ago."

"Then what did cause the Peshtigo and Chicago Fires?"

"It wasn't just one cause." Edwina waved the thought away with a flick of her wrist. "Although the weather was primarily responsible for the fires, five different factors converged."

"Okay, let's start with the weather. October's usually gorgeous in Wisconsin." Chloe hunched her shoulders. "What was so different that month in 1871?"

"Drought, for one thing. Prolonged and widespread drought combined with high temperatures caused the fires." Edwina sipped her laced coffee. "High winds were also reported. Because of that, some contend a cyclone spread the flames, creating firestorms in its path."

"Weather was one factor. What were the other four?"

"Fire was considered a friend, a tool. Farmers used it to clear land for crops."

"'Slash and burn' was common?"

Edwina nodded. "Before today's earth moving machinery, fire was the only effective way to clear fields for crops, but the logging industry was also to blame. Loggers intentionally set fire to trimmed branches from the virgin pines. Either that or they simply left the piles to dry, creating tinder ripe for spontaneous combustion."

"Okay, that's three. What were the last two factors?"

"Railroads were given the right-of-way through many thousands of acres. When they cleared the land for the tracks, they left the cut trees and brush where they fell."

"Let me guess. Sparks from the wood burning steam engines set brush fires, right?"

Edwina nodded. "Finally, since timber was so plentiful, sawmills and wood turning factories had enormous inventories of raw logs, lumber, charcoal, furniture, and assorted items."

"Which must have produced mountains of bark and sawdust."

"Yes. They did everything to get rid of it, even dumping it in the lakes and streams, but still the mounds of sawdust grew. They had nowhere to put it, so they used it any way they could, even paving their streets with it and using it as flooring."

"Yikes, they couldn't see the forest for the . . . lumber and sawdust."

"Wood was so cheap, they used it for everything: log cabins in the country, frame construction in town, fences, and boardwalks."

"And no one minded living in a timberland, while all these people started fires and left them burning unattended?"

"Stories are recorded about the smoke being so thick some days, people could barely breathe. The smoke actually blotted out the sun. At midday, the light-house had its light burning so the ships could navigate the bay."

"Yet people stayed." Sighing, Chloe slowly shook her head. "Common sense is a flower that doesn't grow in everyone's garden."

"No," said Edwina, frowning at her. "Don't judge those people by today's standards. Remember, transportation was slow, primarily through the forests on rabbit paths, not interstate highways. Escape was difficult, and fire was a daily companion, a tool. People were used to flames licking at the bases of trees and fires smoldering. Usually, it passed by."

"But not this time."

"Definitely not this time." Edwina's face was grim. "The stories survivors told are atrocious." She swallowed. "These aren't things that took place long, long ago in faraway galaxies. My own mother survived the Peshtigo Fire." Edwina cleared her throat. "What my grandmother told me about it, I'll never forget."

"Like what?"

"She told of a neighbor, Mr. Lempke, who had tried to escape with his wife and children in a horse drawn wagon. A tree fell in their path. He jumped down from the wagon to move it aside so the horse could get through. He heard screams, and when he looked up, he saw his wife and children on fire, flames shooting from their hair and clothes. He tried to save them, but it was too late. The flames were so intense, the wagon, his wife, and children were reduced to cinders within minutes."

"So the only reason he was saved was because he was closer to the ground?" Grimacing, Chloe closed her eyes, trying to drive the image from her mind. "How horrible."

Edwina continued in a monotone. "From what I've heard of the fire storms, that scenario wasn't uncommon. Grandmother told of a small child surviving when her parents, one on each side of her, burned to death."

"How awful. What did they do with the orphans, the injured?"

"The survivors took them in as best they could." Edwina hunched her shoulders. "Grandmother told of the combined remains of what had been three adults that were found so thoroughly burned their ashes were placed in a two-quart container. Nearby, the remains of a man were found. All that was left was a knife blade, a ring, a few pieces of his skull, and a couple teeth. She said the entire body could be held in the palm of your hand."

"Ohmigosh!" Feeling nauseous, Chloe swallowed hard.

"The wind's direction kept changing, alternating between the southwest, west, northwest, and then back to the south. Throughout the firestorms, a series of whirlwinds showered cinders and sparks in every direction. Steam whistles from the mills and tug boats in the harbor blew their alarms, but the winds overtook nearly everything in their paths."

"Yet somehow your mother and grandmother survived."

Edwina took a deep breath as she nodded. "Yes. Although they lived too far from the bay to run toward the water, Grandmother thought quickly. She lay face down in a plowed field, holding her newborn baby, my mother, beneath her. They escaped what she said 'Seemed a certain death.'"

"What a strong woman." Chloe bit her bottom lip. *Wish I was more like her.*

Edwina surveyed her before she spoke. "Our family's always had strong women. We've had to be, but Grandmother didn't consider her actions anything unusual. She called herself a 'typical pioneer mother.' She felt blessed, not brave."

"What about her husband? Did he survive?"

"My grandfather, Dan O'Hare, happened to be visiting family in Champion at the time." Tilting her head to the side, Edwina smiled. "Here's where our family history again parallels that of Our Lady of Good Help."

Chloe leaned forward. "How so?"

"As the fire raged toward them, Dan and the family led all their livestock to the church. They prayed and prayed to be saved from the firestorm. Adele Brise helped them form a procession to beg Our Lady to intercede for them. First, they processed on their knees outside, circling the church, saying the rosary and carrying a statue of Our Lady before them. Later, as the firestorm became too much to bear, the people went inside, and the livestock stayed outside, within the fenced, consecrated grounds. Inside the chapel, the people prayed before the Eucharist."

"So Dan survived?"

"Yes. The next morning, in the light of day, he and the rest of the people walked outside. They saw devastation in all directions. What had been a small clearing in the middle of an enormous forest was now the only remaining area untouched. Fire had destroyed all the virgin pine outside the grounds. The tall trees had been reduced to cinders. All they could see was flat land with smoldering ashes for miles in every direction. Everything around the fence had burned. Nothing was left. Yet somehow the flames arched over and around the chapel."

"So they were saved."

"Flames had licked at the outside of the fence and blistered the wood, charred it, but inside the fence, the paint was untouched. In fact, even the grass inside the fence was green. Grandfather said it was like a sea of green in an ocean of gray ashes. All the livestock on the grounds and all the people within the church of Our Lady of Good Help survived. Grandfather called it a miracle. He and Grandmother went on to have another nine children, five more daughters and four sons."

"Our ancestors sure were lucky."

"Blessed," said Edwina, opening the scrapbook to another page. "Grand-mother saved this article from the *Eagle Extra*, dated October eleventh." She handed the scrapbook to Chloe. "My eyes are getting too old for this. Read it aloud, would you?"

Chloe looked at the yellowed, brittle piece of newspaper and squinted, trying to read its faded print.

"Standing amid the charred and blackened embers, with the frightfully muti-lated corpses of men, women, children, horses, oxen, cows, dogs, swine, and fowls—every house, shed, barn, outhouse, or structure of any kind swept from the earth as with the very besom of destruction—our emotions cannot be de-scribed in language. No pen dipped in liquid fire can paint the scene—language 'in thoughts that breathe and words that burn,' gives but the faintest impression of its horrors."

Chloe handed back the clipping. "It's impossible to imagine a natural disaster on that scale."

CHAPTER 4

"Two words. Three vowels. Four consonants. Seven letters.
It can either cut you open to the core and leave you in ungodly pain or it can
free your soul and lift a tremendous weight off your shoulders.
The phrase is: It's over."

– MAGGI RICHARD

The next morning, when she logged into work, Chloe saw the email from her supervisor. Over breakfast, she mentioned it to Edwina.

"I have to spend a couple days at the office in Milwaukee. Apparently, the product development manager wants me to assist onsite with the UAT testing." What she did not mention was the manager's name: Aaron. *Breaking off our relationship is harder than I thought.*

"When do you have to leave?"

"In the morning. Will you be all right while I'm gone?"

"I'm perfectly capable of taking care of myself, thank you. You don't need to babysit me." Scowling, she poured another cup of coffee, lacing it with brandy.

Chloe swallowed her smile. "I'll go grocery shopping today so you'll have plenty of veggies for salads and frozen dinners to microwave."

"And don't forget coffee." She sipped her hot drink. "And brandy."

⸺⸺ ❖ ⸺⸺

When Hud rang the doorbell that evening, Chloe's heart skipped a beat. *Saying goodbye is going to be tough.* Stepping onto the front porch, she closed the door behind her and kissed him.

As they finally pulled apart, he gazed into her eyes. "That was quite a hello."

Grimacing, she said, "Actually, it's an early goodbye. I have to go to Milwaukee for a few days." Then, laying her head on his chest, she threw her arms around him. "I miss you already. This is ridiculous. We've only just met and I . . ."

He hugged her to him, and they stood, silently communicating in their embrace, until Edwina called through the screened window.

"The way you two carry on, you'd think she'd enlisted and was going off to war."

Chuckling, they broke apart.

"Hello, Miss Ed," he called to the window.

"C'mon in."

Chloe opened the door and led him inside. Edwina was sitting in her rocker, going through another photo album.

"Miss Ed, how would you like to come to dinner at Pop-pop's tonight?"

"Jake's?" Edwina's eyes opened wide as her jaw hung slack. Then, clearing her throat, she said coldly, "No thank you." Without another word, she resumed studying the photos, turning the pages. He had been dismissed.

Hud blinked and worked his jaw but said nothing.

Rolling her eyes, Chloe tried to smooth over the rebuff. "Aunt Ed's already had dinner, but thanks so much for inviting her." Then she linked arms with him. "C'mon, we don't want to be late." She turned to Edwina. "I should be back in two hours. Do you need anything before we leave?"

Edwina answered without looking up from her album. "There's no need to coddle me. Just because my arm's in a cast doesn't mean I'm an invalid."

Chloe took a deep breath and counted to five. "Okay, then I'll see you in about two hours." She stopped in her tracks. "Almost forgot the tart cherry cobbler I made for dessert." She grabbed the rectangle cake pan. "I left a small pan in the fridge if you'd like some, Aunt Ed."

Edwina grunted without looking up.

"See you," she called as they closed the front door.

Once inside Hud's pickup, she turned toward him. "I apologize for her rudeness, but there's been bad blood between Aunt Ed and your grandfather for the past sixty years."

He glanced at her. "I knew there was tension between our families, but outside of a few rumors I'd heard, I've never known what caused it."

"Aunt Ed's told me her side of the story, but I'm not sure what really happened, either." She grinned. "Did you know they were childhood sweethearts?"

Keeping his eyes on the road, he smiled, his dimple in clear view. "No, I'd never heard that. Maybe Pop-pop will tell us what he recalls about it."

"You mean, tell us his side?" She pressed her lips together. "It's a mystery. As Aunt Ed goes through the old photo albums and scrapbooks, she's teaching me so much about our family history, yet whatever happened between her and your grandfather is still a puzzle." She thought of Celestine as she reached for her galena pendant and then thought twice. *Maybe she'll shed some light on it . . . after I meet Jake.*

As they stopped in front of a frame house, Chloe suddenly felt butterflies in the pit of her stomach. *Ohmigosh, I'm meeting Hud's family.* A second thought quickly followed. *I'm meeting Aunt Ed's old beau. A double whammy.* She took a deep breath.

Hud looked at her and chuckled. "Relax. This isn't a lion's den."

"What do you mean?" Her breathing came fast.

"You look like you're saluting the emperor as you enter the Colosseum. You know. 'We who are about to die . . .'"

She laughed at the image. Then she took a deep breath, and her breathing returned to normal. "Now that you mention it, I guess I am just a little nervous."

"Don't worry." His dark eyes homed in on hers. "They'll love you."

She stared at him. "Why do you say that?"

"Because I love you."

As her mouth fell open, she heard Rose's voice.

"Chloe, I'm so glad to see you."

Still dazed, Chloe turned toward her, the cake pan in her hands.

"Oh, you brought dessert. What'd you make? Oh, here," she said, taking the pan from her. "Let me carry it for you."

Feeling giddy, Chloe took Hud's offered hand as she stepped down from the truck.

"It's great to see you, Rose. Aunt Ed especially wanted me to thank you for the irises." She crossed her fingers behind her back. "That was really thoughtful."

"I can show you where I got them. Then you can pick them anytime you want. Maybe tomorrow?"

She grimaced. "Have to go to Milwaukee for a few days. How 'bout when I come back?" As they crossed the porch, Chloe saw a silver-haired man standing just inside the door, staring at her.

"You must be Edwina's grandniece." Taking her hand in his, he said, "Looking at you is like reliving my youth. You're the spitting image of Edwina."

She grinned. "Funny, that's what Aunt Ed said about Hud and you." Looking at the man's silver-white hair, it was easy to imagine Hud in sixty years. Then, his recent words flashing through her mind, she felt a grin lift a corner of mouth. *Hud loves me.*

Jake's head tilting to the side, he gazed at her. "You even have her Mona Lisa smile." He shook his head, seeming to marvel at the similarities. Then he opened the door for her. "I go by two names, so you have a choice. Would you rather call me Jake or Pop-pop?"

She smiled at his warm welcome, staring into the eyes that reminded her of Hud's.

"You make me feel like family, but at least for now," she said, hunching her shoulders, "how about I call you Jake?" Then she remembered the galena pendant. "And thank you so much for wire wrapping this stone."

She accidentally touched the stone, connecting with it, and saw Celestine was pulling at Jake's arm.

"Jake, Jake, I'm over here. Look at me." Then she seemed to feel Chloe's eyes on her, and she turned toward her. "Tell Jake I'm here."

Gasping, Chloe pulled her hand away. Trying to cover with a bright smile, she quickly added, "I love it. Can you tell us where you found it or why Celestine treasured it so much?"

He tilted his head quizzically. "Why do you say Celestine treasured it?"

"I found it in a jewelry box she had hidden away. It must have been important to her."

Jake hesitated, thinking. "Come on in and sit down while I tell you the story."

Chloe sat on the sofa. Jake sat across from her, while Hud sat beside her. A middle-aged woman appeared at the kitchen door, wiping her hands on a towel.

"Just finishing up dinner," she said with a wide smile. "I'm Hud and Rose's mother, Barbara."

As she approached the sofa, Chloe stood up.

"Hi, I'm Chloe."

Barbara held out her arms as Chloe held out her hand. Immediately, Barbara moved her hand to shake Chloe's, as Chloe tried to hug her. In the process, they both began laughing and ended up hugging.

"I'm so glad to meet you."

"You, too." As the two women separated, Barbara said, "I've heard so much about you from Hud and Rose, I feel like I already know you."

"Oh, that is so sweet." Chloe put her hand to her heart as she felt her chest cave. Mentally groaning, she compared her warm welcome with her great-aunt's response to Hud. "It's easy to see where Hud and Rose get their dispositions." She looked from one face to the next, already feeling at home. "I'm so very glad to meet you."

"Can I get you something to drink? Lemonade?"

"Perfect, thank you."

Jake said, "Have a seat while I tell you the story about the stone."

"All my great-aunt told us is that the three of you went on a picnic, and you stumbled across this piece of galena."

He nodded. "Celestine was an impressionable young girl at the time." He sighed as he rubbed the back of his neck. "She liked to tag along with us. If we didn't invite her, she pouted and felt left out. Finally, Edwina and I decided we'd so something that included her, so one day . . ."

"How would you like to go on a picnic with us, Celestine?"

"Would I ever!" Her eyes lit up as she glanced from Jake to her sister and back again. "When? Now?"

Jake nodded as he shared a grin with Edwina.

"You've been talking nonstop about your school project," said Edwina, smiling.

"My mineral collection." She made a face. "I've got every mineral on the list but galena."

"Then how would you like to find a piece of galena to add to your collection?" asked Jake.

"Yes!"

"To pass the time along the way, we sang or played games, like who could find the most red, white, or blue cars, and of course we looked forward to reading the Burma-Shave signs."

Jake turned to Rose. "Do you know what Burma-Shave signs are?"

"Nope." She shook her head.

"They were little red signs spaced out as you drove along," said Jake. "Each one had a word or two printed on it, but read together, they formed a jingle."

"Like 'HER CHARIOT . . . RACED 80 PER . . . . THEY HAULED AWAY . . . WHAT HAD . . . BEN HUR . . . . BURMA-SHAVE,'" said Barbara, bringing in the lemonade. "I remember those . . . barely."

"Thanks." Chloe took the lemonade from Barbara with a smile.

"Or how about this one," said Jake. "A MAN . . . A MISS . . . A CAR - A CURVE . . . HE KISSED THE MISS . . . AND MISSED . . . THE CURVE . . . . BURMA-SHAVE.'"

They all groaned.

"But finish your story about Celestine and the galena," said Barbara. "I've never heard this one."

Jake's smile drooped. "I hadn't thought of it in a long time. Okay. Finally, we arrived at Shullsburg."

"Shullsburg?" asked Rose. "Where's that?"

"Clear across the state. We're on the upper northeast corner of Wisconsin, and Shullsburg's on the lower southwest corner. It took us at least four hours to get there. A friend of mine owned a farm with an old galena mine on it, and he let us sift through the mining rubble.

"First Celestine, Edwina, and I had a picnic under a big maple tree. Then we walked along the tractor roads, loosening up after the long drive. Finally, pails and shovels in hand, we began picking through the mining waste. Mostly, we found crushed stone. Occasionally, we found a few small, square crystals." Jake glanced up with a grin. "Then I found the mother lode."

As he gestured to Chloe's necklace, her hand unconsciously flew to her throat, touching the stone, connecting with it. Immediately, Celestine appeared, sitting on the floor at Jake's feet, listening raptly. Chloe pulled her fingers away before Celestine felt her eyes on her.

"What happened then?" asked Rose.

As Jake's ears turned red, he rubbed the back of his neck. "Although I thought of her as a kid sister, I think Celestine had a schoolgirl crush on me."

"Why do you say that?" asked Rose.

"When I showed her the stone . . ."

"Oh my goodness," said Celestine. "That's gorgeous. No one at school's going to have one in their collection like this."

"Then I'm guessing you want it?" Jake chuckled as he met Edwina's eyes in a private smile over the girl's head.

"Do I? Oh, I do! I do!" Jumping to her feet, she threw her arms around him, stood on tiptoe, and kissed him on the lips. "Jake Beaulieu, I'll love you 'til the day I die."

Blinking, he pulled back his head out of her reach. Then, removing her arms from around his neck, Jake laughed self-consciously.

"No need for all that." He stepped away, glancing at Edwina.

Her arms crossed over her chest, she was scowling at them. Her silence spoke volumes.

Jake cleared his throat. "Here. It's yours." He held out the stone at arm's length, keeping his distance.

"Oh, thank you, Jake." Celestine stepped toward him, as if to kiss him again, and he took a step back.

"I think Jake realizes your . . ." Edwina sneered, "gratitude. You've got your stone. Now let's leave." Not waiting for an answer, Edwina turned on her heel and began walking back to the car.

"Where the four-hour drive down had flown by," said Jake, grimacing, "the four-hour drive back took an eternity. Edwina refused to speak to either her sister or me." He looked off into space, as if recalling something. He sighed. "I think that was the beginning of the end."

"The end of what?" asked Rose.

"Things were never the same between Miss Ed and me after that." He seemed lost in thought.

"Well," said Barbara, standing up, glancing at Jake. "All this talk about picnics has made me hungry." She gestured toward the dining room. "Dinner's ready. Shall we eat?"

⁂

"Dinner was wonderful. Thanks again." Chloe hugged Hud's mother goodbye.

"And dessert was delicious," said Barbara. "Next time you come, you'll have to give me the recipe."

"It's easy, just four ingredients. Pitted, tart cherries." She grinned. "That's the only hard part, pitting them. Then cake mix, butter, and pecans."

"That's it?"

"That's it." Chloe shrugged. "I told you it's easy."

"Okay, how do you make it?"

"Add four cups red cherries to a greased nine-by-thirteen pan. Sprinkle the dry cake mix over the pitted cherries. Drizzle a half-cup melted butter over that. Sprinkle a cup of chopped pecans over all, and bake at three-fifty for about forty-five minutes."

"And it tastes like you spent all day baking it," said Jake, hugging her goodbye.

Chloe laughed. "I should've kept it a trade secret."

"Don't forget," said Rose. "As soon as you're back from Milwaukee, let me know. I'll show you where to pick the best irises."

"Okay, it's a date." Chloe hugged her goodbye and stepped into the truck. She waved and then, leaning over, gave Hud a hug. "Thank you so much for tonight. It was wonderful. I absolutely *love* your family."

His dimple working in his cheek, he asked, "How do you feel about me?"

She looked up through her lashes and grinned. "What a leading question."

"I've already told you I love you."

Out of nowhere, a feeling filled her chest. Much more than merely drawn to him, she felt magnetized. Throwing her arms around him, she met him in a kiss that left her feeling breathless. *Ohmigosh. What is this?*

As they drew apart, she shook her head. "We hardly know each other. Why do I . . . ?"

"Why do you what?" Again, his cheek dimpled as he grinned. "Why do you love me?"

"You said it, not me." As she met his eyes, she slowly nodded. "But yes, I do love you." Then she groaned. "Which makes it even harder to leave for Milwaukee tomorrow."

"We can call each other."

"Maybe Skype every night."

Still parked in the driveway, they noticed his family grinning, waving goodbye. He waved back as he started the engine.

"I know a beautiful lookout over the bay where we can say goodbye in private."

Ten minutes later, they were parked in the moonlight. She turned toward him. "Hud?"

"Yeah?"

"I've been thinking. Could Celestine somehow be causing us to . . . ?" She frowned. "Could she be behind our attraction?"

"Why do you ask something like that?" Arms crossed over his chest, eyes narrowed, he pulled back his head and looked at her.

She hunched her shoulders. "I don't know. I've just never experienced anything like this. It's all happening so fast. We just met last week, but I feel I've known you forever. It's as if we've loved each other before, and now we're back together again."

He nodded. "You've heard about love at first sight. Maybe that's what this is."

"Maybe." Her eyes narrowing, she gave a frustrated sigh. "But I think it's more than just that."

"Just that?" His dark eyes glimmered in the moonlight.

She playfully punched his shoulder. "You know what I mean."

"The funny thing is, yes, I do. I know exactly what you mean because I've wondered about it, too."

She took a deep breath. "What if we try to see Celestine again tonight?"

He glanced up through the windshield. "No aurora borealis that I can see."

Hand poised over her necklace, she looked into his eyes. "Should I?"

He grinned back. "Go for it."

She touched her hand to the galena, and Celestine appeared in the back seat. Her crossed arms on the headrest, propping up her chin, she leaned over the front seat into their space.

"She's here," Chloe whispered.

His eyebrows shot up.

"Don't whisper," said Celestine. "I can hear you whether you whisper or shout. I can hear you whether you're touching the necklace or not."

Chloe took a deep breath. "Okay, we have a bit of an attitude here."

"Look, I finally get it." Touching Hud's shoulder, Celestine shook her head. "He's not Jake, is he?"

Glancing at Hud, Chloe shook her head. "Nope."

The girl sighed. "When I first saw you and Hud together, I thought . . . I thought somehow time had gone back to when Ed and Jake were about your age. I'm the one that caused their breakup, interrupted nature. They'd have had kids by now, grandchildren. I wanted to make up for it, get them back together again." She grimaced. "Scratch that, I wanted to get *you* back together again . . . let nature take its course."

Chloe repeated Celestine's words as she watched Hud swallow hard, his Adam's apple bobbing. Then she turned toward the girl. "You know now we're not Aunt Ed and Jake."

Celestine nodded. "To answer your earlier question, I may have 'helped' your natural attraction in the beginning, but you two fell in love all by yourselves."

"But you admit you did something. You helped it." Chloe tilted her head. "What did you do?"

Celestine shrugged. "I just wished hard that you two would fall back in love."

"Fall *back* in love?" She stared at the girl. "Could you explain that?"

"Well . . . I wished you'd both remember Ed and Jake's feelings for each other." Grinning, she pantomimed shooting arrows. "You might say I played Cupid."

Chloe nodded. Looking past the girl, she stared into Hud's eyes. "Celestine admits helping us 'remember' Aunt Ed and Jake's feelings for each other."

He shuddered. "You're telling me there's a ghost in this truck that somehow tricked us into recalling their memories?"

"I wouldn't call them memories," said Celestine, "just feelings."

"'Feelings,' she says."

"I'm not 'she.' I told you. My name's Celestine."

Chloe rolled her eyes. "We seem to have a very temperamental ghost."

"Don't call me temperamental. I'll show you temperamental!" With that, she disappeared.

Suddenly, the truck's cab became icy. Chloe could see her breath. She shuddered, but not from the cold as much as from the feeling spiders were crawling down her back.

"Euwww." She turned to Hud. "This is what I felt in my closet before I dis-covered Celestine's jewelry box hidden in the floorboards." She met his eyes. "This is proof. Somehow, she can affect our feelings."

"Celestine," said Hud. "Stop it! This sort of behavior isn't going to help you, Miss Ed, Jake, or us." He turned to Chloe. "How old was she when she drowned?"

"Fourteen."

He raised his voice again as he glanced around the cab, trying to talk to the girl. "At fourteen, you should act like a young lady, not a child."

"I'm not a child," she said, straddling the console between them.

"Is she here?"

Chloe nodded.

"Celestine, you help us, and we'll help you. The other night, you said you wanted to make some kind of confession."

She nodded. "It was my fault Ed and Jake never married. It wasn't his fault I drowned. It was an accident . . . and I want to set the record straight."

Chloe repeated her words.

Hud stared at the back seat as he spoke. "In that case—"

"Celestine's sitting beside you on the console."

He turned to blindly address her. "Let's work together."

"No," she said, arching her back, posturing. "Let's play together."

Chloe repeated her words.

"What do you mean, 'play' together?" Hud looked through her at Chloe.

"That's for me to know and you to find out."

"Okay," said Chloe. "Can you give us a hint?"

"A Christmas hug . . . A birthday kiss . . . Awaits . . . The woman . . . Who gives this . . . . Burma-Shave."

Chloe repeated her words, adding, "She's giving us 1950's Burma-Shave clues."

"Why can't you simply tell us how to help you?" Hud swallowed a sigh.

"Heaven's . . . Latest . . . Neophyte . . . Signaled left . . . Then turned right . . . . Burma-Shave."

"Signaled left, then turned right." Chloe thought for a minute. "Are you saying you changed your mind?"

"Oh, good, we're playing Ten Questions." She clapped her hands. "You're getting warm."

"Does this have something to do with your drowning?"

"Warmer."

Catching Celestine's eye, Chloe heaved a frustrated sigh. "At this rate, we'll be here all night."

"The whale . . . Put Jonah . . . Down the hatch . . . But coughed him up . . . Because he scratched . . . . Burma-Shave."

"Down the hatch, but coughed him up. Are you saying you fell into the water and then . . . ?" At a loss, Chloe looked to Hud for help.

"Okay," he said, "you fell into the water, and you tried to get back up into the canoe?"

Celestine smirked. "You're lukewarm. Substitutes . . . Are like a girdle . . . They find some jobs . . . They just . . . Can't hurdle . . . . Burma-Shave."

Chloe repeated the words to Hud and tried again. "Just can't hurdle. You fell into the water, tried to get back up into the canoe, but you weren't able to climb back in?"

"Warmer. It has a tingle . . . And a tang . . . That starts . . . The day off . . . With a bang . . . . Burma-Shave."

After Chloe repeated her words, Hud tried. "You fell into the water, tried to get back up into the canoe, but something hit you with a bang?"

"Warmer. Don't lose . . . Your head . . . To gain a minute . . . You need your head . . . Your brains are in it . . . . Burma-Shave."

Chloe said, "You fell into the water, tried to get back up into the canoe, but something hit your head?"

"Very warm, but you're at question number seven," said Celestine. "Three more strikes, and you're out! He saw . . . The train . . . And tried to duck it . . . Kicked first the gas . . . And then the bucket . . . . Burma-Shave."

Chloe repeated her words.

Hud said, "You fell into the water, tried to get back up, something came at your head that you tried to duck?"

"You're lukewarm, and that was question number eight."

"Think for a minute." Chloe looked at Hud. "If she were trying to climb into a canoe, what could hit her on the head?"

"The canoe itself," he said, thinking aloud, "or—"

"*Or*, you're warmer, and that was question number nine. One more *strike*, and you're out!"

"Or . . . OAR . . . strike . . . I got it," said Chloe. "You fell into the water, tried to get back up, and the paddle struck your head?"

"Close, but no cigar." Celestine made an obnoxious sound of a buzzer going off. "Ten questions. You lose."

"No," said Chloe, raising an eyebrow and her voice. "Hud and I were discussing, not questioning you. It's still at question nine."

Celestine sighed. "You needn't get so huffy. All right, to prove I'm a good sport, *unlike some people*, I'll give you one last hint and one last chance. These three . . . Prevent most accidents . . . Courtesy . . . Caution . . . Common sense . . . . Burma-Shave."

"Common sense. You didn't use common sense," said Chloe. "You didn't fall, you jumped in the water, tried to climb back in the canoe, but it overturned, and the paddle struck your head?"

"Bingo! Give that girl a cigar!"

"That's the right answer?" he asked, catching Chloe's eye.

Chloe nodded. "Now, if we could prove this to Aunt Ed, she just might get over her feud with your grandfather." She turned to Celestine. "We need proof. Is there anything we can show your sister to make her believe your death was an accident?"

"So you want the *letter* of the law," said Celestine, climbing into the back seat, "not the *spirit* of the law?"

Chloe repeated it for Hud's benefit.

"Did you leave a letter somewhere?" he asked the console.

"She's in the back seat now," said Chloe.

He turned his head to blindly speak in her direction. "Or maybe you left a suicide note?"

"THIS IS NOT . . . A CLEVER VERSE . . . I TRIED . . . AND TRIED . . . BUT JUST . . . GOT WORSE . . . . BURMA-SHAVE." Celestine scolded them, "You're getting sloppy. You already know it was an accident, not a suicide. RHYME AND REASON . . . EVERY SEASON . . . YOU'VE READ . . . THE RHYME . . . NOW TRY THE REASON . . . . BURMA-SHAVE."

Chloe relayed her words to Hud. "Reason. Did she mean, what was her reason for jumping, or we have to use reason to figure this out by ourselves?" She shook her head, trying to clear it. "It's getting late, and I told Aunt Ed I'd be back in two hours."

"IN CUPID'S LITTLE . . . BAG OF TRIX . . . HERE'S THE ONE . . . THAT CLIX . . . WITH CHIX . . . . BURMA-SHAVE." Celestine leaned over the front seat until her eyes were level with Chloe's. "Bag, box . . . that clix," she hissed.

Chloe passed on the latest information to Hud. "Box that clicks. Could she be talking about her jewelry box?"

<hr />

When Chloe got back home, Edwina was still awake.

"I have an idea."

Chloe brought out the jewelry box and set it on the dining room table.

Edwina sighed. "We've looked through everything in this box at least twice."

"I get the feeling we've missed something." She opened it but saw nothing except jewelry and photos—no letters, no notes. Then she checked the back of each photo, hoping for a written clue, but nothing came to light. She picked up the box and turned it upside down, looking for a secret compartment, but nothing rattled or opened. She turned it upright and checked the satin lining.

"What are you looking for?" Edwina eyed her actions suspiciously.

"I don't know." She shook her head. "Just something we've missed. I think this box holds the clue."

"Clue to what?"

Chloe hesitated discussing it, not wanting to reopen her great-aunt's wounds by bringing up details of Celestine's death.

"I just get the feeling there's something in this jewelry box we've missed."

Edwina sniffed. "What's the definition of insanity? Doing the same thing over and over but expecting different results."

Chloe sighed but said nothing. Then, searching the lining with her fingers, she gasped.

"What?"

"I think I feel something." She brought the box over to her aunt. "Do you see this lump here? It's got a sharp corner that's pressing against the lining. Feel it."

Edwina ran her fingertip over the square edge inside the lining. She looked at Chloe and nodded.

"I'm going to see if there's an opening or tear in the lining. Chloe gently tugged at the lining's edges—first one side, then the second, and then the third. "I don't want to rip the lining. I could tear whatever's in here." When she pulled at the fourth seam, the satin material slipped out. "The stitches have been removed. See? The lining was simply tucked into the edge."

She gently reached inside the lining. When her hand connected with something, she opened her eyes wide.

"Did you find something?" Edwina looked at her.

"Yes. If I could just get hold of it without damaging the lining." Gradually, she pulled out an envelope. Turning it over, she saw it was a letter. "It's addressed to you." When she glanced at her aunt, she saw tears streaming down the woman's wrinkled cheeks. "What's wrong?"

"It's Jake's handwriting."

Chloe glanced at the postmark. "It's dated September ninth, 1955."

"The day before Celestine drowned." Edwina swallowed as Chloe handed her the letter.

"Do you want to read it in private? I can go."

"Stay. After all these years . . ."

Her voice fading, her hands trembled as she opened the envelope's flap and pulled out the yellowed letter. She read silently as she swiped at her tears. Then she slumped in her chair, letting the letter fall to the floor.

Chloe picked it up and handed it to her, but she shook her head.

"Read it. Go ahead."

Dear Edwina,
I don't know how to convince you other than swear I know nothing about the missing hundred-dollar bill. Please realize I'd never do anything to hurt you. We're one.
I love you and always will,
Jake

Chloe caught her breath. "So it was that hundred-dollar bill that made you break up with him."

Edwina drew in a long breath. "Almost, but not quite. We fought, but eventually I would have forgiven him, despite the fact we never found the money. It was my sister's death that drove us apart." She shook her head. "For that, I can never forgive him."

Chloe bit her lip to keep from speaking up. *Without proof, Aunt Ed will never believe Celestine's death was an accident, let alone believe it was her ghost that told me. But maybe . . .* Chloe touched her galena pendant and immediately saw Celestine standing over her sister.

When the girl met her eyes, she said, "Look again."

Nodding, Chloe wedged her hand between the jewelry box and its lining.

"What are you doing?" Edwina sat up in her chair.

"Acting on a hunch." She reached inside until her hand connected with another piece of paper. "Found something." She eased it out and gasped.

"What?"

Without a word, Chloe placed it in her hand.

"The hundred-dollar bill." Her hand to her forehead, Edwina sank back in her chair, staring at the ceiling.

<hr />

The next morning over breakfast, Chloe said, "I hate leaving you here alone while I'm in Milwaukee, especially after what we discovered last night." *If only Aaron weren't so pigheaded.* "Bad timing, but if you feel uncomfortable about being here alone, tell me. I'll see if there's some way to get out of the UAT testing."

"No." Edwina shook her head as if in a daze. "I'll be fine. You go ahead."

"The fridge is stocked. I made your favorite dinner, lasagna. The laundry's done. It's just you being alone that worries me. I'll call you every day, and Hud said he'll look in on you after work each evening to see if you need anything."

Edwina sat up and scowled. "Don't fuss over me. I'm not a baby. I've been taking care of myself for eighty years."

As her irascible spirit resurfaced, Chloe swallowed a smile, convinced her great-aunt could, indeed, take care of herself. *Strong women in my family. If I could just be more like them.* She groaned inwardly, thinking of having to work with Aaron for the next few days.

On the drive to Milwaukee, Chloe thought about the letter and hundred-dollar bill.

Wish I'd had more time to talk with Aunt Ed before leaving. Imagine learning a sixty-year grudge was built on lies.

If Celestine had not taken the money or hidden Jake's letter, Edwina would have married her childhood sweetheart and taken an entirely different path through life. Jake wasn't negligent in Celestine's death. I have to convince Aunt Ed of his innocence. But how? Maybe Celestine will help.

Chloe thought of touching the pendant around her neck, then thought again. *Not while I'm driving.* But even without touching it, she began sensing Celestine's presence. More than imagining, she could almost hear her recite the Burma-Shave jingle: STATISTICS PROVE . . . NEAR AND FAR . . . THAT FOLKS WHO . . . DRIVE LIKE CRAZY . . . ARE . . . . BURMA-SHAVE.

Celestine. How much heartache her mischief caused Aunt Ed and Jake. Chloe shook her head. *But how much trouble is she causing Hud and me? Things have happened so quickly between us. Are our feelings for each other real, or is our attraction some sort of game Celestine's playing?*

And speaking of games, why won't Aaron take a hint? He doesn't want me when I'm here, yet he won't let me go when I try to leave.

As she approached Milwaukee and began recognizing the landscape, she sighed. She had taken I-43 south from Green Bay, which merged with WI-57, which merged into WI-32. Once in Mequon, commuting to Milwaukee was routine. She had driven the same route every morning for the past three years.

Monotonous but routine. Normal. That's what my life was until I met Celestine. Now it's paranormal. Are Hud's and my feelings for each other real, or are we being influenced? Infatuation and the supernatural. So much has changed since the last time I drove this stretch.

CHAPTER 5

"Sometimes good things fall apart so better things can fall together."
– MARILYN MONROE

As she walked into the office, Chloe felt disjointed, disconnected, as if she had been gone for months. *Has it only been two weeks?* For over three years, she had enjoyed the camaraderie of the office—the feeling of belonging, of being part of the organization's whole. It had lent a sense of stability to her life. Now, it seemed foreign, oppressive.

She sat down at her cube and began logging on when she heard Aaron's voice. "Welcome back, stranger. Missed you."

Without looking up, she could tell by his honeyed tones he was leaning over her cube's half wall, speaking quietly, so only she could hear. She peered up at him.

"Why don't you speak up? Afraid Jennifer will hear?"

For nearly three years, she and Aaron had been an office item. Whatever project he had been assigned, he had requested her assistance. They had spent most of the work week together, including working lunches and overtime. After work, they'd gone to happy hours and often shared dinner together. Her cubemates had called Aaron her "office husband" and asked when he going to make it official.

He had more than made her feel they were a team. Time and again he had told her they were partners, broadly hinting at making it permanent, inside the office and out. Feeling his equal partner in the projects, Chloe had always gone the extra mile for him—always crafted his PowerPoint presentations, edited his white papers, and made him shine in front of upper management.

In the beginning, he had shared the credit with her, but gradually she became his silent partner. She did all the work, while he basked in the glory. In the beginning, he had been courteous and supportive, but over time, his tone became increasingly sarcastic to the point it became emotionally abusive. Humiliating her became his favorite pastime, publicly and privately.

The problem was, he could be charming one minute and cruel the next. Just when she would be ready to call it quits, he would win her over with flowers and promises. Always ready with an excuse, he would tell her how sorry he was—that he had been tired, overworked, misunderstood, whatever the reason du jour.

That scenario developed into everything becoming her fault. No matter what went wrong, he blamed her. She became his scapegoat—first at work, and then later during their personal time together. She could not do anything right. Nothing pleased him. His tactics were insidious. Slowly, he eroded her self-confidence to the point Chloe began believing him some of the time, and then most of the time.

In rare moments of self-respect, she would stand up for her rights. Then Aaron would either turn on the charm, depicting himself as the victim, or threaten to leave. Either way, it reduced her to tears and ground away her self-confidence until it disappeared.

The coup de grâce came when the company president's daughter joined their project. The more time Aaron spent with Jennifer, the less he spent with Chloe, both in the office and out. They still dated occasionally, but as their dates became fewer and farther apart, their time together dwindled.

In her company, Aaron could be charming, promising her a wedding just as soon as he finished this or that project. He could also be domineering, emotionally abusive, finding fault with her figure, her dress, or her actions. Either way, Chloe eventually realized he was manipulative. She tried to break up many times, but each time he would win her back, only to repeat the process again.

Then Chloe caught him kissing Jennifer in the copy room. She backed out without being seen and did not mention it until their dinner date that night.

He waived away the accusation. "It was an innocent peck on the cheek."

"I saw it." She stared at him coldly, arms crossed. "It was not innocent, and it was not on the cheek."

He took a deep breath. "If you must know, she'd just been promoted to manager. It was a congratulatory kiss, nothing more." Then his eyes narrowed. "She's trying to make something of herself, unlike you. Jennifer's going places. Again, unlike you."

"Sure, she's going places," Chloe sneered, "to her daddy's office to ask for the promotion." She stood up. "I'm sick and tired of your criticism." She threw her napkin on the table. "And you're wrong about me. I am going places . . . *out of here.*"

For the next few days, she ignored his calls, texts, and instant messages. At meetings, she carefully chose seats at the opposite end of the conference tables.

Then, an office memo had circulated about Aaron's promotion to product development manager. That afternoon, two things happened. Jennifer showed up at work with an enormous engagement ring, and Edwina called Chloe, mentioning her fall and broken wrist.

That had been the last she had seen of Aaron until he showed up on Edwina's doorstep. Then she had received the email from her manager, telling her Aaron needed her assistance in Milwaukee, and now he was leaning over her cube wall, intruding on her space.

"Don't be silly," said Aaron. "I'm not whispering."

Chloe looked up at him, scowling. "Excuse me?"

"Touchy, touchy." He smiled his most charming. "I'm just glad you're back. I missed you."

"What do you want?"

He leaned closer. "You."

"A: I broke up with you. B: you're engaged to Jennifer. And C: my manager said you need my assistance with UAT testing. What are we testing . . . *besides my patience?*"

His lip curling, he smiled slowly in his arrogant, self-assured way. "If UAT testing is what it takes to bring you back from Door County, you can test all the applications from now until doomsday, but it's you I want. Here, not a hundred and twenty-five miles away."

"You're not my manager." She sneered.

"But since he reports to the president . . ."

"You mean reports to Jennifer's daddy." She took a deep breath, counting to five.

"You get the picture." His smile warmed. "But not the whole picture. Jennifer is just a means to an end, and Milwaukee's just a stepping stone. My eye is on corporate . . . and you. You're the one I want to take with me."

"I'm sure Jennifer and her daddy would be interested to hear that, but I really don't care what or who you want." She stood up, abruptly eye to eye with him, forcing him out of her cubical. "I resent you sending me on a wild goose trip, wasting company time and my time. If you'll excuse me, I need to have a little chat with my manager. He and I need to look over the test plans, see if any of the SQA team could better assist you."

"Chloe, you're overreacting. Relax," he said, blocking her exit from the cube. Then he handed her a thumb drive. "Here's my presentation for upper management. Look it over, tighten up its weak points, give it back to me by close of business, and we'll forget all about the UAT testing."

"Is that what this urgent trip is really about? You want me to do your work?" Grunting, she shook her head. "You couldn't find anything but fault with me when we were together. Now you want my help?"

"Need your help." He looked at her with big, sad eyes. "Won't you take a look?"

She rolled her eyes. Then she took another deep breath. "Fine. I'll look over your presentation, but this is the last time. This afternoon I'm having a little chat with my manager. In the future, don't bother me with your personal needs during business hours . . . or after hours. If you do, I'll take your harassment to HR and file a complaint. That blemish on your record ought to look good to upper management . . . and Jennifer's father." Scowling, she looked hard into his eyes and was surprised to see a grudging respect.

How about that? I stood up to Aaron. Huh! Will wonders never cease?

After editing Aaron's presentation and meeting with her manager, Chloe decided to leave early and beat the rush-hour traffic. Instead of staying the night, as she had intended initially, a little voice urged her to hurry back to Door County.

As she drove, a feeling of impending doom closed in on her. *Why? This trip to Milwaukee resolved the problem I've had for the past three years: Aaron.* She gave a sigh of relief, but a general feeling of apprehension returned. She could not shake it off, so she stepped on the gas.

More than imagine, she could almost hear Celestine recite the Burma-Shave jingle: "IF DAISIES . . . ARE YOUR . . . FAVORITE FLOWER . . . KEEP PUSHIN' UP THOSE . . . MILES PER HOUR."

With a sigh, she took her foot off the gas. *Fine!* Still the general feeling of overwhelming anxiety remained.

Two hours later, she pulled into Edwina's driveway. The door was locked, so she used her key.

"I'm home!" She heard nothing. "Aunt Ed, I'm home!" Silence. She called a third time and thought she heard a feeble response coming from the kitchen.

She walked in and found Edwina crumpled on the floor beside an overturned stepladder. She rushed to her.

"Aunt Ed, what happened?"

"I . . . I fell." She pointed to the ladder.

"Oh, no." Chloe debated whether to call an ambulance or help her up. "Can you stand if I help you?"

"Maybe."

Chloe put her arms around her. "Grab onto me, and I'll help you up." Edwina tried but winced and slumped back down. "I'm afraid to move you, Aunt Ed, just in case anything's broken. I'm going to call an ambulance. Just give me a moment, and then I'll get you a pillow for your head."

Chloe dialed 911 and gave them the address. Then she got a pillow and gently placed it under Edwina's head.

"They'll be here in a few minutes. How long have you been lying here?"

"Two-and-a-half, maybe three hours."

About the same time I got the feeling something was wrong.

"Glad I didn't have to stay overnight. Can I get you a glass of water or anything until the ambulance gets here?"

"No, I just feel like sleeping."

She heard a knock on the door. *That can't be the ambulance already.* Peeking, she saw Hud, swung open the door, and flung herself into his arms.

"Oh, am I glad to see you!"

"Me, too," he said, grinning as they pulled apart from a kiss. "I didn't expect to see you until tomorrow or the next day. I was just checking in on Miss Ed."

Chloe's smile drooped.

"What's wrong?"

"She fell while I was gone."

"Oh, no. Is she all right?"

Chloe drew in a long breath. "I don't know. She can't get up."

"Is . . . ?"

She nodded. "The ambulance is on its way."

"It's a good thing you got back early." He grimaced. "If she hadn't let me in, I'd have had to call you, but who knows? Time might be of the essence."

Biting her lip, Chloe nodded. "Come on inside." Then she stopped and listened. "Is that the siren?"

A moment later, the ambulance backed into the drive. Two paramedics brought a stretcher into the kitchen. They checked Edwina, testing for painful areas, and then lifted her onto the stretcher.

"We'd better take her to the hospital for X-rays, just to be sure," said one paramedic. "Do you want to follow?"

"I'll drive," said Hud, gently taking her hand in his.

<hr />

Three hours later, the doctor met with them. "Nothing showed up in the X-rays," she said, "but I'd like to keep her overnight for observation.

Chloe took a deep breath. "That's understandable. At eighty, Aunt Ed's no spring chicken. But she is a tough old bird."

The doctor grinned. "Good, I'm glad she's strong. Like I said, I don't see anything, but soft tissue doesn't show up in X-rays. I want to make sure she has no internal injuries."

After the doctor left, Chloe and Hud visited Edwina, but she was asleep.

"Guess the muscle relaxant's kicked in," said Chloe, turning to Hud. "Thanks for staying with me through this. I really appreciate it."

"Just glad to be of help." He took her hand in his, entwining their fingers. "You're important to me, you know."

<hr />

As Hud parked in front of Edwina's house, Chloe asked, "Want to come in for dinner?"

"I'm sure you don't feel like cooking. Maybe you'd like to go out for something."

She shook her head. "I made a big batch of lasagna for Aunt Ed before I left, and I wouldn't want it to go to waste." *Besides, it'll be fun to play house, pretend we're married.* She smiled up at him mischievously.

"What are you grinning about?" He chuckled. "You're not planning to poison me or anything?"

She laughed. "My cooking's not that bad."

She reheated the lasagna in the microwave and found a bottle of Chianti. As they sat next to each other at the round dining room table, it occurred to her she had not told Hud about the finds in the jewelry box.

"So much has happened since the last time I saw you, I forgot to tell you. Remember when Celestine told us that Burma-Shave jingle about a box that clicks?"

"Yeah." Nodding, he helped himself to another serving of lasagna.

"Aunt Ed and I checked. She was talking about her jewelry box."

He turned to her. "What did you find?"

"Here, let me show you."

She got the jewelry box and brought it to the table.

"What's this?" He glanced at her.

"Did Jake ever tell you why he and my great-aunt never married?"

He ran his fingers over his chin as he thought. Then he shook his head. "No. I'd overheard rumors, but Pop-pop never discussed it with us. It was a taboo subject, obviously something that hurt him deeply."

Chloe took a deep breath. "I can see why."

She relayed the story Edwina had told her about the hundred-dollar bill. Then she opened the jewelry box. The letter and bill rested on top of the pictures.

"This is *that* hundred-dollar bill?"

She nodded.

"How do you know?"

"Celestine told me to look behind the lining."

Gently pulling out the tucked-back fabric, she showed him where she had discovered it.

"Wow." He took a sip of Chianti. "How different Pop-pop and Miss Ed's lives would have been if they'd found it sixty years ago."

"It's so sad."

"No wonder Celestine's conscience bothers her."

Chloe raised her eyebrow as she nodded. Then she handed him the letter.

"Jake's handwriting," he confirmed.

"This was hidden in the lining with the money."

"Celestine again?"

"Yup." She refilled their wine glasses as he read it.

"What would make her do something like this?"

"I don't know." Shaking her head, she made a sour face. "We know she likes games, but this is taking a joke way too far."

"What do you want to do about it?" He watched her face.

"I think it's only fair to let Jake know." She met his dark eyes. "Don't you agree?"

"Let's show him these after dinner."

⁘

They found Jake sitting in the backyard, watching the moon rise.

"What an unexpected surprise," he said, standing up to greet them. Then he looked at their expressions. "What's wrong?"

"For one thing," said Hud, "Miss Ed's in the hospital."

"What?" He looked from one face to the other. "What's wrong? What happened?"

Chloe told him about the fall and the doctor's need to keep her overnight for observation.

"Is it serious?" His face suddenly looked haggard, older.

"Nothing's broken, but it's a wait and see game," said Chloe. "Hopefully, we'll know if there are any soft tissue injuries by morning. I imagine, as long as there's no internal bleeding, we can bring her home tomorrow."

"Let me know as soon as you hear anything," said Jake. He watched as Chloe and Hud exchanged a look. "Is there anything else?"

"You'd better sit down," said Hud.

Jake paled. "What's wrong?"

Chloe handed him the hundred-dollar bill.

"What's this?"

"Look at the denomination and series number."

"Nineteen-fifty-five . . ." His eyelids flew open. "Is this . . . ?" She nodded. "Then you know about . . ."

Again she nodded. "Aunt Ed told me the story."

"Where did you find it?" He listened quietly as she told him the story, a dazed expression on his face. He handed her back the bill. "Sixty years," he mumbled. Then he looked into her eyes. "Does Edwina know?"

"Yes." She handed him his letter. "She read this last night."

He glanced at its contents, folded it, and returned it.

"I'm glad she finally knows the truth." He took a deep breath. "If only . . ." He sighed.

"Only what?" Hud grimaced. "That sixty years hadn't passed in bitterness, or that Miss Ed knew of your innocence in Celestine's drowning?"

79

"Both." Jake gave a mirthless chuckle. "What a mess."

"Chloe and I know it was an accident." He put his hand on Jake's shoulder. "We know you're not to blame for her death."

Another mirthless laugh. "I appreciate your belief in me, but how would you *know* something like that? The only person who knows what really happened was Celestine, and she's dead and gone."

"Dead," said Chloe, "but not gone."

Jake glanced at her. "What do you mean?"

Chloe and Hud shared another look.

"I can see Celestine," she said.

"Now?" Jake's eyes opened wide.

"When I touch this galena pendant you made, I somehow connect with her." She made a sour face. "Although, today it seemed I could hear her without touching it. Her voice enters into my thoughts."

Jake cocked his head. "Show me."

"Okay." She touched her fingers to the stone and waited for Celestine. Nothing happened. Looking around, she cleared her throat and touched it again, this time encircling it with her hand. Nothing. She gave a nervous laugh. "This is embarrassing."

Jake raised his eyebrow, but Hud looked up at the sky. "The aurora borealis is showing overhead."

"Oh." She shared a knowing look with Hud. Then she turned to Jake. "For whatever reason, the northern lights wreak havoc with seeing her."

"Apparently, some electromagnetic interference," said Hud.

"You can see her, too?"

"No," said Hud, "but I've felt her."

"What do you mean you've felt her?"

"She can influence feelings, sensations."

Jake slowly shook his head. "I'm not following."

"She's made me feel icy cold. She's made my skin crawl. She's given me the willies." Hud shared another look with Chloe.

"She can also influence your emotions, subconsciously." Not wanting to share all their personal secrets, Chloe neglected to mention how much Celestine affected her emotions. She glanced at Hud as a shiver passed through her.

He nodded in agreement. "If you want proof, think about where Chloe found the hundred-dollar bill and letter."

"Celestine told me to look in the lining of her jewelry box. That's how I found it."

"And tell him where you found *that*."

"She'd stashed the jewelry box beneath a floorboard in the closet."

Chloe watched Jake's eyes gradually open wider, as his mouth relaxed its suspicious smirk.

"That's substantial evidence." He nodded. "I believe you."

"For whatever reason, I can see Celestine. That is, usually. Just not tonight." She rolled her eyes. "Maybe I can see her because I'm her namesake. I'm the only daughter of her brother's son, the only female born in the past two generations of my family. Maybe she can relate to me. Maybe that's our connection."

"Celestine was an interesting kid." Jack looked at the two of them. "She always seemed like a kid sister to me. We got along just fine until the last few months before she drowned. She changed from a sweet girl into . . ." He broke off, grimacing. "It's not right to talk about the dead." He turned to Chloe. "I'm sorry."

"No, please tell us all you know," she said. "Maybe we'll get to the bottom of this, find out how to help Celestine." She glanced at Hud. "She obviously wants to right the wrongs she caused."

"Maybe she's stuck here until she can make amends," Hud said.

"Stuck between heaven and earth." Chloe looked off into space without seeing. Then her eyes focused on the sky overhead. "I don't see any northern lights." As she spoke, she put her hand to her galena pendant.

Instantly, Celestine appeared. She was staring intently at Jake, her face only inches from his. "I wish I could tell him."

"Tell him what?"

Celestine spun around. "Tell Jake Beaulieu I still love him. That I've loved always him, even beyond the day I died. That I'll never stop loving him."

"Then why did you accuse him of stealing the money?"

"Is she here?" asked Hud.

Chloe nodded, then turned toward Jake. "Celestine says she's never stopped loving you."

Squinting, Jake blinked. Then he shook his head. "I always liked Celestine. Loved her like a sister."

Celestine screamed into his ear. "Don't you get it, Jake? I loved you. I love you." When Jake did not flinch, Celestine began shouting louder and louder. Still, he did not hear her. Finally, she gave up trying to get through to him and turned to Chloe. "Do you have any idea how frustrating this is?"

"I guess not."

"I can see and hear everything, yet I'm invisible. No one can see or hear me. Except you."

"Why is that?" Chloe held out her hands, palm up. "Why me?"

Celestine's eyes opened wide. "Don't you know? When you were born, you and your parents came to live here."

Chloe searched her memory. "I don't recall them ever telling me that."

"I used to tell you stories, sing to you," said Celestine. "You were open to everything. No one had told you things like, 'There's no such thing as ghosts,' or 'Seeing's believing,' or 'It's not much if you can't touch.'"

Chloe spoke slowly as memories emerged. "I vaguely remember odd dreams when I stayed here summers as a child."

"Yes!" Smiling, Celestine clapped her hands. "That was me, too, but by that time your mind was partly closed. You didn't believe in ghosts anymore."

Chuckling, Chloe nodded. "I remember my father telling me not to worry about things I couldn't see. He said I was too old to believe in ghosts, that I had to learn the difference between fact and fiction."

"When you were a baby, you could see me, hear me easily. As a child, you still saw me in your dreams, but after you grew up, you forgot all that, lost that ability."

"You're saying, after I stopped being receptive to the idea of ghosts, my mind shut them out. Since I didn't believe in them, I couldn't see them. I couldn't see *you* anymore."

Celestine nodded. "Somehow, that stone lets you see me. Until it opened your eyes, I thought I was stuck here forever."

Chloe's ears perked. "Where's 'here'?"

Celestine held out her hands indicating the space around her. "Here, in this lonely no man's land."

"Why do you call it a no man's land?"

"I'm nowhere. I'm not really on earth, and I'm not in heaven. I'm stuck *here*, nowhere, with nothing and no one . . . almost no one."

"You mentioned how the stone lets me see you. Hud said galena helps communication, which might explain that part, but why me? Other people have touched the stone. Why can't they see you?"

"Maybe because of our history."

Chloe gave an uncomfortable laugh. "Other than being related and having the same name, *what history?*"

"I've known you from nearly the moment you were born."

Chewing her lip, Chloe considered that.

"What?" Hud searched her face for clues. "What's she saying?"

"Sorry, I forget you can't hear Celestine." Chloe grimaced. "She says I'm sensitive to her because she imprinted on me when I was a baby."

Hud creased his forehead. "Has she said why she accused my grandfather of stealing the money?"

"No, not yet." Shaking her head, she turned toward Celestine. "Why—?"

"I heard him." Her arms crossed, the girl scowled at her. "You don't have to repeat everything."

Chloe rolled her eyes. "Sorry."

She pursed her lips. Then her scowl turned into a mischievous grin. "I know. Let's play ten questions again."

"No, let's not. Playing games is what got you into this."

"But I'm so bored, so tired of this no man's land." Celestine's voice sounded childish, yet brittle.

Chloe heard her unspoken cry for freedom. "Then how can we help you?"

"I want to right my wrongs. I want to get out of this prison, this lonely, Godforsaken jail."

"Okay, help us help you. Why did you accuse Jake of stealing the money?"

"Simple. I loved him."

Chloe scoffed. "That doesn't make sense."

"Yes, it does. It makes perfect sense. I didn't want him to marry Edwina. I wanted him for myself."

"So you—"

"Did everything I could to break off their engagement." Celestine nodded. "Yes."

As Chloe relayed the information, Jake slumped back in his chair.

"What about the drowning?" asked Hud.

"You'd said the other night it wasn't Jake's fault, that it was an accident." Chloe's eyes homed in on Celestine. "What happened?"

Sighing, the girl stared at Jake. "I'd just found and hidden his letter. It looked like they'd get back together. I couldn't let that happen, *wouldn't let that happen,* so I made one last effort."

"What do you mean?"

"I figured if I told Jake I loved him, he'd forget all about Edwina and marry me. I went to his boat shop, pretending to rent a canoe, but when I saw him, I lost my nerve. Then, to build myself up, I tore him down."

"Edwina's better off without you." Celestine sneered. "Any one of her new friends at college will be a better provider than you'll ever be. They'll all have college degrees. You don't even have a high school diploma. Think what they can offer and you can't. You're nothing but a dropout, a loser."

"You know I had to quit school. I didn't have a choice. I had to take that job at the mill to help my family."

Shoulders back, chin high, she scoffed. "Your family, that's another thing. You're a half-breed Indian."

"Quarter," he said, his eyes blazing momentarily. "And that's Native American."

"Sorry," she rolled her eyes, implying just the opposite. "But that means something to my sister, to my parents." Her self-confidence returning, she took a step closer. "Now, none of that means a thing to me." Sidling up to him, she put her hands on his pectorals and then wrapped her arms around his back, pressing her body against his.

Immobile, his eyes wide, he stared at her.

"You're all that matters to me, Jake." Misinterpreting his silence, she lay her head against his chest, listening to his heartbeat, thinking it sounded like a tom-tom. She lifted her lips to his, reaching for him, grazing his lower lip with hers. "You're all that matters."

As he recovered from his shock, he looked down at her. His eyes flashing, he pulled her arms from around his back and held her small hands between his rough palms.

"I don't know what you're up to, Celestine, but understand this. I love your sister." Then he shoved her away. "Find someone else. Better yet, find someone your own age."

"Jake," called a customer. "I need some fish bait."

"Be right with you," he answered. With a parting glance at her, Jake hurried toward the boat house.

"You'll be sorry," she called. She threw a silver dollar after him. "If you won't help me, I'll help myself."

He cupped his hands against the wind, calling, "The water's too rough for canoes. A storm's coming. Wait 'til tomorrow."

While he was inside helping the customer, Celestine took one of the canoes. Crying, she paddled out into the bay, tucked the paddle safely in the bottom of the canoe, and jumped into the deep water.

"Jake! Jake!"

As she tread water, she kept calling for help, expecting him to come to her rescue, but he was inside the shop and could not hear.

She dog-paddled and called until she finally realized he was not coming. Nothing had worked out.

She tried to climb back into the canoe, but the wind had picked up. The waves had gotten too high for her to pull herself out of the water. Finally, she put all her weight on the canoe's side, but it gave way, flipping over on top of her. As the paddle swung out from the base of the canoe, it caught the side of her head and knocked her unconscious.

"So, you see," said Celestine. "Jake was innocent. It was an accident."

When Chloe relayed the story, Jake shook his head. "The police investigators never could figure out how it happened. This explains it."

Celestine stood in front of Jake, looking directly into his eyes. "Can you ever forgive me?" When he did not respond, she turned to Chloe. "Ask him for me."

Taking a deep breath, Chloe said softly, "Jake, Celestine is asking you to forgive her."

He spoke without hesitating. "Of course I do. She was just a foolish kid with a schoolgirl crush on me."

Celestine shook her head. "Not a crush. Tell Jake Beaulieu I love him."

After work the next day, Chloe and Hud brought Edwina home from the hospital.

"You're lucky you came through this unscathed," said Chloe.

Edwina snorted. "The doctor said I have the constitution of a sixty-year-old."

"You're a tough old bird." Chloe smiled warmly. "Hope I've inherited your genes."

"I'm just glad you weren't seriously hurt, Miss Ed." Hud grinned at her.

She gave him a begrudging smile, then turned to Chloe. "You know what I sure could go for? A nice cup of coffee."

Chloe shared a sly grin with Hud. "Okay, let's sit at the kitchen table while I get it started." As she scooped the grounds into the coffee maker, she glanced at Edwina. "Out of curiosity, what was it you were trying to get down from the cabinets?"

Edwina flushed. "Nothing."

Chloe frowned. "Is this 'nothing' so important you'll try to reach it again?"

Edwina pursed her lips, making a sour face, but kept silent.

"Well, is it?" Chloe stared at her. "Because if you're determined to get it, you might as well save us all the trouble of you falling again. Next time you might not be so lucky. Tell me what it is you want, and I'll reach it for you."

Wrinkling her nose, Edwina sighed. "If you're going to be pigheaded about it, there's an old Saltine cracker tin on the top shelf in the back."

"Do you want it now?"

Edina jerked her head in a quick nod, and Chloe pulled the step ladder over. She tried to reach it, but couldn't.

"Let me get that for you," said Hud, trading places with her. He reached as far as he could, even standing on one foot and leaning into the cupboard.

Chloe gasped when the step ladder teetered. "Be careful."

His hand finally knocked it but could not grasp it, so it slid to the floor with a clatter. The tin cover popped off, scattering yellowed letters and old-fashioned cards across the kitchen floor.

Hud and Chloe started gathering them, but one Valentine's Day card caught her eye. It showed a little girl driving a Model T Ford reading "YOU AUTO BE MY VALENTINE" and signed "Jake" in a child's scrawl.

Chloe swallowed. She quickly gathered it, along with the other letters, and gave her stash to Hud, who placed them in the tin.

"Here you go," he said, handing it to Edwina. "Good as new."

Edwina eyed them both caustically. "Did you two gawk enough at my personal effects?"

Chloe shared a look with Hud but said nothing.

"Since you already got an eyeful, you might as well know. Yes, I saved every single letter from Jake, everything." She grimaced. "I just haven't looked at 'em in fifty-sixty years." Then she scowled. "Isn't that coffee ready yet?"

Swallowing, Chloe found her tongue. "Almost." She again glanced at Hud for moral support. "I'm glad you told us because it'll make the next thing I have to say easier."

Lowering her chin, Edwina leveled her eyes at her, glaring. "And what might that be?"

The doorbell rang.

"Here he is now."

Edwina's eyes widened. "Who?"

Hud and Chloe caught each other's eye. "I'll get it." Hud crossed into the dining room and opened the door.

"Am I too early?" asked Jake's voice.

"No, no," Edwina's lips mouthed, but no sound escaped.

"Aunt Ed," whispered Chloe, "Jake asked to see you. Just hear him out."

The older woman shook her head. "No. It's been too many years, too much bitterness."

"Don't you think it's time we put that behind us?" Jake stood at the kitchen's threshold, a bouquet of irises in his hand.

Edwina swallowed. Her eyes turned to his, and a youthful look of wonder came over her face. Sixty years fell away, along with her wrinkles. For a moment, Edwina looked twenty.

Chloe stared. *The look of love.* She reached for Hud's hand.

Then Edwina's expression hardened. Her eyes narrowed as the wrinkles returned to her furrowed brow. Her jaw tightened, and the creases returned to her lips.

"What do you want?"

Jake took a deep breath. Extending the flowers, he took a step toward her. "Rose picked these for you."

Before Edwina could make a caustic remark, Chloe said, "Let me find a vase."

Never taking his eyes off Edwina, Jake nodded as he took another step toward her, still holding the flowers at arm's length, like a shield.

Edwina hesitated, her fingers reaching for and then falling back onto her lap as she seemed to waffle between accepting and crushing them. Finally, she gently accepted the irises with her casted hand.

"Thank you," she mumbled into her chest.

Chloe breathed a silent sigh of relief. She brought the vase over and held it as Edwina placed the flowers in the water.

"Can I get everyone coffee?"

At their nods, she poured the coffee and brought Edwina's flask.

"Isn't there any coffee cake?" Edwina's voice was gruff.

"As a matter of fact, yes, but I thought we'd have it for dessert. After dinner." Chloe winked at Hud. "Tell you what, why don't you and Jake go into the dining room and get reacquainted, while Hud and I finish making dinner?"

"Can I carry your cup, Ed?" asked Jake.

Edwina considered it, then shrugged. "Guess it'd be all right."

Chloe shared a quick grin with Hud.

⚬⚬⚬⚬⚬ ☾ ⚬⚬⚬⚬⚬

By the time Chloe brought out dessert, she noticed Edwina and Jake were talking like ordinary neighbors. *It's almost as if Aunt Ed has called a truce to their feud.* As she set down the cake and began slicing it, she wondered about Edwina's true feelings.

"You should come with us sometime," said Jake.

"Come where?" Chloe glanced at him.

"We go to Our Lady of Good Help's church."

"Isn't that the one with the connection to our family?" Chloe turned to Edwina.

"The same," she said, lacing her coffee.

"Let me see if I remember the story correctly," said Chloe, glancing at her great-aunt. "My great-grandmother, Teresa Malone—"

"No, she was your great-great-grandmother," said Edwina. "When Teresa was seven years old, she accompanied Adele Brise during two of Adele's visions of the apparition."

"I didn't know that." Jake looked from one woman to the other.

"Tell them about our family's other connection to Our Lady of Good Help, Aunt Ed." Chloe handed her a slice of cake.

Edwina sipped her coffee and then said, "My grandfather, Dan O'Hare, and the family took refuge inside the church during the Peshtigo Fire."

"The livestock stayed outside, but within the fenced grounds of the church," said Chloe, handing Hud his cake, "as the people inside prayed."

"And they survived?" Hud looked from Chloe to Edwina.

"Yes," said Edwina. "The next morning, they saw devastation in all directions.

What had been a small clearing in the middle of an enormous forest was now the only remaining five acres the firestorm had left untouched."

"What about the livestock?" asked Jake.

"The outside of the perimeter fence was charred, blistered, but its inner side was untouched. All within survived. Grandfather called it a miracle." Edwina sipped her coffee.

"Your family's connected to two miracles at Our Lady of Good Help."

"But I've never seen it." Chloe handed Jake a slice of the coffee cake.

"Well, let's change that." Jake looked from one face to the next. "What do you say we all go to church there Sunday?"

CHAPTER 6

"'The Hour of the Wolf' is the hour between night and dawn.
It is the hour when most people die. It is the hour when the sleepless are haunted
by their deepest fear, when ghosts and demons are most powerful."

— INGMAR BERGMAN

Sunday morning, Hud drove to Champion with Chloe in the passenger's seat and Edwina and Jake in the back.

Edwina kept nodding off, then waking with a start.

"Why don't you put your head back and nap until we get there?" asked Jake.

Frowning, Edwina shook her head. "Just woke up at three and couldn't get back to sleep."

"The hour of the wolf." Sighing, Jake nodded.

"What's the hour of the wolf?" asked Chloe, turning to face them.

"It's the hour between three and four. Some say it's when most people die and most babies are born. It's when sleep should be the soundest, but it's also when those awakened are visited by night terrors and anxieties."

Chloe watched her great-aunt. Though Edwina said nothing, she nodded her head almost imperceptibly.

"Last year," said Jake, "I was involved in a group discussion of Divine Mercy at Our Lady of Good Help. One of the members said she woke every morning at three filled with fear and a strong sense of evil. After praying the chaplet and rosary, her panic would fade, and she'd fall asleep."

Again, Edwina nodded her head almost imperceptibly.

"During the same time frame, I was listening to Relevant Radio while driving back and forth to Our Lady of Good Help. Several call-in discussions touched on the subject. Others reported the same experience. According to the broadcast, intense spiritual warfare occurs during the hour of the wolf. Satanic cults hold 'black masses' at that hour, the connection being it's the opposite of three in the afternoon, when Christ died."

Edwina exhaled quickly.

"Many have even reported an overwhelming presence of evil when they wake at that hour."

"What do they do?" asked Chloe.

"Pray. Their response is prayer. Some actually leave their house and go to a Perpetual Adoration Chapel to do combat."

Edwina turned to him. "Have you ever felt those terrors at three in the morning?"

Jake nodded.

"What do you do?" Edwina watched him closely.

"I say, 'Jesus, I trust you.'"

"That's it?" Edwina eyed him caustically, then sniffed. "That doesn't seem like much ammunition to arm yourself against evil."

"You don't have to be an electrician to turn on a light switch," said Jake softly. "You don't have to understand. Just trust and believe in God. Every moment's an invitation to make an act of faith or trust."

"That's so passive." Twisting her mouth, Edwina made a sour face.

"It isn't passivity." Jake shook his head. "This is how God speaks to us, moment by moment. Everything," he slowly repeated, "*everything* in life should be welcomed as His expression. There's really only one rule. Live in the present moment. God wills or permits everything. There must be something He—"

"Night terrors are evil." Edwina's eyes grew large. "I can't believe God allows them."

"If He doesn't intervene, it means it's what He thinks is best for you at that moment."

"Best for me?" Curling her lip, Edwina shook her head. "This isn't making a bit of sense."

"It doesn't have to make sense." Jake smiled gently. "It didn't to me at first, either, but I've learned, if God allows it, there's something He wants you to experience or overcome. My guess with these night terrors is He wants you to trust that, if you move forward with a happy spirit, things will work out."

"Happy spirit," Edwina mumbled under her breath. Scowling, her eyes were defiant. "What do I do at three in the morning when all my old worries, my *if-onlys*, come back to roost?"

"Realize that's where God wants you to begin trusting and believing Him. There's real power in faith, enough power to overcome your night terrors . . . and anything else."

Edwina sneered. "Who do you think you are . . . some kind of self-proclaimed shaman or guru?"

Hud glanced at Chloe. She responded with an uncomfortable half-smile and faced forward. Cringing, she tried to give the back seat what little privacy she could, but she could not tune out their words.

Jake spoke with quiet fervor. "Don't you think I've had to overcome a few things in my life? You, of all people, should understand my *what-ifs*."

Edwina said, "You're not the only one with regrets."

After several minutes of ear-splitting silence, Hud glanced at Chloe. "Did you know the Shrine of Our Lady of Good Help was declared a miraculous site in 2010? It's the only site recognized in the United States and one of only fifteen in the world. Champion, Wisconsin, is in the same league as Fatima, Lourdes, and Guadalupe."

"I didn't know that." Creasing her brow, Chloe shook her head. "I'm not even sure what a miraculous site is."

"When the Catholic Church authenticates a shrine," said Hud, "it means the Church recognizes actual, physical cures can occur during a visit to the shrine."

"Are you saying miracles are possible at Our Lady of Good Help?"

"Not only possible, miracles occur," said Jake in a quiet voice from the back seat. "Even I've felt the hand of God."

Chloe turned toward him. "Really? How so?"

He gave Edwina a sidelong glance before answering. "Many years ago, a series of events happened to me where I felt like Job, afflicted and overwhelmed. I'd been accused of theft and negligibility in the death of a loved one. Through no fault of my own, I'd lost the love of my life, and . . ." He swallowed. "I came close to taking my own life."

Edwina's breathing became shallow. Her chest rose and fell quickly as she listened.

"I prayed at that Shrine for answers: 'Why did You let these things happen? What should I do?'"

"Did you receive answers?" asked Chloe.

"What I received," Jake took a long, deep breath, "was peace. It was there I learned how to live with a God-given purpose. It was no longer 'my life' but God's. Living moment by moment, I began welcoming everything as God's personal communication to me. It was there I learned, if I could just believe, miracles would happen."

Lips pursed, eyes narrowed, Edwina raised her eyebrow, silently appraising him.

"What caused this change?" Chloe could not help comparing Jake's serene composure with her great-aunt's patent skepticism.

"*Abandonment to Divine Providence,*" he said. "Written in the eighteenth century and translated in 1921, that book transformed my life. Basically, it said God designed the perfect path for each of us in our everyday lives."

"That's what changed your outlook?"

He nodded.

"How?"

"As I began searching for God in the ordinary, I realized there are two ways to be holy. You can either be sculpted, like stone, which can take a lifetime of being chiseled into a work of divine art, or you can be melted, like metal, and poured into a mold." He grinned. "That's the more painful way, but it's faster."

"You learned that at the Marion Shrine of Our Lady of Good Help?" Edwina met Jake's eyes.

He nodded. "Consecrating your ordinary, everyday life to Our Lady is your unique path to God. It's assigning a holy purpose to your daily life."

"The Marion Shrine, Our Lady," Edwina said, her tone dismissive. "I can believe in God. I can *even* accept Jesus as the son of God, but in no way can I believe in His mother as a divine entity."

"She's human, not divine, but can you accept her chronologically as being born before Christ and giving birth to Him, introducing Him into our human events?" Jake watched her expression.

"Of course."

"Then it's no stretch of imagination to say Our Lady was the dawn preceding Jesus. I turn to her so she can continue to lead me to Christ and the Father, especially in moments of crisis."

"That may work for you, but not for me." Edwina's jaw tightened as the creases deepened in her pinched lips.

"Blessed are those who haven't seen but believe. Your own family's seen her miracles twice." He smiled gently. "By extension, I should think you'd at least acknowledge her."

Edwina scratched her head. "When you phrase it that way, I realize it's not only Our Lady I have trouble believing in. It's the whole human part of divinity that troubles me." She peered into Jake's eyes. "Why would God debase Himself to come to earth?"

Jake thought a moment and then said, "You'd mentioned one of the miracles your family experienced at Our Lady of Good Help was being saved from the Peshtigo Fire. Did you know Peshtigo is a Native American word meaning 'river of the wild goose'?"

"That's a *non sequitur* if I ever heard one." She scowled at him. "What's that got to do with our discussion?"

"You asked why God would demean Himself to come to earth. Let me tell you a story about wild geese."

Not far from here, in fact, just off New Franken Road, a man didn't believe in Jesus, but his wife did. One snowy Christmas Eve, his wife was going to the Christmas Eve service at Our Lady of Good Help. She invited him to join her, but he refused.

"That Christmas story's ridiculous," he said. "Why would God debase Himself to come to earth as a man?" So she left, and he stayed home while the gentle snowfall developed into a blizzard. As he sat in front of the fire, he heard a thump, then another. Something had hit the window.

He peered through the frosty glass but couldn't see anything, so he dressed and went outside. Apparently, a flock of wild geese had been flying south and gotten caught in the storm. Lost, they flew in low circles—blindly, aimlessly. Several had flown against his window.

Feeling sorry for them, he opened his barn doors and watched, waiting for them to take shelter, but the geese did not understand. He tried to get their attention, but it scared them away. He broke up pieces of bread and made a bread crumb trail to the barn. They still didn't get it. Nothing convinced them to go inside the barn.

Finally, he took one of his domestic geese from the barn and carried it, circling behind the wild geese. When he released it, his goose made a beeline into the barn, leading the wild geese to safety.

As the man recalled his earlier words, the Christmas story began making sense.

Wearing a grin, Jake peered at Edwina. "So the moral of the story is: we're the geese, blind and lost. God sent His Son to become one of us, so He could save us from wild-goose chases."

"Speaking of wild-goose chases," said Edwina, "Hud's parked the car. Are we here?"

Chloe noticed Edwina's scowl looked more like a smirk. *How much of her cynicism is just a front?* Then she watched Edwina's smirk relax into a smile, answering her question. *She's not quite the tough old bird she pretends to be.*

———— ◇ ————

They walked to the side door and down the flight of stairs, leading to the crypt. Inside, they saw a crowned statue of Mary on the altar built over the stumps, marking the exact location of the apparition.

Chloe immediately become aware of a peaceful sense of the divine. She felt moved to tears, but she couldn't express why. Several people were praying, and a deep hush permeated the chapel. Its intimate serenity flooded her senses, overwhelming her. As she kept her eyes on the altar, she led their group to a pew in front of it and, crossing herself, knelt in prayer.

Minutes passed in silent contemplation. Chloe thought of her great-great-grandmother, who had been a blind witness to Adele Brise's vision. She thought of her great-great-grandfather taking refuge inside the church during the Peshtigo Fire. *How closely entwined my family's been with the miracles of this church, yet it's the first time I've ever been here.*

Then thoughts of Celestine politely knocked at her mind's door. Chloe touched her pendant, and Celestine appeared in front of the altar.

As Celestine rose from her kneeling position, she seemed subdued, not her usual flamboyant self. Instead of proclaiming her love for Jake or wanting to play word games, she simply said, "Pray for me. Help me right my wrongs, and pray for me." There one minute, gone the next, she disappeared like a heat mirage.

Chloe silently asked for Celestine's spirit to be at rest. Then she asked how she could help. Surprisingly, thoughts flooded her mind. *Are these ideas mine, or are they divine inspiration?* She looked to the altar for answers.

She glanced at Jake and Aunt Ed, both deep in prayer, their heads bowed together. Then she gave Hud a sidelong glance, smiling when his eye caught hers. Gesturing toward the exit with her head, she crossed herself and stood up, silently heading up the stairs to the door. Hud followed, but they did not speak until they were outside.

"Celestine appeared, asking for our help."

"What does she want us to do?"

Chloe smiled to herself as she shared with him. Hud took the statement in stride, nodding as nonchalantly as if she had said Edwina needed help.

When did speaking of spirits, speaking to spirits, become so 'normal'?

"She wants three things." Counting on her fingers, she held up the first. "She wants us to pray for her."

"That's easy enough," he said.

"She wants us to help reunite Jake and Edwina," Chloe said, holding up the second finger, "and . . ."

"What's the third?" Hud peered into her eyes, waiting.

Squirming, Chloe took a deep breath. "How can I put this?" Scratching her ear, she took another deep breath. *Here goes.* "Celestine considers us . . . you and me . . . an extension of Jake and Edwina."

"So . . . ?"

She swallowed. "She feels she . . . interrupted nature's course."

Squinting, he shook his head. "I'm not following. What does she mean by 'nature's course'?"

"Because Jake and Edwina are past the age of having children, and she considers us their younger counterparts."

Grinning, he put his arms around her and drew her to him. "I think I get the picture."

"We wondered if she was influencing our emotions," Chloe sighed, "and this confirms it. It also makes me question how much of our feelings for each other are our own or are Celestine's projections."

She looked into his eyes, trying to read his thoughts. What she saw was love.

But is it real, or is it Celestine's handiwork?

"To hear you talk, you'd think she'd been pouring love potions and aphrodisiacs down our throats." He chuckled. "Relax and enjoy it."

She grinned, recalling their earlier conversation in the car. "What was that Jake said? Live in the present moment. God wills or permits everything."

Tightening his grip around her shoulders, he said, "Who knows? Who says Celestine isn't a messenger of God? If this is how God speaks to us, everything in life should be welcomed as His expression." He stared at her lips and lightly began kissing them in-between words. "I say, never look a gift horse in the mouth."

Her lips pressed against his, Chloe started chuckling, which started Hud chuckling until they were both laughing in each other's arms.

Holding her head back to look at his entire face, not just his lips, Chloe surprised herself by saying, "I love you, Hud Beaulieu."

He stared at her a moment and then brought her to him in an all-embracing clinch. "I love you, too, Chloe Clark." Then he kissed her, leaving no doubt.

Projections, messengers from God? Uhn-uh. This is the real thing.

The sound of someone clearing his throat interrupted their kiss. Still in each other's arms, they turned their heads in time to see Jake stifle a laugh.

"Glad to see our families enjoying life." His eyes twinkling, Jake held the door for Edwina as she joined them outside.

"Enjoying what?" Edwina asked.

"Life," said Chloe, meaning it.

"Mass doesn't start for a few minutes," said Jake. "Why don't we look around the grounds?"

They noticed a small cemetery near the crypt and wandered over to explore.

"This is Sister Adele's grave," said Chloe, reading the headstone. "Died in 1896, twenty-five years after the Peshtigo Fire." She looked up at them. "I wish there were a museum here about the fire."

"There is," said Hud, "in Peshtigo."

"Really? I'd love to do research there, see if I can't learn more about our family after the fire."

"It's definitely worth a trip if you haven't seen it." Jake looked from her to Hud and back. "Maybe you two would like to take a road trip one of these days?"

"Sounds like a great idea." Hud's face was an open invitation she could not resist.

"It does." She smiled up at him.

"Saturday?" His eyes flashed.

Hiding a chuckle, her smile turned into a grin. "It's a date." *He always has a way of making good times better.*

They filed into church just before Mass began.

Chloe's ears perked at the first reading: First Kings, chapter nineteen, verses eleven through thirteen.

"Then the Lord said, 'Go outside and stand on the mountain before the Lord; the Lord will be passing by.' A strong and heavy wind was rending the mountains and crushing rocks before the Lord, but the Lord was not in the wind. After the wind, there was an earthquake, but the Lord was not in the earthquake. After the earthquake, there was fire, but the Lord was not in the fire. After the fire, there was a tiny whispering sound. When he heard this, Elijah hid his face in his cloak and went and stood at the entrance of the cave."

Whispering. What a perfect follow-up to our earlier discussion of how God speaks to us. Chloe caught Hud's eye, and he nodded.

"Does God speak to us?" asked the priest from the pulpit. "Or is that something that only happened in the Old Testament? And if He does still speak to us in this day and age, how does He do it? Is it a deafening roar, a soft whisper, or a strong sensation that it's God who's speaking in our mind?

"Have you ever noticed how noisy our world's become? We celebrate holidays with fireworks and enjoy sports events with roaring crowds. Televangelists broadcast their messages over amplified networks. Televisions on in the house, radio on in the car, something's always on in the background. With traffic, sirens, construction, and, as the Grinch so aptly put it, 'all the noise, noise, noise, noise' of civilization, we might think God would need to shout for us to hear Him.

"As Elijah discovered, God's voice isn't like a strong wind, earthquake, or firestorm. Instead, it's a whisper, so we need to listen carefully. We need to be alert for His voice, wherever we find it. Maybe He speaks through a friend or relative—or through reading, meditation, or prayer. Maybe He speaks through rustling leaves in a breeze. Maybe God speaks through good thoughts in our minds, but it's God guiding us, drawing us closer to Him, and assuring us of His love.

"God speaks most fervently during Mass, when we celebrate together as a family to worship Him. We hear God most clearly while we sing hymns, read Scriptures, hear homilies, and especially, take Communion.

"Don't miss God's tiny whisper because you're expecting a deafening roar. Quiet your mind during the liturgy. Jesus truly is here, waiting to speak to you. Ask Him to open your heart and mind so you can hear His voice as you meditate on His word. Believe you can hear His subtle murmurs, and you'll hear Him."

Chloe reflected on the message. *Believe you can hear Him, and you can. Is God speaking to me through Celestine?*

After Mass, she asked Jake what he thought of the homily.

"I liked Father's discussion of listening for God's voice, but he never touched on embracing God's will." Jake held the door for her as they left the church. "Hearing Him's only half the equation. Embracing God's will, doing God's will, is the other half."

She blinked, computing. "I never looked at it that way."

"Resistance is the cause of all our troubles." Jake stopped beneath a tree, waiting for Edwina and Hud to catch up. "Submission to divine will is what's given me peace. Sixty years ago, I can tell you, I was a different man—bitter and resentful—but by embracing God's will, I received His peace."

"I can understand accepting God's will . . . up to a point." She raised her eyebrow.

"Patience." He smiled gently. "God only wants you to do the part you can do with your temperament, your abilities. God's created the perfect mold just for you." He winked. "And it isn't like anyone else's mold."

Chloe smiled, thinking of outlandish assignments.

"What if God wanted me to become a missionary in Yemen or join the French Foreign Legion? I don't think I could do those things."

"Accept God's will without saying, 'I wish such-and-such was different.' If what God gives you is unacceptable, how will you ever find peace?" He looked her in the eye. "Do you know better than God?"

She chuckled. "No."

"God will give you the flexibility to go beyond your comfort zone, to do whatever He wants you to accomplish, along with a bonus: peace of mind." He smiled. "But only if you embrace God's will."

"There's a meditation path with Stations of the Cross," Hud said, joining them, "and there's a display of crutches and other mementos of thanksgiving for prayers answered. Where would you like to go first?"

Chloe turned to Edwina. "Do you feel up for a walk?"

"After sitting all morning, a stroll sounds good." Edwina cocked a half-smile. "Just no marathons, please."

"This stroll's for meditative purposes only. No sprinting. You have my word of honor." Chloe held up her right hand, scout's honor, as she grinned at her great-aunt. "Besides, this isn't the right time or place for sprinting."

"To the servant of God, every place is the right place, and every time is the right time, or so said St. Catherine of Siena." Jake grinned at them as he held out the crook of his arm for Edwina.

She gave him a coquettish glance and then, smiling to herself, shyly took his arm.

Chloe studied the couple, imagining what they had looked like sixty years before. Raising her eyes, she saw Hud watching her, an amused smile softening his chiseled features. With a gallant flourish, he held out the crook of his arm, mimicking his grandfather. Chloe chuckled and linked arms with him, gripping his taut bicep with her fingers. She looked up into his face.

"There's a certain air about this place, a peaceful feeling."

He nodded. "I can't help but believe miracles and prayers leave behind impressions. Maybe that's what we're sensing."

An American Goldfinch flitted through the trees, rustling the branches. Chloe breathed deeply, inhaling the fresh scent of the pine needles. Then three Canada geese flew overhead. She thought of her aunt's response to Jake's story.

"Wonder if they're on a wild-goose chase."

Hud looked at her questioningly, and she laughed, feeling relaxed—safe on these hallowed grounds.

After making the meditation path's loop, they found themselves back at the church. For some reason she couldn't fathom, Chloe felt drawn to the crypt.

"Let's visit the chapel again before we leave."

"We've seen it once," said Edwina, her lips pursed, her eyes glancing around nervously.

"I know but . . ." Wondering why she felt attracted to it, Chloe searched her mind for a plausible excuse. "We never saw the crutches left behind by the grateful healed."

"It's getting late," said Edwina, her eyes shifting back and forth. She licked her lips. "We should be getting back."

"A quick prayer, and then we can leave." Chloe wondered why she felt so compelled, but all the lessons of that day told her to follow her instinct. "Five minutes."

"I suppose."

They descended the short stairway, entering the Crypt of the Apparitions. This time, Chloe noticed the candles. Votive candles were everywhere. Racks of votive candles twinkled along every wall. *It's a wonderland of holy light. Why didn't I notice this the first time?*

Again, Chloe led them into the pews, but Edwina sat apart, up a row, on the other side of the central aisle, just within Chloe's peripheral vision. Again, Chloe felt compelled to touch her pendant, and Celestine appeared. She said one word as she glanced at her sister.

"Watch."

Then Celestine faded.

When Chloe turned slightly to better see Edwina, she noticed a bright light. Two women sat beside Edwina, one on each side. Heads huddled together, first on one side, then on the other, they seemed to be whispering. *Funny, I didn't notice anyone come in.* She glanced at the entrance, but it was empty. Shrugging, she turned back to watch Edwina.

From her great-aunt's rapid head movements, turning from one side to the other, it appeared two contradictory conversations were occurring simultaneously. Edwina would nod, then turn and shake her head. The woman on her left seemed to almost glow. Tilting her head, Chloe squinted. *What's going on?*

Then, their backs to her, the three women rose and walked toward the crypt's foyer. Chloe followed a few steps behind them. There, she saw the many pairs of crutches neatly tucked behind a glass case.

The three women appeared so caught up in their conversations, they did not notice her. Concentrating, Chloe began to hear their whispers.

"He loves you. Let bygones be bygones."

Edwina nodded. Then, as the other woman spoke, Edwina half turned toward her.

"Don't forget, he's ignored you for sixty years. Never forget, he's to blame for Celestine's death."

Edwina wrapped her arms around herself, nodding.

As it occurred to her who they were discussing, Chloe gasped. *Jake.*

The three women turned toward her. For the first time, she saw the other two women's faces. One had been badly burned, disfigured. Sparse patches of thin hair hung from her scalp, and she wore a coarse brown dress that brushed the floor.

The features of the second face were bland, undefined, like a face covered with a nylon stocking. She wore a fabric that gleamed in the candlelight, illuminating the small room, so bright its reflected light eclipsed her face.

Chloe blinked. When she opened her eyes a fraction of a second later, the two women were gone. *How could they have gotten past me? I'm blocking the exit.* She peered around. There was no sign of them having squeezed by her, up the stairs. The racks of votive candles continued to burn without flickering, showing no sign of anyone having breezed past.

But she felt cold, as bone-chillingly cold as she had felt in the back of her closet. Shivering, she turned toward her aunt. Before she could question her, Hud and Jake appeared in the vestibule.

Hud smiled until he saw her face. Then his eyes narrowed suspiciously, and he crossed to her.

"You okay?"

Nodding, too shaken to speak, she motioned to him to follow her outside.

"Did you see anyone leave the tiny room before you entered?"

"No. Why?"

Before she could tell him, Jake and Edwina interrupted, her aunt insisting it was time to go.

The ride home was quiet. When Hud and Jake walked them to the door, Chloe invited them in for dinner.

Edwina put a hand to her forehead. "If you don't mind, I'm just going to bed. I have a splitting headache."

Hud and Jake glanced at each other.

"Maybe another time, when Ed feels better," said Jake, "but thanks for asking us."

Hud gave Chloe a quick peck on the cheek, whispering, "Meet you tomorrow for a perch fry?"

She nodded. "Five?"

As they left, Chloe turned to her great-aunt. "Who were those women you were speaking with at the crypt?"

Raising her eyebrow, Edwina shook her head. "I wasn't talking to anyone."

"In the chapel, and then in that vestibule, I saw you talking with two women."

Tongue in cheek, as if picking her teeth, again Edwina shook her head.

"Nope, you're mistaken, but I really do have a headache. I'm going to lie down a bit, take a nap."

Chloe watched her great-aunt walk to her bedroom and close the door. She sighed. *I couldn't have imagined it, yet Hud didn't see anyone, and Aunt Ed's denying it.* Then, remembering Celestine had told her to watch, she touched her pendant. *Celestine will confirm what I saw.*

The girl appeared, kneeling, her ear pressed against Edwina's door.

"Cel—"

Finger to her lips, the girl shushed her. "Listen," she mouthed more than whispered, and she vanished.

What's going on? Grimacing, feeling like a spy, Chloe grudgingly listened at the door. She heard whispering. *Who's she talking to?* She put her ear against the old-fashioned keyhole.

"Move on," said a calm voice.

A raspy voice hoarsely stage whispered, "Don't forget. Never forget. It's his fault she drowned."

Chloe's jaw hung loose. *Aunt Ed still believes Jake's responsible for Celestine's death.*

Chloe peeped through the keyhole. Edwina was alone, yet she'd turn one way and then the other, apparently listening to the voices Chloe heard.

Maybe this is the right time to tell her.

Chloe knocked on the door. The whispering stopped, and once again she felt a blast of arctic air, but Edwina did not appear. She knocked a second time.

When Edwina still did not answer, Chloe called, "Aunt Ed, there's something we need to discuss."

Finally, Chloe heard her shuffle toward the door.

"Can't this wait?" Edwina opened the door. "I really do have a headache."

Chloe narrowed her eyes, distrusting Edwina. *She's lied about these . . . entities. What else isn't she telling?*

"Aunt Ed, it occurred to me you might still blame Jake for Celestine's drowning."

Edwina's eyebrows shot up. "Why would you bring that up?"

Chloe took a deep breath, deciding which tact to take. *Honesty's always the best policy.*

"I heard you just now."

"You heard what?" She tilted back her head, appraising Chloe.

She was unsure how much to disclose. "I heard you talking to . . . yourself."

Edwina seemed to relax, as if that satisfied her. Then she shrugged. "Just mumblings. It's nothing important."

"It isn't Jake's fault Celestine drowned. It was an accident."

Edwina's face turned beet red. "How would you know? Were you there?"

Chloe worried about her aunt's blood pressure. "Of course I wasn't there, but I talked to someone who was."

"Who? Jake?" Edwina's narrowed eyes homed in on hers.

"Yes." Chloe took a deep breath, gathering her nerve. "But I also spoke to Celestine."

Edwina weaved on her feet.

"Aunt Ed!" Chloe leaped forward, placing her shoulder under the woman's arm, bracing her up. "Lean on me. Let me help you to bed."

Chloe staggered under the older woman's weight but got her onto the bed safely. *I shouldn't have sprung this on her.*

"What was it you wanted to tell me?"

Chloe slowly shook her head. "Maybe this isn't the best time to discuss it."

"Make up your mind!" Though the woman lay prone, the anger in her voice was clear.

Chloe struggled with her conscience. *I don't want to irritate her, but Aunt Ed needs to know.* Mustering her courage, Chloe told her about the galena pendant and Celestine.

⸺⸺ ◇ ⸺⸺

"So it really wasn't Jake's fault?" Edwina looked up at her.

Chloe shook her head. "No. According to both Celestine and Jake, it was just an accident."

"And the rest of it?" asked Edwina. "Was the rest of it all Celestine's doing?"

Chloe tilted her head as she looked at Edwina, still prone in bed. "What rest of it?"

"The lipstick," said Edwina, peering at her skeptically. "You said you can see her." Edwina sat up in bed. "Ask her."

"You mean Celestine?"

At her aunt's nod, Chloe touched her pendant. Celestine appeared, sitting on Edwina's bed.

"Is she here?" asked Edwina, her eyes wide.

"Yes, and she can hear you. Ask her yourself."

Edwina looked at the space beside Chloe.

"No, Celestine's sitting at the foot of your bed, here." Chloe gestured with her hand, and Edwina shifted her eyes.

"What about the times you mentioned lipstick on Jake's collar?"

"None of it was true." Chloe relayed Celestine's words as she spoke them.

"But I saw the lipstick once." Edwina's eyes narrowed. "If you're really here, Celestine, tell me how that happened."

As Chloe relayed Celestine's words, she watched her great-aunt's changing expressions. *Celestine's answer is Aunt Ed's way of judging whether I'm telling the truth.*

"I wanted to make you suspicious," said Celestine. "One time, after Jake left, I asked if you'd seen lipstick on his collar. Of course, you hadn't seen any because there wasn't any, but I made sure you'd see lipstick the next time I questioned you about it.

I watched where Jake stashed his clean shirt when he worked at the canoe rentals. Then I sneaked in the back door when he was busy at the front desk with customers. Holding his shirt to my face, I caressed my cheek with it as I breathed in his scent. I pressed his shirt against my chest and cuddled it as if he was in it, wishing he was.

104

Then, remembering Jake belonged to you, I crumpled it and grazed its collar against my lips, leaving an unmistakable red smudge.

When Jake stopped by to take you to the drive-in, I said, "You should be more careful when you kiss him. Look. You got lipstick on his collar. You saw the lipstick that time, and it started a fight that ended with you telling him to leave."

When Chloe relayed the story, Edwina stared into space, her face ashen.

After several minutes passed in silence, Chloe asked, "Aunt Ed, are you all right?" She nodded.

"That was a test, to see if I was telling the truth, wasn't it?"

Again, Edwina nodded.

"Now do you believe me?" Chloe watched her.

"Yes." She looked up at her niece, her eyes red. "Is she all right?"

Chloe exhaled as she pressed her lips together. "Her soul's not at peace, if that's what you mean. She wants to make amends for what she did to you and Jake."

Sighing, Edwina's shoulders slumped.

"Ask her about the two voices," said Celestine.

"Who was that you were whispering with when I knocked on your door?"

Instantly, Edwina's expression changed. Her eyes narrowed as she scowled at Chloe.

"No one. I was talking to myself."

"Aunt Ed, I saw you talking to them in the crypt, and I heard you in here. Who were they?"

Edwina spun her head to look at her. "You saw them?"

Chloe nodded. "In the crypt, not here."

"Describe them." Chloe nibbled her lip as she tried to recall. "One was wearing a shimmering gown. It was so bright, it dazzled, seeming to attract and reflect light. I had to squint to see. The gown's brightness blinded me to her features. The other's face was scarred badly, as if she had been burned. Thin, wispy clumps of hair tufted out from her head, and she wore a coarse burlap gown."

Edwina blinked. "I've never seen them," she said in a faint whisper, "only heard their voices."

"I never saw them until I . . . until after I . . ." Celestine's voice faded off.

"After you died?" asked Chloe.

"Yes." Celestine whispered. "Before that, I only heard them talking to me, advising me."

Chloe looked from one to the other. "You both say you've heard them?"

Edwina nodded. "It's almost like an angel on one shoulder and a devil on the other."

"Exactly," said Celestine. "It's voices in your head, telling you what to do. Only they cancel each other out."

"Sounds like clairaudience, hearing voices," said Chloe, "although some people associate that with schizophrenia."

"It feels like it." Edwina lifted an eyebrow. "One voice tells you one thing, while the other tells you the opposite. They contradict each other."

"That's pretty much what Celestine just said." Chloe looked from one to the other. "When did you start hearing these voices?"

"They began a few months before Celestine drowned," said Edwina slowly, thinking.

"I began hearing them just before . . . just before I . . ." Celestine's voice trailed off.

"Before you died?" Chloe asked again.

Celestine nodded. "After I . . ." she swallowed. "Now I can see them."

"What are they?" Chloe looked from one to the other.

"One's an angel," said both sisters in unison.

"And the other?"

"Whatever's the opposite of an angel," said Edwina, shrugging. "A demon, I guess."

Celestine shook her head. "I'd call the other a dark soul."

"What do you mean 'a dark soul'?"

The girl grimaced, as if searching her mind. "She's a spirit caught in no man's land, like me, but there's more. There's hatred, evil. I call her a dark soul." She shook her head. "I don't understand it, but she's the reason I'm here. She's the one who put the thoughts in my mind, told me to do things."

"What kind of things?"

Creasing her brow, Chloe cocked her head to one side, trying to understand.

"Smear lipstick on Jake's collar, hide the hundred-dollar bill and letter, take the canoe out on rough water, want Jake for myself." Celestine looked up at her, pleading. "I'm afraid of her. She still tells me to do things. She bullies me, and I want to get away from her."

"I thought you said you were lonely, bored."

Celestine nodded. "I am alone . . . usually, except when she wants to control me."

"What do you want?" Chloe searched the girl's eyes.

"I want to right the wrongs I did, but she . . . it wants revenge."

Chloe grimaced. "Misery loves company."

"This *thing* is so bitter, so filled with hatred," said Celestine. "It wants to drag everyone down with it."

"Down?" Chloe squinted, trying to understand. "Down where?"

Celestine looked down through lowered eyelids. "I don't know. Maybe hell?" Then she looked up, her eyes wounded, her posture stiff. "This *thing* is evil, and it frightens me. Help me get away from it." The girl vanished.

"I remember when this started." Edwina sat propped up on pillows, her back leaning against the bed's headboard.

Still reeling from Celestine's disclosure, Chloe slowly turned toward Edwina. "What?"

"I remember the day I began hearing voices, the same morning Celestine changed. It was the time our mother took us to the field where your great-great-grandmother saved her from the Peshtigo Fire."

"Is that near here?"

The older woman nodded. "What had been a freshly plowed field in the 1870s was a community park in 1955, when we visited it. Mother wanted us to see it, remember it. As Mother told us the story, Celestine explored the area, finding ways to keep herself amused."

Maria, their mother, pointed to a clearing between two picnic tables.

"It was here my mother lay facedown on the freshly plowed field. Covering me with her body, she protected me from the firestorm that roared around us."

"You and grandma were here alone?" Edwina watched her mother.

Maria nodded. "Your grandfather had gone to Champion the day before. I was their first child, a baby, but your grandmother told me the story so often, I almost 'remember' it."

"It was just you two here in this field?" Edwina looked at the manicured picnic area, trying to imagine the fiery scene.

"No. Mother's sister, Letty, lay facedown just a row or two away, holding her baby."

"Over here?" Celestine ran to the picnic tables and began looking around them, beneath them.

Maria pointed to the grassy space between them. "Yes. Somewhere in the area between this first table and the next."

Edwina thought out loud. "So her baby would be Celestine's and my aunt or uncle." Then she turned to her mother. "Who is it? Do we know her or him?"

"The baby would have been your aunt, but, unfortunately, neither she nor her mother survived. Less than two feet from us, they were both burned beyond recognition. All that was left were several metal eyelets, a few teeth, and part of Aunt Letty's spine. Mother said she nearly lost her mind at the grisly sight and stench of her sister and niece's remains after the firestorm passed."

Edwina grimaced. "Wouldn't she have heard her screaming?"

"According to her, the firestorm was a tornado, a whirling wall of flames. It sounded like a freight train roaring by. Mother always said she had been to hell twice. Once during the fire and again afterwards, when she saw the charred remains of her sister and niece."

"You said it happened over here?" called Celestine, kneeling on the grassy area.

"About there," Maria called. "What are you doing?"

Celestine grinned mischievously. "Looking for four-leaf clovers."

"How could they have been two feet away from you and been burned alive?" Edwina shook her head.

"The heat was that intense. According to Mother, survivors told of neighbors just raising their heads an inch or two higher to keep from smothering in the soil and being burned alive, while they lay beside them, unscorched."

"It must have been an inferno."

Celestine came running over and placed a tarnished copper circlet in her mother's hand. "What's this?"

"I'm not sure." Maria turned it over and rubbed off bits of caked clay. "It looks like an old brooch of some sort."

"Do you think it's from the Peshtigo Fire? A treasure?" Celestine's eyes sparkled.

"I don't think it's that old," said Maria, "but it could be."

"Maybe it was Grandma's sister's brooch." Celestine's eyes lit up at the thought. "Maybe it's haunted."

Maria handed it back to her. "And maybe it belongs to someone who'll come looking for it. Better put it back."

Celestine frowned but, mumbling under her breath, walked back to where she had found it.

"Mother and I chuckled at Celestine's excitement over finding something she thought was haunted." Edwina looked up at Chloe. "I always thought she'd done as Mother told her, returned it, but . . ." She grimaced. "I saw that brooch in the jewelry box you found."

"Really?" Several ideas entered Chloe's mind, but she immediately dismissed them. "I can't believe there's any connection between that brooch and the dark spirit. It'd be too coincidental."

"Nothing's coincidental. Truth's always stranger than fiction. You just told me how the galena you found in the jewelry box lets you see and hear Celestine." Edwina hunched her shoulders, shrugging. "Why couldn't the brooch be connected to your great-great-grand-aunt Letty?"

Chloe blinked as she thought it through. "You're right. It's the same rationale. Where's the jewelry box now?"

"I put it in my old cedar chest in your closet." Edwina pointed.

"I'll get it."

As Chloe approached her room, she felt chilled. Shivering, she grabbed the flashlight from her dresser, but as soon as she entered the closet, the light flickered and went out.

No, no, not again. This hasn't happened since I found the jewelry box. Celestine, stop it!

She touched her pendant, but Celestine did not appear. Recalling what had worked previously, she laid the flashlight on the floor and moved aside her clothes on the front rack. As she peered into the back at Edwina's cedar hope chest, she shuddered, reminding herself *it's a chest, not a coffin.*

Taking a deep breath, she began humming Tchaikovsky's "1812 Overture." Then she dashed under the front rack of clothes and raced to the chest. When she lifted its lid, it was too dark to see inside. Humming loudly, she groped with her hand, grabbing what felt like the jewelry box. Then, slamming down the top, she raced back into her room, shivering.

"Euwww." *Feels like spiders crawling on me. If you're doing this, Celestine, stop it!*

She breathed deeply, steadying her nerves before taking the jewelry box into Edwina's bedroom. As she walked in, she noticed the sunny day was beginning to cloud over. Instead of sunshine pouring through the window, the sky appeared dark. Glancing out, she saw roiling clouds gathering just above.

She looked at her great-aunt. Her eyes closed, Edwina leaned against the headboard.

"Are you awake?"

Edwina's eyelids fluttered open. "Just resting my eyes."

"Here it is." Chloe placed the jewelry box beside her.

As Edwina opened the box, her eyes fell on the tarnished copper circlet. She gently lifted it out, placed it in the palm of her hand, and studied it. As if the sun had set, the room became dark.

Again, Chloe glanced out the window and saw twilight.

"Let me flip on the lights. Looks like a storm's brewing." She turned on the bedside lamp.

Edwina silently stared at the brooch, her eyes bloodshot, brimming over with tears. Then she gasped, clutching the brooch to her chest.

"Aunt Ed." Chloe sat on the side of her bed. "Are you all right?"

Nodding, the woman swallowed her tears before speaking. "I'm fine. It's just . . . it's been so long since I remembered Celestine as my baby sister. I'd forgotten. I loved her. All I remembered was the hatred I bore Jake. She was a sweet kid who . . ." Edwina opened her hand and looked at the brooch. Then she looked up at Chloe. "This brooch is just a piece of burned metal. How could it be evil?"

Chloe glanced at the deepening darkness outside the window.

"Not the brooch, maybe it's the connection to it that's evil."

"What are you thinking?"

"If this brooch was Letty's when she was burned to death," said Chloe, "maybe it captured her last thoughts, memories."

"Is it possible she could have left some kind of 'imprint' on it?"

"It's a cliché in movies, but can it really happen? I suppose anything's possible."

Holding the brooch in the palm of her casted hand, Edwina lightly caressed it with the fingertips of her other hand.

"Did this pin really survive the blaze? Could it have captured the last horrible moments of Letty's life like a kind of camera?"

"Hud and I are going to the Peshtigo Fire Museum. Why don't I take it there? Maybe someone can date it for us or at least see if this brooch is from that era."

Chloe held out her hand, and Edwina placed the brooch in it. As it touched her skin, Chloe thought she saw movement from the corner of her eye. Both women turned their heads as a shadow seemed to race across the wall. *Strange.*

Chloe placed the pin in the jewelry box and closed the lid. Glancing outside, she noticed the clouds were letting up. *Weird.*

"Do you still need this lamp on?"

"No," Edwina leaned back, "but I think I will take a nap. I feel drained."

CHAPTER 7

"Courage is fire, and bullying is smoke."
— BENJAMIN DISRAELI

Saturday, Hud picked her up early. The sun was shining brightly. The sky a robin's-egg blue, it was a perfect morning. Chloe smiled at Hud beside her, glad to be alive.

"The entire area we're driving through this morning was part of the million acres burned during the Peshtigo Fire," he said.

She glanced out the car window at the greenery. "We've only driven a few miles. How many miles to go?"

"About eighty," he said, checking the odometer.

"Nearly ninety miles of flame." Shaking her head, she tried to wrap her mind around it. *How awful for the people caught in it.*

"No one's certain, but they estimate twenty-four hundred square miles were burned during the fire. The death toll in Chicago was about two hundred and fifty people. Some say the death toll here during the Peshtigo Fire was nearly ten times that."

"Wow." Inhaling, she shook her head. Then she heard a child's singsong voice in her mind.

"ASHES TO ASHES . . . DUST TO DUST . . . KEEP WISCONSIN GREEN . . . OR WE'LL . . . ALL GO BUST . . . . BURMA-SHAVE."

Chloe turned to Hud. "We have a visitor." He took his eyes from the road long enough to glance at her with an upraised eyebrow. "Celestine's here," she answered.

Nodding, he turned back to the road.

"The blackened Forest . . . Smolders yet . . . Because . . . He flipped . . . A cigarette . . . . Burma-Shave."

Celestine sat between them on the console, looking from one to the other.

"Haven't seen you in awhile," said Chloe. "Where have you been?"

"Laying low." Celestine seemed to shrink as she hunched forward.

"Who are you hiding from?"

"Letty."

"Why?"

She dangled her feet, her toes kicking behind the dash. "You know."

Chloe turned to Hud. "Celestine says she's been hiding from Letty." She told him the story of Celestine finding the brooch and how, soon after, odd things began happening. She also recounted what she had seen and heard.

Taking a deep breath, he raised his eyebrow again. "Maybe it wouldn't be a bad idea to stop off at church." He glanced at her. "A little holy water can do wonders. If we're lucky, maybe we can find the priest and ask him to bless it . . . just in case."

Just in case. Chloe nodded. Then she turned toward Celestine, but she had gone. She looked out the windshield. Clouds were gathering. The sunny skies had turned gray. *Could that be because of the brooch?* She reached into her purse for the plastic baggie containing the pin.

Yelping, she jerked her hand out and looked at the blood oozing from her fingertip.

"Dang it!"

"What?"

"I just pricked myself on the pin." *Was it my fault, or did the brooch . . . ?* She frowned. "Yes, I think it'd be a good idea to bless this pin."

<hr />

As they parked in front of the church, the dark sky opened up. Hail thundered down on the truck's metal roof. Though the skies were dark, the air was white with hail as far as they could see.

"Where'd this come from?" Hud ducked to peer at the sky through the windshield.

Chloe glared at the baggie containing the brooch and then held it up to show him.

"I wouldn't be surprised if this has something to do with it. As weird as it sounds, it seems this doesn't want us to go into the church."

"Let's wait it out," he said. "The hail will stop in a minute."

Chloe raised her eyebrow but said nothing. Ten minutes later, she looked at the white mounds collecting on the ground.

"It's coming down just as hard as when it started." Shaking her head, she sighed. "Let's make a run for it."

Hud looked out the window and grabbed a quilt from the back.

"That hail's the size of golf balls. Let's at least cover our heads."

Holding the quilt over his head, he opened the driver's door and jumped out. Then he tented the quilt as Chloe climbed over the console and followed him out. Even under the quilt, the hail beat against her calves as they raced into the church.

When they got inside the vestibule, Chloe looked at the red welts where the hail had struck.

"Should've worn jeans, not capris."

He sucked air through his teeth, making a hissing sound. "That's going to leave a mark."

"Bruises at the very least." Grimacing, she looked for the holy water font. "Let's not waste any time." Entering the church, she dipped her fingers in the holy water and, yelping, quickly jerked them out.

"What?" He turned toward her, his brow wrinkling.

"The holy water just stung my finger where the pin pricked it," she whispered. Pursing her lips, she held up her index finger, showing him an angry, red sore.

His eyes met hers. "It sure seems that brooch or something doesn't want us here."

Again, Chloe dipped her finger in the holy water and quickly made the sign of the cross mumbling, "In the name of the Father, the Son, and the Holy Ghost."

This time she sprinkled some of the holy water on her calves. Then she pulled the pin from her purse and took it from its baggie. Holding it carefully, she submerged it in holy water for a count of three before lifting it out. Again, carefully holding it by its latch, she made the sign of the cross. "In the name of the Father, the Son, and the Holy Ghost."

Chloe took a deep breath. "Hope that's that."

"Let's say a prayer," he whispered, motioning toward the pews with his head.

She nodded and followed him, where they prayed silently for a few minutes. Then, genuflecting and making the sign of the cross, they started for the exit. When they reached the vestibule, a young priest welcomed them with a warm handshake.

Hud introduced him as Father David.

"I've been watching you," he said, his dark eyes serene, never leaving her face.

Chloe shot Hud an uneasy glance. "Really?"

With a gentle smile, he nodded. "Would you care to tell me what's going on?"

Again, she glanced at Hud uneasily. He gave her an encouraging nod, and she summarized what had prompted them to bless the pin with holy water. Hunching her shoulders, she ended by saying, "This brooch just seems . . . for lack of a better word, possessed."

Father David listened thoughtfully. Then he invited them to his office, gesturing to two chairs with his upturned palm. "Have a seat." Sitting behind his desk, he turned to Chloe. "So you think the brooch is possessed."

"I hope not, but I think so."

He scratched his forehead. "There are three forms of demonic influence: possession, obsession, and opposition."

Chloe mentally repeated the three forms.

"Demonic possession's very rare, but demonic *obsession* is common."

"What's the difference?" Chloe looked from Father David to Hud and back again.

"Demonic possession is when a demon controls a person so he or she can't resist. Demonic obsession is when a demon only influences a person's behavior, but it can lead to jealousy, fear, rage, or compulsive behavior, like drug addiction or alcoholism. Obsession can be treated with deliverance."

"By deliverance," Chloe narrowed her eyes, "do you mean a person's released from this obsession?"

"Yes. The person's set free from the spirit's bondage."

She showed him the brooch. "What if this is an *object* that's haunted, not a person? Is there anything we can do?"

Father David's smile faded. "Truly haunted objects are classified in the third kind of demonic influence, opposition. This happens when either a restless or an evil spirit possesses an object."

"I'm unfamiliar with the terms." She smiled uneasily. "What's the difference between the two?"

"Restless spirits are often people who died with unfinished business and want to communicate with their loved ones. Without a physical body, they can't communicate verbally, so they appear in dreams or leave signs, such as a locked door or a familiar scent. On the other hand, evil spirits try to frighten or possess the people. Not only can they move objects and make noises, they can create conflict, mistrust. Either way, they're crying out for help."

"How can we help?"

"I recommend blessing them."

"What happens during a blessing? What do you do?"

"I pray for the spirits, assuring them they are loved, and I pray for their past memories to be healed."

Chewing her lip, Chloe took off her necklace and handed it to him along with the brooch. "Can you bless these for us?"

Father David nodded solemnly. Taking the two objects in his left hand, he made the sign of the cross with his right.

"Let us pray. O God, at Your word all things are made holy. Pour Your blessing upon these objects, which You have made. Grant that whoever gratefully makes use of them according to Your will and law may, by calling on Your holy name, receive from You health of body and salvation of soul, through Christ our Lord. Amen."

Again, he made the sign of the cross over them. "In the name of the Father, the Son, and the Holy Ghost." Then he handed them back to Chloe.

She took a deep breath, filling her lungs. Hand on chest, she smiled.

"Thank you. I feel better already." Putting the necklace on, she added, "Hope this helps Celestine and Letty."

⚜

Back on the road to Peshtigo, Chloe looked out at the passing scenery. The hail had melted. The roads were clear, and the sky was blue again. She recalled Hud saying the Peshtigo Fire had engulfed the entire area, and she tried to imagine what it had looked like prior to that, when it had been a virgin forest. Thoughts of Letty and Celestine followed. She touched her pendant, wondering what would happen now that it had been blessed.

"MANY A FOREST . . . USED TO STAND . . . WHERE A . . . LIGHTED MATCH . . . GOT OUT OF HAND . . . . BURMA-SHAVE." Celestine sat on the console between her and Hud, looking from one to the other.

"You're still here." Chloe smiled wryly, glad to see her little friend but sorry her soul was still not at rest.

Hud glanced at Chloe, his eyebrow raised. "Celestine?"

Chloe nodded and glanced down at the girl. "Do you feel any different?"

Celestine hunched her shoulders. "I feel better." She affirmed it with a nod. "I'm not afraid of Letty anymore."

"That's a good thing, but you're still here. Why?"

"I don't know." Again, the girl shrugged. "Maybe, like he said, I just have unfinished business. When it's done . . . I'm done . . . here." With that, she faded.

⸺⸺ ◇ ⸺⸺

When they arrived at Peshtigo, it was still too early for the museum to open. Taking her hand, Hud turned toward her.

"Let's walk around the cemetery until the museum opens."

They strolled along, reading the tombstones' inscriptions wherever they were still visible, where they had not weathered away.

"Ida, Wife of Frank, Her spirit smiles from that bright shore and softly whispers weep no more," read Chloe. "She was twenty-one." She frowned.

"Here's the grave of a child," said Hud. "He was two and a half. John, son of James and Ann, One loved, One less on earth, One angel more in heaven."

"And of a woman, who was thirty-five," said Chloe, reading. "As a star that is lost when the daylight is given, she has faded away to shine bright in heaven."

It reminds me of Celestine . . . if she was in heaven. She sighed.

They stopped near a tombstone and read the nearby plaque.

"Lempke. Aunt Ed told me his story. Ohmigosh, this is where he was buried." Chloe turned toward Hud. "Aunt Ed said her grandmother had told her about him. Mr. Lempke had tried to escape with his wife and," she read, "*five* children in a horse-drawn wagon. He had jumped down from the wagon to help the horse get through. A wave of fire passed, and he saw flames shooting from his wife's hair and his children's clothes. He tried to beat out the flames, but it was too late. The fire was so intense, his wife and children were burned alive."

They stood in silence a moment, looking from the plaque to the grave to the surrounding greenery. Birds chirped and called to each other. A nearby tree was beginning to bloom.

Hud squeezed her hand. "These plaques bring the people's stories to life."

Lips pressed together, she nodded. Then they strolled over the grassy knoll, stopping in front of the mass grave of the fire victims. Staring at the fenced-in area, Chloe felt waves of emotion. A lump rose in her throat. Swallowing hard, she blinked back tears as she thought of the unnamed hundreds of incinerated persons, their charred remains tossed together.

It's like the crypt of the apparition. It's so moving, so powerful. It's heartbreaking.

"No one knows for sure how many are buried here," said Hud. "Estimates range from a hundred and fifty to over three hundred and fifty. Most of the fire victims' identities were unknown, burned beyond recognition." He pointed at the road. "According to eye witnesses, wagons carrying the victims were lined up for three miles, waiting their turn for the remains to be interred here."

She looked up at him. "So this was a public cemetery?"

He shook his head. "No, it belonged to the Congregational Church. The church was destroyed in the fire, but the surviving congregation members decided to open the cemetery to anyone needing a grave site."

She glanced at the annual flowers, carefully planted in neat rows.

"Looking at this manicured town, it's hard to imagine the horrors that took place here."

"Reports say the fire was an inferno, reaching up to two thousand degrees Fahrenheit."

"And that heat was accompanied by a tornado." Chloe shook her head. "It's amazing anyone survived."

"The Peshtigo Fire occurred in 1871, a year after the US Census was taken. Records were sketchy, but they figured a minimum of seventeen hundred people from this town disappeared in the fire. Most residents were newcomers, immigrants, or itinerant laborers that had not been included in the census." Hud raised his eyebrow as he sighed. "The number was probably much higher."

Looking at the mass grave, Chloe thought of Letty. *Wonder if she had the benefit of a Mass said for her or a decent burial.*

"Because of smoke inhalation and burns, many more died in the following months," said Hud. "Simply surviving, healing, rebuilding took everyone's time and energy. And those that survived had to bury the dead, care for the ill, take in the orphaned children, and rebuild their destroyed homes, all the while trying to feed their own families and those of their less fortunate neighbors."

Thinking aloud of Letty, Chloe asked, "What about the scars they carried? Not only the external, but the emotional scars?"

"Maybe some wore their scars proudly, like badges of honor won on a battlefield."

"Or maybe they hid their scars, ashamed of their disfigurements." Chloe counted on her fingers. "We're five generations removed from the Peshtigo Fire, yet here we are, still dealing with the losses even though the stories have been partially lost, only partly retold." Her shoulders slumping, she grimaced. "It's still sad."

They strolled toward the historical marker in thoughtful silence.

"Wisconsin's very first marker," said Hud, reading. "On the night of October eighth, 1871, Peshtigo, a booming town of seventeen hundred people, was wiped out of existence in the greatest fire disaster in American history."

They stopped in front of a wooden sculpture of warped and painted lumber.

"It even looks like a fire," she said. "How appropriate to represent the firestorm with its main fuel, wood."

Then they heard voices. Looking toward the museum, they noticed several people at the front door. Hud checked his watch.

"Looks like they're opening up."

They walked up the steps of the Peshtigo Fire Museum, a reconverted church. Inside, long glass counters displaying row upon row of artifacts from the fire greeted them. They saw exhibits of period relics arranged into rooms, showing what life had been like in the early days. Charred items from the fire were on display, but what drew Chloe's attention was a glass-enclosed fossilized *Bible*. Alongside broken dishes and molten glass were the carbonized and petrified remains of the holy book.

"Is this sign right?" asked Chloe. "Is this *Bible* petrified?"

The volunteer nodded her head. "Yes. In fact, if you tilt the light just so, you can read the print." She adjusted the lamp.

"You're right!" Chloe gasped as the hairs stood up on the back of her neck. "It's open to Psalms one hundred six and seven."

"They discovered this in 1995, in debris beneath the drug store."

"That's only a little more than a hundred years after the fire." Chloe narrowed her eyes. "Doesn't petrification take millions of years?"

"Normally, yes, but it was buried quickly beneath the ash. Because paper's a wood product, minerals from the surrounding material seeped into and re-placed the paper's cells with calcite, marcasite, pyrite, and silica." She smiled. "It's petrified."

"Wow. I wonder who turned the *Bible* to that page." *What were the circumstances? Did they die there?* Chloe shuddered as her eyes swept the room. "What stories must be hidden in all these artifacts."

"There are several newspaper accounts that actually do tell the stories," said the volunteer, pointing to the movable racks.

"I'll be sure to read them, thanks." Then Chloe recalled the brooch. "Inci-dentally, would you or someone else be able to tell me the date of this pin?"

Taking it from her purse, she handed over the baggie.

The woman examined it carefully. "I'm no authority, but this looks similar to something else we have here." Leading them to another display counter, the volunteer brought out a tray of tarnished and scorched jewelry. "This is all from the late nineteenth century." Holding it near another brooch, she studied the two, comparing them.

Chloe gave a low whistle. "They're close."

"Nearly identical," said Hud. "They could have been made from the same mold."

The volunteer nodded. "Again, I'm no expert, but this certainly appears to date from the late nineteenth century." She handed the brooch back to Chloe. "Family heirloom?"

Chloe creased her brow, wondering if it had been Letty's. "Maybe." Then remembering Celestine had owned it, she added, "Actually, yes, it is."

"Every artifact is a remembrance of those lost," said the volunteer.

A man joined them. "People weren't just 'lost' in the Peshtigo Fire," he said drily. "People were incinerated. Breathing in superheated air, people spon-taneously combusted. Folks were cremated in the two thousand degree air where they stood. They were reduced to ashes in the flames. Their hair and clothes caught on fire. Their lungs were scorched so badly, each breath was excruciating. Their eyeballs singed. They were left to wander blindly. Panicked livestock trampled them. Collapsing buildings and trees crushed them. Flying debris dropped out of the swirling firestorm, impaled folks, and lit them up like torches before they expired. People weren't just 'lost.'"

"This is our local historian, Jacob Dawson," said the volunteer, "also my uncle. If there's an authority on the Peshtigo Fire, it's Jacob, the town mayor for nearly fifteen years."

"This was a fire of biblical proportions," said the elderly man, warming to his topic and apparently glad for an audience. His cataracted blue eyes lit up with the intensity of a young man as he spoke. "This fire was so extreme, it created its own weather: firestorms and fire tornadoes. It picked up loaded railway cars and flaming, hundred-foot-tall trees and threw them like unguided missiles, streaking out of the sky and falling on unsuspecting victims. And there was something else."

"What?" Chloe watched his eyes darken.

"Something that no one's ever been able to explain." The elderly man's eyes homed in on hers. "Black balloons, they called them. Swirling, black objects that came out of nowhere, shooting through the sky and exploding on contact with any material it touched, even flesh. The way folks described it, it sounds like napalm."

"Some people speculate it was balls of pine sap," said the volunteer, "exploding out of the burning trees and then carried with such force by the winds, they compressed and detonated on impact, like bombs."

"Others think these balloons were methane gas or charcoal, but they whirled and spit out from the advancing flames where they collided with objects, creating loud booms and spreading fire in all directions. Folks tell of a family huddled together in a field. When one of these black balloons exploded on them," he swallowed, "the whole family burst into flames."

"What do you think it was?" Chloe watched his pale, cloudy eyes.

"Meteorites," he said. "Those black balloons were red hot remnants of the disintegrated Comet Biela. Records indicate fires started simultaneously in Michigan, Wisconsin, and Illinois. From a starting point of East Michigan, I believe those meteorites bombarded the Great Lakes region in a less-than shape that spread from Chicago to Peshtigo." He held up his right thumb and forefinger to make a less-than sign.

Chloe recalled Edwina telling her the idea was bogus astronomy.

"I heard the Impact theory had been disproved."

He shook his white head. "Here's proof it was a meteor shower. They found a fifty-eight pound meteorite on the east side of Michigan, near Lake Huron.

I believe that was the point of impact, with shards spreading across the entire Great Lakes region."

Chloe did not want to argue. "Whatever caused it," she said, remembering Edwina's stories, "I'm told my great-great-grandmother called it hell."

"Many thought it was the end of the world. They didn't even try to escape. Some committed suicide." Jacob nodded. "Roughly a thousand folks died in the fire."

"That's just in the flames," said the volunteer, "but another fifteen hundred or so perished from hypothermia in the water or from the effects of the fire later that night or the next day. The same cold front that fanned the fire's flames caused the temperature to drop forty degrees. From a burning inferno, the temperature plummeted. People's clothing had either burned away or hung dripping wet from the cold water. Those whose body temperatures dropped below ninety-five degrees, died."

Jacob nodded. "One young man, holding his brother under one arm and his sister under another, found that, although he'd save them from the fire, they'd died from the cold. Right in his arms."

"Those who survived in the river had to deal with the aftermath," said the volunteer. "They literally had to push away the burned and bloated corpses floating past them along with the thousands of dead fish floating belly up."

Chloe squinted, thinking. "Why would the fish die?"

"With all the ash from the burned forests, the water was turning to lye," said the volunteer. "So many had died, human cadavers and carcasses of livestock and wildlife lined the beaches. When the flames finally subsided and people began to emerge from the river, the survivors tripped over the bodies as they made their way to shore."

Chloe shook her head. She closed her eyes against the images in her mind.

"The rains they'd prayed for finally came," said Jacob. "Too late to put out the fire, the downpour only added to the survivors' misery, draining more ash from the burned land into the river and drenching their nearly naked bodies in the frigid October temperatures."

"Nothing was left," said the volunteer. "There was no shelter from the rain, and there was no food. The fish were dead. The birds were gone. The livestock and wildlife were dead or dying. Any provisions or crops had been reduced to ashes. The trees were smoldering cinders for miles. Even the soil had burned or blown away. What once had been fertile, loamy soil was now barren sand and rock."

"The survivors were surrounded by death and total destruction." Chloe looked from one face to the other. "What did they do? Where did they even begin?"

"They began by burying their dead," said Jacob, his lined face grim. "The remaining sawmills began churning out lumber for coffins. The dead were everywhere. Some were nothing but carbonized bones, brittle to the touch. Others were piles of ash with a melted button or coin mixed in. Some appeared unharmed by the fire. Those had died of smoke or heat inhalation. Some were cremated in the firestorm and simply blown away, and many were never found or identified."

"What about the spirits of those who died?" Chloe thought of the brooch. "Has there ever been any paranormal activity around Peshtigo?"

Jacob exchanged a glance with the volunteer.

"Oh, there's plenty of ghostly activity here," the man said. "Many of the spirits seem confused, disoriented. They don't realize they're dead. They're bound to an object or a place, normally the area where they died, but unless their bodies have been put to rest, they can't be free."

Chloe glanced at Hud and then looked at Jacob. "What if their bodies were burned to ashes and never found? How could they be buried?"

"Sometimes a memorial service is held as a tribute to their life, so the soul, though gone, is not forgotten."

Hud's eyes brightened, as if he recalled something.

"My grandfather once mentioned a place where they planted lilacs—"

"As a memorial to the lives lost in Birch Creek during the fire, yes," said the volunteer, nodding. "Their remains were buried where their bodies were found but with no markers or headstones. The lilacs are a living monument to them. If you have time, stop and see it." She gave them directions.

They saw the church tabernacle that Father Peter Pernin had saved by plunging it in the Peshtigo River. Not flames, not smoke, not water had harmed it. Then they saw the portrait of Father Pernin that had lain hidden behind another painting for a century. It only came to light when the owner had taken the painting to be reframed.

⁓⁓⁓ ❖ ⁓⁓⁓

After they finished touring the museum, Chloe and Hud decided to drive the fifteen miles to Birch Creek, Michigan. They had barely left the parking lot when Celestine appeared between them, sitting on the console.

"DON'T LEAVE SAFETY . . . TO MERE CHANCE . . . THAT'S WHY . . . BELTS ARE . . . SOLD WITH PANTS . . . . BURMA-SHAVE."

Celestine gave Chloe a dirty look until she fastened her safety belt.

"I was getting to it."

"Huh?" Hud turned toward her.

"It's Celestine reminding me to buckle up for safety." He began chuckling. Finally, Chloe turned toward him. "What?"

He took his eyes off the road to glance at her.

"You don't find a certain humor in a ghost that taunts you as she haunts you?"

"THE SAFEST RULE . . . NO IFS OR BUTS . . . JUST DRIVE . . . LIKE EVERYONE ELSE . . . IS NUTS . . . . BURMA-SHAVE." Celestine tried to push his head until he faced forward. "Tell him to watch where he's going."

Chloe chuckled. "Now she's scolding you. She said to keep your eyes on the road."

A snort passing for a chuckle, he rubbed his cheek. "Did she just touch my face?"

"Yes, why?" She listened to the sound of his hand brushing against his five-o'clock shadow.

"I thought I felt something."

"What did it feel like?"

He lifted a shoulder in a shrug. "A light breeze skimming across my cheek or the tip of a feather tickling me."

Chloe nodded thoughtfully. "We've both felt emotional sensations, but that's the first time either of us has physically felt her."

He glanced at her. "What about the cold and the sensation of spider webs and spiders crawling on you?"

She raised her eyebrows. "You're right. Maybe it is the same thing. I just wondered if her ability to physically affect us is increasing."

Within a few minutes, they found the memorial at the intersection of the crossroads the volunteer had mentioned. Pine trees their backdrop, thick green grass grew up to the lilac blossoms. Though June, the lilac bushes still bloomed, their laden branches perfuming the air.

Chloe inhaled their sweetness. Again, she shook her head at the disparity between the lushness before her and the destruction these lilacs represented. She swallowed, recalling the stories Edwina and Jacob had told her.

"You okay?" Hud's hand reached for hers.

Tilting her head against his arm, she nuzzled him. "Yeah, just . . ." She sighed, looking at the lilacs. "All this beauty now. It's hard to imagine the horror of the Peshtigo Fire." Then she felt her index finger throb from where the brooch had pricked it. She frowned.

"What?"

She showed him her index finger. "Maybe we need little reminders, so we don't forget those who died." *Maybe that's exactly what Letty's doing. Reminding us.*

<hr/>

On the way back to Door County, they stopped at the Copper Culture State Park in Oconto.

"This is a pretty park," said Hud, "a good place to stretch our legs."

They toured the farmhouse museum and then hiked, hand-in-hand, along the Oconto River, talking.

"Doesn't hearing how so many died in the Peshtigo Fire make you stop and think?" Chloe gave Hud a sidelong glance.

He turned toward her. "What do you mean?"

She took a deep breath, trying to put her thoughts into words. "My great-great-grandmother was younger than I am now when she survived the fire and saved her baby. Doesn't it make you wonder about your own mortality, your purpose in life?"

"Grandfather always told us, 'There's only one rule in life: the duty of the present moment.'"

She grinned as she swung his hand. "That's why they call the present a gift."

They stopped beneath a pine tree on the river, watching the swift water carry a branch downstream.

"To use more clichés," he said, "enjoy the ride." He tilted his chin toward the bobbing branch. "Be like that bough. Dance like no one's watching."

She did an impromptu set of moves and caught his eye, chuckling.

"You mean, like that?"

"Not exactly. If you even consider who's watching, *whether* anyone's watching, you're not in the moment. You're not dancing."

She scoffed. "If that wasn't dancing, what was it?"

"Performing." He lifted his eyebrow. "You have to simply accept the moment for what it is."

"Okay, mister maharishi of the moment, how do you do that?"

"For one thing, notice what's around you." He knelt down on one knee. "For instance, look at this flower."

She knelt down with him. "Okay, now what?"

"Really study it. What kind is it?" At her shrug, he stifled a smile. "It's a blue violet, but the point is, look at its petals. Count them. Notice its leaves, kind of sawtoothed. You've probably got some conversation going through your head that hasn't got a thing to do with this flower, this moment. Let that conversation go. Focus on this flower, this moment."

Lifting her eyebrow, she glanced up at his face. "And what does focusing on this flower do?"

"It reminds you to get outside yourself, outside of your internal conversation that either anchors you to the past or yanks you into the future. Focusing simply reminds you to slow down and savor the moment. Embrace God's will in the moment. That's always within your reach."

"Okay, so studying flowers is a trick to center yourself. What else?" She crossed her arms over her chest.

"Not just a flower, examine anything—your senses, for instance, your sense of sight," he said, twirling the violet in his fingers. "Or pay attention to the sounds. Listen."

They stopped talking. Chloe heard the breeze gently sighing through the pine tree above them. She heard the gurgling water beside them. A bee buzzed in the flowers nearby.

"Use your sense of smell." He took a deep breath, and she followed suit. "Smell the pine?"

Snickering, she nodded. "I get it. Stop and smell the roses. Wake up and smell the coffee."

He smiled at her patiently. "More clichés, but basically, that's the idea. My point is, the 'moment' is all around you. As grandfather says, 'Everything's to be welcomed as the expression of God.' Use your senses of sight, smell, touch, sound, taste, and use your voice." He glanced at the blue sky. "Thank God for the beautiful day. Even that's an act of faith."

Her hands outstretched, palms up, she hunched her shoulders. "All I did was wonder about our mortality, our purpose in life. What's that got to do with faith?"

He shook his head. "You were worrying about the future. You were worrying about not living up to Miss Ed's standards. That's not living in the moment.

When you find yourself wishing this or worrying about that, just be thankful for what you have, what God's given you."

Pressing her lips together, she took a deep breath. "I understand what you're saying. I'm just not there yet."

He cocked an eyebrow as he surveyed her. "Where's 'there'?"

"Oh, I don't know." She sighed. "Maybe after Aunt Ed's cast comes off, when I'm back in Milwaukee—"

He grunted.

"What?"

"Have you ever heard of destination addiction?"

She shook her head.

"It's believing happiness is the next place, the next job, home, partner, or whatever. You fill in the blank." His mouth twisted in a wry grin. "Until you get over the idea that happiness is somewhere else, it'll never be where you are."

"Huh." She nodded. "What you're saying is 'be in the moment.' Be *here*."

He caught her eye, and she stared at him, as if seeing him for the first time. She looked at his tanned face, the flash of his white teeth as he parted his lips in a smile. She stared deep into his dark eyes, the color of chocolate. She watched his body lean into her. As he bent his head toward hers, his dark mane of hair falling forward, tickling her face, his lips reached for hers. She caught her breath.

Oh, I'm in the moment.

On the drive back to Door County, Hud turned toward her.

"Earlier, you'd said something about after Miss Ed's cast comes off, when you're back in Milwaukee."

"Yeah?" She watched his profile. "What about it?"

"Have . . ." He took his eyes from the road to watch her reaction. "Have you ever thought about staying in Door County, making it your home, and not going back to Milwaukee?"

She took a deep breath as she gazed into his eyes. Then she swallowed.

"I . . . I really hadn't thought about it. Aunt Ed's cast comes off in two weeks. I figured . . ." She shrugged. "I guess I figured I'd just go back to my old life."

He nodded slowly, as if mulling something over. Finally, he gave her a side-long glance.

"Think about staying here." He gave her a wry smile. "Just saying."

Raising her eyebrows, she stared at him. *What's going through your mind, Hudson Beaulieu?*

—————— ◇ ——————

As Hud walked her to the door, he stopped and turned toward her.

"Usually, I like piloting sunset cruises, but not tonight."

She looked up at him. "Why? What's different about tonight?"

His dimple showing, he gave a self-conscious chuckle. Finally, he put his arms on her shoulders.

"I don't want to say goodbye. I don't want our day to end."

With a silent sigh, Chloe felt her chest cave in. Then she put her arms around his back, feeling him against her, heart to heart.

"I don't want you to go, either."

He lifted her face and then leaned down toward her. His hair tickling, his five-o'clock shadow grazing her cheek, Chloe closed her eyes and stood on tiptoe to meet him in a kiss.

"To kiss . . . a mug . . . That's like a cactus . . . Takes more nerve . . . Than it does practice . . . . Burma-Shave."

Her lips still pressed against his, Chloe started laughing.

"What?" His eyes wide, he looked at her as if she was crazy.

"Celestine's reciting Burma-Shave jingles in my ear."

"What's Cel—"

"Chloe," called Edwina from the living room, "is that you?"

"Yes, I'm home." Looking at Hud, she swallowed a giggle. "Do you need something?"

"You just got a call from work."

"On Saturday?" She made a sour face. "Who was it?"

"Someone named Glenn Gerard."

"My supervisor," she whispered to Hud, frowning. *What could he want on a Saturday?*

"He's at the Green Bay office and needs you to bring him a copy of some APO or POA or something like that."

"What?" Pursing her lips, she worked her jaw. *Aaron?*

"He apologized, but—"

"Just a minute, Aunt Ed, don't strain your voice. I'll be right in." Chloe turned to Hud. "Sorry, it looks like work's calling us both. Maybe—"

Hud spoke as she did. "What if—?" They both chuckled. "Sorry, you were saying?"

"Maybe we could get together tomorrow?" she said.

"My thoughts exactly." He grazed her lips with a gentle kiss. "I'll call you tonight." Taking her hand, he squeezed it as he began walking away. "Talk to you later."

She hung on to his hand as long as she could. Then, as they parted, she raised her hand in a wave. Her eyes following him as he backed out the driveway, she gave him a final wave before going inside.

"What was that you were saying, Aunt Ed?"

She read from a note. "Glenn Gerard apologized for bothering you on a Saturday, but he said he needs you to bring him a copy of the OPA."

"The OAP. He wants me to hand deliver the operational acceptance plan?" She shook her head. "That doesn't make any sense. I'll just email it."

"No, he specifically asked that you attend the meeting. He wants you to capture the changes."

"On a Saturday afternoon?" She raised her eyebrow. "Something's fishy here."

"He said he's been texting you all day, but you haven't responded."

Skeptical, Chloe pulled out her phone to check. *Sure enough, there must be half a dozen messages from him.* She groaned. "I must have been in a dead zone. Thanks, Aunt Ed. I'll text him, but can I get you anything first?"

"No, thanks." Edwina shook her head. Then, a smile starting at the corner of her mouth, she asked, "Did you have a good time with Hud?"

"I did. In fact, I didn't want the day to end."

Edwina smiled to herself. "It doesn't seem so long ago, I felt the same way about . . ." Her voice trailed off. "Glad you enjoyed yourself."

Chloe answered her supervisor's text. Will email OAP.

Back came a text. Servers down for quarterly patching. Please deliver OAP and capture changes. Meeting in forty-five minutes.

She printed out three copies of the document and grabbed her laptop.

"Aunt Ed, looks like I have to go to a meeting. Can I get you anything before I leave?"

"Can you put another pot of coffee on?"

Chloe grinned to herself. "Sure."

CHAPTER 8

"'Oh yes,' he thinks, 'Women. With their subversive sexual tactics
have no place in this game. It is no accident that the queen is the deadliest of
pieces; the manly pawn: the weakest.'"

— LUIS CAMARA SILVA

Chloe hurried into the main conference room of the Green Bay satellite office. Purposely walking past Aaron, she sat beside her manager and distributed copies of the operational acceptance plan. Aaron texted her as she logged on to her laptop, but she ignored it. Stifling a sigh, she refused to meet his gaze.

She captured the customer's changes online, and within an hour, they concluded the meeting.

Glenn smiled after the customer left. "Chloe, I appreciate your quick response, especially on a Saturday afternoon."

"Not a problem." Chloe shrugged. "I'm just glad it all worked out."

"Without your help, we couldn't have finished this transaction until next week."

"Which would have put us behind schedule," said Aaron.

Glenn looked from her to Aaron and back. "How about dinner? It's the least I can offer you two."

Chloe shook her head. "Thanks, but it's getting late. I really should be back before dark."

Aaron checked his watch. "Sunset's not for another two and a half, three hours." Lifting his eyebrow, he caught her eye and smiled.

Chloe recognized Aaron's nonverbal invitation. Looking into his eyes, she saw the person he had been, the person she had loved. She took a deep breath, hesitating.

"There, it's settled," said Glenn. "A good steak, and you'll be on your way in an hour."

She shook her head. "No, I've been gone all day. I'd better get back to my aunt. Thanks, but—"

Aaron held the door open for her. He tilted his head and grinned.

"One hour, come on. Glenn and I owe you."

Against her better judgment, she heard herself say, "Okay." Something nagged at the back of her mind, but she dismissed it with a shrug. "I guess an hour won't make a difference."

⁂

They found a steakhouse around the corner. Aaron pulled out her chair for her and sat across the table, next to Glenn.

Throughout dinner, she felt his eyes on her but ignored him, talking business with her manager. When she looked for the salt, Aaron slid the shaker to her before she could reach for it. When her glass was empty, he asked the waiter to refill her water. When Glenn excused himself to take a call, Aaron leaned across the table.

"I've missed you, you know."

"You miss my revisions." She deadpanned. "So, how's Jennifer?" She pretended to study her manicure.

He gave her a wry grin. "Then you haven't read my text. We broke up."

She curled her lip into a caricature of a smile. "And I should believe you because . . . why? Remind me."

He took a deep breath. Closing his eyes, he nodded. "You're right. I deserve that." Then he looked at her, his eyes open, sincere. "You only miss someone once they're gone."

Chloe tried to read his eyes but saw a brick wall behind them. She sniffed. "C'mon, Aaron, I've known you too long. What are you hiding?"

"She's leaving." His voice caught. "As in leaving me behind, moving on."

Impassive, her eyes narrowing, Chloe surveyed him. "You mean, she's beating you at your own game?"

He gave a dry laugh. "Technical writers, you always know how to cut through the crap, straight to the facts." He looked at her sideways and shook his head. "No wonder we made such a good team, with me always hustling and you . . ." Leaning across the table, he homed in on her eyes. "You always keeping us on track. I'd get the idea. You'd make it happen with spreadsheets, schedules, and statistics."

She shrugged. "Anyone could have done it."

Shaking his head, he leaned closer. "Not just anyone, you . . ."

She blinked. For a moment, she saw the man she had fallen in love with, the man who had taken away her breath. *And who left me gasping without a respirator. Don't forget that.*

She crossed her arms. "You obviously want something, and you want it badly enough to put on this act. What is it?"

He changed chairs, sitting beside her, leaning into her space.

"You, and it's no act. I was wrong, so wrong, to ever let you go."

Tilting her head back from him, she pulled away, squinting, scrutinizing him.

"Do you live in a fairy tale? You didn't 'let me go.' You left me for Jennifer. You left me in a black hole, a vacuum with no oxygen. You left me fighting for my next breath." Looking down at the table, she breathed deeply, recalling the memory so vividly it affected her breathing. "Apparently, you have no idea how deeply you hurt me. Either that or you don't care." Looking into his face, her eyes challenged his.

He took her hand in his. "Chloe, come back with me for a nightcap. I promise I'll make it all up to you."

Jerking her hand away, she opened her eyes wide as she analyzed him. "Come back? Come back where with you?"

"My hotel room."

"That's it. I'm out of here." She stood up just as her manager approached the table. "Glenn, I want you to know, I'm copying you on my complaint to HR."

Raising his eyebrows, Glenn looked from her to Aaron and back again. "I was gone five minutes. What happened?"

"Aaron just invited me up to his room for a," she grimaced, "nightcap."

The picture of misunderstood innocence, Aaron spread out his hands and opened his mouth, as if speechless. He gave a dry laugh. "Cap? I said *cup* . . . a cup of coffee, not a nightcap."

Chloe sneered. "Coffee, if that's your story, stick to it, but realize something. You've just admitted you invited me to your room."

His eyelids shot up. "I . . . I said no such thing. I said . . . you should *have* a cup of coffee before you drive home." He turned to Glenn. "My only concern was for her safety."

Ignoring him, she addressed her manager. "I hope you'll understand if I don't stay for dessert."

Glenn nodded as he turned to Aaron. "I see."

Aaron took a deep breath. "Good, I'm glad you understand."

Glenn's face was devoid of a smile. "I see you've moved to the seat beside Chloe, and I've been watching your body language while I've been on my call." Then he turned back to her. "When you copy me on your complaint tomorrow, I'll be sure to add my observations." Glancing at Aaron, he added, "Somehow, I think Jennifer and her father will find it provocative reading."

Lips pursed, Chloe nodded her thanks, picked up her laptop and purse, and headed for the door.

Once outside, she noticed the sky. Clouds were gathering into thunderheads. She saw a streak of lightning while walking through the parking lot. A fraction of a second later, she heard its thunder. She gasped, and the scent of ozone was strong. She inhaled the fresh, pungent aroma. Then, glancing at her watch, she double-checked the time.

A little past six, but the sky's as dark as nine.

A drop of rain splashed in her eye and then another. She ran to her car and slammed the door just as the rain began pelting the car. By the time she reached the highway, her windshield wipers were going at maximum speed. One, two, one, two, they drummed a throbbing beat, but still they could not keep up. Torrents of driving rain poured down on her windshield. Each swipe of the wipers only splashed more water on their returning swing.

It's like looking through waxed paper.

She strained to see through the driving rain as she tightened her grip on the wheel. Then the inside of the windshield began to fog up. She wiped at it with one hand, but between the fog, rain, and deepening darkness, she could barely see the road, let alone anything on it.

Suddenly, a figure dashed in front of her. *A wolf? Letty?* Screaming, she swerved onto the road's muddy shoulder to avoid it, slid off the road, and crashed through the underbrush into a tree. As the airbag inflated, all she heard were the sounds of the rhythmically beating windshield wipers and the screeching of the car horn.

She opened her eyes and saw smoke. *Fire!* She pulled at her seat belt, but it stuck. Images of the Peshtigo Fire burned in her mind. *I'm not going to die in flames!*

With that thought, she tore the seat belt from its buckle and yanked at the door. Despite the smoke, she could see the crumpled metal of the car's front wedged against the door. *The impact must have forced the hood back into the doors, crushing the metal and locking me inside.*

She pulled and pushed at the door until she heard its lock release. Then she swiveled in the driver's seat, put both feet on the door, brought up her knees, and kicked with all her might. *I'm not going to die in flames!*

The door popped open, and she fell out into the mud. Despite the driving rain, she crawled away from the car, afraid it might catch fire. She felt for her phone on her belt and tried to dial 911, but after pressing the first button, everything went black.

Minutes or hours later, she was not sure, she opened her eyes. Blinking through the drizzle, she saw her car smashed against a pine tree, accordion style. Instead of the hood leading out from the car, it was concave, indented up to the wheel chassis. She looked at the door, not sprung on its hinge but swinging on a four-inch fold of bare metal.

Did I do that? Adrenaline's a marvelous drug.

She gave a mirthless laugh. Feeling her arms and legs for broken bones, she realized she felt no pain. Nothing hurt. Nothing seemed broken. Other than a whopper of a headache, she felt fine. She tried to stand up, but she got dizzy and fell down backward, hitting her head. Again, she blacked out.

When she came to, she tried to focus, but unless she squinted, she saw double. Weaving, she tried to sit up, but her head throbbed. She tried again, this time propping her back against a tree. The headache made her wince, but she found, if she did not move a muscle, the pain was bearable, and she drifted off.

It was still dark when she woke, but otherwise, Chloe had no sense of time. Propped up against the tree, she tried to focus her eyes but gave up. Instead, she held one eye shut as she peered through the other. Through it, she saw a woman standing by the wrecked car, cackling a patois of words and laughter. Her clumps of wispy hair tufted out from her head, hanging in scraggly strands, and she wore a coarse burlap gown.

Letty? Why can I see her? How can I hear her?

"Feeling poorly?" The old woman cackled, her mouth open wide, exposing receded gums with only two crooked teeth left in their sockets. "Didn't Aaron suit your fancy?" Again, she cackled, seeming to enjoy the situation.

"Letty? How . . . ?"

"Can't believe your eyes, dearie?" The woman chuckled, her eyes wide and her mouth gaping. Her two opposing teeth reminded Chloe of a macabre jack-o'-lantern.

Feeling sick to her stomach, she swallowed the bile she suddenly tasted in her throat.

"Why can I see and hear you?"

"All in good time, dearie. All in good time." The woman's eyes narrowed as she scratched her chin. "First, you need to answer my question."

"What question?"

"Are you daft?" The words hissed between Letty's two teeth. "Didn't Aaron suit your fancy?"

Chloe scowled. "Of course not. Why should he?"

Again, Letty cackled her open-mouthed laughter, her body shaking as if convulsed.

"Then I suppose Hud's more to your liking?"

Closing one eye, Chloe squinted to see one of her.

"What's it to you?"

The woman rushed to her, shouting into her face. "I ask the questions here . . . dearie!"

The reek of burned, putrefied flesh was overwhelming. Chloe gagged.

"What's the matter, dearie? Aren't feeling well?"

"Why are you doing this?" Chloe breathed through her mouth to avoid the stench. "What do you want?"

"What do I want? I want my life back. I want my child back. I want to *be!*" The final word sounded like metal grinding on metal.

Chloe put her hands to her ears until the shrill screech subsided.

"I feel your pain, but you're dead. Letty, you've been dead nearly a hundred and fifty years. You've got to accept that, move on."

"*No!*" This time her cry sounded like a wolf howling into the wind.

Again, Chloe put her hands to her ears. When she slowly lowered her hands, she realized the sound continued. *That's not Letty. That's the car horn still blaring.* With that knowledge, she fell into a fitful sleep.

"You're so easily manipulated." The woman sneered.

"What?" Chloe opened her eyes and looked around. *I'm still in this dream.*

"Just like your great-aunt, Celestine, you're so easily manipulated." The woman cackled, exposing her two teeth. "If not Aaron, Hud. If I can't live, I can live through you."

"What?" Chloe winced as she rubbed her head.

"You have the impudence to tell me I'm dead, as if I didn't know?" Letty bent down until her hollow, bloodshot eyes peered into Chloe's. "Not yet seventeen, I was burned alive in that fire. Incinerated. Not dead, the better truth is I never lived."

The woman's decayed flesh reeked. Chloe tried to move away from the stench, but the effort made her head throb. She groaned.

"Stop it! I feel your pain, but my head's about to explode."

"It wasn't fair. Your great-great-grandmother lay a foot or two from me, yet she and her child survived. I protected my baby with my own body, but we were both burned alive. Roasted. Nothing was left to show I had lived. No body to bury, no grave or marker, no child, no descendants, no one to mourn or remember me."

In pain, nearly in tears, Chloe was frustrated she could not grasp the implication. "What do you want?"

"I want to be remembered. Remember me . . . remember me . . ." Letty's last word screeched like a siren, shrieking in Chloe's ear, resonating in her mind.

Chloe saw flashing lights. She heard voices far in the distance, as if through a tunnel or pipe. They echoed, reverberated, but she could not understand the words.

"What? What?" She tried to rouse herself. Then everything went dark.

When she opened her eyes, it was light. *What time is it?* She turned her head to see the clock on her nightstand and winced from the sudden movement. Instead of her room, she saw a wall of windows.

"Where am I?"

"You're in the hospital."

Turning her head slowly, Chloe followed the sound of the voice.

"Hud, what . . . ?"

Her eyes swept the interior of the room. Then she saw Edwina, sitting beside the bed.

"Aunt Ed, how did you get here?" She lifted her head to look up at Hud, flinched from the pain, and fell back on the pillow. "What happened?"

He brought a chair over and sat down so she could see him more easily. "Is that better?"

"Mm-hmm. What happened?"

"You've been in an accident."

"An accident?" She tried to sit up and winced. Then she remembered the rain and swerving to avoid the figure in the road. "A tree. I hit a tree, and the car horn was blaring so loud, it gave me a headache."

"That's understandable." Hud gave her a wry smile. "You have a concussion."

She groaned. "Is it bad?"

"The CAT scan didn't show any serious damage."

"But they want to keep you here for observation," said Edwina, "just in case."

"For how long?" Chloe looked from her aunt to Hud.

"Just overnight." He lifted a corner of his mouth in a half-smile. "Consider it a vacation. They'll wait on you hand and foot."

"What about my car?"

He grimaced. "Totaled. Sorry."

She sighed. "That's just great."

"Don't worry about it." Hud gently took her hand in his. "That's what insurance is for." His smile drooped into a grim twist. "Your only job is to rest and recuperate."

"I'm sorry, folks," said an attendant, poking her head into the room. "Visiting hours are over in five minutes."

"Over?" Chloe looked from face to face. "What time is it?"

"Six," said Hud, checking his watch.

"It can't be." Chloe scowled, trying to remember. "I left Green Bay at six."

Hud spoke gently. "That was yesterday."

Chloe groaned. "I've been asleep for twenty-four hours?" Squinting, she peered into his face. "It can't be."

"It is." He gave her a wry smile.

"How did I get here? What happened?"

"Don't you remember? You dialed my cell."

Chloe tried to shake her head, but the movement made her head throb.

"No . . . I . . . I recall trying to call 911, but then everything went black. What happened?"

"Apparently, you pressed my number." He shrugged. "And your phone speed-dialed it. I could hear your car horn blaring in the background. When you didn't speak, I worried you were in some kind of trouble."

"That's when Hud called me," said Edwina. "He wanted to know where you'd gone."

He nodded. "Then I called the police, gave them what information I had, and picked up Miss Ed." Avoiding her eyes, he pursed his lips. "Thought she should be along, in case they needed a relative to sign any paperwork."

Edwina's voice shook. "A patrol car saw your skid marks, but if your horn hadn't been blaring, they might not have found you as quickly as they did."

"Wow." Chloe took a deep breath. "So if my phone hadn't dialed Hud, and the horn hadn't been blaring . . ."

"Who knows when they might have found you." Edwina's chin quivered as she completed the thought.

"Sorry, folks," said the attendant, entering into the room. "Visiting hours are over."

Hud nodded. Then he leaned over Chloe, brushing her lips with his. "See you in the morning."

Edwina squeezed her hand. "See you tomorrow."

Chloe felt her eyes well up with tears.

"Thanks for . . . everything." She swallowed and cleared her throat. "It's good to know who I can depend on, who cares about me."

Hud hurried back to give her a hug. "Love you," he whispered.

"You, too." Chloe responded automatically, but as she looked up into his eyes, Letty's words echoed in her mind.

"Just like your Great-Aunt Celestine, you're so easily manipulated . . . . If not Aaron, Hud. If I can't live, I can live through you."

Does Hud really love me? Do I love him, or is this all some game Letty's playing?

As Hud backed away, he squeezed her hand.

"See you in the morning."

She waved goodbye until they were out of sight.

I feel so empty inside. Why?

It occurred to her how alone she was. If Hud's feelings were only controlled responses, no one cared for her. No one was immune to Letty's maneuvers. Not Celestine. *Not even Aunt Ed.*

As she drifted into an uneasy sleep, Letty appeared, cackling, parroting Hud. "'Love you.' Kissy, kissy."

Chloe's head ached, and all she wanted to do was sleep.

"Leave me alone."

Letty tossed her head, her few strands of tufted hair waving.

"Miss high and mighty, has it ever occurred to you?"

"What?"

"Without me, you'd have no social life."

Chloe scowled. "What are you blabbing about?"

"You want me to 'leave you alone.' Without me, no one would care about you—not Edwina, not Aaron, not Hud." She smiled, her open mouth leering. "If anything, you should be grateful. Without me, you'd have no one." Her hollow, bloodshot eyes bored into Chloe's.

Chloe blinked, recalling how Hud and Edwina were the only ones to show concern. *Could that be true?*

"Of course, it's true."

Chloe looked up at her. "You can read my mind?"

Nodding, Letty cackled her shrill laugh.

"Why? Why are you doing this to me?"

"You feel so sorry for yourself, yet you've lived such an easy life."

Chloe scowled. "How would you know?"

"You sort through your memories like an old photo album, returning to your 'favorite' wounds and injustices time after time." Letty tilted her head, peering into her eyes. "What you dwelled on became your focus. I know your history because I can read your mind." Letty's lip curled in disgust. "So you had an unhappy childhood. Boo hoo. You're not the first to have had a less than ideal youth."

Not just childhood. Chloe swallowed hard, thinking of Aaron.

"You're wondering why you attracted him."

Chloe's eyelids flew open. "Who?"

Letty snickered. "Who do you think? Aaron."

"How . . . ?"

"Your mind's an open book." Letty cackled. "Because you relived those negative childhood memories, you attracted destructive people to you. Don't you understand?"

"What are you getting at?"

"You attract what you think. It's a simple matter of cause and effect. Your thoughts caused the effect—in this case, Aaron's exploitation."

"No." Beginning to see Letty's plan, Chloe narrowed her eyes. "You mean your manipulation. Stop playing your mind games."

"Oh, the pup barks." Letty snickered. "You think you've had a hard life? I was born with a bad stutter, too shy to talk to anyone. I married the first man who looked my way—a Civil War veteran, hardened by war, ten years my senior. When he proposed, I said yes without a second thought. I was barely sixteen. By seventeen, I had a baby and was pregnant with my second." Suddenly falling silent, she stared off into space.

"Then what happened?"

"What happened?" Letty scoffed. "The fire."

Chloe tried to find the right words. "I know you were only a foot or two away from my great-great-grandmother when you died, but what happened? How did she survive when you didn't?"

She took a deep breath, the sound resonating like wind rustling through dry leaves.

"My sister Teresa led a charmed life. Where she had beaus, I had no one. Where she married the love of her life, I married the only man who ever asked. Always pretty, outgoing, Teresa made friends easily, while I stood in the background, too shy to open my mouth and stutter. Just before the fire, she befriended a neighbor, a Métisse."

Chloe cocked her head. "A what?"

"A Métisse. A woman who was part Menominee and part French. Élise walked with both peoples, knew both cultures. She lived with a foot in each world. She also walked with the spirits, believing everything had a soul. Even a rock, a tree, had a soul. Élise warned her a fire was coming."

"So my great-great-grandmother knew about the fire ahead of time?"

Letty nodded.

"Why didn't she share that information with you?"

Curling her lip, Letty scoffed. "She did, but I didn't listen to the repeated words of a mixed blood."

"Mixed blood." Chloe opened her eyes wide. "You mean, you disapproved of Menominee/French intermarriages?"

"Did then. Do now."

Creasing her eyebrows, Chloe scowled. "Is that why you didn't want Aunt Ed to marry Jake?" Blinking, she thought it through. "And is that why you're interfering with Hud and me?"

Letty shrugged. "I didn't believe Élise's warning any more than I believe Hud's hollow words."

"Yet Élise's advice is what saved your sister and her baby." Chloe followed the thought. "It's why my ancestors survived, why I'm here today. What did Élise tell your sister to do?"

"She said the Menominees sensed a fire was coming. They could hear a distant roar, smell heat on the wind."

"You mean, they smelled smoke."

Letty shook her head. "Not smoke. They could smell the dryness, the scorched sap, the readiness of the land. They knew the risk for fire was high."

Chloe searched her mind for possibilities but could think of none.

"How?"

"The Menominees trained their teenaged boys to camp out, to keep animals away from their corn, pumpkin, and bean patches." Letty caught her eye. "Remember, they believed everything had a soul."

Chloe squinted. "I'm not following."

"It was part of their tradition, the boys' rite of passage to becoming men. They were largely on their own, but an older man stayed with them, teaching them. It was how they passed on their knowledge. While there, the boys learned what to do in case of wild fire, and they kept watch. As soon as they sensed fire coming, they alerted the camp."

"What advice did Élise give?" Chloe struggled to sit up, hanging on Letty's words.

"She taught my sister what the Menominees did during fires. First, they burned the prairies."

"Back burned." Barely moving her head, Chloe nodded.

"They destroyed all the brush and dead leaves, so the fire had no fuel to feed it. They made sure the area was near a spring or river, and then they dug trenches in the sandy soil. That's where they ran during the fire."

"It makes perfect sense." Chloe cocked her head. "Why didn't you listen?"

Letty's hollow eyes opened so wide, Chloe felt she was looking into the empty sockets of a skull.

"We had a log cabin and a shed for our livestock. We couldn't set fire to what we'd worked so hard to build."

"Then couldn't you have burned the fields near your cabin?"

"What fields?" Letty's lip curled. "We had small clearings in the virgin timber that we'd planted into gardens. We couldn't burn what we'd cultivated."

Chloe pressed her lips together in a grim line.

"Did Élise tell your sister anything else about survival, something you could have done besides burn your cabin and crops?"

Letty nodded. "She said the Menominees soaked bear skins in water. When the fire came, they'd cover the trenches they'd dug with the wet skins."

"Wouldn't the heat from the firestorms have scorched everything, lungs included?" Chloe peered at her.

"They'd tent the wet skins, leaving space beneath them so they could breathe. Then they'd cover them with sand."

"I doubt my great-great-grandmother had any bear skins. What did she use?"

"She made do with quilts soaked in a barrel of water." Letty became sullen. "Teresa listened to her Métisse friend. She convinced her husband to plow up the crops, and they dug shallow trenches. Then she hauled that barrel of wet quilts and water into the center of the clearing, as far away from their log cabin and the surrounding forest as she could."

Chloe nodded slowly. "What a resilient woman." She bit her bottom lip. *Wish I was more like her.*

"Like I said, Teresa led a charmed life." Letty shrugged.

"It sounds to me like she did all she could to be prepared."

Letty shook her head. "Just dumb luck."

Lying back on the pillow, Chloe surveyed her.

"If I recall, Aunt Ed said my great-great-grandfather was away in Champion when the fire came."

"He was, along with my husband. They were selling produce in town."

"Is that why you were with my great-great-grandmother?"

"While our husbands were gone, we kept each other company, especially since I was pregnant."

Chloe was afraid to ask but felt compelled. "What hap—?"

"My husband survived and remarried." Scowling at her, Letty's eyes looked like hot embers.

Chloe took the hint. "What I don't understand," she paused, choosing her words carefully, "is how your sister survived, yet you didn't."

Letty took a deep breath, the sound like dead reeds rustling in the breeze.

"When th-th-the fire came, th-th-there was no time to th-th-think. Instinct told me to stay in th-th-the cabin. I th-th-thought it would protect us."

Chloe's ears perked at the sudden stutter.

"Yet you ended up beside Teresa in the field. How did that happen?"

"Th-th-the cabin caught fire." Letty snickered. "I ran out into th-th-the field and th-th-threw myself beside her, but it was too late. With-th-out any wet quilts to cover us, my baby . . . actually, both babies and I were burned alive."

Chloe lifted her head, unconsciously leaning toward her. "Oh, Letty, I'm so sorry."

Letty shrugged. "It's past."

"But it obviously isn't over for you." Chloe found herself sympathizing with her. "Why? Why haven't you been able to move on?"

Letty's face darkened, like clouds gathering into a thunderhead. When she erupted, it sounded like a thunder clap.

"It was Teresa's fault. Don't you understand? It was Teresa's fault I died. I can't forget th-th-that . . . or forgive it."

"But your sister shared the information with you." Chloe tried to reason. "You chose to stay in the cabin, so how—?"

"How dare you question me?"

Raising her eyebrows, Chloe opened her mouth to speak, but before any words came to mind, Letty continued.

"You weren't th-th-there. You didn't face th-th-that hellfire."

"Well, no, but—"

"I wasn't supposed to die in th-th-that firestorm. My world ended, yet I was little more than a child myself. I never lived! I was robbed of both life and death."

Chloe tried to shake her head, but it brought back the ache.

"What do you mean you were robbed of death?"

"I had no funeral, no grave, no tombstone. I had no children to mourn me, no family to remember me. It's like I never was." She hissed the final word, the sound like steam escaping.

Chloe massaged her forehead, trying to think, trying to rub away the pain.

"If I recall, Aunt Ed said parts of you survived the flames. Didn't your husband or family bury your remains?"

"Th-th-they th-th-threw th-th-them in a mass grave and covered everyth-th-thing with lye."

Chloe's shoulders slumped. "From what I've heard, they had to act quickly to bury the dead. I'm sure they mourned you. They were just trying to survive the aftermath."

"No respect." Letty groaned, the sound like a draft howling through a cold chimney. "All th-th-that's left of me is th-th-this brooch."

Chloe tried to make sense of it. "Could that brooch have captured your last thoughts somehow, like a camera taking a snapshot?"

Letty peered at her from behind drooping eyelids. "What you see is a dim reflection of what I once was."

Suddenly, the room filled with light. Squinting, shielding her eyes, Chloe strained to see through the glare.

"What happened?"

"Good morning," said the nurse, adjusting the blinds. "Hope you had a restful night."

"Where . . . ?" Looking around the room, Chloe remembered where she was. She winced as she rubbed her temples. "Guess I was dreaming."

The nurse approached her. "Does your head still hurt?"

"Yeah." When she tried to sit up, she flinched from the pain.

"The doctor's making her rounds. She'll be here in a minute."

"Okay, thanks." Chloe closed her eyes. A moment later, she heard voices.

"Why didn't you stop her?" asked a calm voice.

Chloe tried to open her eyes, but the glare was blinding. *Why don't they close those blinds?*

"I wanted to, but she scares me."

She squinted until her eyes adjusted. *Celestine? Who's she talking to?*

The woman's face was blurred, as if a heavy veil covered it. She wore a fabric that gleamed in the sunlight, illuminating the hospital room, so bright its white light eclipsed her features.

"If you want to move on, you've got to right your wrongs, not make things worse."

Celestine nodded.

"You've got to stand up to my sister."

My sister? Chloe gasped. *Is this bright being my great-great-grandmother Teresa?*

She half sat up, resting on an arm. "Teresa?"

The woman in the white lab coat said, "No, I'm Doctor Franks." She chuckled. "You could call me Linda, but not Teresa."

Chloe put her hand to her forehead. "I must have been dreaming again."

The hospital released her a little past noon. Though she had a clean bill of health, Chloe was grateful for Hud's offered arm as they walked down the steps.

"Just feeling a little wobbly." She gave him a sheepish grin.

"Understandably." He grinned back. "I'm glad it's all that's wrong with you." He leaned over to kiss her cheek.

His hair tickled, and she chuckled.

"What's so funny?"

She gave his arm a friendly squeeze. "I'm glad to be alive, glad to be holding you."

"That accident must have shaken you more than I realized."

Her smile sagged. "The accident could have been much worse, but when I was knocked unconscious, and then again last night while I was dreaming, I saw how forlorn Letty is. Not here, not there, she's caught in a shadowy existence." After recapping their conversation, she sighed. "I'm beginning to pity her."

"Didn't the blessing help?"

"Hard to say." Taking a deep breath, she pressed her lips into a thin, white line. "I'm guessing it helped, but her spirit resents Teresa's family, *my* family, so much she can't let go." She glanced up at him. "I think it'll take more for her memories to be healed."

Hud helped her up into his truck. "What makes you say that?"

"Letty envied her sister. She counted Teresa's blessings, not her own. Apparently, Teresa was popular and outgoing, while she was withdrawn."

"A case of sibling rivalry?"

"More than that." She turned toward him. "When I asked how Teresa survived and she didn't, Letty got defensive. She became so angry, she began stuttering."

"Why?"

"She blames her sister, even though it sounds like Teresa tried to help her." She sighed. "Letty made her own choices."

"But she doesn't see it that way?"

Chloe tried to shake her head, then winced. "No. She blames Teresa and the Métisse, who taught her how to survive." She turned toward Hud, creasing her forehead as she thought it through. "And she's taking this vendetta down through the generations. First Celestine, then Aunt Ed and Jake, now you and me."

"We know she was behind Celestine's death."

"And Jake's accusations of guilt."

Inhaling through his nostrils, Hud raised his eyebrows. "Her reason for being, for not moving on, is so destructive." He turned toward her. "You called it a vendetta."

Chloe grimaced. "Maybe that's too harsh a word."

"No, I think it characterizes Letty's hostility perfectly."

"How so?"

"She seems to blame everyone but herself," he said. "I've never taken a psychology course in my life, but she sounds so . . . human, so caught up in base motives. I'll bet she still won't accept the fact, let alone admit, she's at fault."

"So she can't forgive herself?"

"Exactly." Nodding, he met her eyes. "Some souls aren't ready to move on because of a lower vibration, a negative energy. Call it what you want, but she can't let go because she can't absolve herself."

Chloe tilted her head back as she studied him. "So what are you saying? Help Letty resolve her issues?"

"If Letty could forgive herself and let go this vendetta."

"And Celestine could right the wrongs she committed while under Letty's influence."

Hud met her eyes. "I'll bet both souls could move on."

"Something else." Caught up in his gaze, she added, "I must have been dreaming, but I saw what I think was my great-great-grandmother Teresa."

"What was she doing?"

"She seemed to be coaching Celestine."

"That would make sense. Teresa would have been Celestine's grandmother, right?"

Chloe nodded. "I wonder . . ." She stared into space, trying to work out the pieces.

"What?"

"If Letty's the spiteful sister, could Teresa be her opposite?" She thought of Edwina in the chapel. "I just got a mental image of a devil on one shoulder and an angel on the other, each whispering advice. Could Teresa be Letty's compassionate counterpart?"

"You said she was guiding Celestine." Hud raised an eyebrow. "Maybe she's trying to help her move on." He grinned as he started his truck. "And speaking of moving on, let's get you home."

Home. She gave a wry chuckle.

"Did you say something?"

"Just wondering where 'home' is, anymore."

He gave her a warm smile. "Not sure this is the right time, but speaking of your home."

Chloe's cell rang. "Sorry." She reached into her purse to turn it off, but her fingers fumbled, and she pressed the speaker by mistake.

They heard a muffled "Chloe, are you there?" coming from her purse.

Wincing, she mouthed more than whispered, "Sorry, it's my manager." Then she found her phone and clicked off the speaker. "Hi, Glenn. What's up?"

"A Hud Beaulieu left a message this morning that you'd been in an accident and would be out of work a day or two. I hope it's nothing serious."

She glanced at Hud and smiled. "I'm okay. A concussion, but no broken bones. In fact, Hud just picked me up from the hospital."

"What happened?" She could hear Glenn's concern over the phone.

"I swerved to avoid something in the road driving home from Green Bay last night and ended up hitting a tree."

He groaned. "Tough break. Is your car damaged?"

"Totaled."

"Oh, no. Sorry to hear that. Look, I don't want to keep you. You need your rest, but I do want to put your mind at ease. I'll speak to HR about sick leave and also about . . ."

"Aaron?" She filled in.

"Yes, him too, but also about your working remotely on a more permanent basis. After your sick leave runs out, telework. Take as long as you need to recuperate. Just come into the office, say once a month, for face-to-face meetings."

"That's very generous, Glenn."

"Well, I feel partially responsible, so I'd like to make your recovery as easy as possible."

"Thanks, I appreciate your help."

"Keep me updated."

"I will. Thanks again. Bye." She took a deep breath as she ended the conversation and turned toward Hud.

"What'd he want?"

"Looks like my manager answered my question."

He took his eyes from the road to glance at her. "What question is that?"

She gave him a crooked smile. "'Home' will be here for awhile." She filled him in on the details.

Though he kept his eyes on the road, Chloe could see his cheek dimple.

"What are you grinning about?"

"Funny how things work out, whether it's the right time or not." He glanced at her, and she saw the twinkle in his eyes. Then she watched it fade. "What was that about Aaron?"

She raised her eyebrows as she took a deep breath. "I hadn't wanted to mention this, but maybe it's best you know." She told him about Aaron's behavior the night before.

Hud nodded. After a moment of silence, he said quietly, "You never did tell me about your history with him."

She looked out the window, gathering her thoughts. Then she turned to him.

"For three years, Aaron and I were an item. During that time, he gradually became emotionally abusive and manipulative to the point I lost my self-respect. When he started dating the boss' daughter behind my back, I finally broke up with him. A few weeks later, he got a promotion and announced his engagement to Jennifer. The same day, Aunt Ed called about her fall and broken wrist." She grimaced. "This is what I meant when I said I wasn't as selfless as you. When I came here, I was running away from Aaron as much as I was helping Aunt Ed."

He drove silently for a few minutes. Then he glanced at her.

"You know, you and Celestine have a lot in common."

"Besides our names?" She gave a nervous laugh. "What do you mean?"

"You've both been manipulated, and now you're both trying to escape your harassers so you can move on."

"Wow." She felt like someone had knocked the wind out of her. Crossing her arms tightly, her shoulders hunched forward, she inhaled through her nostrils. Thinking, she slowly relaxed and then nodded. "There's a lot of truth to that."

As he glanced at her, his eyes narrowed, prying. "So have you broken free from Aaron's grip?"

She looked inward, asking herself the same question. "When I started dating him, he said he shared my interests." She met Hud's eyes. "As the differences emerged, his golden halo began to corrode."

He gave her a wry smile. "So his shining armor began to rust?"

She nodded, relieved by Hud's sense of humor. *Didn't know I cared so much about his opinion.* As the thought took hold, her jaw relaxed, and she found herself staring at him.

He glanced at her and chuckled. "Why do you look so surprised?"

"You're taking this all in stride. You're not blaming me for . . ." She struggled for the words.

"For what, trusting someone who didn't deserve it?"

First grimacing, she gradually raised her eyebrows as the thought took hold. "Yes. That's it exactly. Guilty as charged." She chuckled. Then she took a deep breath, feeling freer, better about herself than she had in a long time.

As they pulled into her driveway, her smile drooped.

"I just wish I'd helped Aunt Ed for the right reasons."

"Don't be so hard on yourself." Turning off the engine, he stared at her. "Whether or not you were completely selfless, you helped her. Your actions speak louder than your doubts."

She grinned.

"That's better. It's good to see a smile on those lips . . . that look so irresistible." He leaned over the console and kissed her.

As they drew away from their embrace, Chloe studied him. *Maybe this isn't Letty's doing. Maybe we truly care for each other.*

His face dimpled in a grin. "Why are you looking at me that way?"

"Just wondering." Shrugging, she felt the heat rise to her cheeks. "When I was knocked unconscious and 'spoke' with Letty, she said our attraction is all her doing."

"What?" He burst out laughing. He laughed so hard, Chloe found herself chuckling along with him. When he finally caught his breath, he wiped his eyes. "That's a good one. You must have been hit on the head harder than I realized."

His words warmed her heart. Again, she filled her lungs, feeling more self-possessed than she had in awhile.

Still smiling, his eyes became serious. "Your problem is, you overanalyze things."

"Why do you say that?" She tilted her head. "Name one thing."

He held out his hands, gesturing to the two of them. "Us, for instance. We're simply falling in love. No one, no 'thing,' is manipulating us. Maybe your analytical mind's an occupational hazard."

She rubbed her forehead, thinking. "I do have to compare, contrast, and classify everything for my job."

He nodded. "And a second thing: your worry that your motives for helping Miss Ed are tainted. You just read too much into things." He put his arms on her shoulders. "You're a good person, Chloe." He grinned. "I'm not saying perfect, but you're a good soul."

Again, she felt her cheeks burning. "Thanks."

He noticed a brochure he'd left on the dash.

"I've got an idea"

As he handed her the pamphlet, his eyes sparkled mischievously.

"What's this?" Taking it, she scanned the title. "Burn Rehabilitation Center?"

He nodded. "I volunteer there once a month and happen to know they need a new brochure."

She looked into his eyes, reading his thoughts. "You want me to create it?"

He shrugged. "This would prove you're unselfish . . . to yourself. You'd gain nothing by helping them other than a sense of satisfaction."

She tilted her head, thinking. "I've got several days of sick leave . . . with nothing to do."

"Except heal." He caught her eye. "You'd be helping the burn victims and hopefully helping yourself."

She smiled slowly and then nodded.

"That's a great idea. Just let me know what they want included in the brochure."

"I've got a better idea. Why don't you come with me tomorrow? Take a tour of the facilities, meet some of the patients and volunteers, and get a feel for it."

CHAPTER 9

"There are wounds that never show on the body that are deeper
and more hurtful than anything that bleeds."
– LAURELL K. HAMILTON

The next morning, Hud picked her up and took her with him to the Burn Rehabilitation Center. After a quick tour, Hud introduced her to one of the volunteers.

The first thing Chloe noticed about Jerry was his tattoos. His arms and legs were nearly covered in them. Then she noticed the raised and red scarred skin beneath and around the ink.

As he watched her, he grinned. "You like the 'tats'?"

"The what?"

"The tattoos." His grin widened.

"I can appreciate the artwork on others."

"Just not yourself?"

Returning his grin, she shook her head. "Needles scare me, and I don't like pain."

"Jerry's a survivor," said Hud. "Over fifty percent of his body was burned."

Her grin drooped a she glanced at his tattoos. "Is this to cover the scars?"

"Actually, no, it was a hobby before the accident, but after I recovered, it became a business."

"He's got his own shop," said Hud.

He nodded. "Owning a place was a goal that kept me going through the long months of healing."

"Were you in an accident?"

"An industrial explosion." He chewed his lip. "They kept me in an induced coma for a couple months. When I came to, I couldn't move. My muscles had atrophied. I saw double, and I couldn't even talk."

"Wow." Chloe swallowed, remembering seeing double for a few hours. "It's hard to imagine taking so long to get your vision back."

"Which is why I volunteer at the center. I know how important a support group is. No burn injury survivor should have to feel they're alone during the healing process."

Hud said, "Jerry also volunteers at The Phoenix Society and the Burn Survivor Support Group."

Chloe studied him. "Where do you find the time?"

"It's become a way of life. The accident changed my whole perspective." He grimaced as he shook his head. "I don't take anything for granted, anymore."

Chloe inhaled as she regarded Jerry, thinking of the Peshtigo Fire victims. *A hundred and fifty years ago, they didn't have the luxury of burn centers or support groups for the survivors.* Then Letty came to mind. *Or for those who didn't survive.*

<hr />

On the drive back, Hud glanced at her. "Think you'll have enough material to create a brochure?"

Nodding, she smiled. "Counting the graphics they gave me, plenty. I'm thinking of making a four panel fold, double-parallel brochure."

He chuckled. "Whatever that is, am sure they'll appreciate it." When she did not answer, he peeked at her. "Are you okay?"

She flinched. "Yeah. I was just daydreaming. Meeting Jerry and some of the others reminded me of the Peshtigo victims."

"In other words, you were thinking of Letty."

She gave him a sheepish smile. "You're starting to read my mind."

"Your mind's an open book."

Her smile faded. "That's exactly what Letty told me in a dream."

Hud gave her knee a playful squeeze. "That's all it was, a dream. You'd just been in an accident. You had a concussion, and they'd given you a sedative. Don't be so sure it was Letty that spoke to you."

"Maybe. But after seeing some of the burn victims today, I'm beginning to understand her torment."

He scratched his head, as if thinking. Then he put on a bright smile.

"Maybe you need to get your mind off such serious topics." His eyes lit up. "How would you like to visit the Oneida Powwow tomorrow?"

She looked up at him, grinning. "I'd love it."

"Have you ever been to one?"

"Nope."

"Indian tacos, dancing, crafts," he nodded his encouragement. "I think you'll enjoy yourself."

"I know I will." Then she spotted a sign: U-PICK CHERRIES, ONE MILE. "Oh, Hud, can we stop?"

He started to roll his eyes, but instead smiled. "Sure."

He turned at the sign, and ten minutes later they were carrying plastic buckets from tree to tree.

She looked from the laden, red-dotted trees to Hud.

"I've never picked cherries before."

"I haven't since I was a kid."

"These pretty red 'balls' remind me of Christmas decorations." She laughed. "Picking them, I feel Christmas has ended, and we're taking down the tree."

He chuckled. "Do you like sour cherries?" She nodded, and he popped one in her mouth. "Watch the pit."

"Mmm . . . delicious, but different from the sweet cherries, aren't they?"

"A little tart, but according to my grandfather, sour cherries are good for you."

She turned toward him. "We should invite him and Aunt Ed to the pow-wow tomorrow."

When they pulled into her driveway, Hud indicated a parked car with his chin.

"Pop-pop's here."

They walked inside to find Edwina and Jake sitting at the dining room table, quietly chatting over coffee and cake.

Edwina gestured to a vase of crimson and cerise flowers.

"Look what Rose picked."

Chloe grinned. "Roses, what else?" She held up a brimming bag of cherries. "Let me rinse these, and we can add even more red color to the table."

"Grab some cups and saucers, while you're at it, and join us for some cherry coffeecake."

Edwina smiled, looking younger, happier, *something*. Chloe could not put her finger on it. *Something's changed.* Knitting her brow, she gave Hud a puzzled look as they headed for the kitchen.

A minute late, when they returned to the table, Edwina said, "Jake was just starting to tell me about the time he raised a wolf."

"Really?" Again, Chloe shared a private grin with Hud, recalling the howl from their first date. "I'd like to hear it."

Jake nodded. "A couple, who came into my boat shop, ran a road-side," he grimaced, "'petting zoo.' We got into a conversation, and they mentioned one of their wolves had had a litter of pups, but the runt probably wasn't going to make it." He took a deep breath. "Their indifference bothered me."

"Why?" Chloe looked up at him.

Jake glanced at his grandson and then back to her.

"Hud may have told you. We belong to the Wolf clan. Native Americans have great respect for wolves."

Hud nodded.

"I couldn't allow a wolf pup to die, not if there was anything I could do to prevent it. The next day, I visited their road-side attraction. When I saw the weakened condition of the pup, my heart sank. He could hardly move. When I picked him up, he was all fur and bones." He took another deep breath.

"'He won't last long,' said the women. 'It's too bad. He's such a friendly little thing. Everyone would've wanted their picture taken with him.'"

"Friendly." He shook his head. "He was so weak, he was near death, yet he tried to lick my face. I asked the woman, 'What are you going to do with him?'"

"She shrugged. 'Let nature take its course.'"

Jake glanced at Chloe and Edwina. "This was in the late sixties, before the Endangered Species Act. Back then, there weren't rules or regulations about keeping wild animals."

Chloe felt her jaw go slack. To cover, she asked, "But by owning a wild animal, wouldn't you also have been doing the wolf an injustice?"

Jake's eyes went cold. "Remember, those pups were born in captivity. That litter was part of a road-side attraction, there only for amusement and profit, and the owners were going to stand by idly while he died."

Nodding, Chloe drew in her breath. "You're right. Times were different then, and you were only trying to help." She glanced up at him. "What happened to him?"

"Long story short, they said I could have him for thirty-five dollars."

Chloe scoffed. "This was the same pup they were going to let die?"

He nodded. "I paid them and drove Mahwaew straight to the vet's."

"You told them he was a wolf?"

"Times weren't *that* different then." He arched his eyebrow. "The vet didn't ask, and I didn't offer any information he didn't specifically request."

"What was wrong with Mah . . . Mah . . . ?"

"Mahwaew. Ma-hwow." He spoke the syllables slowly. "It's Menominee for wolf."

"What was wrong with him?"

"Mostly, a poor diet, and he was riddled with worms. Plus, the vet prescribed an arginine supplement for him."

"What's that?"

"It's an amino acid. Wolf milk contains more of it than puppy milk substitutes, so he needed a boost."

Chloe squinted, trying to understand. "Why's it so important?"

"If wolf pups don't get enough arginine, they can develop cataracts."

She grinned at Hud and Jake. "So the vet *did* know he was a wolf."

Jake's eyes twinkled. "Guess he did, at that."

"So what happened?"

"I brought him home. An older German shepherd of ours took him under his wing." He chuckled. "Woof and Wolf, I called them. They became inseparable— sleeping together, playing together. I had to hand-feed Mahwaew until he was old enough to eat meat. Then I built a pen for them with platforms, a sand box, trees, a shelter, and a water trough. All through this time, I tried to socialize him as best I could."

"What do you mean 'socialize'?"

"I knew he could never be turned loose in the wild. The best I could do for him was bring him back to health and socialize him with as many experiences, places, and people as I could—not only with males, but also with females." He glanced at Edwina as he took a deep breath. "My wife and I took turns feeding and handling him."

Edwina blinked, nodded silently, and looked down at her coffee.

As the pause lengthened, Chloe sensed the growing tension. To relieve it, she asked, "Why did you want to socialize Mahwaew?"

"Since I couldn't let him loose in the wild, I trained him to be an ambassador."

"You'd said he was friendly when you first met him."

"He was, and that gentleness grew. He loved people, especially children."

"So he survived?"

Jake sat up straight. "Not only survived, he thrived. When he was a couple months old, we stopped by the couple's 'zoo.' Mahwaew was twice the size of his litter mates."

"Really?" Chloe looked at him. "Why was that?"

Jake grimaced. "Probably they'd had no medical attention and not enough to eat." He glanced at her. "Wolves don't eat ordinary dog food. They need meat, and a lot of it. An adult wolf eats two to five pounds of meat every day."

She gave a low whistle. "Did he eat you out of house and home?"

"No, but he did escape from his pen once. Got a call from the neighbor, saying our dog was in his backyard, playing with his kids."

She gasped. "Oh, no."

"Oh, yes." He took a deep breath. "My heart was in my mouth, but when I got there, he was playing with the kids, just like any other dog." He chuckled. "Our neighbor said he was the best behaved dog he'd ever seen. In fact, they wanted to keep him."

Chloe laughed.

"Such irony." Hud shook his head.

"How did he get out of his pen?"

Jake's eyes smiled. "Wolves are smart. They watch. He saw how I lifted and unlocked the latch. Then he figured a way to use his paws and mouth to open it."

"So you kept him at your house?"

Jake shook his head. "Woof and Wolf's pen was in the backyard—that is, until he learned how to escape."

"What a liability," Chloe said. "If he'd hurt anyone, it could've been a disaster."

Jake's eyes opened wide. "I couldn't let that happen. I'd never have forgiven myself." He sighed.

Chloe watched his face cloud over, wondering if he was thinking of Celestine.

"What did you do with Mahwaew?"

"I built him and Woof another pen on some property we own outside of town."

Hud caught her eye and grinned. "Where we watched the aurora borealis."

Chloe gasped. "You mean, that wolf we heard . . . ?"

"Was probably a descendant of Mahwaew's." Hud nodded, his dark hair drifting behind his head's movements. "A wolf used to visit him. She'd stand within view of his pen and howl."

"Was that the white wolf you mentioned?"

"More likely, one of his descendants." Hud's dark eyes lit up. "Whenever I see a white wolf, I *know* it's one of his."

She turned toward Jake. "So he mated with this wild wolf?"

He nodded. "When he reached puberty, he escaped one night. I found him the next morning, his chin resting on his front paws, just outside his pen. I let him back in and added a padlock, but that day I began calling all the wildlife authorities, all the wolf sanctuaries. Finally, I found one that would work with him, train him to become a friendship ambassador. The next weekend, I drove him to a wolf sanctuary in South Carolina, but every now and then I'd catch sight of his friend and her litter on the fringe of the property, along the tree line."

"How do you know it was Mahwaew's pups?"

"He was pure white," said Jake. "His mate was gray, but the pups were all white, too."

"We keep a water trough on the property that automatically refills," said Hud, "so the wolves and other wildlife always have a fresh water source. Once in awhile, we spot one of them drinking from it."

"Though you found him a home, it had to be bittersweet to lose him." Chloe grimaced.

Jake shrugged. "He was never 'mine,' and he no longer belonged in the wild, but he wasn't domesticated, either. My role was to heal him and help him move on."

Hud caught her eye. "As you know firsthand, we still hear his offspring. Sometimes we even catch a glimpse at dusk or early morning."

Chloe nodded as she mentally replayed Jake's words. *My role was to heal him and help him move on.* Celestine and Letty came to mind. Then she glanced at Jake.

"Did you ever hear what became of him?"

He nodded. "The sanctuary groomed Mahwaew to become a wolf ambassador. He was a great favorite of groups of children and tourists who visited the sanctuary, and he lived to the ripe old age of fourteen."

Hud added, "Wolves in the wild live to be nine or ten." After a lull in the conversation, he glanced at Jake and Edwina. "We're thinking of visiting the Oneida Powwow tomorrow. How would you like to come along with us?"

Jake bit his lip. "I'd sure like to, but I promised to volunteer at Our Lady of Good Help's gift shop." He turned to Edwina. "Why don't you go with them?"

"Are you going to be there very long?" Ed asked.

Hud shrugged. "Just a few hours. Why?"

Edwina stared down at her coffee and spoke in a quiet voice. "Maybe I'll go along with you."

Though he said nothing, Jake's eyebrow arched. Chloe swallowed the grin she shared with Hud.

<hr />

That night, Chloe lay awake, thinking of the Burn Rehabilitation Center and Jerry. That led to thoughts about the Peshtigo Fire victims and Letty. Though she tried to will it, sleep would not come. She was too keyed up. Finally, she decided to get up and begin work on the brochure. By three o'clock, her eyes were burning, but she had completed a rough draft.

So much for resting and recuperating.

She crawled into bed and turned off the lights. Just as she was drifting off, Letty appeared.

"There's time enough for rest when you're dead, dearie."

Chloe groaned. "Leave me alone. I just want to sleep. I'm dead tired."

"I'm dead, and I'm not tired. I want to live, but I never got the chance. I was seventeen when the fire claimed me, barely getting started." Sneering, Letty put her face against Chloe's. "If I can't live myself, I can live indirectly . . . through you."

The reek of burned, putrefied flesh was overwhelming. Coughing, making a face, Chloe waved her hand, blowing away the stench.

"Gee, it must be great having supernatural powers."

"Not really."

"Go away!"

Chloe put a pillow over her head, trying to block out Letty's voice and stale breath.

"Sometimes a person's spirit can't go away, can't move on. I don't have a choice."

"Yes, you do." Chloe tossed away the pillow, grumbling, "This isn't doing any good." She thought of the rehabilitation center's burn victims. "Letty, you *can* move on. Other people have. Even I survived a car wreck. Just deal with it. Now, please let me sleep."

"No!"

Instantly, all the lights in the room turned on, and Chloe sat up in bed, blinking, squinting.

"Okay, okay, I get the message." Then, getting an idea, she walked over to her computer. "Okay, Letty, if you won't leave me alone, let me show you something."

"What?"

Chloe heard her skepticism as she showed Letty a "before" picture of Jerry.

Letty shuddered and closed her eyes. "I can't look at this. It's too painful, too close to what I . . ."

"You're a big girl. What, a hundred and fifty years old? Look!" Next she showed Letty an "after" picture of Jerry. Then she showed Letty several pictures of other patients in various stages of recovery. "See, they're getting on with their lives. You didn't even have to live through the pain of healing as they did, *so move on*. Quit playing these mind games. Stop manipulating!"

Letty faltered. "This is all I've done for so long . . . all I know."

Chloe yawned. Then she shook her head, trying to shake off her sleepiness. "If you think you're so tough, show me. Move on!"

"No! You're the only grip on life I have left. I'm staying with you, for better or worse."

Chloe rolled her eyes. "Letty, that's a marriage vow. I don't believe it applies to hauntings." She yawned again. "Can't you just cross over, move on, whatever?"

"No, that would mean I'd see God."

Chloe's chuckle was humorless. "That's the point, isn't it?"

"No! I hate Him. I never want to see Him."

Chloe was too exhausted to think. "Why?"

"How could He let Teresa live while He let me die? No! I do *not* want to see any God that's so inhuman."

"Of course He's inhuman. He's divine." Chloe stifled yet another yawn.

"He's cruel. I never want to see a God that's so heartless."

"That's it." Chloe threw up her arms. "I'm done trying to help. I'm going to sleep." She turned off the lights, crawled into bed, and put her fingers in her ears. Though she saw Letty's mouth move, she heard nothing. "I'm not listening to you. La-la-la-la-la-la-la."

Maybe that's it. I have to consciously tell Letty I'm not listening so she loses interest and goes away. With that, Chloe yawned and drifted into an uneasy sleep.

The next morning, on the drive to Our Lady of Good Help, Jake mentioned he was going to go to confession.

"Anyone want to join me?"

"Confession." Scowling, Edwina spit it out like a curse word. "Why do you want to go to confession? Why should you have to tell your sins to a person? Cut out the middle man."

Sitting in the front seat, Chloe couldn't help but overhear their conversation. When she heard Edwina's quarrelsome tone, she turned to face forward, giving the back seat as much privacy as possible.

Jake answered patiently. "In the Book of Matthew, the apostles were given the authority to bind and loose sin. 'Whatever you bind on earth shall be bound in heaven, and whatever you loose on earth shall be loosed in heaven.'"

Edwina sniffed. "Maybe the apostles had that authority, but not ordinary, everyday men."

"You mean priests? Who are the priests and bishops but the apostles' successors?"

Edwina dropped her pose and stared at him. "Says who?"

"Says the *Bible* and over two thousand years of tradition. Think of the Gospel of John, when Jesus breathed on his apostles, giving them the power to forgive sins. 'Receive the Holy Spirit. Whose sins you forgive are forgiven them, and whose sins you retain are retained.'"

"How would they even have known someone's sins?"

"Simple, through the sacrament of confession." Jake chuckled.

Edwina scoffed. "Semantics. You're begging the question."

"I can't see any other way of interpreting John twenty, twenty-two and twenty-three."

"If you think about it . . ."

"About what?" Jake watched her.

"Sin, evil . . . It's all God's fault," said Edwina.

"What?!"

"God lets terrible things happen to good people. Why?" Edwina's tone became belligerent. "How could a 'loving' God allow such suffering in the world?"

Chloe raised her eyebrows as she recalled Letty's rant in her dream. *Was that just a few hours ago? Aunt Ed has more in common with her than she may think.*

In the silence that followed, Chloe heard Jake draw a deep breath. Finally, he asked in a monotone, "What you're really talking about is Celestine's death, isn't it?"

"No!" Then she paused. "Yes . . . maybe I am . . . now that you mention it."

"Don't you think I've asked that same question a thousand times?"

Chloe heard the desperation in Jake's voice.

Edwina's chuckle was dry. "I thought you were the one with all the answers." Her sarcasm hung in the air like thick smoke.

"No, I'm the one who's always asking the questions. As far as answers go, I get them from here."

Chloe heard him thump a book. Turning slightly to her left, she gave the back seat a sidelong glance and saw him page through a well-worn book titled the *Catechism of the Catholic Church*.

"I'll paraphrase," he said, alternating between reading and glancing up. "As intelligent and free creatures, humans have to journey toward their destinies by their own free choice. Yes, they can stray. Yes, they can sin. That's how evil entered the world, but in no way is God the cause of that evil."

Curling her lip, Edwina sneered but kept still.

"God permits sin and evil since He respects His creatures' freedom." Jake paused, a smile coming into his voice. "Oddly enough, He even knows how to wrench good from it."

"Good?" Edwina rolled her eyes. "What 'good' can come from evil? What 'good' came from my sister's drowning?"

Chloe heard Jake suck in his breath. His breath ragged, he said, "St. Paul wrote, 'We know that in everything God works for good with those who love Him, who are called according to His purpose.' Good comes from not only the positive in our lives but the negative, as well."

"Platitudes. I ask what 'good' came from my sister's death, and all you give me are clichés."

Jake sighed. "I don't pretend to understand the Lord's ways, so I can't explain them. None of us will know God's providence until we meet Him, but during the bleak times, we have to 'walk by faith and not by sight.' When everything's going right, it's easier to trust Him than when everything's going wrong, yet crises, tragedies are what help us grow closer to Him."

"Losing my sister didn't bring me closer to God." Edwina scoffed. "It pushed me further away."

"That tragedy was an opportunity to begin trusting God." He smiled gently.

"There's real power in faith—enough power to overcome loss, bitterness, regrets . . . anything." He shrugged. "When there's nothing you can do, you have two choices. Either turn toward or turn away from God."

Edwina frowned in distaste. "I turned away."

Jake shook his head. "I've already told you how I turned to Him after your sister's death." He gave Edwina a sidelong glance before continuing. "As you know, many years ago, I was accused of theft and negligibility in the death of a loved one. I lost the love of my life, and . . . I came close to ending my own life."

Edwina's breathing became shallow. Her chest rose and fell quickly as she listened.

"I knelt in prayer at that shrine, demanding answers. 'Why did You let these things happen?'"

"What answers did you get?" asked Chloe, joining the conversation.

"Not answers," Jake took a long, deep breath. "What I received was an understanding. It was no longer 'my' life, but God's. I began living moment by moment, welcoming everything as God's personal communication to me. Sometimes it isn't until we're brought face-to-face with our own mortality that we realize we're not in control. God is."

Lips pursed, eyes narrowed, Edwina raised her eyebrow, silently appraising him. Finally, she asked, "How long are you going to be at confession and your volunteer job?"

Jake looked at his watch. "My shift doesn't end until four hours from now." A hopeful glow lit up his eyes. "But I get an hour for lunch. Maybe we could meet for a picnic, eat in the shade?"

"That ought to give me enough time."

Jake cocked his head. "Enough time for what?"

Wearing a sassy grin, Edwina reached for the catechism book in his lap.

"Enough time to beat you at your own game."

⚬

Hud pulled into the parking lot of Our Lady of Good Help.

"All ashore that's going ashore."

Jake, Edwina, and Chloe all opened their doors.

"Hey, where are you going?" Hud caught Chloe's hand. "I thought we were off to the powwow."

162

"We are. But after a dream I had last night and then hearing Aunt Ed this morning, there's something I have to do first."

Hud nodded and turned off the motor. "Mind if I come along?"

She squeezed his hand. "Was just about to ask you."

"Can somebody help me down from this truck?" Aunt Ed's tone was ornery.

Chloe stifled a chuckle. "One sec." She hopped down, took the book Edwina handed her, and then held out her other hand.

"Thanks, Chloe, I'll help her from here." Jake came around the truck and offered his elbow. "What are you going to do while I'm in confession?"

Edwina took hold of his elbow and then grabbed the catechism.

"Like I said, I'm going to read this book of yours so I can prove you wrong about God."

Chloe took a deep breath. *Has Aunt Ed always been this way, or has Letty influenced her?* She glanced at Hud and shivered. *How much has Letty manipulated all of us?*

"You do that." Jake's smile was twisted. "Let me show you my favorite place to meditate. It's quiet, in the shade, and just in front of the St. Francis and wolf statues."

Chloe's ears perked. "Wolf statue? Why would there be a statue of a wolf by St. Francis?"

Jake looked at her. "You've never heard the story of the Wolf of Gubbio?"

Chloe shook her head. "I know St. Francis is the patron saint of animals and ecology, but I've never heard of any connection to wolves."

"Why don't you come with us? I'll tell you about the Wolf of Gubbio on our way."

Hud and Chloe exchanged a nod. "Okay."

"When Francis lived in the Italian town of Gubbio, a wolf was terrorizing the area. No one would venture beyond the town walls. Finally, Francis made the sign of the cross at the town's gate and went out to meet the wolf. When it saw him, it rushed at him with its jaws wide open. Francis again made the sign of the cross and told the wolf to stop molesting people and livestock in the name of God. The wolf approached him, lay down at his feet, and rested its head in St. Francis' hands."

"Oh, this is a fairy tale." Edwina sniffed.

"No, this is a hagiography."

"A what?" asked Chloe. "A hag . . . ?"

"A hagiography, a biography of a saint. This story of the wolf demonstrates St. Francis' influence over nature and animals."

Edwina sneered. "Like I said, a fable, a folktale."

"Ah, you need evidence. As Our Lady of Good Help told Adele, 'Blessed are they that believe without seeing.'" He glanced at Chloe and Hud. "Let me finish the story, and then I'll give Edwina her proof."

They nodded.

"St. Francis made a deal with the wolf. 'You're hungry. That's why you've killed people and livestock. Stop molesting them, and we'll make a pact with the citizens of Gubbio to feed you every day.' The wolf placed its paw in St. Francis' hand. Then the two met with the townspeople. St. Francis and the wolf made the pact again, this time publicly. The wolf lived another two years, eating handouts from the townspeople. Never again did it hunt or kill."

"Was that your evidence?" Edwina scoffed. "That the wolf allegedly never killed again."

"No." Jake seemed to swallow a smile. "The proof came later. Tradition held that Gubbio built the Church of Saint Francis of the Peace at the wolf's grave site. During repairs to the church wall in the 1870s, they found the skeleton of a wolf beneath a slab."

Edwina grunted.

"What did they do with its remains?" asked Chloe.

"They reburied them inside the church." Jake stopped in front of the statues. "Here we are."

Chloe looked at the grassy garden retreat. Graceful, wrought-iron benches faced the concrete statues, where buttercups and petunias blossomed at their feet. Birds sang from the nearby trees as a butterfly landed on the wolf sculpture.

"I can see why this is your favorite place to meditate," said Chloe.

Jake nodded. "You'll be comfortable here, Ed. It's shady, quiet." He checked his watch. "I'll be back in two hours to join you for lunch."

Again, Edwina grunted. Then she waved goodbye without looking up at them. Glancing at each other, the three turned and walked back toward the shrine.

Chloe took a deep breath. "Maybe this is none of my business, Jake, but Aunt Ed's so crotchety. Why are you so patient with her?"

He looked at her, grinned, and then paused, as if gathering his thoughts.

"You didn't know Edwina when she was young. She was easygoing, soft-spoken. She had a ready smile, a glow in her eyes."

Chloe shook her head. "I love Aunt Ed, but the person you describe is hard to imagine."

"After Celestine drowned, Ed's personality changed. She became the bitter, sharp-tongued woman you see, but what broke my heart was watching the glow disappear from her eyes. Whether or not it was my fault Celestine died, I always felt responsible for the light fading from her eyes."

"The windows of the soul." Hud glanced from Chloe to his grandfather.

Jake nodded. "It was almost as if Edwina's soul left her and something else entered her psyche."

Chloe thought of Letty as they walked in silence. When they approached the crypt, Chloe slowed.

"There's something I have to do." She glanced at Hud. "Will you come with me?"

Smiling, he took her hand. "Sure." Then he turned to Jake. "We should be back from the powwow in about five hours. Should we meet you by the wolf?"

"Perfect. Have fun."

Chloe and Hud walked down the flight of steps and entered the chapel. Candles flickered in the dim light, welcoming them, beckoning to them. Chloe lifted Hud's fingertips to her lips and slowly let go his hand. As she walked toward the altar alone, she paused to light a candle.

She felt a rush of cold air, and she caught her breath. Cupping her hand around the newly-lit flame, she looked left and right for a sign of Letty. Then she heard the air conditioner fan click on. Chuckling with relief, she shook her head at her superstitions.

Still, the flame seemed weak, flickering in the draft. Rather than try to read anything in the snuffed candle's meaning, she cupped her hand around the flame, guarding it until it was strong enough to burn on its own.

Chloe thought of what Jake had said about the light going out of Edwina's eyes. *What 'draft' had snuffed out her inner light?* Again, Letty came to mind.

She knelt in front of the altar, crossed herself, and whispered so softly only God could hear.

"Help Letty overcome her bitterness. She's not evil. She's just . . . resentful. Please help her move on. Help her let go her grip on Aunt Ed and Celestine."

Chloe crossed herself and stood up. Just before leaving, she thought she glimpsed Letty out of the corner of her eye, standing near the candles, watching her. She turned her head quickly, but all she saw were flickering flames.

As they approached Nicolet Drive, Hud took his eyes from the road.

"The powwow doesn't start for another hour. Want to stop by the Bay Beach Wildlife Sanctuary?"

"What's there to see?"

"Wildlife, obviously," he chuckled as he caught her eye, "but also the Nature Center, Wildlife Habi-Trek Trail, Lookout Tower, and Woodland Building. Are you . . . game?" His eyes twinkled.

"Sure. Why not?" She met his smile and raised him a wink. "Let's live in the moment."

With a laugh, he turned on the blinker, took a right, and reached for her hand. "I love you, Chloe Clark."

Her heart soared, but she asked, "Really? Why?"

He chuckled.

"No, really. Why?"

He pursed his lips. "Why does the sun rise? Why do birds fly? It's nature taking its course, and you're," he sighed, "helping it along with the way you look, the way you are."

Again, her spirits rose, but she persisted.

"Five weeks ago, we hadn't even met." She leaned over and kissed his cheek. "Don't get me wrong. I adore you, but there's this nagging thought."

"You're overanalyzing again."

Raising his eyebrow, he pretended to give her a stern look, and the two of them burst out laughing.

Ten minutes later, they were walking through the Nature Center, hand in hand. From there, they strolled along the Wildlife Habi-Trek and climbed the Lookout Tower to scan for coyotes. Finally, they stopped into the Woodland Building to watch the otters play. Animal tracks painted on the floor led them from area to area. When they came to the back door, Chloe glanced up into Hud's eyes.

"Do we exit here or backtrack to the front?"

"Not sure."

He pressed the handle, and the door opened. Before them was a pen surrounded by a twelve-foot, chain-link fence. Inside it were tawny canines.

"Ohmigosh . . . wolves." As Chloe looked at them, she spoke in an awed, hushed tone. "Except for their slanting eyes, they look like dogs."

Opening the door wider, they saw a caretaker getting ready to feed them.

"Sorry, folks, this area's off-limits to visitors."

"Oops." Chloe hunched her shoulders as she closed the door and turned to Hud. "It's a shame we can't see them up-close, but wasn't it a coincidence, just happening onto those wolves like that?"

He shook his head. "There's no such thing as coincidence. A wolf's presence is a symbol of guidance."

She nodded. "I recall your mentioning that."

"In Menominee tradition, wolves play an important role. They often appear when you're faced with a difficult decision."

Chloe thought of Letty. "Interesting."

Hud glanced at his watch. Then he grinned at Chloe, his dimple showing.

"And if we don't make a decision to leave soon, we'll be late getting to the powwow."

A half-hour later, they were walking over freshly-mown grass toward the concession stands.

"Have you ever tried an Indian taco?"

"I've had tacos." Chloe looked up into Hud's dark eyes. "Are they anything like that?"

He smiled. "Only slightly."

They stepped up to the counter, and he ordered two.

Chloe watched them deep-fry the bread bases and then add toppings of chili and grated cheese. Over that, they sprinkled chopped tomatoes, shredded lettuce, and jalapenos.

Chloe looked at the fried bread and grinned at Hud.

"No calories, right?"

"Right."

She watched his dimple deepen as they carried their tacos to a shady picnic table. She could not help but watch the passing parade of people and costumes. Feathers, bells, fringe, breastplates, and headdresses were everywhere. One man in full regalia looked like he had stepped out of the eighteen hundreds, except for his sunglasses and glow-in-the-dark running shoes. A mother and daughter duo wore matching ceremonial dresses. A woman at the next table wore an intricately beaded vest with buckskin fringe.

"How's the taco?"

Chloe grinned sheepishly. "I haven't tried it yet. There's too much to look at."

Hud surveyed the scene. "It is colorful, isn't it?"

"I'll say." She picked up the plate-sized taco, staring at it, holding it first this way and then that. "How do you eat this thing, anyway? It's too big to bite into."

He laughed. "Just go for the gusto, like this." He opened his mouth wide and sank his teeth into it.

"Thanks, but I'll try pulling off bite-sized bits." Chloe chuckled as she broke off a piece and popped it in her mouth. "Delicious."

When they finished, they strolled past the vendors, stopping to look at the different arts and crafts.

Chloe picked up what looked like a rope of braided grass.

"What's this?"

"Smell it."

She breathed in its sweet aroma.

"It smells like freshly-mown grass."

She breathed it in again, filling her lungs.

"It's sweetgrass."

"Descriptive." She grinned. "What's is used for?"

"Smudging. They use it like incense at ceremonies to purify the area and attract positive energy. Some people carry a small braid as an amulet."

"Interesting." Thinking of Letty, she handed the sweetgrass to the vendor. "I'll take it."

They walked past a tent filled with tables of hats and T-shirts. The walls were draped with T-shirt samples of assorted colors and graphics. As one caught her eye, Chloe pulled at Hud's hand, straining to see.

"Look at that wolf shirt."

He chuckled. "Would you like to stop?"

"Yes. It reminds me of the wolves we saw this morning. I can't take my eyes off it." She moved closer to get a better look. "It's almost as if it's calling to me."

Hud stared at her. "This is the second time today a wolf has crossed your path. If you don't buy it, I will."

She chuckled. "As long as you put it that way, okay."

They strolled, hand in hand, through the tents, looking at all the beaded crafts and paintings. Then Chloe noticed a sign: Henna Tattoos. Pictures of different designs and graphics lined the tent walls.

"Oh, Hud, look."

Again, she pulled him back. Following the direction of her eyes, he laughed out loud.

"Wolves, again."

"I've never had a henna tattoo, but this one . . ."

"Calls to you. I get it." He nodded. "Nothing's a coincidence. Go for it. Listen to the call of the wolf." He looked at the crowded working area filled with women painting women's hands. "How 'bout I wait for you over here?"

"It'll just take a few minutes." Smiling, Chloe handed him her packages. Then she turned to the girl, who was waving her over. "I'd like that image," she said, pointing. "The one with the wolf howling at the moon."

She sat down facing the girl and placed her hand on the pillow between them. The girl hand-drew the scene by squeezing a small bottle of wet henna. The thick, reddish ink began to take the shape of a wolf. Then she drew a crescent moon with stars overhead.

Chloe admired her hand.

"You're good."

The girl finished her artwork by sprinkling fine glitter over the moon and stars.

"Come back in about fifteen minutes so I can spray on the fixative."

Chloe nodded. "Okay."

"And be careful," called the girl. "Don't smudge it."

"I won't." Chloe grinned, happy with the world. "Nothing could spoil this day." She thought of Hud and, despite the warm, sunny day, felt a shiver run up her spine. Waving with her tattooed hand, she admired the wolf artwork again. "See you in a few minutes."

Winding her way through the maze of women being henna tattooed, she walked out into the bright sunshine. For a moment, the glare blinded her, and she blinked. As her eyes adjusted, she scanned the area for Hud.

Then she spotted him. His back toward her, she called, but he did not hear. He was talking to a young woman. When Chloe saw her grab his arm familiarly, she went cold. She tried to laugh off her fears. *They're probably old friends.* But as she approached, she saw their body language. The woman's eyes were locked on his as her fingers kneaded his arm.

"Amy's having a party Saturday. I was wondering if you could make it."

A sudden lump caught in her throat, and she gave a small cough.

Hud did an about-face, throwing off the woman's hand in the process.

"Chloe, this is Cherie."

Though she smiled, Cherie's eyes narrowed.

"Are you a friend of Hud's?"

"I'm not a foe, if that's what you mean."

Chloe meant it as joke, but it came out surly. She forced a smile.

Cherie's eyelids lowered as she appraised Chloe. Then she turned to Hud.

"Hope to run into you again . . . soon."

Wearing a twisted smile, she nodded to Chloe and walked away.

Chloe glanced at her retreating figure and then turned toward Hud. The silence was deafening.

Finally, he said, "Let me see your tattoo."

She held out her wrist.

"Nice."

He nodded his approval. She sniffed.

"Want to see the rest of the vendors before the dancing starts?"

She shrugged. "'Kay."

They fell into step, neither speaking.

Finally, Chloe gave him a sidelong glance.

"You'd asked me about Aaron. How about you? Had you been involved with anyone before we met?"

He took a deep breath. "Cherie and I dated a few times, if that's what you mean." He glanced at her. "But it wasn't anything serious."

"That's not the way I saw it."

He caught her eye. "I meant, nothing serious from my perspective."

Her eyes narrowing, she scrutinized him. *Then how serious is he about me?*

"What?"

She shrugged. "I didn't say anything."

"You didn't have to." He gave her a grim smile. "I could hear the wheels of your mind grinding away."

She sighed. "Something Letty said to me in the dream."

"Refresh me."

"That she's manipulating you, influencing our thoughts, feelings. She said she's the reason behind my social life."

He grimaced. "She's just playing mind games with you." He tried to put his arm around her shoulders, draw her to him, but she shrank away, letting his arm fall. He raised his eyebrow. "Chloe, I don't know how to make you believe me. What we have is real, not something imposed on us."

"I'm not so sure about that. I thought what I had with Aaron was real, but I totally misread him . . . for years. And something else. I honestly wonder if I was over him. I can't help wonder if I was ready to start a relationship with you." She swallowed the lump in her throat. "I just want our relationship to be honest . . . real."

"It is real." Exhaling, he shook his head. "What can I say or do to convince you?"

She bit her lip. "This Cherie brings up more questions. Maybe Letty was behind your breaking up with her, or maybe you were on the rebound from her. I don't know your history, and I don't know what to believe. I just don't want either of us to be manipulated, pushed into something that's not . . . tangible."

He took her in his arms. "Oh, it's tangible all right."

Stiffening, she turned her face away until he let go.

"I'm not so sure."

She glanced at the wolf motif on her hand and grimaced.

"Be right back. They have to spray this with a fixative."

As she waited her turn, she swallowed the sudden lump in her throat. *What have I done? What if he really does love me?* She blinked back tears. *What if I really do love him?*

When she returned a few minutes later, she had to press her lips together to stop them from trembling. She wanted to feel his arms around her, hear him tell her everything would be all right, everything was all right, but she did not know where to begin.

Worse, he seemed to be holding back. When her hand brushed against his, he didn't clasp it as he normally did.

"Now what?" His voice was flat, emotionless.

She sniffed back tears. *Somehow the sunny day doesn't seem as bright.* Hunching her shoulders, she shook her head.

"I don't know."

She looked away as she swiped at a tear, hoping he had not seen.

He glanced at his watch. "It's still another hour before we have to leave to pick up Miss Ed and Pop-pop." He looked at her. "They're starting the dancing in a few minutes. Want to grab a seat and watch?" When she did not answer, he added, "We're here. We might as well."

Swallowing another lump in her throat, she nodded, unable to speak.

Then he looked into her face. "Are you all right?"

"No." She turned toward him, trying to hold back tears.

He pulled her to him, holding her tightly.

She threw her arms around him and buried her head in his shoulder. Chest to chest, feeling his heart beat against hers was the only thing that eased the pain. Neither spoke. Then, drawing a ragged breath, she looked up at him.

"I honestly don't know whether I can trust my judgement or not, but Hud Beaulieu . . ."

His eyebrow raised, he watched her, waiting. Finally, he gave her a skeptical grin. "Yes?"

She smiled sheepishly and whispered, "I love you."

He closed his arms around her and whispered back. "And I love you, Chloe Clark. No one, nothing's 'forcing' me to feel it or say it. I love you."

Finally, the ache left. Her heart still against his, she sighed.

An announcement over the loudspeaker told the dancers to begin lining up for the opening event.

He took her hand. "C'mon, let's find some seats while we still can."

Smiling, she swiped at her tears and nodded.

They climbed the sloped hillside surrounding the natural arena and found two grassy seats beneath a sugar maple tree. Chloe leaned into him as he put his arm around her shoulders.

He leaned over, kissed her neck, and whispered in her ear. "I really do love you."

She nuzzled against him. "You, too."

The Master of Ceremonies introduced the groups, the drummers, and the chiefs. After an opening prayer, he invited the veterans to lead the dance. The drummers began the beat, with the singers' voices joining in. First, the veterans entered the arena, encircling it at the widest edge.

Then the MC invited the chiefs to join, followed by the various groups of dancers, each one being named as they joined the lengthening line that began spiraling into a circle. As groups continued to join, the circle of dancers wound into more and more concentric rings.

Finally, the MC invited the "young braves and Indian princesses" to join the line until the arena was filled with people moving and gyrating in rhythm to the beat. When the music ended, the MC asked all to leave the arena but the first set of Smoke Dancers.

A group of colorfully costumed men in feathers, buckskin, and bells began dancing to the beat of another drummer and singer. Then another group danced and another, each dance more intricate than the previous.

A young man selling drinks stopped and asked, "Rosewater lemonade?"

Hud turned to her. "Want one?"

"Rosewater lemonade?" She squinted. "Don't think I've ever tried it."

"Then it's high time." Hud winked and turned to the boy. "We'll take two."

Chloe took the icy cup, inhaled its aroma, and grinned.

"The name fits. It smells like lemony roses."

"Try it."

She took a sip, tasting it first carefully. Then she took a long drink.

"It tastes the way roses smell, but with a lemon twist."

Hud smiled. "How is it?"

"Wonderful." She tapped her plastic cup against his. "To us."

He touched his cup to hers. "May we always find something new to share together."

She watched the corners of his eyes crinkle in a private smile as she drank in the moment.

Then the MC invited everyone who wanted to dance to join them in the arena.

Hud's eyes lit up. "Would you like to dance?"

"Yes!" She downed her rosewater lemonade and scrambled to her feet. "Let's go."

People began joining the dancers from all sides of the arena. It became one large dance floor, with everyone moving and dancing in a circular pattern. Young people, children, elders, couples, mothers with babies, dancers in regalia, everyone and anyone who wanted to dance joined the rotating throng.

At first, Chloe felt self-conscious, and she simply walked in time to the beat. But as others began dancing, she relaxed, moving her body and dancing in rhythm with the group. She looked at Hud and started laughing from sheer joy. Finally, the drumming stopped.

"That was fun."

His eyes flashed. "Glad you enjoyed it." Then he checked his watch. "Hate to say it, but—"

"It's time to go?"

Grimacing, he nodded. When he reached for her hand, she felt an electric shock run up her arm.

Interlacing their fingers, she smiled up at him.

"This powwow was a great idea. Wonder how Jake and Aunt Ed made out at Our Lady of Good Help."

CHAPTER 10

"A confession has to be part of your new life."

– LUDWIG WITTGENSTEIN

An hour later, they found Edwina where they had left her, sitting on the bench near the Saint Francis and wolf statues. Deep in discussion, their backs to the path, she and Jake did not see them approach.

Chloe started to call out, but Hud put his finger to his lips. *Wait*, he mouthed.

"What's the value of confessing to a priest?" Edwina stared at Jake. "Why not confess directly to God?"

"What kind of value do you mean, psychological or sacramental?"

She shrugged. "Okay, what's the psychological value?"

Jake scrutinized her. "It's hearing the priest's words, 'I absolve you of your sins.' Hearing those words reaffirms, reinforces the peace we feel in our hearts when we confess directly to God."

She nodded, seeming to think it over. "I've heard Catholics don't need psychiatrists when they have priests." Edwina chuckled mischievously. "Any truth to that?"

Jake smiled gently. "Whether or not it's true, I've heard that, too, but the most important reason for confessing to a priest is the sacramental grace you receive through reconciliation."

"What do you mean?"

"Confessing becomes more than simply telling God you're sorry. It becomes something sacred, a sacrament. Through penance, God not only forgives you your sins, He gives you His grace, His blessing."

She held back her head, her eyes challenging him. "Define grace."

Jake paused, as if reflecting. "Think about all the poor choices you've made, all the mistakes and wasted years."

She nodded slowly.

"Grace is God's solution to the mess, the private hell we each create."

Taking a deep breath, she closed the book of catechism she had been reading. She swallowed, as if digesting what she had heard.

"After reading this book and talking with you, I'll admit confessing to a priest does seem to have its advantages." Then, peering at Jake through narrowed eyes, she snapped at him, "But even if reconciliation makes sense, don't you think for one minute I'm buying the rest of your hogwash."

Jake's eyes twinkled as he calmly replied. "Certainly not." Shrugging, he checked his watch. "You know, Father David's still here. Maybe you'd like to chat with him?"

Edwina's eyelids flew open. "I'm not making any confession, if that's what you're implying."

"I understand that." Jake hunched his shoulders. "Thought maybe you'd like to discuss the principles of the sacrament with him."

She frowned, seeming to think it over. Then she tapped the book.

"Having read up on the subject all afternoon, I'm armed to debate him." She nodded. "Maybe I will, at that. Bring him on. I'm ready to do battle."

Jake swallowed a smile as he stood up. Then he noticed Chloe and Hud.

When Edwina saw them, she flinched.

"How long have you two been standing there, gawking?"

Chloe crossed her fingers behind her back. "Just got here."

Edwina scrutinized her. "There's something I have to do. Back in a minute."

Chloe kept a straight face as she fingered her pendant. "Take your time."

"We're in no hurry." Hud caught Chloe's eye.

"We'll meet you at your truck," called Jake.

When they were out of sight, Chloe grinned.

"How about that? I do believe Aunt Ed's experiencing some kind of conversion."

"WHY DOES A CHICKEN . . . CROSS THE STREET? . . . SHE SEES A GUY . . . SHE'D LIKE . . . TO MEET . . . . BURMA-SHAVE."

"Celestine?" Chloe raised an eyebrow. "Haven't seen you in awhile. Where have you been?"

"THIS IS NOT . . . A CLEVER VERSE . . . I TRIED . . . AND TRIED . . . BUT JUST . . . GOT WORSE . . . . BURMA-SHAVE."

"Celestine's here?" Hud opened his eyes wide.

Chloe nodded. "She's speaking in riddles again." Then she turned toward the girl. "What do you mean, you tried and tried but just got worse?"

Celestine shook her head. "I tried to see you, but Letty can be such a bully."

"But you're here now. How come?"

"Something's happened to Letty."

Chloe squinted, trying to understand. "I'm not following."

"Something's changing her."

Chloe shook her head. "What happened?"

Celestine shrugged her shoulders. "I don't know, but she looks different, acts different."

Chloe sighed. "What are you trying to say?"

"You know those little tufts of hair on her head?"

Chloe nodded.

"They're starting to connect, and her face doesn't look as scarred anymore."

Chloe raised her eyebrows.

"What's she saying?" Hud studied her.

"Aunt Ed doesn't seem to be the only one undergoing some sort of conversion. Apparently, Letty's experiencing something herself."

"And she's not as mean, anymore." Celestine pressed her lips together in a wry smile.

"In what way?"

"When I tried to appear just now, she didn't chase me away like she usually does."

"So that's why we haven't heard from you lately." Chloe turned to Hud. "Letty's been interfering."

"But this time, Letty almost," she hesitated, "smiled. That's when I noticed her face and hair. It's like she's growing new skin and hair."

"Why? How?"

Celestine shook her head. "I don't know. For some reason, she's just changing."

"And what did you mean with your chicken-crossing-the-street riddle?"

"WHY DOES A CHICKEN . . . CROSS THE STREET? . . . SHE SEES A GUY . . . SHE'D LIKE . . . TO MEET . . . . BURMA-SHAVE." Clapping her hands, Celestine giggled. "My sister, silly. Ed's falling in love all over again."

"What?" Chloe raised her eyebrows.

"This conversion you mentioned?" Celestine studied her.

Chloe nodded "Yeah?"

"You're right. It's a conversion of Ed's heart, but it's part religion and part romance." Celestine squealed like the teenager she was. "I have a feeling."

"About what?"

She spoke in a childish, sing-song voice. "That's for me to know and you to find out."

Then, with a wink, Celestine was gone.

⸻ ◇ ⸻

When Edwina and Jake met them at the car, Chloe noticed how refreshed her aunt's face looked. Grinning, she glanced at her watch and gave a low whistle.

"That must have been some debate. Who won?"

Jake and Hud chuckled, but Edwina seemed detached, as if her thoughts were elsewhere. She smiled pleasantly but said nothing.

As soon as they got into the back seat, Edwina lay her head against Jake's shoulder and drifted off. Jake put his arm around her shoulders.

"She wore herself out."

"What happened?" Chloe glanced behind her. "I've never seen Aunt Ed react this way before."

"It started out as a debate with Father David. Turned into a discussion."

His eyes twinkled, and then he chuckled to himself.

Chloe could not help smiling along with him. "Then what?"

"One thing led to another." He shrugged. "Long story short, Ed went to confession."

"What?"

"Father David's smooth. Poor Ed never saw it coming." He chuckled again.

"How long has it been since she's gone to confession?"

"Not sure." Jake shook his head. "From what she said during our initial conversation with Father David, I'm willing to bet it's been sixty years."

Hud glanced at her through the rearview mirror.

"Maybe that's why she looks so peaceful."

Jake looked down at her sleeping form and smiled.

"Maybe."

⸺⸺ ☙ ⸺⸺

When they stopped in front of the house, Edwina opened her eyes.

"Where are we?"

"Home," said Chloe.

She looked at Jake's shoulder that she had been using as a pillow and sat up straight.

"Oh, I must have nodded off."

Chloe shared a secret grin with Jake.

"Why don't you two come in for some coffee and cake?"

"Sorry," said Hud. "I've got a sunset cruise starting in an hour."

As Edwina stifled a yawn, Jake glanced at her. "Maybe another time. Ed's tired." Then Jake's eyes twinkled again. "But Saturday's the Fourth of July. Why don't we go into Green Bay for the fireworks?"

"Fire Over The Fox Fireworks." Nodding, Hud turned to Chloe. "What do you think?"

"Great idea. Think you'll be up for it, Aunt Ed?"

"And why wouldn't I?" Her eyes challenged Chloe's. Then, grimacing, she heaved a sigh. "Actually, I think it's a fine idea." She turned to Jake. "Let's plan on it."

He smiled. "Want to hang on to that book awhile?"

Edwina looked down at her hand. She was still holding the catechism.

"Maybe."

She gave him a twisted grin, and he chuckled to himself.

As they waved goodbye to Hud's truck, Chloe turned to Edwina.

"How about you? Could you go for some coffee and cake?"

"I could at that. Maybe it'll wake me up." She took a deep breath. "Today took a lot out of me."

"Why is that?"

Chloe unlocked the door and held it open.

"It's been nearly sixty years since I've been to confession. During that time, I've railed against God, against man," she turned to Chloe, "against one man in particular, and against people in general."

"So what made you decide to go today?"

Chloe started the coffee maker and set out cups.

Edwina gave a half grin as she set down the book.

"I don't know. I started out reading the catechism to prove Jake wrong." She gave a wry chuckle. "Then the more I read, the more it made sense."

"Yet, when we arrived, you were arguing with Jake?"

Edwina gave her a sharp look. "You said you hadn't heard."

Chloe bit her lip. "Maybe just a little."

Edwina grumbled. "After sixty years, I couldn't give in without a fight."

"So that's why you wanted to debate Father David?"

She shrugged. "Who knows? Maybe it's been so long I needed to think I was controlling it." Her smile was twisted. "Maybe I just needed an excuse to meet with a priest, test the waters."

"So how were the waters?" Chloe glanced at her as she sliced the coffee cake.

Edwina took a deep breath. Though her eyes rested on the kitchen table, she seemed to be looking inward.

"The hardest part was facing myself." Edwina glanced at Chloe. "The next hardest thing was facing the person who was standing in for God." Edwina muttered, "*In persona Christi.*"

"Was Father David intimidating?" She set plates in front of them.

Edwina shook her head. "Not at all. He was very patient while I stumbled through the past sixty years of transgressions and failings." Then Edwina chuckled. "The strange part was, a fire extinguisher was just inside his office door. I kept wondering if he'd need it after hearing all my sins."

Chloe grinned. "Did he?"

Edwina fell silent. After a moment, she whispered, "The truth?"

Chloe nodded.

"When he asked if there was anything else . . ." Edwina's lip trembled.

Chloe debated whether to hug her or pretend not to notice. She brought over the coffee cake, giving her aunt time to collect herself.

Edwina gulped. "I burst into tears."

"Oh, Aunt Ed."

Chloe sat across from her, taking her hand.

Her face screwed up, as if she was about to cry, but Edwina took a deep breath, composing herself.

"Father David handed me a box of tissues and said . . ." Tears formed in her eyes, but she cleared her throat and barked, "Isn't that coffee done yet?"

Chloe jumped up and poured.

Again, Edwina took a deep breath. "Chloe, I've probably broken every commandment over the course of my life, yet . . ." She cleared her throat. "Do you know what he said to me?"

She shook her head.

"He said, 'That was beautiful.'"

As the tears rolled down Edwina's cheeks, Chloe put her arms around her.

"I'm sure he meant it."

Her eyes red, her lashes wet, Edwina looked up at her.

"Those words came from his heart." She swallowed. "And when he absolved me, I felt surrounded by love and light. I could almost feel my grandmother and my sister holding me, hugging me."

Chloe smiled inwardly. *Maybe they were.*

⚬

The next morning, Rose stopped by.

"Ready to scavenge?"

"Scavenge?" Chloe chuckled at her choice of words.

Rose shrugged. "All right, ready to find some herbs and wildflowers?"

"I sure am."

Chloe followed Rose along a sunny path that led to a county road. The roadside was dappled with showy, white blooms on tall, purple stalks.

"What're these?"

"White Wild Indigo." Rose smiled. "Pretty, aren't they?"

Nodding, Chloe inhaled the blossoms. "But they don't have any scent." She turned toward the girl. "What do they use these for, besides bouquets?"

"They used to boil the roots to treat eczema."

Chloe looked at the red and yellow flowers nearby. "What are these upside-down flowers called?"

"Columbine."

"Were they used for anything medicinal?"

"They used the crushed seeds for headaches." Then, her eyes twinkling, Rose gave her a mischievous grin.

Chloe smiled back. "What?"

"They also used to make love potions out of them."

"Really?" Chloe's mind touched on Hud.

"But use only a little. Too much is poisonous."

Swallowing a grin, Chloe scrutinized her. "Do you think I might use it on . . . anyone you know?"

Rose pursed her lips and hunched her shoulders. "I don't know." Avoiding looking at her, she added, "I think my brother likes you."

"You do? Why?"

She shrugged. "He just spends a lot of time with you, even more than he spent with Cherie."

At hearing the name, Chloe inhaled sharply. She remembered the girl from the powwow.

"Had she been his girlfriend?"

Rose nodded without meeting her eyes.

Chloe bent down, pretending to study the red and yellow blossoms. Then she noticed her henna tattoo and recalled their argument over Cherie.

"What happened to her?"

"I don't know."

"Well, when was the last time you saw her?"

Rose shrugged. "Just before you moved here."

The sun slipped under a cloud. Chloe glanced up at the sky and saw a passing cloud overhead. *Letty, was this your doing after all?* She turned to Rose.

"Haven't you seen her since?"

"Once, in the grocery store." Rose met her eyes. "I'm glad he's not going to marry her."

Chloe squinted. "Why?"

"I want him to marry you."

Chloe opened her mouth but did not know what to say.

"That's sweet of you, Rose, but . . ."

"But what?"

Grinning, she met Chloe's eyes. Now that she had mentioned what was on her mind, Rose seemed to be her usual, outgoing self.

Chloe wore a half-smile. "No one's said anything to anyone about marriage."

———— ◇ ————

The Fourth of July dawned sunny and bright. Chloe made a waffle brunch with strawberries, blueberries, and whipped cream.

"Red, white, and blue." Edwina's eyes opened wide. "It looks so festive."

"I know how much you like berries." Chloe smiled. "Might as well enjoy them while they're in season."

"Gather ye rosebuds . . ." Edwina's eyes lit up.

After breakfast, Chloe took coffee onto the back porch, where Edwina sat, smoking her cigar. Then she cleared the table and put the finishing touches on the brochure for the Burn Rehabilitation Center.

When she finished, she smiled. *I think Hud'll like this.*

That afternoon, Hud knocked on the door. When Chloe answered, he lightly kissed her lips.

"Ready?"

She nodded. "But first there's something I want to show you." Taking him by the hand, Chloe led him to the dining room table and showed him the brochure. "This is a four panel fold, double-parallel brochure."

"I'd wondered what it would look like."

She glanced up at him. "Think the center's staff will like it?"

His dimple deepening, he grinned. "It's great. They'll love it." Then he set down the brochure, put his arm around her waist, drew her to him, and whispered in her ear. "Just like I love you."

She grinned as she extricated herself from his grip. "Let me get Aunt Ed. She's napping on the back porch."

He nodded. "Meet you in the truck."

"Aunt Ed?" She saw Edwina sitting in her rocker, her head resting on her chest, the ashtray in her lap, her hand still holding her cigar.

Chloe raised her eyebrows. "Aunt Ed!"

"Huh?" She lifted her head and looked around.

"Please be careful about smoking." She glanced at the long ash on Edwina's still smoldering stub. "You could have started a fire."

"Nonsense. I've been smoking since long before you were born."

Chloe rolled her eyes. "Promise me you'll be more careful."

Grumbling, Edwina snuffed out the ember in the ashtray and stood up.

"Is Jake here?"

Chloe nodded. "He and Hud are waiting for us in the truck."

⸎

They parked near Broadway and Shawano so Edwina would not have far to walk. Then they strolled along the farmer's market, stopping to look at the assorted fruits, vegetables, arts, and crafts.

"Oh, look." Chloe pulled Hud to a stop as they came to a produce stand. "Those purple and golden-orange heads. Are they—?"

"Cauliflower." Hud nodded. "They taste like the regular white heads, mild and sweet, but the orange and purple heads are supposed to be higher in antioxidants."

"Their colors are stunning."

They passed another vendor with a long line of people. Chloe read the sign painted on the truck.

"Booyah." She turned to Hud. "What's booyah?"

"Originally, it was a corruption of the French word bouillon, just easier to spell." He grinned.

She chuckled. "That's for sure."

"But now even the recipe's different. Bouillon was just a broth. Now, it's a chicken-based soup with carrots, potatoes, onions, and even bits of beef or pork." He squeezed her hand. "Want to try some?"

She looked at the long queue. "Judging from all these people, it's good stuff." She smiled up at him. "Sure. Why don't you get in line while I find a table for Aunt Ed and Jake? Be right back."

Chloe found a picnic table in the shade and helped Edwina get settled. When she returned, Hud was talking to the people in front of him. She slid her hand into his and smiled until she saw who was chatting with him.

"You remember Cherie," said Hud.

How could I forget? She raised an eyebrow and then forced a stiff smile. "Of course."

"And this is her sister, Amy, and their friends, Frank and . . ."

"Steve," said the second man. "I didn't catch your name."

"I'm Chloe," she glanced at Cherie. "Hud's friend."

Chloe did her best to be polite, chatting until their orders came.

184

"Enjoy the fireworks," Hud called after them as they left with their food.

Cherie turned back to him and winked. "We'll probably run into each other before then." She smiled. "Why don't we watch it together?"

"Wish we could," called Chloe, "but we have other plans." She forced another smile, then turned stony eyes toward Hud as she let out an exasperated sigh.

"What?" He hunched his shoulders.

"This is the second time I've left you for a minute to come back and find you connecting with Cherie."

"They were in line ahead of me." He opened his dark eyes wide. "What was I supposed to do? Ignore them?"

"Aren't you the one who said there aren't any coincidences?"

He shrugged. "Sometimes there are."

They stood silently in line until their order was ready. Then Chloe led the way back to Jake and Edwina, who were deep in conversation.

When Edwina saw them, she checked her watch.

"That was fast."

"Not really." Chloe pinched her lips together as she set down the cups.

"This smells so good," said Jake, inhaling, grinning. "Don't remember the last time I had booyah, but it reminds me of my youth." He shared a smile with Edwina.

Raising her eyebrow, Chloe looked from him to her aunt and back again. *What's going on here?*

Jake said grace before they began eating. Then he turned toward Edwina.

"Do you remember when our gang used to make booyah together?"

She nodded slowly, as if the details were coming back gradually.

"I recall a bonfire and a big kettle on a tripod, bubbling away over an open fire. Everybody brought something—salted pork, potatoes, carrots, or cabbage." Her eyes sparkling, she smiled, looking years younger. "Depending on what we brought, the booyah was different every time." She glanced at Chloe. "We didn't have a recipe."

"We just boiled water and added whatever people had." Jake caught Edwina's eye, and they chuckled together, reminiscing.

Chloe looked on silently. Refusing to catch Hud's eyes, she turned inwardly. *Letty? Celestine? Are you up to something?* She touched her necklace, but Celestine did not appear. She sighed.

"What's wrong?" Hud reached for her hand.

"Nothing."

Twisting, pretending to look at something, she pulled her hand out of reach.

After finishing the soup, they walked around the farmer's market another hour, looking at the produce, flower arrangements, arts, and crafts.

"I know a waterfront restaurant, where we can sit on the patio and watch the fireworks in comfort." Hud looked from face to face. "Is anyone else ready to sit down?"

Edwina groaned. "Sounds good."

"That would be perfect." Jake's eyes twinkled.

Chloe squinted as she watched them. *What is Jake up to?* She touched her necklace, and Celestine appeared, grinning ear to ear.

With a girlish squeal, she asked, "Can you believe it?"

Not wanting to speak out loud, Chloe shrugged.

"This is it!"

Again, Chloe shrugged.

"This is what I've . . ." Celestine grinned. "I've just realized lately . . ."

Chloe mouthed, "What?"

"This is what I've been waiting for."

Chloe's eyebrow shot up. She mouthed more than asked, "What about Jake?"

Celestine contemplated.

"I thought he was what I wanted, but that was Letty thinking through me." She glanced at Jake and Edwina and smiled. "*They* are what I want, not *him*."

"Want to come with me to get the truck?" Hud gave her a slow smile.

Chloe glanced at him. When she looked back, Celestine was gone.

"Okay."

His smile turned into a grin. Then he turned to Jake.

"Why don't you and Miss Ed meet us at the corner? We'll bring the truck around so you don't have to walk so far."

Nodding, Jake's eyes lit up. "Perfect."

As Hud and Chloe walked back to the truck, he turned to her.

"I hope you're not going to let a simple coincidence ruin our night."

Sighing, she hunched her shoulders. "I don't know what to think." She looked up into his dark eyes and wanted to hold him, hug him. Instead, she told him Celestine's revelation. "Something's going on. I can feel it. I just don't know what it is."

"Why do you say that?"

She took his hand. "Hud, I can't help believing, not the two of us, but the *four* of us are being manipulated. Wouldn't you agree Jake's behaving peculiarly?"

"He's just enjoying himself . . . the way you should be." He smiled as he gently squeezed her hand. "You're reading way too much into this. Relax and have fun tonight. Remember, you're still supposed to be recovering from the accident."

She nodded. "You're right." Giving him a kiss, she let go his hand and took his arm instead, drawing him closer. "Thanks for reminding me."

"That's more like it."

As they brought the truck to the corner, Chloe watched Edwina and Jake. They were holding hands like teenagers.

Jake helped Edwina up into the truck and then went around to the other side.

"Where's this restaurant you mentioned?" Jake asked.

"On the other side of the river, right along the waterfront." Hud glanced at Chloe and whispered, "Just hope we can get seats on the patio. They don't take reservations."

Twenty minutes later, the maître d' was seating them at a table overlooking the Fox River. They situated their chairs so they could all watch the fireworks. Jake sat on the outside with Ed next to him. Chloe sat beside her with Hud on her right.

"Perfect." Hud looked out across the water and glanced at them. "It's just about dusk. The fireworks should be starting any minute."

They ordered platters of munchies. Edwina and Jake ordered coffee.

"I'll have a chocolate lab porter," said Hud.

"A chocolate lab?" Chloe grinned. "It sounds like a dog."

He laughed. "Maybe, but it tastes wonderful. Try one."

When the waitress brought their order, Chloe agreed. "Delicious."

Aunt Ed brought out her flask and poured a little brandy into her and Jake's coffee.

Just as the sun set, Jake turned toward Edwina.

"Before the stars come out tonight, I want to give you one of your own."

"A star?" Tilting her head, Edwina looked up at him.

Smiling mischievously, Jake handed her a small box.

As she opened its lid, she gasped. "A star sapphire." She held it in the candle-light, and a star reflected in its surface."

Edwina turned toward him. "It's beautiful but . . ."

"Ed, I tried to do this sixty years ago."

Bringing her hands toward her mouth in a prayerful pose, Edwina gasped again.

"I'm hoping you'll say yes again, the second time." Jake watched her closely.

Chloe touched her pendant, and Celestine appeared, dancing around their table.

"This is it. This is it!"

Chloe glanced at Hud. His jaw slack, he seemed as taken by surprise as she. She turned back to watch her aunt.

As Edwina smiled, years fell away from her face. In the candlelight, Chloe glimpsed the young woman she had once been.

"Yes, Jake Beaulieu, I'd be honored to be your wife."

Her hand still on the pendant, Chloe watched Celestine skip around the table, jumping for joy.

"Finally. Finally!"

As Chloe watched the girl, her eyes narrowed. *She'd been so adamant about loving Jake.*

"What?" Celestine stopped hopping about. Her broad smile dissolving, she stared at Chloe.

A shout drew everyone's attention as the night's first firecracker soared and exploded in the sky. And then another and another.

Chloe pretended to drop her napkin. Motioning to Celestine, she leaned down to whisper.

"Until tonight, you'd said you loved Jake, yet you seem happy for Aunt Ed. Why?"

"I also said I wanted to right the wrong I caused. The only way that can happen is if Ed marries Jake."

"But you seemed so passionate about your undying love for him."

"Like I said earlier," Celestine sighed, "I thought he was what I wanted, but now I understand Letty was thinking through me. *They* are what I want, not *him*. Letty made me think her thoughts were my own. She made me 'feel' things I didn't actually feel."

Chloe opened her eyes wide. "Like thinking you loved Jake, feeling you'd never stop loving him."

The girl nodded.

Chloe grabbed her napkin and sat up, looking left and right to see if anyone had noticed her absence. Most people were too busy watching the fireworks. Jake was kissing Edwina. But, an eyebrow cocked, Hud was watching her.

Chloe leaned toward him and whispered, "Celestine's happy about the proposal." Both of his eyebrows shot up. "She is? Why?"

"Apparently, Letty's been manipulating her, Jake, and Aunt Ed for decades," she grimaced, "which worries me."

Hud's eyebrows knitted together. "Why?"

She took a deep breath. "I can't shake the feeling she's behind 'us.'"

"What do you mean, 'us'?"

"Us." Gesturing to the two of them, she hunched her shoulders. "You and me, our attraction to each other—I feel Letty's behind it. After seeing you with Cherie . . . twice . . . it's obvious her feelings for you aren't over."

He rolled his eyes. "Chloe, let's not start this again."

Taking his eyes off Edwina, Jake turned to them. "What do you kids have to say?"

Chloe put on a happy face. "Congratulations, you two!" Standing up, she first gave Edwina a hug and then Jake.

Hud stood up to shake his hand and then leaned over to hug Edwina's shoulders.

"Couldn't happen to two nicer people," he said.

"Hope you realize you're making a lot of . . ." Chloe chose her word carefully, "souls happy with your marriage."

Jake looked up at Hud. "Now I have something to ask you. Will you be my best man?"

Hud grinned. "It'd be my privilege."

Edwina glanced from Jake to Chloe. "Would you—?"

Chloe smiled ear to ear. "I'd be thrilled."

"To do what?" Edwina pretended to give her a sharp look. "I was going to ask you if you'd go shopping with me." Then she grinned. "Just kidding. Would you be my maid of honor?"

Chloe grinned back. "I'd be happy to do both." She hugged her again. "I'm so glad for you, Aunt Ed." She took Jake's hand. "For both of you."

"It's high time we got married." Jake squeezed her hand as he glanced at Ed. "I've been waiting sixty years to make this girl my wife."

Several fireworks went off in close succession. Chatter paused on the patio as everyone watched the sky.

"Have you set a date?" Chloe looked from one to the other.

"I say the sooner, the better." Ed caught Jake's eye. "We've wasted too much time as it is."

Jake reached out for her hand. "Is tomorrow too soon?"

"Tomorrow's Sunday," said Edwina. Nothing's open on Sunday—"

"Except church." Jake smiled. "We can talk to Father David, make the arrangements."

Chloe thought of Letty and Celestine. "Could we go early?"

"Why?" All three looked at her.

"Let's just say it's a 'God prod.'"

Hud grinned. "A what?"

Chloe returned a shy smile. "I call it a 'God prod.' You know, when a little voice inside tells you to do something?"

Hud put his arm around her shoulders. "Sure."

Another burst of fireworks made them look skyward. As the sparks drifted into the bay and new bursts appeared, Hud turned to them.

"This star-spangled night calls for sparkling wine."

He motioned to the waitress. When she returned with champagne and glasses, Hud proposed a toast.

"To Miss Ed and Pop-pop. May their wedding be worth every moment of its wait."

—— ◊ ——

After Hud dropped them off at the house, Edwina sat at the dining room table.

"There's a bottle of wine in the pantry. Why don't you bring it out and have a glass with me? I'm too wound up to go to bed."

Though Chloe was tired, she smiled.

"Sure. Tonight's definitely your night to celebrate." She brought out the wine and a plate of cubed cheese. After pouring, she lifted her glass. "To you and Jake. May you enjoy many happy years together!"

Ed nodded slowly as she glanced at her casted arm. Then she looked at Chloe.

"None of this would've happened if I hadn't broken my wrist and you hadn't come to stay with me."

Chloe smiled, swirling the wine in her glass. "Funny how life works out, isn't it?" She inhaled and then drank, savoring her wine.

"It's more than 'worked out.'" Edwina sipped her wine. "I think you've worked a miracle."

Chloe's smile turned into a snicker. "I didn't do anything except stumble across Celestine's old jewelry box."

"But you were receptive to it, open-minded." Edwina sighed. "I wasn't."

Chloe shook her head. "It wasn't just me. It was . . . conditioning. Celestine told me I used to live here."

Ed nodded as she sipped again. "For the first few months after you were born, you and your parents stayed here."

"Celestine said I could see her, hear her, when I was a baby. She said she used to tell me stories, but as I got older, my mind partly closed. Although I could still see her in my dreams as a child, I had lost the ability to communicate with her when awake. Maybe it was that early connection that let the stone work for me."

"Is she here now?"

Chloe touched her necklace, and Celestine appeared, doing a cartwheel. Grinning from ear to ear, she was bursting with enthusiasm.

"Tell Ed I'm so happy for her!"

"Oh, she's here all right."

"And that I'm happy for her. Tell her. Tell her!"

Chloe swallowed a grin. "And she's delighted for you and Jake."

Edwina sighed. "I'm glad to hear it. Maybe now she can find peace."

As she heard the words, Celestine sobered. "Peace." She blinked, as if processing the concept. Then she turned toward Chloe. "Before you saw me, I was so lonely. Except when Letty bullied me around, I just wandered alone in a no man's land. I wasn't here. No one could see me, hear me. But I wasn't 'there,' either. All I could do was think the thoughts Letty forced on me, or regret the wrong I'd done to Ed and Jake."

Edwina watched Chloe's face. "What's she saying?"

"Celestine had been lost, caught in a kind of limbo."

"And now?" Edwina watched intently.

"Now?" Celestine stood between them, in front of Edwina, trying to communicate directly. "Once my wrong's righted . . ." She stopped mid-sentence, her eyes narrowing, as if she was trying to work out a puzzle. "I don't know why, but once things are as they were meant to be, I believe I can move on."

"You mean," Chloe asked, "after Jake and Aunt Ed marry, you can move on?"

Celestine nodded.

"Move on?" Edwina looked right through her into Chloe's face.

"Whether it's self-imposed or enforced, Celestine hasn't been able to leave her shadow world. Her guilt has held her back." Chloe gave a wry smile as Celestine stepped aside so she could see Edwina. "Your marriage to Jake will return events to where they should have been, and she believes that will set her free."

"After all these years." Edwina nodded thoughtfully as she sipped her wine. Then she glanced at Chloe. "In a way, I've been caught in a shadow world, too."

"How so?"

Edwina gestured to their surroundings. "Not living, just existing here in bitterness for the past sixty years, I was only a few blocks away from Jake, yet I never spoke to him. Instead, I blamed him, resented him for things he never did." She sighed. "We each create our own self-imposed hell."

Chloe smiled. "And now?"

"Now?" Edwina's eyes lit up like a young girl's. "At the ripe old age of eighty, I can finally begin to live."

Both Ed and Celestine spoke in sync. "I'll be free."

CHAPTER 11

"When you were born,
you cried and the world rejoiced.
Live your life in a manner
so that when you die
the world cries and you rejoice."
— NATIVE AMERICAN PROVERB

The next morning, the four of them attended Our Lady of Good Help. Just before Mass, Chloe spoke privately with Father David. When she returned to the pew, she knelt in prayer, not speaking to anyone.

As Father David stepped up to the pulpit, he gazed over the congregation and smiled.

"The Mass is a place where you can lose yourself. For an hour, you don't have to control your life. You can let go and let God. On this very spot, in 1859, Our Lady asked Adele Brise to bring the good news of Jesus Christ to others. Today, the Mass calls upon us to do the same thing through a series of requests and replies. The first part of Mass, the reading of the Word, is an invitation, as well as a challenge." He raised his eyebrow. "It calls us to respond.

"Next, the Creed asks us to believe, to accept Jesus as our Lord and Savior, and to live our lives in faith. The Offertory requests that we give of our time, our talent, and our treasure. From all God's given us, what will we return in love?

"The Eucharist is the Body and Blood of Christ, where we become one in spirit with Him. It asks if we'll receive the Body of Christ to become His hands and His voice in this world. It's spiritual, yet it's visceral."

Visceral. The word resonated with Chloe. *Spiritual, yet visceral.* Nodding to herself, she recalled the Sunday she had felt nauseous yet had forced herself to go to church, thinking the nausea would pass. As the Mass progressed, she had felt worse and worse. Then she received Communion. When she swallowed the Host, she immediately began feeling better. Within moments, the nausea had left. *It impacted me directly, physically.*

"Finally, the Dismissal assigns us our role in the world. It asks us to carry out the unique mission God's given each of us for making His Word come alive for others."

After he finished the Homily, Father David's eyes momentarily rested on Chloe.

"Today's Mass intentions are for Celestine Clark and Letty Malone."

Chloe felt Hud's eyes on her. Jake and Edwina, in the pew in front of them, half turned, but she did not look at them. Instead, she clasped her pendant and smiled to herself when Celestine appeared. No cartwheels, no riddles, the girl wore a solemn half-smile.

"Your prayers are a gift, Chloe. Thank you." As she faded, she motioned toward Edwina with her chin. "Watch."

As had happened in the crypt, Chloe saw two women seated beside Edwina, one on each side. Heads huddled together, first on one side, then on the other, they seemed to be whispering to her.

From her great-aunt's head movements, it appeared two conversations were occurring simultaneously. Edwina would nod to her left, then tilt her head to the right, as if listening. A light radiated from the woman on Edwina's left, seated between her and Jake.

Again, the three women seemed so caught up in their conversations, they were in their own world, but by concentrating, Chloe again began to hear their whispers.

"Jake loves you. He always has."

Edwina nodded. Then, as the woman on her right spoke, she half turned toward Edwina.

"Let bygones be bygones."

Chloe caught her breath. *It's Letty, but she looks and sounds so different.*

Along with the sparse patches of thin hair hanging from her scalp, Letty's hair seemed to be growing back. Chloe glimpsed a side view of her profile. Even her badly disfigured face seemed less scarred, but it was Letty's words that astounded her.

"Let bygones be bygones."

As she "heals" outwardly, could it be a reflection of her soul?

After Mass, Chloe shook Father David's hand.

"Thank you for saying this Mass for Letty and Celestine."

"All souls need prayers, especially the troubled ones."

"And that other thing we discussed." Chloe raised her eyebrow. "If it's all right with you, let me ask Aunt Ed the name of the cemetery, and I'll email you."

Back in the truck, Hud turned to her. "What was that conversation with Father David all about?"

"Something Celestine said gave me an idea, another 'God prod.'" She turned toward the back seat. "Aunt Ed, where's Celestine buried?"

"In the family plot in Sturgeon Bay. Why?"

"Father David and I were talking and . . ."

⁓ ❖ ⁓

The following Wednesday, the four of them met Father David at the cemetery. When Edwina led them to Celestine's grave, they saw that a deep, narrow hole had been dug in it.

Chloe took Letty's pin from a small silk bag and handed it to Father David. He said a short prayer over it, sprinkled it with holy water, and handed it back.

"May you finally be at peace, Letty Malone." Slipping the pin back in its bag, Chloe closed it. "We're your family, and we haven't forgotten you. Your 'remains' are buried in the family plot, on consecrated ground. You'll be surrounded by family for eternity."

With that, she dropped the bag in the earth.

"May her soul, Celestine Clark's soul, and the souls of all the faithful departed through the mercy of God rest in peace." Father David led them in making the sign of the cross.

"You go on," said Edwina, not lifting her eyes from the grave. "I'll join you in a couple minutes."

Jake, Chloe, and Hud walked Father David to his car.

"Would two weeks from today be too soon to hold the wedding?" Jake watched Father David's reaction.

His smile came easily. "As long as we meet for the pre-Cana discussion, it'll be fine."

Jake shook hands with him. "We'll see you first thing tomorrow morning."

When Edwina joined them, her eyes were red and swollen. Jake put his arm around her shoulders and, sighing, drew her to him.

For several seconds, no one said a word.

Finally, Hud broke the silence. "How about lunch?" He looked from face to face. "Is anyone in the mood for pizza? I know a café at the marina that serves the best wood-fired pizza in Door County."

After a ten-minute drive, they parked by the waterfront. Then they climbed to the second floor and found a table on the deck overlooking the harbor. Below them, they watched the tall ship and yacht owners tote their belongings from ship to shore in small carts.

As a stiff breeze blew through Chloe's hair, Hud leaned over and brushed a wisp from her eyes.

"Do you think blessing and burying Letty's 'remains' on consecrated ground will put her spirit to rest?"

"Hope so," Chloe lifted her shoulders, "but I'm not sure."

"I should think burying her brooch in Celestine's grave would give her closure."

Sighing, Chloe answered mechanically. "Time'll tell."

"Where are you?" Hud focused his dark eyes on hers. "You seem miles away."

His words broke her trance. She blinked and then met his eyes.

"Sorry, I just can't stop thinking how Letty's manipulated Celestine, Aunt Ed, Jake . . . even you and me."

Hud watched as the waitress brought the sizzling, deep-dish, Chicago-style pizza to the table.

"This ought to take your mind off her."

Inhaling the scents of the cheese and sausage wood-fired pizza, Chloe nodded.

"You're right. It smells wonderful. Suddenly, I'm starving."

⁓⁓⁓ ◊ ⁓⁓⁓

After finishing their late lunch, they sat back, chatting quietly, watching the ships sail into harbor and dock.

Then Chloe noticed the traffic backing up on the bridge across the bay.

"What's going on?"

Hud grinned. "They're getting bridged."

"Bridged?" She squinted. "What's that?"

"Watch."

His tone reminded her of Celestine's advice. She looked, but instead of seeing two women seated beside Edwina, she saw the drawbridge raise to let a tall ship pass through.

"How interesting."

"I just love ships." Jake strained his neck to see. "Always have."

"You have, haven't you? The Mariners Museum is just across the street." Edwina caught his eye. "Since you like ships so much, do you want to see it?"

"Sure."

As Chloe watched Jake's eyes light up with enthusiasm, she saw the similarity to Hud. *He must have looked just like him in his younger days.*

In the museum, they wandered through the rooms—watching the dioramas, listening to the recordings, and reading about the history of watercraft built in the area, from dugout canoes to modern ships.

Hud suddenly looked at his watch. "Time to go."

"What?"

As they turned to look at him, he grinned and held up four tickets. "The Chicago Fire Boat tour leaves in five minutes." Pointing out the window, he added, "That's it. The fire-engine-red boat docked out back."

Opening her eyes wide, Chloe glanced up at him. "When did you get these tickets?"

"When you were busy watching the sea dogs video."

She watched Jake's eyes light up. Then she reached up to kiss Hud.

"You're really thoughtful. Something tells me your grandfather's going to love it."

As soon as they walked aboard the gangplank, the first mate began the tour, showing them around the 1937 retired Chicago fireboat. Within minutes, they were underway, cruising along the canal connecting the waters of Green Bay to Lake Michigan.

At the mouth of Sturgeon Bay, near the Green Bay side, they spotted a lighthouse.

"That's the Sherwood Lighthouse." The first mate gave them a mischievous smile. "Anyone here believe in ghosts?"

Their foursome exchanged looks but said nothing. Several other passengers giggled, while three people raised their hands.

"I'm not saying I do, and I'm not saying I don't believe in ghosts." The first mate grinned. "But a lot of people who've visited Sherwood Lighthouse believe it's haunted. Residual energy, they call it, something left behind after Minnie Hesh died suddenly."

"I remember hearing of her," whispered Edwina. "My grandmother knew her."

"Minnie was one of the few women to keep a lighthouse, and she kept it spotless. Years later, after it was automated, the lighthouse became a vacation getaway for Coast Guard members and their families. One time, a vacationing couple, who was too tired to do the dinner dishes, left them for the next morning. After they went to bed, they heard footsteps, a woman's voice, and laughter, and then the sound of clattering pots and pans coming from the kitchen.

"'Damn it, Minnie,' called out the husband. 'If you're going to make that much racket, you might as well do the dishes.'"

"Did she?" asked a young passenger. "Do the dishes, I mean?"

The first mate nodded. "As the story goes, she did. Guess she was some kind of clean freak."

Chloe raised her eyebrows as she looked at Edwina. "Is that true?"

Edwina shrugged. "Who's to say?"

"Is this the only lighthouse around here?" asked a passenger.

"There are two more on the Lake Michigan end of the Sturgeon Bay Ship Canal," said the first mate. "The North Pierhead Light, called Big Red, and the 1899 Ship Canal Light."

"Do we see those?"

"No, sorry, not on this cruise," said the first mate. "But you can drive there."

His face animated, Jake looked from Hud to Edwina to Chloe. "Want to go?"

Hud chuckled. "Sure. Why not?"

⚓

Several hours later, they turned into the parking lot of the Sturgeon Bay Ship Canal's east entry. They could see the lighthouses in the distance, but the Coast Guard station and especially the "Private Property - No Access" sign made them hesitate.

"The driveway to the Canal Station light tower's open," said a coast guardsman, pointing to the painted stripe down the center. "Keep to the left side, the public side. The right side belongs to the Coast Guard station."

They followed it to the cement causeway, walking along the canal pierhead. The last rays of the sun were still glimmering in the sky when Big Red began glowing a fire-engine red.

Chloe grabbed Hud's arm, hugging him toward her. She reached up and kissed him on the neck.

Smiling, he put his arm around her shoulders. "What was that for?"

"Nothing. Everything. Just because." She grinned back at him.

Jake called to them. "It's getting dark." Glancing at Edwina, he added, "Maybe it's time we began heading back."

They retraced their steps and climbed into the truck.

Chloe turned toward the back seat. "Have ships and waterways always held a fascination for you, Jake?"

He nodded. "I would have loved to sail the Great Lakes when I was young. The closest I came was the boat rental and tour business."

Edwina said, "And canoe rentals."

Jake paused. "And canoe rentals."

She grunted.

"What?" Grimacing, Jake peered at her.

Edwina turned toward him. "If it hadn't been for canoes, maybe Celestine would still be alive today."

With a sigh, Jake rubbed his forehead. "Don't you think I've wondered that a thousand times?"

She snapped at him. "Don't you think I have?"

"Today we buried the remains of Letty—"

"In my sister's grave."

He sighed again. "What I meant was, can't we bury the hatchet?"

"I can't forget about Celestine." Edwina winced. "Her death has caused me so much pain. It's hard to let go of the bitterness."

"Letty was the cause of your pain," Jake said softly, "not canoes."

Still facing the back seat, Chloe added, "And not Jake."

"Restless spirits are still so 'human.'" Jake gave a wry smile. "They have issues they want to resolve, yet they're riddled with fear. Those souls aren't ready to accept responsibility for their mistakes. They can't forgive themselves, so they blame everyone else and in the process cause others grief."

Grimacing, Chloe shook her head. "I just hope Letty can find peace."

Edwina took a deep breath. "Restless spirits aren't the only ones who blame everyone else." Wearing a tentative smile, she looked at Jake. "Can you forgive a bitter old woman, who's been a lone wolf all her life?"

Jake kissed her. "It isn't easy to let go thought patterns and beliefs you've held most of your adult life. I struggle, too. Healing doesn't mean the damage never existed. It just means the damage no longer controls you." Then he chuckled to himself. "Lone wolf. In two weeks, you'll go from being a lone wolf to marrying into the Wolf clan."

Chloe grinned at them. "And won't that be something to howl about?"

⎯⎯⎯ ◇ ⎯⎯⎯

After Hud and Jake had seen them to the door, Chloe yawned.

"It's been a long day."

Edwina nodded. "It has, but I'm not tired. My mind just keeps going around and around about what's happened today, what's been happening this whole summer."

"I know what you mean." Stretching, Chloe added, "There've been so many transitions, shifts."

"And the biggest is yet to come."

Chloe smiled at her. "Marriage will be quite an adjustment."

Edwina grinned back. "Marrying *Jake* will be quite an adjustment."

Chloe laughed through a yawn. "Sorry, I can't keep my eyes open. Can I get you anything before I turn in?"

"No, thanks." Edwina shook her head with a wry chuckle. "I'm going to stay up awhile, keep my thoughts company."

Chloe had barely turned off the lights before she fell asleep, but it was a light, restless sleep. She would drift off and then wake from a nightmare with a start, only to have it begin all over again.

She relived the accident and saw Letty standing by the wrecked car. Her mouth open wide, she cackled a babble of words and laughter. Her clumps of wispy hair tufted out from her head, hanging in scraggly strands.

"Letty? How . . . ?"

"Can't believe your eyes, dearie?" The woman chuckled, her eyes wide and her mouth gaping, exposing her receded gums with only two crooked teeth left. As the cackling became louder and louder, Chloe woke in a cold sweat, only to fall back into another twilight sleep.

"You're so easily manipulated." The woman sneered.

"What?" Chloe opened her eyes and looked around.

"Just like your Great-Aunt Celestine, you're so easily manipulated." Letty cackled, exposing her two teeth.

200

"Leave me alone."

Letty tossed her head, her few strands of tufted hair waving.

"Miss high and mighty, has it ever occurred to you?

"What?"

"You need me."

Chloe groaned. "I need sleep. Leave me alone. Stop babbling."

"You want me to 'leave you alone,' yet without me, you'd have no one." Her hollow, bloodshot eyes bored into Chloe's.

I'm still in this dream. With that knowledge, she fell back into a fitful sleep.

"Élise, the Métisse woman, part Menominee and part French, lived with a foot in each world. She walked with the spirits, believing everything had a soul. Even a rock, a tree, had a soul. Élise warned my sister a fire was coming."

"So you knew about the fire ahead of time?"

Curling her lip, Letty scoffed. "I wouldn't listen to the repeated words of a mixed blood."

"Mixed blood." Chloe groaned in her sleep. "You didn't approve of Menominee / French intermarriages?"

"Not then. Not now."

Creasing her forehead, Chloe mumbled to herself. "Is that why you didn't want Aunt Ed to marry Jake? Is that why you're interfering with Hud and me?"

Letty shrugged. "I didn't believe Élise's warning any more than I believe Jake's or Hud's empty words."

"But she told the truth."

Chloe woke with a start, looked around, and then drifted back into a semi-dream state.

"Let bygones be bygones."

"Huh?"

"Let bygones be bygones."

She caught her breath. *Letty?*

Chloe glimpsed a side view of her profile. Along with the sparse patches of thin hair hanging from her scalp, Letty's hair seemed to be nearly grown back. Even her badly disfigured face seemed less scarred.

She looks and sounds so different. Can she be healing? Chloe woke, only to fall back into another twilight sleep.

Celestine said, "Something's happened to Letty."

Chloe squinted, trying to understand. "What?"

"Something's happened that changed her. She looks different, acts different."

Half-asleep, Chloe mumbled. "She what?"

"Those little tufts of hair on her head are connecting, and her face isn't as scarred, now."

Chloe half-opened her eyes.

"And she's not as mean to me, either." Celestine hesitated, adding, "She almost smiled. That's when I noticed she's growing new skin and hair. For some reason, Letty's changing."

Chloe sat up straight in bed and realized she had been dreaming. She rolled over, punched her pillow, and drifted into a troubled sleep.

Then, feeling someone's presence, she opened her eyes to see Letty smiling down on her.

"Your complexion, your face is healed," Chloe said in surprise. "Your teeth are white, restored. Even your hair's grown back. How?"

"Don't you know?"

"No."

"You lit a candle, said a prayer for me. You had a Mass said for me and buried my remains in consecrated ground."

"Oh . . . yeah."

"You said you're my family, and you wouldn't forget me. That I'd always be surrounded by family."

"Yeah . . . I did." Chloe began to doze off.

"Chloe," said Letty. "Chloe!"

"What?" She half-woke and then began drifting.

"I didn't have anything to do with Hud's attraction to you."

Chloe could barely keep her eyes open. "Please, just let me sleep. I just want to sleep."

Letty leaned over and whispered. "You fell in love on your own."

"What? Please let me sleep." Chloe dozed off.

"Chloe," said Letty. "Chloe, wake up!"

"What?"

"Élise said the Menominees sensed a fire was coming. They could hear a distant roar, smell heat on the wind."

Still asleep, she coughed.

"They could smell the dryness, the scorched sap. They knew the risk for fire was high."

She mumbled. "They smelled smoke?"

"Yes, smoke, Chloe. Don't you smell it?"

"Smell what?"

"Smoke! Wake up, Chloe!"

Chloe woke to a thick haze. The moment she opened her eyes, the smoke stung and burned them.

"Aunt Ed!" She began coughing as she ran to Edwina's room. "Aunt Ed! Wake up!"

She flipped on the light switch. Even through the smoke, she could see Edwina was not in her bed.

Could she have fallen asleep in the living room? Coughing, she called out as she ran.

Edwina was slumped over in her chair, her hand dangling near the smoldering box of photographs and albums. Plumes of smoke curled and billowed around her, while flames licked at her chair.

"Aunt Ed, get up! Get up!" Coughing, Chloe shook her, trying to wake her, but she could not rouse her from her deep sleep.

She tried to pull her up, but the woman was dead weight. Instead, she kicked the smoldering box away from Edwina, ran into the bathroom, and soaked a towel in running water. Then she ran back and smothered the fire with the towel. Though the flames died down, she worried about smoldering embers. She filled a pail of water and poured it over the box, sending up a cloud of steam.

Coughing from the smoke and steam, Chloe tried to wake Edwina, but she seemed in a stupor.

She opened the doors and windows, trying to ventilate the house. Then she slapped Edwina's face, trying to wake her. As a last resort, she partially refilled the pail with water and threw it at her slumped head.

Edwina came to, sputtering, coughing.

"Get up, Aunt Ed. Get up! Get up!" Coughing, Chloe pulled at the arm that was not in a cast. "Get up! We need to get you out of here, into fresh air. Now! Get up!"

Shaky, Edwina wobbled to her feet. Chloe bolstered her by bracing her shoulder under the woman's arm. Slowly, they made it out the door and onto the front porch.

"Sit down while I make sure the fire's out. Then I'll get you a glass of water."

Chloe helped her sit on the stoop. Then she went back into the house.

Holding her breath, she put the soggy box into the trash can, covered it, and rolled it outside onto the driveway, away from the house. Then she went in to get Edwina a glass of water. As she passed by her chair, Chloe noticed an ashtray and a lighter.

Oh, no. Did she fall asleep while smoking?

"Drink this, Aunt Ed." Chloe handed her the glass of water. "Are you feeling all right?"

The woman nodded as she drank.

"Let me check something, and I'll be right back."

She opened the rest of the windows in the house and then got a flashlight. Outside, she lifted the trash can cover and focused the flashlight's beam inside. Chloe breathed a sigh of relief when she saw no embers or signs of anything smoldering. Then she noticed the cigar butt.

⚬

Early the next morning, Chloe called Hud and told him the story.

"Are you all right?"

Chloe smiled to herself when she heard his concerned tone. "I'm fine, just not sure how to approach Aunt Ed about this."

"And she's all right?"

"I think so. She's sleeping in, but her breathing seems regular." She grimaced. "I think I got her into the fresh air before the smoke did any damage."

"What woke you? A smoke detector?"

"Nope. Aunt Ed doesn't own one." She stopped to think. "I can't quite remember. I know I had trouble sleeping. Maybe the smoke woke me. Although . . ."

"What?"

She squinted, trying to recall. "It seems I was dreaming about . . . Letty! It was a series of connected dreams that replayed different conversations she's had with me, when I either was delirious or sleeping." Nodding to herself, it began to come back. "Letty woke me in time to save Aunt Ed and the house."

"From everything you've told me about her in the past, that sounds out of character."

"Well . . ." She hesitated, not knowing where to begin. "If it's possible for ghosts to change their appearance, I'd say Letty's undergoing some kind of transformation."

"How so?"

She described Letty's complexion and hair. Then she shared Letty's conversations.

"Did she say anything about us?"

Chloe hesitated. "Why do you ask?"

"Aren't you the one who's been so worried whether she's manipulating us, controlling our feelings for one another?"

"Yes."

"So she did say something about us. What did she say?"

"I . . . I mean, I don't remember." She crossed her fingers. "Parts of the dream are foggy."

"How convenient."

"Don't sound so suspicious. Parts are vague." *Just not that part.* She groaned inwardly. *Why don't I want to tell him? Because I don't know which of Letty's conversations to believe.* She shook her head as she changed the subject. "What I called you about is your advice regarding Aunt Ed."

His chuckle was mirthless. "Simple. First, install a smoke detector. Then, convince her to stop smoking."

She sighed. "Good advice, but what I meant was, should we tell Jake?"

"Of course we should tell him. He's going to be living under the same roof with her. He's got a right to know about it."

"Know about what?"

Chloe heard Jake's voice in the background, followed by Hud telling him about the fire. Then she heard the phone being passed.

"Is Ed all right?"

"She's fine, Jake. Just sleeping in late."

"I'll be right over."

"Jake, she—"

The phone clicked.

She looked at the dead phone in her hand. *I'd better get Aunt Ed up.*

She tapped at Edwina's door and then peeked in. "Aunt Ed, Jake's on his way over." Chloe draped a bed jacket near her. "From the tone of his voice, he'll be here any minute. You'd better put this on."

They heard the doorbell.

Chloe snickered. "He's here."

"Give me a minute to get dressed."

"Then you're all right?" Chloe watched her closely. "No ill effects from last night?"

"Other than a bruised ego?" Edwina grunted as she shook her head. "No."

They heard the doorbell again.

"I'd better get the door before a member of the Wolf clan huffs and puffs and blows it down."

Edwina gave Chloe a crooked smile. "Stall him with a cup of coffee. I'll be out in a minute."

Jake and Hud met Chloe at the door.

"Come on in."

"How is she?" On a mission, Jake started toward Edwina's room.

"She's fine." Blocking his path, Chloe grinned. "Just give her a minute to get dressed, okay?"

Jake took a deep breath. "You're sure she's all right?"

"A bruised ego, that's all." She gestured toward the table. "Have a seat. The coffee's hot, and there's some leftover cherry cobbler." When he hesitated, Chloe added, "She'll be right out."

<hr />

After Edwina and Chloe finished relating the evening's events, Jake silently watched the dappled sunlight stream into the room. Then he turned toward them.

"Midnight never has the last word. Morning's too eloquent." He glanced at Hud. "Tell Ed your ideas."

Hud shared a smile with Chloe. Then he focused on Edwina. "Install a smoke detector and quit smoking."

"Not necessarily in that order." His eyes flinty as he peered at Edwina, Jake reached for her hand. "You're lucky the only things you lost were photographs."

She sighed as she took his hand and met Hud's eyes.

"You're right. I won't argue." She grimaced. "Old habits are hard to break."

Jake's eyes softened. "Have you ever heard the tale of the two wolves?"

Edwina shook her head.

"I've heard Billy Graham first told this parable, and I've also heard it's a Native American story." Jake scratched his neck. "Either way. A wise chief was once talking to his grandson about life."

"Two wolves are struggling inside me," he said. "One's pure evil: self-pity, guilt, anger, and ego. The other's everything good and pure: hope, serenity, and faith."

He looked at his grandson. "These wolves struggle in all of us, even you."

"Which one will win?" asked the boy.

"The wolf you feed."

"Feed your faith," said Chloe. "Starve your fears."

Edwina nodded. "Point taken." She glanced at Chloe. "It seems all the women in our family struggle with which wolf to feed."

Chloe took a deep breath. "We each have our own demons to fight." She gave Hud a wry smile.

"And you say it was Letty that woke you?" Edwina asked.

"I think she finally sees us as family, not foes." Blinking, Chloe looked at the morning sun shining through the window. "Letty's beginning to see the proverbial light. I believe she's undergoing some kind of conversion."

"Maybe burying her remains in consecrated ground worked," said Edwina.

"Maybe, but something occurred to me last night. She's never had a memorial. Her name's not on that tombstone. Celestine's is." Chloe opened her eyes wide and turned toward Hud. "Remember that grove of lilac bushes?"

His eyes lit up as he nodded. "Yes. The living monument in Birch Creek for the souls lost in the Peshtigo Fire."

"Aunt Ed, do you recall the place where Letty died, where Celestine found the brooch?"

She nodded. "Yes. The community park at the south end of town."

Chloe looked from one face to the next. "Do you think anyone would object to us planting lilacs there?"

Hud squeezed her hand. "What a great idea."

"I know someone on the town board." Jake got up from the table. "Mind if I use your phone?"

⁂

Two hours later, they had bought a lilac bush at the local nursery and gotten permission to plant it. The sweetgrass smoldering, perfuming the air, they stood in a circle, watching Hud dig a hole near the park's picnic tables. Chloe carefully positioned the lilac, and Hud tamped the earth around it.

Then Jake took out his *Bible* as he glanced at them.

"I think this passage from Ecclesiastes fits the occasion."

They bowed their heads as Jake read.

". . . before the silver cord is snapped and the golden bowl is broken, and the pitcher is shattered at the spring, and the pulley is broken at the well. The dust returns to the earth as it once was, and the life breath returns to God who gave it.

Vanity of vanities . . . all things are vanity."

"Rest in peace," whispered Chloe as she walked away, crossing herself. Her hand accidentally touched her pendant, and Celestine appeared.

"This is where I found Letty's pin." She made a sour face. "I should have left it here."

"Everything happens for a reason." Keeping her voice low, Chloe turned her eyes from Celestine to Hud. "There's no such thing as coincidence."

"What?" Hud's eyes met hers.

"Celestine's here," she whispered.

He nodded knowingly.

Head tilted back, Celestine observed them. "THE WOLF . . . IS SHAVED . . . SO NEAT AND TRIM . . . RED RIDING HOOD . . . IS CHASING HIM . . . . BURMA-SHAVE."

Chloe began laughing. "Who's Red Riding Hood?"

Celestine glanced from Chloe to Edwina. "Ed." Then she glanced back. "And you. You're both chasing the wolf."

Chloe caught her breath, and Hud looked at her.

"What's she have to say?"

"She's talking in riddles, and she seems to have an attitude today."

"I KNOW . . . HE'S A WOLF . . . SAID RED RIDING HOOD . . . BUT GRANDMA DEAR . . . HE SMELLS SO GOOD . . . . BURMA-SHAVE."

Chloe raised her eyebrow. "Who's grandma?"

"Remember the good angel on Ed's shoulder?"

"Yeah." She squinted, thinking. "Are you saying she was your grandmother?"

"And Ed's."

"Teresa? The same grandmother that left Aunt Ed the hundred-dollar savings bond?"

"Bingo!" With that, she disappeared.

Hud caught her eye. "What did she have to say?"

"She's sorry she took Letty's pin." She gave him a wry grin. "And we were right."

"About what?"

"The good angel on Aunt Ed's shoulder was their grandmother, Teresa. Celestine confirmed it just now."

"You said the angel seemed to be coaching Celestine, guiding her." Hud raised his eyebrow. "Maybe we were also right about her trying to help Celestine move on."

"Once Aunt Ed and Jake marry, Celestine will have put things back the way they were meant to be."

"You mean before Letty interfered and Celestine got caught up in her vendetta."

She peered up at him. "Maybe, after the wedding, Celestine will be able to let go her regrets and move on."

"Feed the good wolf."

"Exactly."

CHAPTER 12

"Trip over love, you can get up. Fall in love and you fall forever."
— A N O N Y M O U S

The next day, Hud's mother, Barbara, joined Chloe and Ed for lunch at their house.

"The stuffed tomato salad was delicious." Barbara smiled at Chloe.

"We're so glad you could come."

"And so glad you offered to make my wedding dress," said Edwina, interrupting.

"It's my pleasure." Barbara grinned at them both. "It isn't every day you see your father-in-law marry the love of his life."

Edwina ducked her head, and Chloe chuckled.

"I do believe you're blushing, Aunt Ed."

Edwina cleared her throat. "Certainly not. I was just . . . brushing crumbs off the tablecloth."

While Edwina went through the motions, Chloe swallowed a grin as she caught Barbara's eye.

"When did you find time to buy the material, Miss Ed?"

"Actually, I've . . . I've had it packed away since the first time Jake proposed."

Chloe opened her eyes wide. "You mean you've stored that material for sixty years? Where?"

"In the cedar . . . in my hope chest at the back of your closet."

Chloe shuddered, recalling the chest that had reminded her of a coffin.

"Are you cold?" Barbara looked at her.

"No, I'm just remembering the drafty closet's creaking floors." She glanced at Edwina. "And it's so dark in there, we'll never be able to see. Why don't I drag it out into the light?" At their nods, she added, "Just give me a minute."

Chloe took a flashlight with her, laid it on the floor, and moved aside the front rack's clothes, as she had done before. This time, she felt no cold spots, no drafts, and no spider webs. *What was I so afraid of?* She grabbed hold of the chest and easily dragged it across the floorboards into her room. Then she opened her curtains to let in the sunlight.

She called, "All set, ladies."

When Edwina saw the large letter E carved into its lid, she lightly ran her fingers over it.

Chloe watched her. *What memories must it hold for her?*

As Ed lifted the lid, they saw neatly folded blankets and quilts on top. One by one, she handed them to Chloe until she reached the bottom of the chest. Then she lifted out a tissue paper covered bolt of material, caressing it with her eyes.

"This is it." Ed lovingly handed it to Barbara. Then she hesitated, holding it a beat too long, as if she was reluctant to part with it. "Do you think time's been kind to it, or has it yellowed?"

Barbara took it from her with a gentle smile and carefully unfolded it on the bed.

"Except for the outer fold, which I can cut off, it's as good as new. Maybe better. Only age can instill this subtle color." She admired the intricate pattern. "It's beautiful."

Chloe looked at the delicate pattern woven into the vintage, ivory-colored lace.

"And this is the satin underlayer." Edwina handed Barbara a second bolt.

"What style wedding gown do you want?" Barbara looked up at her.

"Something simple, tea-length."

Barbara nodded. "I know just the style, and with that length, you should have enough lace left over for a short veil."

Chloe grinned. "Looks like the only thing we'll need to shop for are your shoes." She turned toward Barbara and hugged her. "Thanks to you, Aunt Ed will have everything else she needs, and it'll all be custom made."

"Even the bouquet. That's Rose's gift to you, Miss Ed." Then, as she hugged

Chloe, Barbara whispered. "You and Miss Ed are cut from the same cloth. Fine material that stands up to time." Grinning, she winked. "I just hope you catch the bouquet."

⚬

After work, Chloe and Hud drove to Whitefish Dunes State Park along the scenic county roads. They hiked a sandy trail, following Lake Michigan's shoreline, until they came to a rocky ledge, jutting out over the water. Taking her hand in his, Hud turned to her.

"Want to look at the view?"

"Gorgeous, isn't it?"

Never taking his eyes off her, he smiled. "Yes, it is."

She chuckled as they perched themselves on the stony ridge.

"The wedding's only a week away. How do you feel about your great-aunt getting married?"

Lifting her shoulders, she grinned. "Great. How do you feel about your grandfather getting married?"

He pretended to think about it. "I don't know. Grand?" His smile faded as he gazed into her eyes. Then, reaching out, he tucked an errant strand of hair behind her ear. "How would you feel about making it a double wedding?"

Blinking, she became quiet as Letty's words came to mind.

"I didn't have anything to do with Hud's attraction to you."

Then she recalled Letty's earlier words.

"Just like your Great-Aunt Celestine, you're so easily manipulated . . . . If not Aaron, Hud. If I can't live, I can live through you."

Which is true? Does she or doesn't she control our feelings? Chloe pressed her fingers into her forehead, trying to rub away the sudden ache between her eyes.

Hud chuckled nervously.

"Don't keep me on pins and needles. There are enough of those at home, what with my mom making Miss Ed's wedding dress."

Chloe noticed how his smile deepened his dimple. She wanted to kiss that dimple, kiss those lips. *But is he voicing his feelings or Letty's projections?*

"The longer you take to answer me, the less secure I feel."

He wore a wry smile, but a small V appeared between his eyes.

"I don't know what to say."

212

He stiffened as a nervous laugh escaped his lips. "Say yes."

She grimaced. "I . . . I have to think about it."

"What's to think about? You know how I feel about you."

"That's just it." She sighed. "I honestly don't know how you feel. I can't help thinking it's Letty speaking through you."

"You've got to be kidding, Chloe." Turning her toward him, he looked into her eyes. "Please believe me when I tell you I love you."

"But what if you only think you do, like Celestine thought she loved Jake for so many decades?"

Rolling his eyes, he sighed. "It's not . . . the same . . . thing."

"How can you be so sure?" Then, as his tone registered with her, she scowled at him. "And don't use that patronizing tone of voice with me."

"Chloe, I'm trying to propose to you, not start an argument." He groaned in the back of his throat. "You can just be so darned infuriating."

"Really? Well, in that case, there's no need to continue this conversation, is there?" She scrambled to her feet. "Now, if you don't mind, I'd like to go home."

As her hand brushed against her pendant, Celestine appeared, shaking her head.

"Big mistake . . . Many make . . . Rely on horn . . . Instead of . . . Brake . . . . Burma-Shave."

Edwina was cantankerous the morning of her wedding.

"I can't get my hair right." She scowled at her wrist. "Ever since the cast came off, I've been all thumbs."

Chloe tried to hide her sigh. "Be patient. Your wrist was immobilized all those weeks. It'll take time for it to limber up again, but it will." She picked up the brush. "In the meantime, let me help."

Edwina glared at their reflection in the mirror.

"I wish Barbara would get here. What's keeping her?"

Chloe glanced at the clock. "She isn't due for ten minutes. Relax. There's plenty of time to finish the veil."

The doorbell rang.

"Who could that be?"

Shaking her head, Chloe chuckled. "It's probably Barbara."

As she reached the door, her pendant brushed against her neck, and Celestine appeared.

"MANY A WOLF . . . IS NEVER LET IN . . . BECAUSE OF THE HAIR . . . ON HIS CHINNY-CHIN-CHIN . . . . BURMA-SHAVE."

Chloe ignored her as she opened the door. "Come on in, Bar—"

Instead of Barbara, Hud stood in the doorway—rumpled, unshaven, and yawning.

Her eyebrows shot up. "Rough night? Are you just getting in, or what?"

"Good morning to you, too." He grimaced.

She shrugged. "I just meant, you look like you didn't sleep last night."

"I didn't."

"That explains the bloodshot eyes." It was the first time she had seen him since their fight. *Wonder what kept him up . . . or who.* Grimacing, she opened the door wider. "Might as well come in."

"I can't stay. I'm just delivering this." He picked up the box and brought it in. "Mom and Rose are right behind me."

"SHE EYED HIS BEARD . . . AND SAID, NO DICE . . . THE WEDDING'S OFF . . . I'LL COOK THE RICE . . . . BURMA-SHAVE."

"Not now, Celestine."

"She's here?"

"She's been here all morning." Nodding, she pointed to her neckline. "It's just low enough that my pendant keeps touching my throat."

"THE CHICK HE WED . . . LET OUT A WHOOP . . . FELT HIS CHIN AND . . . FLEW THE COOP . . . . BURMA-SHAVE."

"Celestine, if you don't stop with the jingles, I'm taking off this pendant."

"What's she saying?" His bloodshot eyes lingered on her neck.

"She's making wisecracks about your five o'clock shadow."

As he brushed his hand across his chin, she could hear the stubble. She studied his rugged appearance and—stubble or not, angry or not—she had to admit he was unquestionably the handsomest man she knew. She stifled a sigh.

"I have to run home to shower and shave before the wedding."

She peered up at him through her lashes. "So you *have* been out all night?"

As she studied his finely chiseled face, visions of him with Cherie suddenly flooded her mind.

Wearing a surly smile, he nodded. "Yeah, I've been out all night."

"With Cherie?"

Before he could answer, she heard Rose's voice.

"Hi, Chloe."

She put on a smile and hugged her. "How's the flower girl doing this morning?"

Her eyes dancing, Rose beamed. "This is such a big day. I'm so excited!"

"Has she shown you the bouquet she made?"

Chloe turned toward Barbara's voice. "Good morning. Not yet. Where is it?"

"In here."

Hud lifted up the box flaps, and she peered in. When she looked up, she saw his lips inches away from hers. She caught her breath. Then, remembering her manners, she turned to Rose.

"Aunt Ed's going to love it. It's gorgeous."

No sooner had she spoken the words than she recalled her last conver-sation with Hud. Glancing at him, she caught him staring back, and she looked away quickly.

"I'd better get going." His voice sounding strangled, he held up the box. "Where do you want this?"

"Just set it on the table." She caught his eye, wanting answers, yet afraid to hear them. Silently, her eyes implored him. *Were you out with Cherie? Do you really care about me, or is Letty playing games with us?* Then she saw Rose and Barbara watching them. Biting her lip, she stifled a sigh.

Following her gaze, he glanced at his mother and sister.

"See you at the wedding," he mumbled.

As if a last-minute impulse, he reached over and lightly kissed her neck. Chloe caught her breath—wanting to kiss him back, feel his arms around her. Then she saw Celestine, and it reminded her. *No, these feelings aren't ours. This is Letty's work in action.*

She stiffened and looked away. "Bye."

"Chloe," called Edwina, "is my daughter-in-law-to-be here?"

Daughter-in-law-to-be? Barbara? That's right. After Aunt Ed marries Jake, Hud will be my cousin. Taking a deep breath, Chloe called back, "Barbara just got here." Then she turned to her. "Aunt Ed's worried about finishing the veil in time. She's waited this long. She doesn't want to be late for her own wedding."

Chloe was still getting used to driving her new car as she chauffeured the wedding party's female members to Our Lady of Good Help. To avoid Jake accidentally seeing the bride, she parked near the outdoor chapel, as far from his car as possible. Before opening Edwina's door, she looked left and right.

"Coast's clear."

"Good." Edwina said as she stepped out of the car. "I don't want him to see me before the wedding."

Chloe and Barbara shared a smile.

While Barbara took Edwina to the bride's dressing room for last-minute alterations, Chloe and Rose went to the outdoor chapel. Nestled in the angle between two wings, the covered chapel allowed them to be in church yet a part of nature—a marriage of the supernatural and natural.

As they climbed the steps, Chloe noticed dozens of flower vases lined up behind the altar. "Where did all these big, blue hydrangeas come from?"

"Hud and Pop-pop brought them."

She looked at the girl. "Why hydrangeas?"

"Pop-pop said they were Miss Ed's favorite."

"I never knew that." Chloe raised her eyebrow. *Jake really does know her better than anyone.*

As Chloe and Rose began arranging the flowers around the alfresco chapel, a border collie kept them company, rolling over for belly rubs every time they passed. Then a man showed up with a keyboard.

"Hi. Where should I set up?"

"Hi, Rich." Rose turned to Chloe. "This is my cousin Richard, and this is my friend," smiling sheepishly, she caught herself, "almost cousin, Chloe."

"Glad to meet you, Rich." Chloe pointed to a niche along the red-brick wall. "Maybe you can set up along here? There's an electric outlet."

"Great. Thanks, cuz."

Within minutes, he was playing songs from the fifties. When Rich began "Catch a Falling Star," the melody drew Jake and Hud from the church.

"Congratulations, Jake." Chloe went to shake his hand, but he gave her a hug instead.

"You're welcome to call me Pop-pop, especially now." He winked. "One way or another, I'm glad to call you my granddaughter."

Though the morning was cool, Chloe felt the warmth radiate from him. *It's as if the sun came out.* She looked at the cloudless sky above. Then, smiling, she glanced over Jake's shoulder at Hud.

He was watching her through red eyes. No smile, his face was impassive but haggard.

Rich began playing "That's Amore" on the keyboard, but instead of buoying her, she grimaced and felt chilled. *It's as if the sun went behind a cloud.*

Jake followed her gaze. "Hud, get a cup of coffee. Either that or close your bloodshot eyes. You're bleeding to death."

Hud silently nodded and then turned toward the door to the cafeteria. *What's wrong with him?*

As if reading her mind, Jake chuckled ruefully.

"Poor guy. He's been working on his gift for Ed and me every night this past week. Then, the night before last, the engine blew on the cruise boat. He hasn't had a wink of sleep in over forty-eight hours."

Chloe felt her jaw drop as she watched his back.

"No wonder he acts like he's sleepwalking."

"Can I help with any of the flower arrangements?" Jake looked at her.

"No, thanks. Rose and I are just about done." Then she thought of his choice. "I never knew Aunt Ed liked hydrangeas. They're beautiful."

He nodded. "Ed loved these flowers. Her grandmother used to grow them." He took a deep breath. "I thought it might remind Ed of her, make her feel she's here at our wedding."

"That's so thoughtful." Chloe kissed his cheek. *Wish Hud cared as much for me as Jake does for Aunt Ed.*

Rose handed her a petite corsage of wildflowers.

"I made this one for you, Chloe. It's a mini-bouquet, just like Miss Ed's, only smaller." She grinned and then stood on tiptoes to whisper. "And I hope you catch Miss Ed's when she throws it."

Chloe leaned over and hugged the girl.

"Thank you, Rose. This is lovely. And just think, in a few more minutes, we're going to be cousins." She handed back the corsage. "Here, you put it on me."

"Here's Hud." Her eyes twinkling, Rose handed it to him. "You put it on her."

Chloe straightened up.

"Then here. You hold my coffee." He handed his sister the cup.

As he looked for a good place to fasten the corsage, his eyes swept across her chest and then up her neck until they were staring into each other's eyes.

Chloe caught her breath. Somehow, the act of his pinning on her corsage seemed so intimate, she felt chills.

He hesitated and then, with one hand, delicately gathered a fold of her dress material between his fingers. With his other hand, he fastened the pin through the flower stems to her dress, accidentally brushing against her breast. The touch electric, she glanced at his eyes as he gazed up at hers.

"Sorry."

"No problem," she murmured, the sound of her heartbeat drowning out the music, the people, everyone but Hud.

"Oh, don't they make a cute couple?" Two women stopped to watch.

The voice snapped Chloe out of her trance, and she turned toward them.

"Who? Us?" She gestured toward Hud and herself.

The woman nodded. "Yes. Are you getting married today?"

Chloe shook her head and pointed to Jake, as Hud said, "It's my grandfather who's getting married."

"Ohh." The woman frowned, as if disappointed. "What a shame." Then, as she walked away, she turned to her friend. "And they made such a cute couple, too."

Chloe's eyes shot open as she glanced at Jake, mortified for him.

But Jake and Hud just started chuckling, each feeding off the other, until they were laughing so hard, they had tears in their eyes. Rose started giggling, and even Chloe got caught up in their infectious laughter.

"This seems to be one extraordinarily festive wedding party."

Everyone turned toward the voice.

"Father David." Jake held out his hand to him. "Yes. One big, happy family."

Chloe grinned until she caught Hud's eye. Then she felt self-conscious, uncomfortable in his gaze.

"That's fine," said Father David, nodding, smiling. "Are we about ready to start? Is everyone here?" One by one, he looked over the group. "We seem to be missing the bride."

"I'll get her."

Rose dashed off toward the dressing room. A few minutes later, she reappeared with Barbara and Edwina. As they approached, Jake could not keep his eyes off his bride.

Chloe spoke under her breath. "Wow. Barbara sure did a fabulous job on the dress and veil."

"She did, didn't she?" Hud turned toward her.

Chloe flinched, realizing too late she had thought out loud.

"Miss Ed looks almost as beautiful as you."

She glanced at him as the "Wedding March" began, and their eyes locked. At its first chords, chills shot up her spine. Shuddering, Chloe looked away and joined the ladies, getting in line behind Rose and in front of Edwina and Barbara, who was giving away the bride.

Father David, Jake, and Hud took their positions. Then Father David nodded, the signal for Rose to begin walking toward the altar. After a few paces, Chloe fell into step behind her. Again, after a few paces, Edwina and Barbara followed her.

As Chloe approached the chapel, she could not stop staring at Hud. With his deep tan and dark, flashing eyes, he looked as if he had stepped from the cover of a novel. His eyes caught hers and held them until she took her place at the altar. When she turned to watch Barbara escort Edwina, Chloe flashed Rose a smile. Then she bent her head to whisper.

"The bouquet's sensational. Simple yet seasonal."

"Hope you catch it," she whispered back with a grin.

After the "Wedding March" stopped, Father David began the celebration. When Jake and Edwina exchanged vows, the entire altar lit up, as if flood lights had been turned on.

Chloe turned to see what had happened. She squinted as the sun drenched the chapel with light.

Her pendant touched her neck, and she saw Celestine, dazzlingly bright in the sunlight. Then she noticed the spirit in the luminous dress standing beside her. *Celestine seems to be reflecting her light, or is she radiating light of her own?* Chloe tilted her head, wondering if she was seeing right. The spirit glanced from Edwina to the hydrangeas.

Could that be . . . ? "Teresa?" Chloe moved her lips more than spoke the name.

The spirit turned toward her, and Celestine smiled.

Father David said, "Edwina, do you take Jake for your lawful husband, to have and to hold, from this day forward, for better, for worse, for richer, for poorer, in sickness and in health, until death do you part?"

When Edwina said, "I do," Teresa and Celestine turned toward each other and beamed, igniting the chapel with a burst of bright-white light. Then, hand in hand, they disappeared into it.

Chloe closed her eyes against the intense light. When she reopened her eyes, she glanced around the chapel. Dappled sunlight still filtered onto the altar, but the brilliant glow was gone. *Has Celestine gone, too?* She touched, then gripped, her pendant, but nothing appeared.

"What God has joined," said Father David, "men must not divide." He looked at Hud. "The rings, please."

Hud held out the two gold bands as Father David blessed them.

Then, as Jake placed the wedding ring on Edwina's finger, he said, "Edwina, take this ring as a sign of my love and fidelity. In the name of the Father, and of the Son, and of the Holy Spirit."

Chloe's eyes met Hud's. She watched his Adam's apple bob as he swallowed.

Edwina placed the wedding ring on Jake's finger.

"Jake, take this ring as a sign of my love and fidelity. In the name of the Father, and of the Son, and of the Holy Spirit."

As Chloe watched, she recalled Hud's words.

"How would you feel about making it a double wedding?"

If I'd said yes, we'd be husband and wife now. If I just knew, one way or the other, if Letty was behind this attraction.

Stifling a sigh, she glanced up to catch Hud gazing at her. Silently, her eyes implored his. *If I could only read his mind.*

After the dismissal, Jake kissed Edwina. Then, as they hugged or shook hands with Father David and the wedding party, several bystanders began applauding.

To their apparent delight, Edwina kissed Jake and grinned.

"Where to next?" she asked him.

"Hud's made us a very special wedding gift." Jake smiled at her. "Would you like to see it?"

"After that build up," Edwina laughed, "the sooner, the better."

⚓

Edwina rode with Jake, while the rest of the wedding party climbed into Chloe's car. She turned to Hud in the passenger seat.

"Where are we going?"

"To show you where I've been the last two nights."

Raising an eyebrow, he gave her a caustic stare.

Rose leaned over the front seat. "He's just grumpy because he's tired."

"Between finishing his gift for Miss Ed and Jake and then replacing the engine," said Barbara, "he's exhausted."

Chloe gave him a sidelong glance as she started the car. "Okay, how do I get to where you've been the last two nights?"

He gave a dry chuckle. "Drive out to Jake's pier at Sunset Cruises." Then he pointed to Jake's car. "Or just follow him."

When they arrived and piled out of the cars, Jake led the way down the wooden pier. Docked at the end was his tour boat and a beribboned bottle of champagne.

Then Chloe noticed the boat's fresh coat of paint. Beginning to get the idea, she gave Hud a half-smile.

"Did you do that?"

Grinning, his dimple showing, he winked. "You'll see."

As they got closer, they saw the surprise. Jake's boat had been renamed the *Edwina*.

Edwina covered her face with her hands. Then, peeking through her fingers, she stared. Finally, hunching her shoulders and laughing, she looked up at Jake, her eyes shining.

"You named it after me?"

"I did, indeed, but you can thank Hud for the paint job." Jake grinned at his bride and then gave Hud a warm smile.

"Thank you for all the work you've put into this." Edwina hugged Hud loosely, awkwardly, patting his back instead of pressing against him. "I don't know what to say."

"You've already said it." He grinned. "Welcome to the family."

This time, Edwina put her arms around him and squeezed him to her. She turned her eyes from the boat to Chloe and back to Hud.

"And thank you for all the love you've shown us."

Her chest silently heaving, Chloe glanced down at her feet as she bit her lip.

"We've had the wedding." Jake handed Edwina the bottle of champagne. "Now on to the christening."

Her eyes lit up as she looked from the bottle to Jake. Then she laughed.

"I don't know what I'm supposed to do."

"Easy," he said, going through the motions. "Just say, 'I christen thee *Edwina*,' and then break the bottle against the bow."

Chuckling, Edwina tried to compose herself. "I christen thee *Edwina*." Then, closing her eyes, she smashed the bottle against the boat.

"Well done!" Jake kissed her while the rest of them cheered.

As Chloe applauded, her pendant grazed her neck, and she gasped.

Not Celestine, but Letty appeared. Looking almost healed, her scars had nearly disappeared, and her hair had grown back. Braided, her hair was done up with ribbons and ringlets. Matching ribbons trimmed her white dress. Then Letty's voice rang out over the background chatter.

"I'm beginning to understand what love is." Her face relaxed, almost smiling, Letty gently touched her fingers to her cheek, hair, and dress.

Chloe cocked her head, listing to the lilting voice that no longer sounded raspy or hoarse.

She looks so young and . . . Chloe could not quite put her finger on it. *Content? Certainly less antagonistic.*

"To move on," said Letty, "Celestine needed your prayers, which you gave her . . . and me. She needed Jake and Edwina to be reunited, which they are, but she had another prerequisite." Letty's gaze bored into her.

Squirming beneath her stare, Chloe took a deep breath.

"Do you remember?"

Not wanting to speak in front of the others, Chloe shrugged.

"Because I interfered, Jake and Edwina's children were never born." Letty peered into her eyes, watching her. "Now Edwina's past childbearing age."

"You just said Celestine's moved on," Chloe mouthed more than whispered.

"She made amends for her role in their breakup. She's righted her wrong." Letty's eyes met hers. "But it was my fault Edwina and Jake didn't marry in time to have children."

Chloe cocked her head, beginning to grasp her meaning. Then she turned so only Letty could see her lips move.

"Even if they'd married, there's no guarantee they'd have had kids."

"No, that's up to God—"

"God?" Chloe opened her eyes. "Before, you'd said God was cruel, heartless. Now you're saying—"

"Never mind what I'd said." Letty's gaze faltered. Then, sighing, her shoulders slumped. "Who lives, who dies, who's born, *life* is up to God. If Edwina and Jake had married, the intent to have children would've been there."

Chloe asked, "That's enough? The intent?"

With a grim nod, Letty looked from her to Hud. "You two even look like them when they were your age. Time may have skipped two generations," Letty raised her eyebrow, "but there's still one requirement to fulfill before I can move on."

Chloe's eyes narrowed. "Just a minute," she lipsynched more than spoke. "Hud and I don't owe you a thing. You're dead, so stop trying to control our lives. You interfered in Jake and Edwina's relationship, and now you're trying to concoct something between Hud and me." She shook her head. "Uhn-uh. I want a love that's real, not manipulated by some ghost."

Letty bit her lip. "Guess I've gone about this the wrong way." She surveyed Chloe, as if sizing her up. Then she gave her a wry half-smile. "If seeing's believing, there's something you need to see for yourself."

"All aboard!" Hud grinned at the group as he stepped onto the gangplank. "Hop aboard, and let's begin the wedding party!"

Chloe turned back to Letty, but she had vanished.

"Wedding party?" Edwina looked around. "Here?"

"Everything's aboard the *Edwina*." Jake's eyes met hers. "Are you ready to take her on her maiden voyage?"

Chloe stole a glance at Hud. His eyes met hers in an indulgent smile.

"Come on, everyone," said Barbara. "The champagne's iced, and the wedding cake's ready to be sliced."

Suddenly, strains of "Earth Angel" began wafting from the cabin. Conversation ceased as the group collectively perked their ears.

"Our song!" Edwina gave Jake a wistful smile. "You've thought of everything."

Jake returned her smile and then glanced at Hud. "Did you rig up the sound system, too?"

He shook his head and turned to his cousin. "Rich, is this your work?"

"Nope." He hunched his shoulders. "Maybe someone forgot to turn off a radio."

Everyone wore blank stares as they shrugged and turned to the next, except Chloe as she narrowed her eyes. *What are you up to now, Letty?*

"Besides the radio, we forgot something else." Rose looked from face to face. "Miss Ed still has to throw her bouquet."

Edwina brought her hands together. "That's right."

Rose handed her the bouquet. "Here you go, Miss Ed."

Her grin starting with the flower girl, Edwina's smile widened to include all the females. "Ready, ladies?"

Returning the smile, arms uplifted, Barbara and Rose positioned themselves. Chloe hung back, only going through the motions.

Edwina turned away, closed her eyes, and threw the bouquet over her shoulder. "Who's next to be married?"

Chloe watched the bouquet, suspend in midair as if in slow motion. Sensing Hud's eyes on her, she glanced at him and then did a double take. His eyebrows raised, his gaze steady, his lips seemed to move. *Marry me?*

Am I seeing right? No time to think, she turned her attention to the task at hand. With a rush of adrenalin, she leapt up, snatching the bouquet before it touched Rose's upraised arms.

Giving her a stern look, the girl pretended to be annoyed.

"You didn't even give me a chance to step aside. You grabbed it over my head."

Hud stepped closer. "Chloe . . . will you . . . ?" He glanced uncomfortably from her to Barbara to Jake and back. "Would you like to step inside for cake and champagne?"

Still holding the bouquet at chest level, she slowly lowered her arms and pulled back her head to study him. *Why this sudden edginess?* She shrugged it off. "Sure."

He politely stepped aside, waiting for her to enter the cabin first.

Her eyes adjusting from the sunlight to the dim light as she walked in, she saw a banner hanging across the far wall. A separate poster for each letter, two strung rows read: *WILL YOU MARRY ME, CHLOE?*

The dessert table in front of the sign supported a tiered cake. Chloe took a step closer. Not a wedding cake, its icing spelled out *WILL YOU MARRY ME, CHLOE?* Frosted to the top layer was a square cupcake, shaped like a jeweler's box. Lightly set into its frosting was an engagement ring.

Mouth open in an O, Chloe turned toward Hud.

Down on one knee, he took her hand.

"Chloe, I'm in love with you. I can't imagine going through life without you. Will you marry me?"

Beside him stood Letty, beaming, looking completely healed—her complexion unblemished, and her hair thick and full.

Chloe's eyes opened even wider. *How pretty she is.*

"Now do you believe me?" Letty gestured toward the banner, cake, ring, and grinning well-wishers. "Everyone here sees Hud's love for you. Everyone, that is, but you. His family's helped plan this proposal, but I've had nothing to do with it." She gestured toward his still posture, his rapt attention as he focused on Chloe. "What you see is the look of love."

Her heart racing, Chloe caught her breath as she acknowledged Letty's words with a quick nod.

Still poised on one knee, Hud looked up at her. "Will you be my wife?"

"Yes." She lifted him up and took him in her arms. "Oh, yes." Her eyelids fluttering, she closed her eyes as he kissed her.

The cabin lit up with a dazzling, bright light. Peeking through half-closed lids, Chloe saw Letty flanked by two brilliant spirits in luminous gowns. *Celestine and Teresa.*

Then Letty began radiating a glow of her own, adding to the blaze. As the room ignited in an intense, white flash, Chloe shut her eyes against the burst of light. When she opened them again as Hud released her, the spirits were gone.

She touched her necklace. Nothing happened. She grasped it in her fingers. Nothing appeared.

She looked about the cabin. Once again, it was dim in comparison—lit with only lightbulbs and sunlight streaming through the windows—until she looked into Hud's eyes. There she saw the incandescent glow of his love.

READING GROUP GUIDE
ANGELS FROM ASHES: HOUR OF THE WOLF

Why is the title, *Angels from Ashes: Hour of the Wolf*, significant? Why do/don't you like it? What would you have named *Angels from Ashes: Hour of the Wolf*? Is the title a clue to the theme(s)?

Did you enjoy *Angels from Ashes: Hour of the Wolf*? Why/why not?

What do you think *Angels from Ashes: Hour of the Wolf* is essentially about? What is the main idea/theme of *Angels from Ashes: Hour of the Wolf*?

What other themes or subplots did *Angels from Ashes: Hour of the Wolf* explore? Were they effectively explored? Were they plausible? Were the plot/subplots animated by using clichés, or were they lifelike?

Were any symbols used to reinforce the main ideas?

Did the main plot pull you in, engage you immediately, or did it take a chapter or two for you to 'get into it'?

Was *Angels from Ashes: Hour of the Wolf* a 'page-turner,' where you couldn't put it down, or did you take your time as you read it?

What emotions did *Angels from Ashes: Hour of the Wolf* elicit as you read it? Did you feel engrossed, distracted, entertained, disturbed, or a combination of emotions?

What did you think of the structure and style of the writing? Was it one continuous story, or was it a series of vignettes within a story's framework?

What about the timeline? Was it chronological, or did flashbacks move from the present to the past and back again? Did that choice of timeline help/hinder the storyline?

Was there a single point of view, or did it shift between several characters? Why would Karen Hulene Bartell have chosen this structure?

Did the plot's complications surprise you? Or could you predict the twists/turns?

What scene was the most pivotal for *Angels from Ashes: Hour of the Wolf?* How do you think *Angels from Ashes: Hour of the Wolf* would have changed had that scene not taken place?

What scene resounded most with you personally—either positively or negatively? Why?

Did any passage(s) seem insightful, even powerful?

Did you find the dialog humorous—did it make you laugh? Was the dialog thought-provoking or poignant—did it make you cry? Was there a particular passage that stated *Angels from Ashes: Hour of the Wolf's* theme?

Did any of the characters' dialog 'speak' to you or provide any insight?

Have you ever experienced anything that was comparable to what occurred in *Angels from Ashes: Hour of the Wolf?* How did you respond to it? How were you changed by it? Did you grow from the experience? Since it didn't kill you, how did it make you stronger?

What caught you off-guard? What shocked, surprised, or startled you about *Angels from Ashes: Hour of the Wolf?*

Did you notice any cultural, traditional, gender, sexual, ethnic, or socio-economic factors at play in *Angels from Ashes: Hour of the Wolf?* If you did, how did it/they affect the characters?

How realistic were the characterizations?

Did any of the characters remind you of yourself or someone you know? How so?

Did the characters' actions seem plausible? Why/why not?

What motivated the characters' actions in *Angels from Ashes: Hour of the Wolf?*

What did the subcharacters want from the main character, and what did the main character want with them?

What were the dynamics between the characters? How did that affect their interactions?

How did the way the characters envisioned themselves differ from the way others saw them? How did you see the various characters?

How did the 'roles' of the various characters influence their interactions as sister, coworker, wife, mother, aunt, daughter, lover, and professional?

Who was your favorite character? Why? Would you want to meet any of the characters? Which one(s)?

Was there a scene(s) or moment(s) where you disagreed with the choice(s) of any of the characters? What would you have done differently?

If one of the characters made a decision with moral connotations, would you have made the same choice? Why/why not?

Were the characters' actions justified? Did you admire or disapprove of their actions? Why?

Edwina and Jake both had moments where they struggled with their faith. When was the last time your faith faltered? What helped you get through that time?

If you had a least-favorite character you loved to hate, who was it and why?

What previous influence(s) in the characters' lives triggered their actions/reactions in *Angels from Ashes: Hour of the Wolf*?

Did *Angels from Ashes: Hour of the Wolf* end the way you had anticipated? Was the ending appropriate? Was it satisfying? If so, why? If not, why and what would you change?

Did the ending tie up any loose threads? If so, how?

Did the characters develop or mature by the end of the book? If so, how? If not, what would have helped them grow? Did you relate to any one (or more) of the characters?

Have you changed/reconsidered any views or broadened your perspective after reading *Angels from Ashes: Hour of the Wolf*?

What do you think will happen next to the main characters? If you had a crystal ball, would you foresee a sequel to *Angels from Ashes: Hour of the Wolf*?

Have you read any books that share similarities with this one? How does *Angels from Ashes: Hour of the Wolf* hold up to them?

What did you take away from *Angels from Ashes: Hour of the Wolf*? Have you learned anything new or been exposed to different ideas about people or a certain part of the world?

Did your opinion of *Angels from Ashes: Hour of the Wolf* change as you read it? How? If you could ask Karen Hulene Bartell a question, what would you ask?

Would you recommend *Angels from Ashes: Hour of the Wolf* to a friend?

RECIPES

GREEN BAY BOOYAH

2 pounds beef and/or pork stew meat
3 cups onions, diced
1 stewing chicken (4-5 pounds)
½ cup parsley, minced (optional)
1 tablespoon salt, or to taste
½ teaspoon freshly ground pepper, or to taste
1 tablespoon fresh rosemary (or substitute ½ teaspoon dry rosemary)
1 tablespoon fresh thyme (or substitute ½ teaspoon dry thyme)
½ teaspoon fresh sage (or substitute ½ teaspoon dry sage)
4 cups potatoes, quartered
2 cups celery, sliced
1 cup carrots, sliced
1 cup green beans, sliced (optional)
1 cup fresh peas (optional)
Juice of 2 lemons

Place the beef and/or pork and onions in a large kettle. Cover with water. Slowly bring to a simmer, removing the foam from the top. Simmer for 1 hour. Add the chicken, herbs, and seasonings. Simmer gently, covered, for 1 ½ hours or until tender.

Remove the chicken and meat. When cool enough to handle, remove the bones and cut the meat into bite-sized pieces. Add the vegetables to the bouillon and simmer until tender-crisp. Adjust seasonings. Return the chicken and meat pieces to the broth and heat through. Season with lemon juice and serve steaming hot. Serves 12 to 16.

DOOR COUNTY FISH BOIL

2 pounds red potatoes, quartered
8 small onions, peeled and halved (or substitute 16 pearl onions, peeled)
2 tablespoons kosher salt
Four ½-pound whitefish steaks (or substitute lake trout, striped bass, salmon, or bluefish fillets)
Freshly ground pepper, to taste
2 tablespoons fresh parsley, minced (garnish)
Melted butter (garnish)
Lemon wedges (garnish)

Place potatoes and onions in a large stockpot. Add 2 quarts water or enough to cover vegetables by 2 inches. Stir in the salt, bring to a boil, and cook until the potatoes are tender-crisp, about 15 minutes.

Arrange the fish steaks or fillets in a single layer on top of the vegetables. Partially cover the pot again, lower the heat, and simmer until the whitefish flakes easily with a fork, about 10 minutes.

Transfer the fish with a slotted spoon to a prewarmed platter. Arrange the potatoes and onions around the fish. Garnish with freshly ground pepper and minced parsley. Serve with melted butter and lemon wedges. Serves 4.

TART CHERRY COBBLER

4 cups tart cherries, hulled and pitted
1 box cake mix (vanilla or chocolate)
½ cup butter, melted
1 cup pecans, chopped

Spread the pitted cherries evenly in a greased nine-by-thirteen pan. Sprinkle the dry cake mix over the cherries. Drizzle melted butter over that. Top with chopped pecans. Bake at 350 degrees for 45 minutes or until done. Serves 12 to 16.

HOMEMADE RASPBERRY PANCAKES

2 large eggs
1 cup milk
2 tablespoons corn oil
1 1/4 cups all-purpose flour
1 tablespoon sugar
1 tablespoon baking powder
1/4 teaspoon salt, or to taste
1 cup fresh raspberries

Whisk the eggs. Add the milk and oil to the eggs and mix well. Stir in the flour, sugar, baking powder, and salt. Fold in the raspberries.

Heat the frying pan or griddle. Spray with nonstick cooking spray or add a little oil. Using a ladle, spoon the batter onto the pan or griddle. When the tops are bubbly, turn the pancake to brown the other side. When done, transfer the pancakes to warmed plates. Yields 12 pancakes.

FRESH RASPBERRY SAUCE

1 cup fresh raspberries, washed
1 tablespoon sugar

Combine raspberries and sugar in a food processor; process until pureed. Press mixture through a fine sieve over a medium bowl; discard solids.

(Old-fashioned method: crush the combined raspberries and sugar with a potato masher.)

Cover and chill. Yields 1 cup.

AVOCADO STRAWBERRY SALAD
WITH HONEY POPPY SEED DRESSING

Salad Ingredients

6 cups fresh mixed greens
1 pint fresh strawberries, hulled, cleaned, and coarsely chopped
2 avocadoes, peeled and coarsely chopped
4 ounces blue cheese, crumbled
1/4 cup sliced almonds
Small red onion, peeled and thinly sliced

Toss the salad ingredients together. Yields 10 cups salad.

Poppy Seed Dressing Ingredients

1/2 cup olive oil
3 tablespoons apple cider vinegar
3 tablespoons honey
1 tablespoon poppy seeds
Salt and freshly ground pepper, to taste

Whisk the poppy seed dressing ingredients until blended. Drizzle over the salad and serve. Yields 1 scant cup.

ABOUT KAREN HULENE BARTELL

 Author of *Sacred Gift, Sacred Choices, Sovereignty of the Dragons, Untimely Partners,* and *Belize Navidad,* Karen is a best-selling author, motivational keynote speaker, IT technical editor, wife, and all-around pilgrim of life. She writes multicultural, offbeat love stories steeped in the supernatural that lift the spirit. Born to rolling-stone parents who moved annually, Bartell found her earliest playmates as fictional friends in books. Paperbacks became her portable pals. Ghost stories kept her up at night—reading feverishly. The paranormal was her passion. Wanderlust inherent, Karen enjoyed traveling, although loathed changing schools. Novels offered an imaginative escape. An only child, she began writing her first novel at the age of nine, learning the joy of creating her own happy endings. Professor emeritus of the University of Texas at Austin, Dr. Bartell resides in the Hill Country with her husband Peter and her *mews*—five rescued cats.

Visit Karen at:

Website: KarenHuleneBartell.com
Facebook: KarenHuleneBartell
Twitter: KarenHuleneBart
Amazon Author's Page: Karen Hulene Bartell
Goodreads Author Page: Karen Hulene Bartell

Dear Readers,
If you enjoyed this book enough to review it for Goodreads, B&N, or Amazon.com, I'd appreciate it!
Thanks, Karen

Find more great reads at
Pen-L.com

Made in the USA
San Bernardino, CA
25 March 2016